I0658510

When Darkness Fell

"In a dark Southern, post-WWII tale, Susan Lindsley keenly uses dialogue and setting to drop us uncomfortably into the 1940s, taking the reader to a time when people looked over their shoulder and kept their thoughts to themselves for sins that never should have been sins."

~ **C. Hope Clark**, author of The Carolina Slade Mysteries and The Edisto Island Mysteries

"Susan Lindsley writes in the tradition of the South's best: Caldwell, O'Conner, McCullers and Bragg. She writes about a time and place you had to grow up in to know, and she knows. For writing you won't believe, can't put down and will never forget, dig into *When Darkness Fell*."

~ **Peggy Mercer**, Ga. Author of the Year, 2011
for *Peach When the Well Run Dry*

"Compelling, realistic look at post WWII life in the deep South when racism ruled the lives of everyone, even those few whites who resented and fought against such hatred."

~ **Ken McKowen**, Managing Editor, Publishing Syndicate LLC

Copyright © 2014 by Susan Lindsley, all rights reserved. No portion of this book may be reproduced in any form (stored or transmitted) without written permission from Susan Lindsley and/or ThomasMax Publishing.

This book is a work of fiction, and all characters are products of the author's imagination. Any resemblance to real people, living or dead, is purely coincidental.

ISBN-13: 978-0-9914332-6-1
ISBN-10: 0-9914332-6-2

First printing, November, 2014
Second printing, December, 2014
Third printing, August 2015

Front cover design by Elizabeth Kate Bramlett
Additional cover design by ThomasMax

Author's website: yesterplace.com

Published by:

ThomasMax Publishing
P.O. Box 250054
Atlanta, GA 30325
Website: thomasmax.com

When Darkness Fell

Wish I'd never seen and heard Buck and Molly. If anybody else finds out, they're dead.

Susan Lindsley

ThomasMax

Your Publisher
For The 21st Century

Acknowledgments

Thanks to my life partner and sisters who have always supported me with my work. I owe special thanks to Robert Preston Ward for suggestions that resulted in massive changes to the story. And to Pat Blanks, whose eagle eyes have helped so much in catching my errors. Any that remain are a result of my own oversight.

Special thanks to Elizabeth Kate Bramlett for the new cover design.

I cannot say enough thanks to Lee Clevenger for his faith in my work and his ongoing support.

Dear Reader:

This is a work of fiction, based on facts.

The accounts of the massacre at Moore's Ford Bridge and the funeral of George Dorsey are based on *Fire in a Canebrake: The Last Mass Lynching in America* by Laura Wexler. The only actual people mentioned in this novel are the Malcom and Dorsey families, the Hesters, Loy Harrison and Dan Turner.

The relationship between Buck and George Dorsey is entirely fictional, as is the friendship between "Jackie" and Buck.

Milledgeville, Georgia, was the site of a double murder in 1953, during its sesquicentennial celebrations. The characters in this book, however, are fictional and are not intended to represent those of the 1953 events.

The time of this novel is 1946, a few months before the release of the movie *Song of the South.* It was released on November 12, 1946.

The Northern Lights were visible as far south as middle Georgia on Friday, July 26, 1946.

Susan Lindsley

A Word from the Publisher

You are reading a book that won the ThomasMax "You Are Published" annual contest at the Southeastern Writers Association's annual conference and workshop, an event held for nearly four decades on beautiful St. Simons Island. This is Susan's third time to win this contest. Her non-fiction entry: *Margaret Mitchell: A Scarlett or a Melanie?* was a previous winner. Last year she won for her first novel, *The Bottom Rail*, which went on to gather accolades in the Georgia of the Year competition for best first novel.

Lightning can strike *three times* in the same place.

I make the same remarks about this book as I did *The Bottom Rail:* "It's ironic that the things in this book that are now offensive to many would have been shrugged aside as, 'Well, that's how it was back then' not so long ago. But if you go back to the time period of this book's setting, there would be umbrage also -- for completely different reasons. I won't elaborate; I'll let you, the reader, figure out that one."

If you are a writer, I urge you to attend our annual workshop and conference. We have instructors from many phases of the industry. We always have at least one, sometimes two, novel instructors, and often feature classes on poetry, non-fiction (general or specific topics), writing inspirational works, writing for young readers, writing short fiction and a host of other topics. These topics and the instructors rotate annually. We also will have an agent from a major literary agency to whom attendees can pitch or discuss their projects. In addition, we have contests (the ThomasMax contest results in a book deal, but most of the contests have cash prizes) and *free* evaluations by instructors in up to three different manuscript categories.

The 2015 event will be held June 19-23. Our host will again be Epworth-by-the-Sea. You can find out more about our annual event by visiting our website, southeasternwriters.org.

When we judge contest entries, we have no idea of the author's identity. So when I discovered the author of *When Darkness Fell* was Susan Lindsley, we at ThomasMax were delighted. Susan's past winners have been relatively successful sales-wise. She has also self-published some works with our company . . . and I consider her a close personal friend. But I reiterate, we at ThomasMax had no clue as to her identity when judging the contest entries. All other SWA contests are judged similarly to prevent any personal prejudice.

We hope to see you in 2015 or at one of our future annual events. It's the greatest "bang for the buck" writers' training you will ever receive. In a sequestered atmosphere in a resort setting, both experienced and beginning writers will find friends, contacts and, of course, instruction in ways that have led to success. It's all about *Writers Helping Writers.* Don't just take my word for it, though; do some research and you'll see that it's pretty much a universal sentiment from all those who attend that SWA offers the best instruction in writing across many different fields. As former SWA President, I am a bit biased, but success has come to many SWA participants.

--- Lee Clevenger, President, ThomasMax Publishing

In Memory of
Eva Sloan
Marion Ennis
Pete Bivins

The Families

The Lawsons:
> Sam, younger daughter, the storyteller, aged 12
> Sis, older sister, married to J. D. Stanley, local attorney
>> Infant daughter: Katie
>
> The parents: Professor Lawson
>> Laura, nee Mosby

The Steeles:
> Buck, second son
> Jethro, older son
> Willie Jo, daughter
> Elvira, mother
> Sherman, Elvira's father; worked for the Mosby family. Deceased.
> Pollock, Buck's uncle, Elvira's brother

The Everetts:
> Molly, lives with her Aunt Maude and Uncle Seth
> Maude and Seth, parents of "the boys"
>> Richard, older of two brothers

The Synders:
> Cou'n Phil (Judge Philip Snyder) cousin of the Mosby family
> Martha, Phil's wife
> Sunny, their daughter
> Bertha, Phil's sister
> Carolyn, Bertha's daughter

The Gordons:
> Vicki: Widow, partner of Danny Murphy and attorney for Buck
> Michelle: Vicki's daughter; in Sam's class at school
> Slim: Vicki's brother, a lawman

Others:
Aunt Tessie (nee Mosby): Sister of Sam's mother
Bessie: Housekeeper for Vicki Gordon
Collier Hancock: Local district attorney

Danny Murphy: Attorney for Rufus Flint
Ellie Mae and Amos: Tenant farmers on Lawson plantation
Larry Huntington: Gay antiques dealer
Lillie Mae : The Lawson's maid and nanny for Sis's child Katie
Mattie: Rufus Flint's wife
Mickey (Mick): Killed member of Simpson family
Mule Wilson: Farmer gelding mules and horses, without DVM degree.
Roger Benson: County commissioner, owns candy factory and B&B drug store
Rufus Flint: Businessman. Operates a car lot, a grocery, and a furniture store.
Simpson family: Dairy family. Employed Mick
Uncle Morris: Physician, Tessie's husband

The Horses:
    Dolly: Sam's
    Lady: Michelle's
    Charger: J. D.'s

SAMANTHA

Dear Diary,

It's Sunday, May 25, 1946. I don't know how to keep a diary. I've got some paper already in a book to write in. Can't use but the back of the pages, since all I've got is some of Dad's students' Blue Horse Books from one of their tests. I gotta write down <u>everything</u>.

I wish I had never seen and heard Buck and Molly cause if I hadn't I wouldn't chew on my fingernails like I've started to and wouldn't have the bellyache from worrying over them. If anybody else ever finds out, they're dead.

They're my best friends ever, better friends than Michelle even, but they oughten to kiss up on each other and carry on like that. It's not right. A nigra's gonna get himself killed if he even looks funny at a white girl, no matter who he is. Even Buck. No telling what they'll do to him. They'll do a lot worse than just kill him.

Buck knows better—he has to know better. He grew up here even if he has been off to France in the war. And Molly—oh, Molly, you're fifteen, plenty old enough to know the Klu Klux is gonna get you when they find out.

It all started right after Molly and her Aunt Maude had words. Molly doesn't like living with her Aunt Maude, but it's better than staying down with her daddy who beat up on her all the time.

I'd never of known what was going on if I hadn't gotten bored and for something fun to do had gone up to the barn loft to spy on Molly's Everett cousins. I know those boys rustle our cattle, and I went up there to spy on them. I wanted to hear them planning to steal the cows, so I could help catch them in the act. I by-passed the lower loft and went to the top one so I could see better, across the driveway to their house.

Turned out, I couldn't hear much. Seemed like Maude told Molly to go cut firewood, cause I heard Molly yell cutting wood wasn't her job, it was the boys', that she did all the cooking and cleaning. She ran across to the barn and climbed up to the first loft. I was scared she'd come on up and find me and I'd have to pretend I was asleep or something. But she didn't.

She sprawled out on her back—right under a big wasp nest almost black from the wasps crawling on it. She didn't lie there long, but wiggled away from under it.

I was glad there wasn't a nest over where I was.

Molly is real pretty, almost as pretty as Sis, with her little short nose and freckles. Even when she's been crying. Her long blond curly hair splayed out around her like a big gold umbrella. It reaches almost halfway down her back and falls in rolls kinda like Shirley Temple's, but Molly never has to curl it up on rags. She's got eyes like the sky, eyes that almost always seem to laugh when she's on the school bus, teasing some of the girls. I don't know how she puts up with her family—what with all the men so shiftless and doing nothing but making likker and stealing cows. She's the only one who cares about any schooling.

The way she was laid out, her titties poked up against her feedsack dress so I could tell she didn't have on a petticoat. Mama says a girl has always got to wear a petticoat to keep her pride.

She'd no more than wiped her face dry when I heard the ladder squeak. Whoever it was musta not known where to step to keep it from making noise.

It was Buck.

I thought when he got up high enough to see Molly he'd take off to somewhere else, so I just sat and waited real quiet to keep them from knowing I was there.

Molly heard the ladder too and sat up, looked toward it, backed up a little, and hunched down like she was trying to hide, but there wasn't any place for her to go except to bury down into the hay. When Buck's head came over the edge of the loft, Molly sighed and kinda giggled. Buck's eyes got big, like two big white circles on a target.

Neither of them moved for the longest time. Finally Buck eased down a fraction. Molly whispered, "Buck, don't go. Stay here awhile."

He paused. "Miss Molly, I can't. You're grown up. No way a nigger can stay here with a white woman. It wouldn't be right."

"Nobody'll ever know, Buck. I—please. You and me, we always been friends. I need a friend. Only friend I got to talk to is Sam. She's okay but a lot younger'n me. Aunt Maude don't care what happens to me as long as I tote in the stove wood and fix the turnips and 'taters and sit with Bo while she goes off somewhere almost all the time. Stay. You can tell me more about being in the war. C'mon, Buck, stay. We can talk. Okay?" She patted the hay next to her.

"Miss Molly, it ain't right. I best go."

Buck switched from white-boy talk to niggertalk and back again, and Molly didn't even notice or care, but just kept right on talking to him, like it was right and proper for them to be up in the hay loft together. After all, like she said, they have been friends from way back.

"Didn't you talk to the white folks overseas in the war? All the letters you wrote about the chullun. You liked them, and they were white. Did you meet any grownups? Any girls? You didn't write about meeting any. I hear tell some nigger soldiers up and married some white girls in the war."

"Yes'm, one of the niggers I know married a white girl over in France. But that was in France, and France ain't here. I gotta go."

He stepped down the ladder, but Molly held out a hand to him like she wanted to pull him up there with her. "Buck, don't go. I've been caring for you in my mind ever since I can remember. Don't go. Please."

I sure hadn't figured on Molly caring for Buck like a boy friend. Not even last summer when she came down to help pull trash out of the lakebed when we built the dam. I figured she just wanted to help out and make a little money, but maybe she really wanted to help cause Buck was there every day. They worked good together and laughed a lot. But to stand working when it's brinjin hot, you have to laugh.

They stayed like that for what seemed forever, Molly with her hand out to Buck, and Buck standing on the ladder, like they were both thinking on Molly's words.

Molly went on to say, "Buck, ever since we went to school together on Miz Lawson's porch, I've thought you were special. I always looked up to you cause you're smart and you've always been kind to me and—well, I care about you more'n anybody I know."

Fear turned him almost white. He knows what-all the Klu Klux can do, not just to him, but to Molly and even to his family. If a white man even **thinks** a nigra is uppity, the nigra's got trouble. Lots of trouble. Courting a white girl is sure a whole lot worse for a nigra than just being uppity, and Buck knows he's got plenty of reason to be scared of being seen anywhere around a white girl.

Of course everybody knows it's okay for him to be around me cause he works for Dad and looks after me when I could get in trouble. But it's not the same if he's seen with Molly, cause they got no reason to be anywhere together unless it's working for Mama or Dad down at the house.

Buck finally took another step up the ladder. His face shone with sweat when he moved through the sunbeams that came in between the boards. At first, I wondered if he was sweating cause he was scared, but I sweated too from the heat under the tin roof. The sunbeams danced with dust when he moved through them, and the dust danced its way right up to me and tried to tickle my nose. He sat down with his legs hanging over the edge of the loft, like he was going to jump off, his hands on each side of him ready to push. Molly moved over toward him and sat down, her legs hanging down too, and it was kinda like seeing Roy Rogers and Dale Evans at the picture show last week, sitting side by side and just looking out over the prairie and not talking, just sitting and letting the other person kind of soak into them.

I heard a squealing sound behind me and looked back through the oak tree toward the house, where Tommy, one of Molly's cousins, was drawing a bucket of water. The older boy, Richard, sat on a corn-shuck bottom chair on the porch, tilted back against the wall so the chair was on only two legs. A cigarette dangled from his lips, the smoke curling a faint white storm up into his eyes and making him squint at the stick he was whittling down to nothing but shavings, I reckon to use for kindling in the kitchen stove. The cigarette smell drifted on the faint breeze just enough for me to smell it all the way up into the loft. Their mama, Maude, stood on the porch, hands on her hips, waiting for the water. Tommy trotted the bucket to her and then sat on the edge of the porch. I didn't see anything of Maude's husband, and figured he was off to his still while his no-account boys loafed.

I wiggled down into the hay a little more, even while it itched me, and the stale musty odor made me want to sneeze. I pinched my nose to hold back the sneeze, and it went away when I was about to choke myself.

"Buck, I've wanted to be your girl since I can remember. All in the war, I thought you cared. You were so good to write all the time. I tried to say things in my letters back, to let you know I cared too. But after you got hurt and came home, you wouldn't stop to even say hello. Why? Don't you want to be my friend any more, like we used to be? Seems like the only time I get to see you now-adays is when I go help the professor or Miz Lawson and you're there."

When she stopped talking Buck didn't say a word. He just sat with both hands holding onto the edge of the loft, sweat running off his chin and down his arms.

The quiet got longer and longer before Molly spoke again. "You ever had yourself a special girl, Buck?"

"One time I did, before the war," he said real soft. He still hadn't moved and wasn't even looking at Molly, but down at his bare feet that he kept moving first one and then the other on top. "She married somebody else while I was overseas. I'm just as glad, seeing as how we both changed."

She laid her hand on his shoulder, like she was trying to turn him to face her, and knots popped up all over his arms as he tensed up. Her skin was tan from all the work she'd done in the sun, from washing and making soap and such in the yard, but even so against his darker skin it looked a lot whiter. Buck flinched his shoulder just a little away from her, like he was scared of her touching him and wanted to move away but at the same time didn't want to move from under her hand, kinda like a horse shimmering a fly off his shoulder.

"You oughten to do that, Miss Molly," he said.

"Didn't you have a girl friend in the war? I thought all the soldiers got them a girl while they were overseas."

"Naw'm."

"You got a special girl here, since you've been home?"

Buck sat silent for a long minute or so and then said the same thing again. "Naw'm."

"You any idea how lonesome it gits here, not seeing anybody but them boys excepting when I'm at school, and there I just have to sit in class all day. Them boys don't even want me going to town with them on Saturday."

"I know about lonesome. It was plenty lonesome in the war, Miss Molly, even with all the other soldiers around. Us colored soldiers always got sent up to fight first, and mosta my nigra friends got killed. And a colored boy wasn't allowed to talk to a white soldier. The two best friends I had were soldiers from here in Georgia. Didn't I write you about them? One of 'em lives up by Athens. Other one was an officer, and we weren't supposed to be friends, him being an officer and me enlisted, but we were. He lives in California now, and we still write each other some. But it was pure lonesome."

He'd written me about his friend the officer, who'd been born in Georgia and moved out to California as a baby. Jackie got into one of the big white colleges in South California, where he was famous for playing ball. That nigra got so famous he got to be friends with Joe Lewis the champion boxer, and when Jackie got in the Army, he got made an officer because he was friends with Joe Lewis. Mostly the Army wouldn't let the nigras be officers.

Buck wrote Mama all about how her porch schooling had helped him in the Army, and he had gotten moved up to Sergeant. My uncle the Colonel says Sergeants really ran the war cause by the time they get up to be Sergeants, they are better soldiers than most fresh officers. Buck called those fresh officers "ninety-day wonders." When the white officer over him got shot and he radioed back that their officer was hurt, the big officers forgot he was a nigra and made him an officer because he could talk white folks talk. But when he got back and they saw he was a nigra, they put a white officer over him and moved him back down to Sergeant.

In one of his letters, he said a lot of the country nigras were scared of haints, and he'd had to keep the soldiers from telling ghost stories when they were just sitting around at night.

I had to quit thinking about Buck's letters and get my mind back to what he and Molly were saying.

"Sometimes I gits so lonesome I just come up here by myself and cry. They figure I'll git me a fella if I git to go to town, and if I don't do what they tell me, they'll make me go back home to Pappy. And when he gets some likker in him, my pappy beats on me something fierce."

"You're old enough to have a fella and be married, too, Miss Molly."

"Cousin Richard says I got to wait for him to say when I'm ready to get married. He says I can marry up with him, but I don't even like him, Buck."

"You can't marry up with him. He's your kin."

"He says it don't matter that we're kin. He makes me stay in the back room at night by myself and locks me in. I don't know what to do, Buck. Richard says he wants me to marry him, but I can't stand the idea of having to sleep in the bed with him. He's dirty and always smells bad, and he never takes a bath. He wears the same overalls all week and his hair is always messed up. He don't even use a sassafras root to clean out his mouth. Look at you. No matter how hot it is or how much work you do, you're always neat."

"Oh, I wouldn't say that, Miss Molly. Right now, I'm plenty dirty and sweaty."

"Oh, Buck, but you smell so nice to me. You always have. Like the sunlight and the wind, and like the hayfields and the horses." She grinned. "And like sassafras."

She reached over and touched his shoulder again, and went on, "And I've always wanted to touch your hair." Her hand moved on up to his head, her fingers sort of combing through his hair that was a mat of curls.

"Miss Molly, you oughten to do that."

"But I want to touch you, Buck. Don't you want to touch me, too?"

"You know I can't."

Buck wiggled and squirmed but didn't say anything.

"Well?" Molly said, and we both waited for Buck, who still said nothing.

Buck was all of a sudden being really nigger when he said, "Missy, it jest ain't right you asking me sumpin lak dat."

"Why not?"

"I dun told you, Miss Molly, I's a nigger and you's white. White folks'll kill me iffen I was to—"

"Buck, I'll never tell anybody about you and me. Oh, Buck, can't you see I care for you more'n anybody I know? I've cared for you for it seems like forever, and I was sure glad you came back home last summer when the Army let you out cause you'd been hurt so bad. And will you quit talking like a nigger?"

Molly's voice had a little tremor in it, a little bit of fear, but it was soft and gentle at the same time, like the way I talk to the horses when I break them to lead, like telling a horse I'd take a board to his head if he didn't behave, but at the same time I'd be saying it like I was talking sweet words to him, and I'd give him a handful of sweetfeed to get him to do what I wanted. That's the way Molly sounded talking to Buck.

Her hand slid up and down his arm, and Buck tried to wiggle sideways, but Molly just scooted along by him.

"Don't, Missy," he said. He sounded like he was choking on something, and the sweat ran down him most as heavy as the water he always pours over his head when we haul hay and go to the spring for a drink.

Her hand went to the scar across his shoulder and she said, "Buck, you ain't like other men around here, not like any other niggers and not like them cousins of mine. You're special, just like before you went off.

I've loved you extra special since I was little and I heard you talking to Professor Lawson and his missus about all kinds of stuff. And you've always been good to me. Always treated me like I was special, not somebody just to wait on you, like them boys treat me. You ain't never been mean like they have. So I always figured you liked me."

"I do. I have. Oh, God, Molly, I've loved you since I don't know when." He looked away from her, down at his hands that he now twisted in his lap, and his voice fell almost to a whisper. "That's why I came home. Just to see you whenever I could. Why do you think I come up here when I know you're home?" He turned toward her, and I wished I could of seen his face cause he groaned deep in his throat, and she leaned suddenly toward him, grabbed both his arms in her hands, kissed him on the mouth. Even Roy Rogers and Dale Evans don't do that in the picture shows. Buck didn't move to her or away from her and didn't move her hands from his arms, but when she put her face against his chest, wiggling as close as she could against him, his black hands came up to grab her arms and push her away. He lowered his head, shaking it back and forth, and muttered, "Oh, God, Molly, I've gotta go!"

"No, Buck, no. Stay. Please stay. I've always been your girl, Buck. I got no hankering for anybody else, just you, since I can remember." I could see Molly's face getting soft all over, even her eyes, soft like a kitten's eyes when you pet it and it purrs and rolls over on its back cause it wants you to rub its belly.

"We can't, Molly. We just can't."

"Sure we can, Buck, if you love me."

"Miss Molly, I do love you. God knows I love you," Buck whispered to her and slid his hand up and down her arm. It sure did look strange to me to see that black hand I'd seen so much on a pitchfork and a plow handle sliding against Molly's white arm, as stark as a piece of coal laid out on a fresh sheet. It looked like the winter-black trees against the twilight sky.

"I love you, Buck. Seems like I done cared about you since I can remember. I'm so lucky you care about me."

I thought about what Molly meant about being so lucky to have Buck care for her—she's got lots of kin, but I reckon she thinks they don't care. They probably don't—I've never heard any of them say anything nice to her. Her pa beat on her till Dad got her moved down with her aunt and uncle, and now her Aunt Maude makes her do all the work at their house. I reckon if they had a cotton patch she'd be the one chopping it, just like she's the one tending to the little garden in their back yard. But they'd really be bothered if they knew she was up here in the barn loft with a nigra man putting his hands all over her, and her asking him to.

I figured I better get out-a there right now, and wiggled backwards, out of that peephole. I crawled away on my belly like a snake slithering out of the ground when gasoline is poured down on him. I could feel myself strangling, and my hands were shaking so hard I didn't know if I'd be able to hold onto the oak limbs to swing down out of the loft.

But I did.

I eased my foot out onto the closest limb, felt it sway under me, and I swung out to catch the overhead limb as I dropped onto the next one down. It scratched against the barn, but sounded like a squirrel running on the boards, and I was down the tree and headed home, kicking up dust.

At the train tracks, I stopped, sat down on a rail, and cried. I was so scared for them.

Mama one time told me that when you have a good friend, you have to trust that friend to be doing right—whatever he does is okay even if you can't understand at the time. So maybe Mama would tell me not to think they're doing wrong.

I don't reckon I can ask her, though. I for sure can't ask my teacher cause her husband's in the Klu Klux.

I gotta hide this diary real good. Can't even Mama know about today.

MICKEY

"Hey, nigger," Junior called.

Mickey turned—and kicked the milk can. It tilted, Mickey grabbed, but he and the can tumbled onto the barn floor. White flooded across the red clay floor.

"Damn you." Junior grabbed the back of Mickey's overalls and jerked him up. Before Mickey had gained his balance, Junior slammed a fist into Mickey's face just below his eye. Mickey collapsed onto his side and curled, arms over his head. Junior kicked his back.

Mickey screamed.

"Get up and take ya beating, nigger."

"Please Mr. Junior. I didn't mean to turn hit over. Please suh."

"Get up."

Mickey sat up and scooted back on his butt.

"I said get up."

Mickey rose, pulled his arms up to cover his face.

Junior evaded Mickey's defense and struck his nose. It broke and leaned off to the side.

Mickey covered his nose with both hands. Junior's fist landed upside Mickey's head again.

"Now you git out-a here, nigger, afore I kill ya."

Mickey hurried to the barn door, a wide arched opening that never closed. As he stepped around the wall, he stopped, looked back at the white man who controlled his livelihood and life. "You ain't never gonna hit on me again. I'm gonna kill ya."

He ran. Junior's voice followed him. "You ain't killing anybody. You get yourself back here in the morning or you'll be the one dead."

The walk home was five miles. Mickey had made two when he heard Junior's truck, the muffler sputtering so that everyone knew it a half-mile off. He didn't look back but jumped the ditch and ducked into the brush.

A shotgun poked out the passenger window.

"Uh-ugh. They after me."

Mickey fought the brush in the edge of the woods as he made his way homeward. Darkness fell. Junior's truck sputtered as it passed him on the way back to the barn.

He wanted his daddy's shotgun. Mama was gonna fuss, but he had to go back.

Got to shoot Junior. If I don't, what am I? Junior always calls me "dumb nigger." But I ain't dumb. I know a heap more'n Junior about lots of things. As much about cows, and lots more book learning. The professor loaned me all those books and the Missus made me study that summer, same as she helped Buck learn.

I gotta get those books back to the professor.

As he neared home, he saw the clutter in the yard. Mattresses. The iron bedsteads. Mama's good chair. The few canned goods Mama had put up, the Mason jars busted.

The professor's books.

Ole Red slunk from under the porch, belly-crawling like an egg-sucking hound dog toward him. Red wagged his tail and groveled, head down, waiting for Mickey to touch him.

"What's matter, Red? They whup you? It's okay, boy." He scratched Red behind the ears, and the dog leaped up, paws on Mickey's' chest, tongue slurping over his face.

Mickey looked to the house and took a deep breath.

Mama. The boys. Junior's folks've been here.

He leaped onto the porch and ran inside.

His mother jumped at the sound of his steps. "Oh, thanks be to gawd you be here, son."

His brothers sat in cane-bottom chairs beside the pine table his daddy had made. He realized his mama had been kneeling in front of the older boy. The rag in her hand was bloody. Both boys' faces were swelling and showed cuts that still seeped blood. A single bloody tooth lay on the table.

"Ma, what happened?"

"What happened to you, Mick? Junior hit up on you too?"

"Yeah. But did he—?"

"Junior and his brother cum here and hit up on 'em and told me they'd do worsen iffen you weren't at the barn like you supposed to be tomorrow."

"He can't do this, Ma. He can't come here and beat up on the boys cause he be mad at me. I told 'im I was gonna kill him, and I am."

"Oh, no, Mickey." She shouted. "You cain't do that. They'll kill you fer sure.

"Ma, I gotta. If they kill me, they kill me. But I ain't gonna let a white man beat up on me, and for sure not beat up on my baby brothers, without I do something. I kill 'im, that'll learn some of them white men they better take care."

Mickey set about to gather what he would need while his mother began making cornbread and frying up the chicken she had killed and cleaned just before the men had invaded her house.

"That'air ham's still in the smoke house, son. Go git you a good slab. Git cha a clean Mason jar for water. You can't drink out-a the river. You shoot Junior, you ain't gonna be coming home. You gotta head up nawth."

Before he went to the smoke house, he entered the attached shed, where he cleaned the possums, coons and rabbits he brought home for the family. His shotgun still lay across the pegs where he'd left it after the last hunt.

When he walked in with the ham and shotgun, his mama cried.

Mickey ate with the family, hugged his brothers and mother, and headed back to the milking barn, shotgun in his right hand, the croaker sack with all his food and supplies over his left shoulder.

He'd be there at milking time, for sure.

*   *   *

Mickey sat in the darkness and waited. Moonlight filtered into the barn enough he could see the patterns of browns in the hay he had scattered over the floor before they milked last night. Junior hadn't bothered to muck out the barn.

He fingered the shotgun. His daddy's old Stevens single shot. Loaded with double-ought buck.

Junior wouldn't be along for another hour at least. Mickey nibbled at the cornbread his mama gave him when he left home—and took extra care to catch crumbs. He didn't know when he might get something else to eat. If ever.

He tried not to think about Mama. She begged him not to go. "You gone git yourself kilt. Don't go back. Please, Mickey, don't!" She gripped his arm so tight it hurt.

"Mama, I got to. Maybe—I dunno, Mama. I jest gotta."

He left her standing in the door, watching him. He turned at the bend in the road and looked back. The kerosene lamp outlined her and one of his brothers standing beside her in the doorway.

He took a swallow from the Mason jar. He'd be leaving it here. It wasn't worth the weight to carry and drinking out of the river and creeks was something he did without giving it a thought.

Wonder if I gonna be seeing Mama again.

Time seemed to drag. The moon shadows looked like they didn't move across the floor at all.

Finally, a rooster crowed. Painful excitement grew inside, the kind he got when he knew the dogs had treed and all he had to do was kill. Junior would be treed the second he walked into the barn.

A few of the cows arrived ahead of Junior and stood outside the barn, lowing, ready to be milked. He knew they would not get milked this morning. Another payback to Junior. His cows would go dry.

Junior's barn boots scrunched the dirt outside, and the lantern threw shadows into the barn ahead of him. Mickey stood, clutched the shotgun in his right hand, and let it hang down alongside his leg. He kept his right forefinger on the trigger guard as Junior entered the barn.

Junior switched on the lights, raised the bail on the lantern, blew out the flame and hooked the lantern over a nail.

Mickey coughed. Junior looked up.

"Bout time you got here, nigger. We got milking to do."

"I ain't here to do no milkin', Junior. I come back to pay you fer the beating. I ain't taking no mo from you."

His right eye had swollen shut. Dried blood splotched his back beside the cross of his overall straps. His left arm throbbed.

Mickey brought the shotgun forward so Junior could see it. His right forefinger lay across the trigger, his hand wrapped around the grip. His left hand supported the stock.

"Put that gun down. You crazy? I'll see you hang for walking in here like that.

"You ain't hanging me and you not gonna hang no other nigger either, Junior. I come here to kill ya." Mickey's hands trembled. The barrel of the shotgun seemed to swing in circles because of the pain in his left arm.

Junior laughed and reached for the bucket at his feet. In one motion, he slung it toward Mickey and ducked around the cedar trunk supporting the roof. "You ain't got the nerve, nigger."

He grabbed a pitchfork.

Mickey crept toward the post. Hunkered sideways behind it, Junior was almost hidden. Only the hands holding the pitchfork were visible.

"You done told me I had to take muh beating. Now I'm telling you, you got to take your own beating."

Mickey pulled the shotgun to his shoulder, flipped back the hammer. The pitchfork flew towards him.

He dropped to the floor onto his belly and elbows.

Junior leaped out.

Mickey fired.

Double ought buckshot dropped Junior.

Mickey laid the shotgun on the floor, picked up the pitchfork, and stabbed it into the body.

"You ain't beating up on any more niggers, Mista Junior," he muttered.

He could not move again for what seemed like forever. His body shook, like it had that time he had caught the twenty-pound catfish down at the river.

"Gotta git," he said "Gotta git out-a here."

He lifted the shotgun, broke the singleshot to pop out the empty shell, reloaded, and snapped it closed.

Dogs'll be after me soon as they get 'em from over in Macon. Gotta fool 'em.

Junior's shirt, hanging on a nail since the last cold spell, caught his attention. He grabbed it. *Fool the dogs with Junior's own smell.*

Knowing it would be several hours before Junior was missed, Mickey strode from the barn, back to the road, and trotted off into the growing morning.

As he topped the hill above Hickory Creek, the rising mist enveloped someone fishing from the edge of the bridge. Mickey stepped off the road, into the ditch and behind a clump of plum bushes. Out of sight, he slipped as quiet as the mist until he could identify the man on the bridge.

Buck.

Mickey smiled. At least one friend, a man who could understand. He strode down the hill and was still more than one hundred feet from the creek when Buck rose to his feet, lifted his cane pole and hauled up a catfish. He had pulled out the hook and held the fish by its gills as Mickey neared and spoke.

"Hey, Buck. See you got a nice one fer breakfast."

"Hey. Yeah, I did, Mick. God, man, what happened to you?" Buck almost dropped the fish and the cane pole leaning against his other shoulder nearly wobbled off.

Mickey's left eye was still shut. His dark face was purpling with bruises. His split lip had crusted with blood. His nose twisted off to one side. Dried and fresh blood spattered his overalls. He held a shotgun in one hand, a croaker sack in the other.

"I turned over a can of milk up at the dairy and Junior beat me half to death."

"And then what? Some of that blood's fresh. What he did to your face didn't happen just now. How come you're leaving the dairy this early?" He pointed to the shotgun. "What did you do, boy? You go up there and shoot Junior?"

Mickey nodded. "I had to, Buck. I let him git by with beating up on me, he ain't gonna stop with jest me. He be killing any nigger what goes up there and he think he kin get by with it. Now he can't. He can't hurt nobody again, and lots of white menfolks're gonna think afore they go beating up on a nigger."

"They'll kill you. You know that. You can't go home. You got to get to the river.

"They ain't gonna find me. I got me Junior's shirt. I can't go down Hickory Creek, it's too deep. But I'll lose them. Soon's I hear them dogs, I'll get to a creek and drag Junior's shirt. It'll mess up the dogs noses. They ain't gonna get me."

"You got enough food in that sack?"

"Corn pone, some ham and some fried chicken. I'm gonna be just as good as snuff and nowhere near as dusty." Mickey laughed. "So don't you fret over me none, you hear?"

Buck nodded and smiled. He looked down at the fish still hanging on his fingers. "Let me get this on the string."

Mickey reached down for the stob Buck had shoved into the bank and pulled up the string. It held four other fish.

"Man, you got yourself a load here."

"Yeah. Want me to drop them off with your mama? "

"No, I don't reckon so. You think Junior's brother's gonna mess with Mama again?"

Buck slid the last cat onto the string. "I dunno. I don't reckon so. But I'll tell the professor. He'll know what's best for her. Don't worry, Mickey. We'll see to your mama."

With the catfish in one hand, he reached his other to his friend. Mickey took it.

"Luck to you, Mick. Hope you make it out-a here. Get to the river and get downstream all day. By night, you ought to be safe."

"Thanks, Buck."

The older man nodded, picked up his fishing pole, turned and strode off.

I ain't heading to the river without I see Mama. Get her out-a the house in case they come after her. Like Buck said, maybe she can go down to the professor's, to one of them cabins out behind the big house.

BUCK

Buck knew there was no need to fret over Mickey. The boy would run until he got caught, and if he were to be lucky, luckier'n any nigger boy he knew, he'd make it to the river far enough south that he would be ahead of the hunters.

He shook his head and tried to put his mind ahead. He was going to see Molly before he got home and told the professor about Mickey.

Oh, Molly my love, if you were only a nigger too. Sometimes I think I shouldn't have ever come home from the army. Just gone up to Detroit or out to California.

When he reached Molly's home, he stood in the yard and hollered for her aunt. "Miss Maude? I got some extra catfish. You want some?"

Maude came onto the porch. A thin woman with sparse gray hair, she wore only a dress made from mismatched feed sacks. Her feet were bare, and light from the other end of the hallway at the back door outlined her through the dress.

Molly peeked over her shoulder. She looked him in the eye and smiled. Her blue eyes glistened. Her hand rested a moment on the door jamb and Buck saw it tremble.

Remembering, he shivered.

Buck smiled back. He didn't dare look Maude in the eye, but Maude couldn't see that instead of looking over her shoulder he was staring into Molly's eyes. He approached the porch. "I got all these and I don't need but the smallest one for my breakfast. You want the other four, Miss Maude?"

"I shore do, Buck. Molly, you step down and fetch 'em."

The touch of Molly's hand as she took the string and held it as he removed the smallest fish was the closest he could get to hold her hand today. The professor would have work for him as soon as he learned about Mickey.

SAMANTHA

A deputy sheriff pounded on the back door before we sat down to breakfast, and I got to the kitchen by the time Mama opened up the screen to let him in. My belly tightened up—he was in the Klu Klux like all the deputies were, and I was scared he had come to find Buck to kill him. I went weak in my knees and grabbed the door jamb to keep my balance.

"Morning, Miz Lawson, Miss Samantha. Sorry to bother you, Miz Lawson, but we're looking for that nigger boy Mickey. Works up at the dairy. I don't reckon you've seen anything of him down this way?"

I closed my eyes and took a deep breath of relief.

He looked like he had on yesterday's uniform, all wrinkled up and with sweat smudges on the sleeves where he'd wiped off his face. He hadn't shaved and reeked like a field hand at the end of a brinjin hot July day. Even the smell of sizzling bacon couldn't hide his stink. At least he took his hat off to talk to Mama, but that made him look even worse cause it had ironed his sweaty hair to his head.

"Why no, I haven't. Why in the world are you looking for that sweet boy?"

"Ain't nothing sweet about him no more, M'am. He up and shot Junior Simpson this morning. Killed him."

Mama's jaw dropped, but she got her mouth closed quicker'n I did. Mickey has helped us get hay in every summer since he was about twelve, and he's only sixteen now. He's always had a smile for everybody and I've never seen him the least bit mad.

"What happened?" Mama asked. "What in the world did Junior do that made Mickey mad enough to do such?"

"Didn't have the first reason, M'am. Just up and shot Junior about three-dark-thirty this morning when he walked into the barn. Looked like he'd laid out for Junior all night with a shotgun. He had himself a feast there, even left a chunk of his corn pone and fatback on the floor in the hay when he run off. We got dogs coming from Macon, so don't you fret none. We'll have him caught by dark. If you hear tell of where he's holed up, though, will you call down to the office?"

"We don't have phones out here, deputy. But I can send in word if I hear anything."

"You do that, please, M'am?" He nodded to her and was gone.

What of his rank smell he didn't take with him the rising wind from the window blew out through the screen door.

"Mama, you reckon he'll come by this way to hide?"

"Not too likely, Sam. Come on, I've got to finish getting breakfast on the table. Your dad'll be in with the milk in a few minutes."

Before Mama had the bacon laid out on a paper sack to dry the grease, Dad walked in with a bucket of steaming milk, and while I poured it through the straining rag into a gallon jug, Mama started to tell Dad what the deputy said.

"I heard," Dad interrupted. "Buck told me about yesterday's beating—"

"Beating?" Mama asked.

"Yes. Junior beat Mickey pretty bad." He passed on what Buck told him. And what he had learned from Bessie.

"Bessie told the Simpsons he'd gone to Detroit, so they finally left. But they tore up the inside of the house, threw mattresses and clothes into the yard, and dumped out all the food from the kitchen. They made one big mess. And they looked for guns, took Mickey's daddy's .22 rifle.

"They didn't find Mickey's shotgun, though. It was in the shed where he left it back in the spring. Before I milked, Buck and I went to get Bessie and her other two boys. We moved them into the slave house."

"I'll fix them some breakfast," Mama said.

"Can I take it down to them, Mama?" I asked.

She shook her head at me and said, "No, you have to get ready for school."

To Dad, she said, "Will it ever get any better?"

"I don't know," Dad sighed. "This shooting might make some of the white men a little slower about hitting on the nigras. It's the first time a nigra has gone back after a beating and killed a white man."

"But they'll kill Mickey when they find him," I said. "Why'd he do it? Didn't he know he'd be killed for that?"

"Yes, Sam, he knows. But he had two choices—stand up for what is right or forever be the same as a slave. He'd rather be dead than to be subjected to beatings. But killing's never the answer. One killing just leads to another."

"Where's Buck?" Mama asked.

"At the cottage. I told him to go inside and stay until all this is over. Any nigra out today can expect trouble."

"I'll go see about him," I said.

"No, you've got to catch the bus. Buck'll be fine. I can see about him later. Finish up your breakfast and get dressed for school."

"Bessie needs some things," Dad said as he sat down. "Food, water. We brought the mattresses out of the yard. And she got her chamber pot. Main thing is to keep it quiet. You hear me, Sam? Not a word to anybody. Not even to your friend Michelle."

"You bet, Dad," I said. "I don't want any of those Klu Kluxers around here." I wouldn't tell my best school friend, but when she does find out, she'll wonder why I didn't trust her to keep it quiet.

On the bus, I told the driver that Junior was killed and I didn't reckon any of his family would go to school today, but he drove on up to the Simpson's dairy anyway. "I gotta at least show up, whether they go to school or not. I reckon the two brothers and his daddy'll be out looking for that killer."

We stopped at Maude's to pick up my friend Molly, and after I told her, she sat real pale and didn't say a word. She musta been in a swivet about Buck. She doesn't know I saw them Sunday.

At the Simpson's, nobody was in the yard except a deputy. The driver opened the door and waved at him to come over from where he leaned up against an oak and gripped a shotgun like he couldn't wait to shoot it. On the front seat, I could hear everything. So could Molly.

"Whatcha still doing here?" the driver asked.

"Waiting. Just in case that nigger has the gumption to come back up here. Seen any sign of anything on the road?"

Shaking his head, he said, "I ain't seen the first nigger anywhere. It's like they've all gone into a hole somewhere."

"They know what's good for 'em, they'll stay in a hole. Any nigger shows up around here is a dead nigger. A nigger's gotta take his beating when he does wrong."

"Nobody's got a right to beat on somebody else," I hollered.

"Sam, you quit mouthing off like that. Folks'll call you a nigger lover."

"I'd rather be a nigger lover than a nigger hater like you."

"You get that bus out-a here afore I have ta spank that young 'un," the deputy said.

Before the door closed, I stuck my tongue out at the deputy.

MICKEY

Home was still a mile away when the first sounds came from behind him. Truck. In a hurry.

He ducked off the road and watched Junior's father drive by, with Junior's younger brother in the passenger seat with the end of a shotgun leaning out the window.

Seems like all that young'un does is poke that barrel out the window.

He stayed in the brushes until the dust settled.

No time now to go home. And the way to the river would be covered up with white men. White men with shotguns.

He headed north, away from home. Two miles below the mill, he waded into Mill Creek, soaked his overall legs and rolled them up. He hustled downstream for a good half-mile, and when he scampered up the bank at a cattle crossing, he dragged Junior's shirt behind him. An hour later, he heard the dogs yelping. Same as his possum hounds, on the trail. They quieted when they hit the creek. The handlers' shouts of encouragement reached Mickey, but he felt safe with Junior's scent masking his.

But white men seemed to be everywhere. Trucks roared and rattled both ways on the roads. At some forks, he saw armed men standing around. Men in pairs and on horseback rode the paths. He took to the bushes, and managed to avoid the hunters all day.

SAMANTHA

After school, as soon as I got on the bus, I asked the driver if he had heard anything about Mickey. Lots of the high school boys were on the bus, and all the driver had heard was that the dogs had gotten over here from Macon and were set on his trail from the barn. Mickey had gone to the creek below the millpond, but they hadn't been able to track him after that. I wondered if he was hidden up under the falls or if he could have floated down the middle of the creek on a board or a tree limb. The creek's deep enough for a boat, and there's so much marsh around it in places you can't walk up to the banks. If he got down Mill Creek to the river, he could hold onto a treetop and float way off.

Everybody was still hunting him. Even the solicitor general and the rest of the lawyers were out on horses in the woods, with most every white man around. The bus driver said there were more shotguns and rifles in the woods today than when the damn Yankees had marched across Georgia, and that somebody was gonna get killed. He said white boys were driving their Chevys all over, just hunting for any nigra they could find to beat on or to shoot.

We passed two white men who stood beside a pickup stopped on the side of the road. Both men held a shotgun. They waved at us, and we stopped long enough for them to say there're been no sign of Mickey.

The high school boys on the bus couldn't talk about anything but going "nigger hunting" as soon as they got home.

When I got off the bus, with my shoes in my hand, I trotted over to the cottage to see if Buck was all right. When I ran up on the porch, he musta known my step, because before I could knock, he called out, "Come on in, Sam."

Buck put down his book. He looked a little peaked, even if he did have on clean overalls and had sat inside all day instead of working.

"You heard anything?" he asked.

I shook my head. "No. There's a couple of men up the road aways, holding shotguns. They said Mickey's still free. How'd you know what happened so quick?"

"I ran up on Mickey this morning when I was fishing up at Hickory Creek. He was on the run. And still madder'n any colored man I ever saw. I hope he makes it to the river. I told the professor as soon as I got home from fishing."

Everybody calls my dad "Professor" for being a college professor, but Mama and I call him "Dad." I sat and rocked. My feet pushed me back until they came up off the floor. The wood squeaked a little, almost making me drowsy with the music. Like always, my thumb found the knot in the armrest and worried at it.

"But why? He coulda just run off. "

"Mickey figured the only thing left for him was to kill Junior before he got killed himself."

"They wouldn't of killed him, would they, Buck?"

"He threatened a white man, so the white man has to kill him to keep the rest of us coloreds in our place. Anybody helps Mickey, that somebody is dead, too. Every colored in the county is inside, doors and windows closed."

"Maybe he'll get away," I said. I glanced over to the front windows and saw Buck had closed them. No wonder his house seemed so stuffy and I could smell the cornbread he'd cooked himself for dinner even if he had eaten four hours ago. Sweat ran down his face, and sweat made a little trail down my spine and settled in my underpants. I needed to go to the pond for a swim to cool off.

Shaking his head, Buck said, "He'll never get out of the county. Not unless he got down the river before anybody else knew."

"The dogs can't find him if he went to the millpond. The dogs can't track him in the creek. He can just float away and they'll never find him."

"Mill Creek is big enough, if he can stay in the water and work his way to the river. But he can't swim. And they'll have men all along the river where Mill Creek runs in. I can't hold out much hope for him. Once that many white men get out looking, there's not a nigra around here who can get away."

Was he telling me if they got after *him* he couldn't get away? I shivered and tried to turn my mind away from that kind of thinking.

"You talked to Bessie since y'all moved her down to the cabin?"

He shook his head. "Your mama thought it best I not to go around there just in case somebody drives by. I don't want to do anything to cause your daddy any harm."

"I reckon I'll go on up to the house. You need anything?"

"No, Sam. Thanks though. I'll tend to the chickens and—"

"Oh, no, Buck, you stay inside. I can do all our chores okay by myself. You stay here and stay safe. I couldn't stand it if they shot you."

They'll do more than just shoot him if they learn about Molly.

He laughed. "Okay, Sam. I'll stay here. And you be careful to get everything tended to well before dark, you hear? And watch out for foxes. I hear Mr. Hightower up the road had one in his yard yesterday, slobbering all over the place, and he missed it with his .22. You be careful. You don't want a run-in with a fox."

I sure didn't want to see a mad fox. I promised him I'd be careful and went on up to the house. Sis had come to pick up her baby, Katie, and as I walked in she was telling Mama that her husband J. D. hadn't gone on the hunt for Mick. But most of the other lawyers had. Even our cousin Judge Phil had left his office. Weren't any men lawyers left in town today but J. D. and our friend Danny Murphy. Course, Vicki, my friend Michelle's mama and the only lady lawyer in town, wasn't out there chasing Mickey.

Mama said for me to hurry up with my chores and get back inside. If Mickey was desperate enough, he'd kidnap somebody to help himself get away

"Get Buck to go with you for the cows and take the rifle. Mr. Hightower says there's another rabid fox around."

"Mama, I don't think Mick would bother me. Not really. But I'll take the rifle just in case that fox comes down here."

"Sweetheart," she said, "Mick's trying to stay alive. Anything's possible. I don't want you out alone anywhere, you hear? You get Buck to go with you. Not just for the cows. Get him to help with all your chores, even the chickens."

I trotted down to Buck's and we started our chores at the chicken house. Two trucks ripped up the road, throwing so much dust into the air it was still thick when it had rolled as far as the chicken pens.

"All the white boys are out nigger hunting tonight," Buck said.

We'd put the milk cows in their stalls away from the calves and were walking up the hill to the house when a truck came down the road, raising dust, and squealing as it stopped next to us. Four boys from the Stanleyville Military School, every one of them in uniform and with a gun, jumped out, poking the guns toward Buck. One pushed the end of the shotgun barrel right into Buck's neck.

Buck didn't move, but I did. I screamed at them, "You stop it. Get out of here. Leave us alone."

When nobody moved except for the tallest one, who smirked at me, I yelled, "Git out," the same way I would at a stray dog that tried to get into a hen nest to suck eggs. I brought my rifle up to point right at the boy with the shotgun, the only one of them I knew.

"Terry! Listen to me. Go away. Leave us alone! He's helping me. Can you hear me? Terry?"

Silence. All of us froze as still as the cardboard cutouts over at the picture show. I heard a chuck-will's-widow call from over by the spring. Twilight turned everything blue around us. Even the conjure woman's drum was quiet.

We stood like that for what seemed forever. Until I eased my thumb up to the safety and pushed it off with a loud click.

Terry's lopsided grin sorta jerked wider at the sound and then shrunk off. His eyes squeezed almost closed as if he didn't want me to see him scared of my rifle pointed right into this face. Besides, he knew my daddy would kill him in a second if he bothered me.

The light breeze drifting from the boys toward me was already filled with the rank odor of sweat and old cigarette smoke, but now the stench of fear overpowered everything and stung my nose. I knew we had won as he slowly raised up the end of his shotgun so it pointed up into the trees behind Buck.

"Okay, nigger, she's saved your skin tonight, but you better get your black nigger skin inside your house and stay there if you want it in one piece tomorrow. You hear me, nigger boy?"

"Yessuh, Mista, I hears you, suh," Buck whispered, his face turned to the ground, his eyes looking only at the boys' feet.

"Let's go, men," Terry said. The other three jumped into the truck bed while Terry got behind the wheel and roared off.

"Oh, Buck, they scared me so." I didn't tell him how much my throat burned with my supper trying to come up, but he saw my hands shaking when I tried to put the safety back on.

He reached for the rifle, clicked it on safe, and said, "All they wanted was somebody to push around. Any nigger'd do. They wouldn't of bothered me if your daddy had been with me. Let's get off the road before somebody else comes along and you shoot one of 'em. I can't let you go to jail on my account, Sam."

We ran the rest of the way to his cottage, and just as we got inside, we heard another truck go by, its muffler busted and its manifold roaring. Buck closed the door behind us and turned the latch.

I dropped into his rocker.

"They'll burn crosses all over tonight," Buck said.

"I'm scared they'll come back. Those boys were just from the military high school, and they're meaner'n snakes. I thought they were gonna kill you."

"They won't bother me again, not's long as I don't rankle them. You got to be careful yourself. You point that rifle at some of these men, they'll shoot you. That Mr. Terry was just showing out, but if it'd been Mr. Flint—well, he'd-a just shoved you down, shot me, and gone on his way."

He went to the window as we heard another truck go by. It was pitch dark. Buck said darkness is the best time for people to roam, pretend they're brave, and attack people they are really afraid of in the daylight. He pulled the shade down and turned on a light.

"You best get on up to the house. I'm fine. Once you're gone, I'll kill the light."

"You just gonna sit here in the dark?"

Buck shook his head. "No, I'll sit on the porch in the dark, and just watch and listen. You look out from your upstairs front porch tonight, in about two more hours. You'll see the light from the cross. They'll burn one in front of Mick's house tonight."

"What'll they do to his mama and brothers?"

"Nothing. They'll be safe down to the slave house. Nobody'll look for them down there. And nobody'll bother them once they catch Mick and know his mama wasn't hiding him."

I threw my arms around Buck's waist and talked into his chest. "Oh, Buck, I don't want anything to happen to you. You're about the best friend I've ever had in all my life."

I breathed in his smells, the soap in his overalls, his sweat, and the cow that rubbed up against him at the barn when we fed them a little while ago.

Buck pushed me back a little and looked into my eyes. I could see his worry deep inside his and in the crinkles between them as he frowned. "Don't fret so, Sam. Whatever happens is gonna happen and being scared won't help."

"You can't even go to town or up the road to see your mama or anything."

Smiling, he shook his head. "No, Sam. Not for a day or two. Only place I'll go is up to the big house and out back to see if Mick's folks need something. Or off with your daddy. You best run home before it's any darker, or your mama's gonna be worried."

I nodded, and said, "You stay hidden, okay?"

He cut off the light and we stepped onto the porch; all I could see was his teeth as he smiled back at me and said, "You run along on home, Sam."

Before he handed me Dad's rifle, he took out the bullet, and I trotted all the way back to the house, where I told Mama what he said about the cross. I wasn't about to tell her what happened with those schoolboys or she'd never let me out of the house again. Mama said not to mention the cross or the Klu Klux to Bessie.

She asked me to take Bessie the fried chicken, sweet potatoes and cornbread she had cooked. I took down a quart of fresh sweet milk too, for her boys. It was some I strained just this morning.

The night was dark as pitch-tar with the moon gone behind some thunderheads that sent smells of rain our way. I stood outside calling till Bessie poked her head out the door, a lamp in her hand.

"I got you something to eat," I said. I reached the food up, and she put down the lantern to take it and the milk. "I'll be back in a few minutes with some water."

"Dat's okay, Miz Sam. Your pa, he dun brung us down plenty a water. Tell your ma much obliged for dis-here supper."

I nodded and said, "I reckon I'll see you in the morning. You got enough to sleep on?"

"Your pa brung us down our corn shuck mattresses frum de house. We's much obliged for dat, too, Miz Sam."

"Okay. Good night, Bessie."

"Night, Miz Sam."

*　　*　　*

After we had supper and had cleaned up the kitchen, I went to the upstairs front porch to look toward the hill where Mick had lived. But it was all darkness up that way. Mama and Dad came up to bed while I was out there, and as they came out on the porch, we saw the night suddenly erupt with light.

"They sure went to a lot of trouble for that one," Dad said.

We could see the shape of the cross, flaming almost two miles away on the hill across the pastures and the cotton fields.

I looked down toward Buck's cottage and wondered if he could see the fire from there. We were about sixteen feet higher on the upstairs porch.

But the night wind blew the smells of the fire right to us, the stench of burning rags, a smell that gets into your nose and won't get out.

Bessie had to smell it too, out in back of our house, and she had to know it was up at her place.

"Mama, they won't burn down the house, will they?"

Dad answered. "No, the house belongs to your Cousin Phil. They'll not burn it."

We didn't talk any more, just watched a little while and listened to the conjure woman beat on her drum. It sounded different tonight, like she knew Mick was running for his life and she wanted to tell him he'd be okay.

Mama told me to go to bed, so I came back to my room and tried, but I couldn't go to sleep. I've tried to shut off what I keep seeing in my mind—that big cross on fire, the Klu Klux whipping up on Mick tied to a tree, and the conjure woman off in the dark, watching while she beats on her drum.

I wish she'd put a hex on the whole Klu Klux. I hope they never find Mick and that he gets away.

MICKEY

When darkness fell, the urge to go home pushed him back southward. The night felt safe, like all the nights he had been out with his dogs. He broke from the brush into a cotton field on a ridge overlooking the house.

Fire danced into the night—a cross burning in his yard. He sobbed. What had he done to his mama? They'd burn the house down if it didn't belong to old man Judge Phillip.

He trotted across the field toward home. Panting, he stopped in the edge almost a hundred feet from the yard. No sign of Klu Kluxers there. No truck anywhere. Only so much of his mama's things in the yard, already burned to a pile of stench. The kerosene soaking the cross had burned almost out and the rags smoldered and flared in places.

The moon slithered from behind the clouds, lit up the yard and sent rays of light across the porch. He couldn't see anybody around.

The drum started. Mickey shivered. The conjure woman had pounded dread into the night for as far back as he could remember. Was the woman warning him not to go to the house? She couldn't know he was going home.

Mickey tensed himself to stop the shivers, crossed the yard and stepped onto the porch.

"Mama?" he called through the open front door.

No answer. He stepped in. No sign of his family. Had they killed his mama?

He wandered through the shadowy-dark rooms. No sign of Mama or the boys. He turned and headed back towards the porch. And faced two shotguns.

"Gotcha, nigger," one of the men said, grabbed his arm, jerked him out the door and onto the ground.

Two more men fell on him and pulled his arms behind his back.

Mickey knew he was dead. He just didn't know how bad dying could be.

SAMANTHA

I've lain awake forever, twisting and turning from side to side, sweating on the sheets so much I had to move around to try to find a cool place.

Even with my room at the back of the house, I hear the trucks and the men yelling, so I know Buck can too. I hear them when they turn off the main highway, at least three miles away, and start up our direction.

Off and on, one of the men whoops, probably just to hear himself. He's probably scared of the dark—and of the conjure woman pounding on her drum.

It's brinjin hot, and I have to keep the windows open. Twice I've sprinkled my sheets with water to try to cool off, but I can't. Every time I turn the light off, I get so hot I just get up and sit by the window and listen to it all.

I heard the clock strike two a little bit ago. I got to quit worrying about Mick and Buck and get some sleep or I won't be worth shucks tomorrow.

I hadn't heard any trucks in a while.

Those Klu Klux musta found Mick.

And kilt him.

What'll they do to Buck and Molly if they find out what I saw last Sunday?

Wednesday May 28

The old tom gobbled once and woke me.

The drum started. The conjure woman never, but never, beat her drum in the daylight.

Mick was dead.

I lay in bed and shivered. The pounding got faster and faster and louder and louder. And stopped.

The world went silent.

No trucks rattled up the road. No laughter from nigras walking by on the way to work. The air was so still even the wind musta been scared to blow.

No rooster called to the rising sun. No hens cackled. Even the gobbler and crows were silent.

I knew what it meant to be as quiet as inside a grave.

I hurried to dress so I could help Buck feed the chickens and turkeys and gather up the eggs for breakfast before Dad came in from milking. When I got back to the house Sis and J. D. stood in the yard talking to Mama. Sis held Katie, who slept with her head buried in her mama's neck.

J. D. is Sis's husband and has a Confederate name like all his family—he's Jefferson Davis Stanley.

Sis and I don't look at all alike; she's real pretty and has got reddish-blond hair that curls down over her ears and sometimes falls into her blue eyes, while mine is brown and pulled back in plaits. She wears dresses all the time instead of boys' jeans like me. She stands almost as tall as J. D., and, like him, she keeps her back as straight as if she had a plank stuck down inside her clothes.

"We heard this morning they found Mick, dead. They're saying he killed himself, not even a half-mile from the Simpson's barn. Hanged himself on a big old oak limb," Sis said as I walked up.

"He wouldn't of killed himself," I said.

J. D. kinda wiggled his neck the way he does when he's nervous. He looked real smart in his suit—he seems to always have on a suit and tie, same as Dad when he goes to town. He keeps his hair cut off flat on top, like when he was a Marine, and he looks like the picture of the statue of one of the Roman gods from the history book. He's only been a lawyer by himself with his own office since he came home from the war. He went to law school and worked with Danny Murphy till he enlisted. He didn't wait to get drafted cause he wanted to be a Marine and help win the war. Even with all his schooling, they sent him off like a regular soldier.

He looked over at me, frowning. "Sam, Mick's dead for killing a white man. And you be careful right now, you hear? Everybody's edgy about all this, the nigras as much as the whites. You don't go saying anything about it. Maybe the Klu Klux won't bother you, but they might take it out on your dad or Buck."

"Oh, no, J.D., they wouldn't!" Mama said. "Surely not!" As she raised up her hand to her face, it trembled. I'd never seen Mama scared before.

"Those Simpson's aren't much liked around here, but all the white boys got themselves a chance to go night hunting. This town is all wound up tight as a drum and just waiting for any excuse to do something. I'm surprised at how much some of the lawyers seemed to enjoy going out hunting a person with the idea of killing him."

"But Mick was running. He wouldn't of hanged himself," I insisted.

J. D. nodded. "That's right, Sam. Most likely some of those vigilantes caught up with him somewhere and took him back there to the Simpson's to hang him. But officially, he hanged himself. Nobody's gonna question it, that is no white person. And any nigra that asks is gonna have those hooded bas—bad boys after them."

Mama asked, "Have you heard anything about Mick's house? They burned a cross up there last night."

J. D. shook his head.

Mama said we ought to go up and see about it, see if Bessie could go home. Even if it did belong to Cou'n Phil, they might still have done something to it. Sis said she'd stay at our house with Katie and fix breakfast. So Mama and I got in J. D.'s car. He hadn't parked in the shade, and it was already brinjin hot inside, so the wind blowing in the windows felt good. I kept my eyes closed and my face just outside the window all the way up the road, not pulling back inside until he slowed down and the dust started catching up with the car.

The cross was still in the yard, burned and fallen down into the dirt, where if they'd had grass, the fire would of gotten away and burned down their house. It's just a three-room house sitting on rocks under the corners of each room, but it's their home. Like all the other tenant houses around here, it's just old pine clapboards that have never seen paint. J.D. went inside for a minute, came out, and said it looked like the family had left in a hurry but the house hadn't been wrecked too much; they'd be able to live there if they came back from where they'd gone.

I wasn't gonna say they were down in our yard, but Mama did, and she said, "I just don't know what to do for her. She's got no way to feed those two boys with no grown man in the house."

"Vicki's looking for somebody. She told me just yesterday that her brother Slim is moving to town and will be living with her," J.D. said and smiled. "She said she can't get by any longer without some help since her brother's moving in."

Vicki's been Mama's friend from when she first moved to town a little over two years ago. Her daughter Michelle is my best friend at school. Sometimes she rides her high-stepping Tennessee walking horse mare out to the plantation to ride with me. Of course, we don't see them a lot, since we're almost ten miles out of town.

"I'll ask Vicki to give Bessie carrying rights so she'll have food for the children as well as some income. But it's a long walk for Bessie," Mama said.

"Oh, Vicki said she'd drive out to the country every day if she could find a good woman. I'll tell her about Bessie soon as I get to the office."

"Howcome her brother's coming here?" I asked.

J. D. rumpled my bangs, which always makes me mad. He knows I don't like it, I think, so he does it just to aggravate me. "Slim has been a deputy sheriff down in Florida, where Benson goes fishing. They're friends, so Roger got him a job as chief deputy here. I guess he figures Slim will leave his stills alone. Benson got him here to stop the rustling."

"Think he can?" I asked as we reached his car.

J. D. laughed. "I've met him, Sam. And I think he'll do the job. He cleaned up a town in South Carolina before he moved to Florida. In fact, Danny said Slim would arrest his own mother if she was breaking the law."

Back in our yard, Mama went to the slave house to talk to Bessie, but I went down to see Buck. I couldn't bear to go with her and see Bessie crying over her oldest boy. I wanted to cry over him even if I didn't know him anywhere near as good as I know Buck and his brother Jethro.

Buck met me in his back yard. "What's all the ruckus about?" he asked.

"They killed Mick last night. Hung him over by the dairy. All the white folks are saying he hanged himself."

Buck turned his back for a moment and I thought I heard him snuffle real quietlike, but he seemed like he kinda straightened up a little bit and walked back toward his cottage.

"Buck?" I called after him.

He turned, and I could see the tears sitting in his eyes and trying to get away. "Yes, Miss Sam?"

"I'm so sorry, Buck. I know he was your friend. I liked him too."

He nodded. "Thank you, Miss Sam."

I ran over to him. "Buck, it's not Miss Sam, not now and not ever.

I'm Sam, just plain Sam."

He cut his eyes down to mine and didn't try to stop the tears. "I know, Sam. I just spent all night getting my mind back to where it's gotta be, thinking like a nigger. And hating it that I didn't take that shotgun away from Mick, whomp him over the head, and drag him down to the river and make him leave."

"You couldn't of made him leave, Buck. You know that. He had his own mind made up."

Dad hollered for Buck, so we started up to the yard, where he was already moving the truck down toward the slave house. It was gonna be real late for us all to sit down for breakfast.

Buck and Dad loaded Bessie's few things into the back of the truck while J. D. talked to Bessie about her going to work for Vicki. He said he'd get Mick's body brought down to her so she could bury him.

As Dad drove off with them all, I went into the kitchen where Sis had smelled it up with biscuits and sausages. She and Mama had already gone into the dining room, so I followed the food to the table and made myself a biscuit and sausage sandwich and had two big glasses of icy milk.

I wanted to ask Mama about howcome some of the nigras have the same last name that she did before she got married. I know Buck's mama was a Mosby, same as my mama, and I wanted to ask if we are cousins. but I didn't dare. There're a lot of nigra Mosbys around, and I wondered, too, if Bessie might be one.

*   *   *

Late this afternoon, Larry Huntington, the Antique Man from Savannah I like so much, drove up and brought some fancy things from New Orleans to show Dad. The prettiest was a porcelain candle stick all blue and white that he said was Frankenthal; the top part comes off, so you can burn one candle or put the top on and burn six.

Dad bought it. Larry had some other things he said he was supposed to show to our Cousin Phil tomorrow. Mama asked him to stay to supper, and he said he'd like to, that he didn't have any plans tonight.

He walked out to the front pasture with me to take in the milk cows, and I went to the spring above the waterhole to get a drink. Larry grew up in a town not far off, but he never drank from a spring until today, and I showed him you just bend down and stick your face in the water.

He did, but said he didn't really like looking at frogs and spring lizards while he drank. I laughed at him, and told him he ought to be looking at his reflection in the water.

He says he's part Creek Indian, but I think his nose is too narrow and short to be an Indian nose. I wonder if he's kin to Buck, who's part Creek Indian too. The Creeks lived around here and they made the arrowheads I find when the sharecroppers plow up the meadows.

Larry doesn't sell Indian rocks; he just sells things he can get from France or somewhere like that. But he used to sell things he found in his mama's attic and things he bought from his neighbors, when they let him go through their attics. He finally made enough money to buy things from people in France and England to sell to Dad and Cou'n Phil and other people, both here and down in Savannah, where he's got a big store now. It's in an old house he bought to live in and fix up the same as it was in the early 1800s, just like Dad has redone the part of our house that was all broken windows and fallen plaster when he bought it.

"You're about as pretty as a girl," I told him. His jet-black hair curls a little over his ears and down his neck where he wears it a little bit long. It always tumbles over his eyes, which are as soft a brown as my horse's, and his eyes catch the sunlight like Dolly's too. Larry's always got a smile, and I seem to forever feel happy around Larry. He looks just like a picture show hero ought to look.

"Now, Sam," he grinned. "And I guess you're about as handsome as any boy I've ever known."

"Reckon that's why Dad is always calling me his son who was born a girl?"

He ruffled my bangs and laughed again, but most of the time he doesn't treat me like a kid. "Maybe that's why," he said. "Come on, let's go get those cows to the barn so we can enjoy your mama's supper."

Larry's been coming to see Dad since before I can remember, ever since Cousin Phil told him Dad liked antiques. Except for what Mama got from her mama, most of our things came from Larry. Before Sis got married two years ago, Larry took her out to the picture show some. Mama wanted them to get married cause we all like Larry, but Sis married J. D. Stanley instead, and her baby, Katie, is in direct line from the man our town is named for. That's almost as good as being in direct line from Daniel Boone or Lewis Wetzel.

By the time we got the cows into their stalls, the sun was down. Darkness fell as we walked up the hill, and some clouds scooted over the stars, but the wind blowing the clouds didn't reach to the ground. Even though the moon was just a slice of light way off to the west, we could easily see the wide path of the dirt road gleaming almost white against the deeper black of the trees.

Far off, the conjure woman started beating on her drum, and Larry stopped, his hand touching my arm. "What's that?"

"It's just the conjure woman. She beats on that drum most every night."

"Who?"

"The conjure woman. She puts spells on people. Makes them do weird stuff. She may be casting a spell right now."

"On us? You reckon we better hurry back to the house?" Larry whispered and smiled, and I think he was just pretending to be a little scared, the way some grownups do.

"Oh, no. She's a couple of miles away, off in the woods. Besides, I think she doesn't bother white folks. At least, I hope she doesn't."

"You don't believe in voodoo, Sam? Surely not."

"You can't not believe, Larry. She's done all sorts of things around here. Hexed a woman so bad my daddy had to take her over to the asylum."

"Oh, come on, Sam."

"Really."

He stopped and put his hands on his hips, cocked his head and looked down at me. "Sam, you believe that?"

"Yes, I do. Mama told me it's happened a lot."

He looked off toward the direction of the drumming, a frown coming onto his face. "Maybe I ought to ask her to conjure something for me. You reckon she could conjure me a sweetheart who'll be true forever, never look at another man?"

"I think all her spells are bad and she doesn't hex up a sweetheart. Besides, most white people don't believe. But I do."

Larry laughed. "Well, if you believe, I have to believe, too." He reached over and took my hand. His felt soft, like he never did any hard work, but it felt strong too, like he could pitch hay as good as Buck if he were aiming to.

We walked on to the house, swinging our hands together.

I like Larry, even if he is about ten years older than me. It's not just that he's got a pretty face, but he's always acting like he cares about me and talks to me, like today. His voice is all the time soft, kinda like the way I talk to the horses. The boys at school always kind of yell when they talk, like a peacock strutting around. But Larry is gentle.

He stayed to visit with Mama and Dad after supper, but I came to my room cause they weren't talking about anything I wanted to hear, just about old furniture and stuff like that. I crawled out my window onto the porch roof, leaned against the side of the house, closed my eyes, and listened. The wind was sleeping, and the night throbbed to the distant drumming that seeped into me until my heart pulsed with the same beat.

Thursday, May 29

Like every day this week, Molly just about danced when she got off the school bus. All she thinks about is Buck. She barely talked to me on the bus all week, but mostly sat by the window, her head laid up against the glass, and looked at something inside her mind.

She can't see the Klu Klux just waiting to find out.

She didn't even go into her house today. With it being the next to last day of school, we didn't have any books. Out the back window I watched her skip down the road toward the train tracks—she was going off somewhere to meet Buck. She couldn't of been headed to his cottage cause it's close to the road and almost in our yard, and if they were to meet there, Mama and Dad would know in a minute.

I had a co-cola and some of the chocolate chip cookies Mama had just taken out of the oven so they were still warm and soft and filled up the house with cookie smells before I went to drive the milk cows to the barn. I took two cookies with me and finished the last bite just as I got to the middle big field. When I got halfway across, near the cedar tree, something caught my eye over toward the creek.

A fox.

In daylight.

It looked around, moved its head back and forth, and kinda shifted from one side to the other. It was looking away from me.

I kept on walking, watching the fox, not where I stepped. I snapped a stick. The fox turned toward me.

In the middle of the field, I looked for somewhere to run.

It growled. Slobber dripped from his jaws as he shook his head and trotted toward me.

My stomach knotted up. I started to shake all over. Something bitter came up from my stomach. I took off for the big old sweetgum across the field cause I couldn't outrun that fox all the way to the house. Running as hard as I could, I headed for the one tree that's got limbs almost all the way to the ground. I beat him to the tree and clambered up on the limbs.

The fox kept on growling and carrying on. I didn't know what to do. It was so far to the house nobody'd hear me if I hollered, but I hollered anyhow. I was not going to come down out of that tree even if the fox left. He might be crazy mad, but he could still smell me if he did walk off. Just like I could smell him, a rank and almost choking odor.

I sat on one limb, put my feet on the one below, and tried to get easy so I could sit till dark.

I've never seen a fox so close up before. Never seen a red fox. His tail was thick, his color almost golden like the sunset, his ears small and pointed like my kitty Tip's. But his eyes were scary, frantic, like a horse when you first try to put a halter on it. Foam dripped out of his mouth. He looked thin and poor.

The few minutes I'd been in the tree were enough for the bark to start digging into my hind end. Nobody'd know to look for me until I didn't come in for supper. I yelled. I'd count to a hundred and yell again. "Help! Anybody? Help!" By time I was getting numb all over, I heard voices over on the train tracks across the fence. Feet crunched the gravel. I called again. "Help! Somebody help me! There's a mad fox over here!"

Buck called back. "I'm coming, Sam! I'm coming!"

I heard him scrambling down the bank, sliding down the gravel into the ditch. "Buck! No! Be careful! He's got rabies. Go get help!" But he came on, crashing through the bushes into the pasture.

The fox saw him, growled, and started toward Buck.

He lifted the rifle, shot once and the fox dropped.

"Howcome you never miss?" I asked. He never missed the mistletoe, either, every Christmas, when he shot it down from the pecan tree behind the house.

"You got just one bullet, you can't afford to miss. You all right, Sam? Did he bite you?"

"Yeah, I'm okay. No, he didn't catch up to me. Boy, I sure am glad you were close by." I stood on the limb that I'd rested my feet on. My legs had gone as stiff as my backside, and for a minute I had to just stand up on a limb and shake my legs one at a time to get some feeling back and the tingling out.

"Be careful, Sam," Buck said as I started down.

Molly came into the field from the train tracks.

"Whatcha doing here?" I asked without thinking.

Real quick, Buck said, "I ran up on Miss Molly down by the crossing a minute ago and she said she thought she'd heard you calling, so we ran down here."

He cut his eyes down, not looking at me. Buck is the only nigra I know who looks me in the eye when we talk. He was lying, and he knew I could tell.

Molly didn't even look my way, but kinda twisted the end of one of her curls around a finger and looked to the side.

I wished they could trust me, but they know they can't be sure of anybody not telling on them. They oughtta know they can't keep it secret forever.

Didn't anybody say a word until I got onto the ground, shook some more of the stiff out of my legs, and dusted myself off.

"I was looking for the cows," I finally said.

"We better be getting them to the barn," Buck said. "Your mama'll be looking for you soon and it's almost dark." He reloaded his single-shot rifle and pushed the safety on.

"I thought you never carried it loaded."

He grinned. "Right now, I'm not about to carry it not loaded. And you be mighty careful yourself about going off, even for the cows. Might be you should be toting your daddy's rifle, just in case."

After we got the cows to the barn, we walked back up the hill together in the almost dark. At my driveway, I stopped, wondering what they were going to do. Was he gonna walk her home? Should I offer to go along just in case somebody drove by? Was she gonna walk home by herself? Or was he gonna take her over to his cottage?

"Night, Sam," Buck said. They walked into the night and left me standing there.

June 5, 1946, Wednesday

Dad roared. Pollock and Buck yelled.

I dropped *The Count of Monte Crisco* on the porch floor and took off across the yard. I got to the end of the driveway in only about three seconds. His eyes closed, Dad sprawled flat out on the ground, blood running all over his head, a bloody rock right by him.

Buck held Pollock's arm pulled up behind him, almost to his neck. Pollock leaned so far forward his head reached half way to the ground.

I bent down and put a hand on his shoulder. "Dad! Dad!"

"Leave him be, Sam. Go get your mama. She's got to go get the sheriff and Dr. Morris," Buck said.

"She's not home," was all I could manage to choke out as I pulled my hand away, aware only of the redness and the strong iron smell of the blood running out the side of Dad's head. "Is he—?" I couldn't mouth the word "dead."

"I think he'll be okay, Sam. But I can't turn Pollock aloose. He hit your Dad with that rock. You'll have to go get some help."

"I'll get some rope." I ran back to the kitchen porch and grabbed Dolly's bridle. While I ran back down the drive, I threw the loose ends of the reins over my shoulder so I could untie the plowlines from the bit.

When I got back, Pollock was turned aloose and was on his knees, bent over, his hands covering his face. He cried. Strange, to see such a big man cry. Pollock was about the biggest and strongest man I ever saw. His bare arms look bigger than my legs; his muscles roll down from his shoulders; and his blood vessels stand up and move like ropes under his skin. He seems stronger'n the horse pulling the plows. But now he was on his knees, crying, his body shaking with sobs.

Buck knelt by Dad, wiping his cut head with his own shirt that he had pulled off. When I stopped beside him, he didn't stay a word, just took the rope, stood, stepped over to Pollock, pulled his uncle's hands behind his back, and tied them together.

"I'll care for your Dad, Sam. Take your bike and go get your uncle Doctor Morris."

"Is Dad—? Is he going to be okay?" I was panting, not just from my run, but because I didn't know how bad Dad was hurt. Was he gonna die? What would we do if Dad was dead? Even with Buck we wouldn't be able to keep the farm going. It'd be too much for Mama.

"He'll be okay. Tell your Uncle Morris he'll need to stitch up this cut. Now you get going, Sam."

Glad as I was to hear Buck's words, I didn't slow down going for my bike in the back yard. I pedaled hard and had built up some speed when I came swooshing back down the driveway. Buck didn't even look up from where he was keeping that rag pressed upside Dad's head.

I was more'n two miles up the road when I heard a car coming up behind me. I turned, raised my hand with my palm toward it, and of all the people to come along, it was Roger Benson. I couldn't believe he stopped. He poked his head out of the window and asked through the sound of the car motor and the cloud of dust that settled over him and me both. "Is something wrong, Sam?"

"It's Dad. He's hurt. Pollock whomped him on the head. I'm going after Uncle Morris. He's got to sew up Dad's head."

Benson can't stand Dad ever since Dad tried to get him voted out of being county commissioner. I wondered if he was going to help me, but he said, "You go on along home. I'll stop by and send Dr. Morris along. If he's gone off somewhere, I'll find him. You run along home."

"Thank you," I stammered. He gunned his white Buick off up the road, raising another bunch of red grit that had me coughing before I could get out of it.

Uncle Morris passed me with a wave out the window before I got very far along on the road back home. Right behind him came Benson, who stuck his hand out the window as he passed me. I heard him yell, "I'll send the sheriff out," and he was gone in another roll of dust.

By the time I turned my bike into the driveway, Dad was sitting up and Uncle Morris was about done stitching the cut on his head. Blood on Dad's shirt had set up from the wind and from dust the car had brought off the road.

Pollock slumped sideways against an elm tree, his head hanging down, his hands tied behind his back. Buck stood beside Uncle Morris and held a bunch of little things for him to use. I kinda peeked at all the stuff, but Buck pulled away. "No, Sam. We can't touch any of this."

Uncle Morris always treated me kindly, but today he seemed to be a little cross to me. He's tall, kinda stooped over from age, with a little ring of white hair around his head and rimless glasses that perch on the end of his nose. His long slender fingers look like a woman's, but I reckon they help him stitch up people better being small like that than if he had big hands like Pollock.

"You get out of my light, Sam. Go sit down somewhere."

There wasn't a tree to sit against except over by Pollock, and I didn't want to get close to him, even if Buck had tied his hands good. So I just backed up a couple of steps and checked the driveway for chicken stuff and for the rocks we had put in the mudholes last winter. I sat down, cross-legged, where I was, right in the driveway.

Nobody said anything while Uncle Morris finished up his sewing, swabbed some reddish stuff on Dad's cut, and wrapped a bandage around his head. It sure did look a bright white against Dad's fire-red hair and against the blood that was still caked in streams down the side of his face.

Before Dr. Morris finished with the sticking plaster, the sheriff drove up, with a deputy in another car right behind him. They both stepped out, hitched up their britches, wiggled their pistols on their hips, tugged on their hats, and walked over to Dad.

"That the nigger what hit you up side the head?" the sheriff asked, pointing over to Pollock.

"Yes, he's the one," Dad said.

"What about young Buck over here?" he asked, pointing.

"He stopped it," I said. "He held onto Pollock and saved Dad's life. Don't you even think about bothering Buck."

The deputy put his hand on my shoulder. "It's okay, Sam. We just have to ask."

While the sheriff stood there looking down at Dad, the deputy walked over to Pollock, nudged him with his toe, and said, "Get your sorry self up from there."

Pollock tried to get up, but he couldn't with his hands behind him, and he tumbled onto his face. Buck stepped over to him, reached down, grabbed his upper arm, and helped him stand. The lawman looked at the ropes holding him and silently pushed him over to one of the cars. He slammed the door behind Pollock, turned to the sheriff, and said, "I'll take the nigger on to jail."

"Be right along," the sheriff said.

Dad started to get up, but Dr. Morris said, "Hold on, Professor. You got a bad knock on the head there. You need to sit a bit longer."

"I need to get up," Dad insisted.

But Buck leaned down and placed one of his still bloody hands on Dad's shoulder. "You best be easy, sir. You were out for a long time. All you need do is rest."

"We'll take care of the nigger, Professor," the sheriff said. "Don't you fret none."

"I don't want anything done to him, Sheriff. He's not a bad nigra. He just got upset."

"Any nigger that hits a white man is a bad nigger," the sheriff said. "We'll take care of him in town."

"No. Just lock him up for a couple of days," Dad insisted.

The sheriff turned toward his car. "I'll see about it," he mumbled over his shoulder. He climbed in his car, backed out the driveway, and left.

Buck and Uncle Morris got Dad into Uncle's car and drove close to the back door. From there, Buck half-walked, half-carried him into the house, like he was really stove up bad. I ran upstairs for a sheet to put across the sofa so Dad could lie there without getting the sofa cushions nasty from the blood and dirt stuck all over him.

"Don't let him go to sleep," Dr. Morris said. "Keep him drinking water and keep him awake. At least for a couple of hours."

Dad smiled. "I'll be up and out again in a couple of hours."

"I don't think so," Uncle Morris said. "What happened?"

"I got mad at Pollock. He didn't understand what I wanted him to do. It was really my own fault, but I haven't learned to talk his words. When I got mad and started yelling at him, he just got so frustrated he picked up a rock and hit me. All my fault."

Growing up in the north, Dad never learned to talk like a Georgia nigra cause he never talked to one till after he came here to live and married Mama. They don't always know what he wants them to do. Like the time Dad told Amos to nail the board up horizontally, and he had no idea what Dad meant. Buck is about the only one around who always knows what Dad is talking about.

The back porch screen door squeaked open and closed, and I ran to the kitchen to find Mama coming in, with Vicki behind her.

"What's Morris's car doing at the porch steps?" Mama asked.

"Dad got hurt but he's—" was as far as I got before Mama took off through the kitchen.

"What happened?" Vicki asked, so I told her.

Vicki is the only woman I ever heard of who read the law and didn't go to law college, but passed the test to be a lawyer. Danny Murphy sure taught her good. When they first came to town, Michelle and I got to be school friends, and Vicki and Mama got to be good friends too. When I first called her "Miz Gordon," she told me to call her Vicki. She's the first grown up to tell me to call her by her first name. She calls Mama "Laura," which is Sis's real first name too, only nobody calls either one of them "Laura." Everybody calls Sis just "Sis," unless J. D. calls her something else. And everybody calls Mama "Miz Lawson," except most of the coloreds call her "Miz Laura."

Buck left right after Mama came in, and I followed so I could ask him what was gonna happen to Pollock.

"He'll likely go to jail for a long time," Buck said. "Unless he gets electrocuted. Or even lynched."

"Oh, no. They can't kill him. Not with Dad saying it was his fault, not Pollock's."

"Sam, you know how it is for niggers. Uncle Pollock knew better than to hit your dad, no matter what. We'll just have to wait and see what happens. You go on along, now."

I headed back to the house and sat on the porch steps for a few minutes, then decided to go talk to Buck some more. Only when I got down to his house, I saw him walking toward the train tracks. As soon as he turned off the road and started down the tracks, I trotted down the hill to look, and, sure enough, aways off down the tracks I could see two people walking between the rails. Molly had on that dress with the flowers that Mama helped her make just before school was out.

At least Buck and Molly have got better sense than to be meeting down at Buck's cottage. Even so, all it's going to take is one white man to see them together and Buck'll have more trouble than his uncle Pollock has. He won't be going to jail, he'll get himself lynched. What in the world would we do without Buck here, now that Pollock's gone and gotten himself into trouble?

"Oh, Buck, you've got to be careful, a lot more careful. You oughtta be scared of the white men around here. But you're not even a little bit cautious," I whispered.

I went back to the house to help Mama, and she managed to keep Dad from going back outside to work for the rest of the day. He said at supper that he didn't have a real bad headache, just a little one. Mama told him he didn't lie good.

When I came up to my room to write, I sat over by my window, hoping for a little breeze to break the heat. It is really hot.

A barn owl screamed like a painter and the night went still, so quiet I could almost hear the moon walking across the yard until just a few minutes ago when the conjure woman started on her drums.

The beat was different, like she knew something. I shivered in spite of the heat.

June 6, Thursday

The whooping started while I was on the back porch. Trucks rattled across the train tracks. My stomach knotted when I realized they were coming in the yard.

I slid down from the end of the porch and hid in the pyracantha bush. I almost yelled when my foot landed on a thorn, but I pulled the sticker out and got more careful about where I put my feet.

Three pickup trucks kicked up dirt and threw fumes into the air as they drove up. A cloth-covered cross leaned onto the cab of one. Pollock was tied face down across the cab of another. The third truck held about ten men in the back end. Everybody but Pollock had on a white robe and a pillowcase.

The knot in my stomach turned to fire that rose up and burned my throat. The wind blew the stench of the exhaust fumes right to me.

I wanted to get Mama so we both could run off, but when I tried to climb back up onto the porch, I couldn't. Even when I tried to prop my feet against one of the brick columns holding up the floor joist, I didn't have the strength to pull myself up. That porch was too high. I was trapped. I could only try to stay out of sight and hope that Mama would hear them and come out. I wanted to scream, but I was too scared. I tried to swallow the bitter in my mouth.

They all got out of the trucks and some began to take turns with a posthole digger. One man began to twist a rope around itself, and I recognized a hangman's noose—I've made a lot of them out of the cords for the blinds in the schoolroom so I could have them to hang the rustlers when Roy Rogers and I caught them.

None of them said a word until the hole was finished.

One of them said, "Back the truck up." Another got in the truck with the cross and backed it up until the tailgate was just about over the hole. Four of them crawled up into the truck bed and, with two of them on each side under the cross beams, began inching it off, until it dropped, the butt end going into the hole. The four men kinda "woofed" when the weight of the cross fell off them. While three of them took a minute to rub their shoulders, the other man picked up a half-smashed gas can and emptied it onto the cross. Before they jumped down, I could smell the kerosene.

Pointing to the tall oak just a few yards from the cross, Cou'n Phil said, "That'll do." I sure was glad he didn't know I was there and recognized his voice.

One of the others said, "I got it." He slid behind the wheel of the truck holding Pollock and began backing it toward the tree. Another one of them leaned into the truck, pulled out a short whip, and headed for the oak, reaching it at the same time as the truck. He jumped up over the tailgate.

Pollock quivered as the man popped the whip twice, slamming the leather against the side of the truck. Laughing, the driver got out and scampered up in the back of the truck too. The man who had made the noose came over and flipped the rope into the truck.

"Slide that noose over his head and I'll take off some of his skin," the man with the whip said.

As soon as they had the noose over Pollock's head, one of the men threw the other end of the rope over the tree limb. They got down, took three loops of the rope around the tree, and stood there watching.

A man raised up the skirttail of his robe, struck a kitchen match on the back of his britches, and lit the cross. They walked over to the truck as the flames shot upward; the smell of kerosene and burning rags rose into the clear sky.

The whip sang, and Pollock screamed as the leather cut into his back. Again the whip flew into him, and again he screamed.

I wanted to run inside for Mama, and I wanted to scream. I was too scared to do either. I heard her steps on the porch as she let the kitchen screen slam behind her. Doing what she had forever cautioned me about, she got off the porch with one step, not four, and ran around the pyracantha bush.

The men all jumped like they were scared when Mama yelled, "What do you think you're doing with that thing in my yard?"

Nobody answered.

The wind picked up. I had to choke down my coughs so Mama wouldn't know I was around. For a long minute the only sound was the fire popping and Pollock whimpering.

Cou'n Phil said, "We're gonna hang this nigger right here. Let all of them know they can't hit a white man."

"You wait a minute for me to get back. I got a pot boiling on the stove and I don't want to burn down the house. Let me tend to that and get back out here before you do anything else. Hold up on the beating. I don't want to miss a lick. You hear me, boys? I want to see everything."

I never before thought Mama was full of hate for the nigras, even Pollock. I'd thought she'd want him in jail, not dead. As far back as I can remember, she's always told me that we have a special trust to take care of them and to help them better themselves. But this one had beat up on Dad. Maybe it was just Pollock she hated.

The smoke from the cross was rolling up, spreading out in the still air, stinking as bad as anything. Mama hadn't seen me when she went back into the house. I was even more scared to move, scared she'd see me when she came back outside. And I didn't want to stay there. I didn't want to see Pollock get hung. My insides were all in a jumble, hurting and twisting up. It was like Mick all over again, only this time it was Pollock, Buck's uncle, a nigra who worked for us all of my life.

I felt like I might throw up, the way I was getting weak all over and breaking out in a sweat that made me shiver with cold.

But Mama was back in a minute, with Dad's double barrel shotgun, and she walked right up to Cou'n Phil, poked the shotgun under his chin, and said, "One of you get those ropes off his arms right now."

I wondered if she knew it was Cou'n Phil.

Six of them scrambled into that pickup, and in a minute Pollock's arms were cut loose. Mama told him to get out of the truck, and he pulled the noose over his head. As soon as his feet hit the ground, she pointed the shotgun into the air and cut loose with one load of 12 gauge shot.

"Any of you want to wait around for the next load?"

I never saw grown white men move so fast, all of them jumping here and yonder to get into the trucks. They were a funny sight as they tried to see through those eyeholes in the pillowcases and not fall all over their own feet while they clambered around.

Pollock stood there, not knowing if he was gonna get that second load or not. While the last of the dust was settling from the trucks leaving, Mama broke the shotgun and took out the extra shell. Turning to him she said, "Pollock, you'll have to go back to the jail."

"Yessum, I knows, Miz Laura, but I'se scairt iffen I walks back, dey'll be waiting fer me down de road."

"Then sit there until the professor gets home. He'll drive you."

"Yessum, Miz Laura."

Pollock went over to the oak tree and sat down right under where he would have been hanging if Mama hadn't come out with that shotgun. He raised up his head a little and asked, "Miz Laura, does you wants I should git de water hose and put out dat fire?"

Mama nodded. "That'll be good, Pollock. Then you wait for the professor to get home."

"Yessum." He scrambled up, trotted across the yard to the faucet, and started pulling the hose across the back yard. It wouldn't reach far enough, so he went onto the back porch, got one of the feed buckets, and filled it with water. It was gonna take him a lot of trips back and forth with that bucket, so I came out of the bushes to help.

Mama didn't notice that I was suddenly there and didn't ask where I'd come from. All I did was get the other bucket from the porch and fill it while Pollock trotted the water over to the cross. After about a dozen trips, he went to the tool house and got a hoe to push the cross down. Grabbing the bottom of it, he dragged it, still burning, over toward the hose.

The stench seemed to sink into my nose and lungs long after Pollock got the fire put out. When he got it soaked good, I turned off the outside faucet, and he dragged the cross way down into the woods behind the house. He came back, sat down under the oak again, and waited.

He hadn't moved a long time later when the sheriff gunned his car into the yard. I stepped down off the porch as the sheriff, pistol in his hand, started toward Pollock, and I was just before going inside for Mama when she came out.

"You hold up there, Sheriff," she called. "There's no need to go pointing a gun at Pollock. He's just waiting for a ride back to the jail."

"Yeah? Then howcome he's out here to start with?"

"Oh, come on, Sheriff. You know he didn't break out. The Klu Klux broke him out, and you know it. He's not trying to run off, and he's going to stay here until my husband gets home. I don't want you shooting him and trying to tell us he was attempting to escape. I won't have that."

Dad drove up right then and told the sheriff, "I'll drive Pollock in. And you be sure there's no more breakouts, you hear?"

June 10, Monday

Buck jogged into the yard where I was practicing shooting marbles and called, "Hey, Sam. Where's your dad?"

"Inside. What's wrong?"

He dripped sweat. He leaned over, resting his hands on his knees for a minute while he caught his breath, reached into his back pocket and pulled out his big red handkerchief to swab off his face.

"It's Queen. She's gotten down, just below the barn, and I couldn't get her up by myself."

I left the marbles and ran inside to get Dad. Queen is the best plow horse we've got, and I knew he'd be upset if we couldn't get her back onto her feet real quick. We've got to have her for cutting and raking the hay too. I rode to the barn with them.

Buck jumped from the truck to grab a halter out of the barn, and we drove on to where Queen was laid out on her side. When the truck stopped, she picked up her head to look at us for a few seconds, and let it flop back onto the ground.

"I don't think she's got much chance, Sir," Buck said.

"We'll get her up," Dad said as he walked to her. "She's too good a horse to just let lie there and die. Let me have that halter."

Dad reached out for it, but Buck said, "I've got it." He stepped up to Queen's head, dropped down to sit on his heels, lifted up the mare's head, and pulled the halter on.

"Sam, you hold onto the halter and pull her head up when we roll her onto her belly."

Dad and Buck got to her back and pushed, and sure enough, Queen pulled her front feet under herself and let her head kinda loll onto the ground, making no effort to get up. She needed those front feet stuck out in front to be able to stand up.

Buck came up front, grabbed Queen's halter, and I knelt down to pull her feet forward. I got to her back side to lean against her backbone while Dad moved to grab her by the tail. He and Buck pulled up while I pushed, but Queen only grunted and rolled back against me with more weight than I could hold.

Dad looked at Buck, and said softly, "If we can get her up, maybe we can save her. I sure do miss Pollock. Reckon we'll have to go get Amos and Ellie Mae."

Buck nodded, and we all three got back in the truck and headed off up the road. If only Pollock wasn't in jail, we wouldn't have to look for somebody else to help us. When we pulled into their yard, we didn't see either one of them out in their cotton field or their garden.

Dad told me to run to the door to see if they were inside. Before I got to the house, I could smell something awful, like a privy right there beside the house with no lye put in it. I had almost reached the porch when Amos opened the door and held one hand out like a policeman.

"Stop," he yelled. "Don't you come no closer, Miz Sam. We dun been hexed. Hit cude kill you too."

I stopped, looked at him for a second, and said, "You mean the conjure woman, Amos?"

"Yessum."

"She got no call to be mad at you," I said. "You got to be wrong about that."

Ellie Mae's head showed around Amos. "Hit de trufe, Miz Sam," she insisted. "She dun got mad cause we dun give summa last year's yams to a nigger she dun put her spell on and we didn't know hit."

"But if you didn't know, that's no reason to get mad."

"Hit don't matter no mo howcome she got mad," Ellie Mae said. "We kain't go out-a de house no mo. We gonna die rightchere afore long. She tell us we die miserable iffen we goes acrost her hex line."

The hex line, still white, lay about fifteen feet from the house and ran across the front and down the sides.

"I'll tell Dad," I said. "He can do something."

I trotted back to the truck, told Dad, and he said for me and Buck to wait there, he'd be right back. Buck and I walked toward the house, but again Amos yelled for us to get back, so we went over to sit in the shade of a chinaberry tree.

"I sometimes can't understand some of this conjure woman stuff," I said. "Her threatening them over some sweet potatoes. But if she hexed me, I'd be scared too, I reckon. From the smell, they've not been to the outhouse in days. Just dumped the slop jar out the window."

"I know, Sam. I think it's more than just some yams. It's hard to believe she'd do this over something so nothing. She knows they're simple." He shrugged his shoulders. "But who knows? Maybe she figured they lied to her about not knowing she'd put a spell on that nigra. I know my mama would whup me till I couldn't sit down if she thought I'd lied."

We sat for a minute. Buck broke our silence. "Lots of mamas keep their boys in line by telling them she'll have the conjure woman hex them if they misbehave, and the boys out our way hear her drumming and believe."

"Like the older men believe in haints?" I said.

Buck grinned. "Uncle Pollock always kept his rifle handy, just in case."

"You believe in haints, Buck?"

"Believing is something you learn, Sam, just like you learn to talk. Like believing in Jesus—you get told something enough times, you're gonna believe it. Now there are a few ***nights*** when I do believe in haints, but most ***days*** I don't."

We both laughed. I feel the same way about the conjure woman— scared of her at night but in daytime not sure if I oughtta be scared.

"Howcome so many people believe in the conjure woman? Do you think she really puts spells on people? Or does it just work if they believe it will? I mean, sometimes, at night, when I hear her drum, I get scared. But like you said, in daytime, I almost don't believe."

"Now that, yes, I do believe. Daytime as well as dark. If you think something can happen to you, you do things to make it happen. And somehow, I think the conjure woman does things, too, to make something happen. Most of us coloreds believe in her, and some white folks too."

He smiled. "You probably never heard about my cousin Josie. She got herself in trouble, running around with a white man when she wasn't more'n about fourteen, and the conjure woman got after her. They say when she showed up in the yard looking for Josie she was all dressed up in black, with a long black coat, even though it was late May. When Josie went to the outhouse, she told Josie she'd not be able to sit down again. And Josie couldn't. But only cause she believed."

"She couldn't sit down to—er—I mean—"

Buck chuckled, and I know my face turned red. I felt the blood rising up and spreading hot all over my neck and face.

He answered, "No, not even for that. Her mama walked up to your mama's and Miz Laura drove Josie to the doctor. Stood her up in the rumble seat of her old Pontiac. It was a week before the doctor got her talked into bending over and sitting down again."

"How'd he do that?"

"Got some head doctor from over at the asylum in Milledgeville to come talk to her. I think they hypnotized her. Anyhow, she left for

Detroit the day after she got out of the hospital."

Dad drove up and we walked over to the truck to meet him. He got out, reached back inside, and took out a grocery sack. Walking up toward the house, he called to Amos. "I'm going to take away that spell, Amos. You just look and see. Then you can come on outside."

I meant to ask Dad what he used, but I forgot to with all that happened today. But he walked around the house, bending over, and putting out some stuff. I kinda think it was gunpowder cause it looked like a black powder. But I think you can make sulfa do the same thing. Anyhow, after he got most the way around, he poured the last of the stuff in a small pile, about four inches from where he started. He lit a match to the line. The stuff flared up, sputtering and flashing around the house. When it got right in front of the house, to that little pile, it almost exploded with fire and noise.

All the while, Dad was doing a little shuffle and chanting something. I finally realized he was singing "Brother John," and I reckon it was in French, because I knew the tune but not the words.

When the smoke blew away, Dad stopped chanting and called to them. "You can come out now. The hex is broken."

They each took one step onto the porch. Dad went to meet them. Buck followed. When he crossed the line right behind Dad, they both grinned and came off the porch. They musta not had much to eat in the house cause they both looked skinnier than I'd ever seen them. They've always been on the fat side, from eating a lot of cornbread and fatback. They never had table scraps so they never had a dog or pigs. Dad always let them have a pig in the fall when they helped us butcher ours. He figured a pig was better for them than a little money, and he let them cure it in our smokehouse.

Dad told me to get the can of lye out of the truck and had Amos spread it in the yard where they had dumped their slop jars. The lye whitened the stinking stuff under one of the windows.

They rode in the back of the truck, thank goodness, because they hadn't had any water except for drinking for several days. They were lucky they had gone to the well not long before the conjure woman came by the other day.

This time around, we had a 2x6 board to poke under Queen, and with Ellie Mae on one end of it and Amos on the other, we got Queen onto her feet. But it took all five of us to get her to the barn, where Dad built a rack around her to hold her up. I put food and water in buckets on a board right under her nose, but all she did was rest her nose on the board between the buckets. I knew she was gonna die.

"I don't think she's gonna make it, Dad," I said.

"All we can do is try," he answered. "The rest is up to her."

It's late now, almost 10 o'clock, and I haven't heard the conjure woman's drums. Maybe she doesn't know Dad broke up another one of her spells, or maybe she's just being quiet to honor Dad for being more magical than she is.

BUCK

Buck coaxed the rattling car into his mother's yard, and when the left front tire hit the log his nephew had left under the mimosa tree, the car stalled, rattled, squealed and crashed under the hood.

His mother and sister came into the yard and toward the car as Buck pulled up the hood.

"Damn!" He shook his head and the word roared across the yard.

"You hesh up talking dat way, boy," Elvira said. "You know better."

"Ah, Ma, I'm sorry. It's just. Oh, hel-heck. I was stupid."

"What's the matter?

"Look." He pointed to the space under the hood. "I bought it yesterday, and look. The motor's fallen out. I can't believe—. It's not possible. I mean. How can the motor fall out?"

"Whatcha gonna do?"

Buck slammed the hood closed, turned back to her, and said, "I'm gonna make Mr. Rufus Flint take the damn thing back. I'm not paying him another cent."

"You hesh up that kind-a talk, Buck. I learned you better'n that."

He touched her shoulder. "I know, Ma. I know. I'm madder'n I can remember. Look, I gotta go. I have time to get to town and back. I'll see you soon."

"You be kerful, son."

"I will, Ma."

Buck strode across the yard and onto the road, his legs steady in their march to town. Only six miles. A lot shorter than those army marches.

Flint, however, was not at his car lot when Buck arrived. Sims, Flint's right-hand man and pistol-carrying bodyguard, stood at the office door.

"Where's Mr. Flint?" Buck stared into his eyes.

"Whatcha want him for? Where's that car you bought yesterday? You wrecked it already?"

"Wrecked it? Not quite. It was already wrecked. Where's Flint?"

"Mr. Flint, to you, nigger."

They glared at each other for a moment. Buck dropped his gaze. *Better not keep looking him in the eye no matter how mad I am.*

"Where's Mr. Flint, sir?"

"He's over at the grocery store. You tend to your manners, you hear, boy?"

"Yes sir."

Buck marched down the street, passed the hotel at the corner, and crossed to the west side. Blacks shopped here. He could go in the front door. He was storming when he jerked it open.

An elderly white woman with a bag of groceries had her hand out as if to push the door open. "Oh!"

Buck backed up and eased the door wide. "Sorry, M'am. I didn't mean to frighten you." He stepped back and the lady came out.

"Aren't you Elvira's boy?" she asked.

"Yessum."

"I thought so. She worked for me awhile, before the war. Say hello to her."

"Yessum."

He didn't know her name, and was ashamed to ask. She walked off, and he entered the store.

Flint sat on a stool behind the cash register. Buck stomped over.

"That car you sold me fell apart a while ago," He tried to keep his temper from heating back up. Tried to keep his gaze locked onto Flint's neck instead of his eyes.

"That's your problem."

"No. It's yours. It was no account. The motor fell out the first bump I hit."

"That's your problem. Now get out of here. I've got customers to tend to."

"You won't be having customers when they find out you cheat 'em." He stared into Flint's eyes.

"Hey, you there!" Flint looked beyond Buck. Buck turned. A boy had opened a refrigerator and Buck saw inside, row after row of pint Mason jars filled with yellow liquid.

Buck thought *He really does save up his pee. Wonder who checks it for poison?*

"Close that refrigerator. What you think you're doing?" His voice silenced the room and other customers turned to look.

"I want a co-cola," the boy said as he pushed the door closed.

"There's none in there. You get one out of that cooler over yonder, boy. Don'tcha go opening up anything else, you hear?

"Yes, sir, Mr. Flint. Here's my nickel."

Flint took the child's nickel and pointed him to the co-cola cooler. He turned his attention back to Buck, reached under the counter and brought out a .38 caliber revolver. "I said for you to get out of here, nigger. Now."

Buck looked at the pistol. Nodded. Turned and left.

He wondered if he should talk to Professor about the car. Or like Flint said, it was his problem.

Either way, he wasn't going to pay Flint another penny.

SAMANTHA

June 11, 1946, Tuesday

At breakfast, Dad said Queen looked might poorly when he was down to the barn to milk, and for me and Buck to check on her in a couple of hours. When Buck and I got to the barn, Queen was dead.

"I knew it," I said.

Buck kinda shrugged. "Me too, I guess. She's not the first one I helped your dad put in a rack."

I laughed. "She won't be the last one, either. I'll get the crowbar."

Buck tore off the side of the rack and went to catch Daisy, the only other plow horse we have. We harnessed her up and wrapped the trace chains around Queen to pull her down into the pasture. We left her under an oak by the creek—we never buried the livestock.

As we walked back to the sound of the rattling trace chains and the clump of Daisy's hoofs, I asked if he knew how Bessie was getting along since Mickey got killed. "She's doing fine. Miss Vicki's brother, Slim, got to town yesterday. He'll break up the Black Market."

"Who owns the Black Market? Where is it?"

He glanced down at me, and I'd swear he tried to hide a grin. "It started big in the war when you had to have a ration ticket to buy beef or gas or anything. It meant any store or person who would sell anything illegally. It's not just a store, though. Or even a person. It's all of it—everybody involved—that's called 'black market.' I don't know where the name came from, but probably not cause the white folks blame us coloreds for it."

I just nodded and wished I hadn't asked him cause I felt kinda dumb, still not knowing exactly what he meant.

Seems like Buck knows everything. He's not only smart, he's almost pretty to look at. He's got his mama's Creek Indian face, lean, with an almost sharp nose, and a kindness in his eyes. His lips are wider than mine are, but they seem to be tight most of the time, like he's mad and holding his mouth tight to keep his mad from blowing out of him. He's got on just his overalls today, so I can see his shoulder muscles ripple and flow. If he were a horse, everybody'd want him, even with that bad scar on his shoulder. He's special, lean and hard from the war; he walks like a soldier, head up, and back straight as a pitchfork handle. When the sun's on him in the summer and he's sweating, his skin glows like polished black walnut. He's so fine and proud. But he can't show it anywhere but around us.

He kept Daisy harnessed and went to the hay fields. I went to the house to read.

About time for supper, Buck came to see Dad, and I sat on the porch steps while they talked.

"Professor, since Mick got in that trouble up at the dairy and got killed, Mr. Simpson's been after me to help him with the milking. I told him I work for you, but he needs some help. He came by the fields again this afternoon while I was cutting hay."

Dad won't have much work for Buck once the hay is in the barn by the end of the week. But it's gonna be a busy few days, raking, shocking and hauling. We'll probably have to get Amos and Ellie Mae to come help, since we won't have Pollock any more.

"Not many colored men'll want to work there, Buck. You told me it was his son who started the trouble, beating Mick. You going to feel safe up there?"

"Yes, sir. Word around town is that some of the white men are scared to beat nigras after that happened. They're a mite afraid they'll get shot, too. I'm not afraid of Simpson. He's offering me a half-dollar a day, for milking about thirty cows every morning. I've told him I couldn't help out except mornings cause of the haying, that I got to be back here by the time the dew's dry. And I told him I won't even think of doing it permanent, and that I was going to ask you about helping him out until he can find somebody."

"That's good pay, Buck. You go ahead if you want to. But I will need you to get the hay in. I can't always count on the Everett boys, especially when they're all gone off to Seth's still." We all laughed, cause Molly's uncle and cousins are most of the time gone off to the still or they're out rustling cows.

"Jethro'll be around, Sir," Buck paused, grinned, and added, "if he's not off to his still." After we quit chuckling over Buck's only brother, he went on. "I'll be back here as soon as the dew dries enough to move the hay. I told Mr. Simpson I might could work for him, but if I do it'll be just until he gets somebody regular."

"I'm glad for you to have some extra work. Your new car'll be handy going up to the dairy before light."

Buck wrinkled up his face, half-mad, half-disgusted. "It would, if it'd been any account. The motor fell out yesterday when I drove up to see Mama. I know I was foolish to buy from Mr. Flint. Everybody knows he cheats us nigras, but I thought I had checked it out real good. I never thought the motor wasn't bolted in. I'm stuck, unless I can find a lawyer who's willing to help me."

Dad shook his head. "Let me check with Danny Murphy and Vicki. She might help. I don't think any of the other lawyers in town would help you against a white man."

Buck asked, "Can he help me? I thought he's going to defend Mr. Flint in that trial for killing the colored lady back two years ago."

"Yes, he is. I'd forgotten."

How in the world, I wondered, could Dad forget about the trial? I want to go to it real bad.

Dad went on, "Maybe Vicki can handle it for you. But it's not going to be easy for a nigra trying to break a contract with a white man. Not even with a white man cheating you from the start. I'll talk to Vicki next time I go to town. But how could the motor just fall out?"

Buck shook his head. "I don't know. I drove the car before I bought it, and looked it over, I thought pretty well. It wasn't until about the third time I crossed the train tracks with it that something started making a noise, and just as I pulled into Mama's yard, something started dragging, and the whole motor was on the ground. Somebody had taken the bolts out and musta crossthreaded them putting them back in cause the threads were stripped bad. I just wasn't careful enough. It's my own fault, but I don't like being cheated."

"Howcome you had to buy on time? You spend all your war money?" I asked.

Buck blushed, his deep brown face turning darker, but he answered, "Miss Sam, maybe I was foolish, but over there in France it looked like everybody was a lot poorer than I've ever been and they needed money more'n I did."

Dad smiled, "Would you do it any different today, Buck?"

"No, sir," Buck shook his head. "Don't reckon I would. Anything I can help with this evening?"

"Reckon not, Buck. You be careful around those Simpsons. Watch how you talk."

Buck laughed. "You got no call to fret nun, suh, I kin be de kinda nigger dey wants when I'se up dere wuking."

Dad smiled. "I'll let you know if things get tight here. I'm obliged to you for talking it over with me, Buck."

"Yes, sir," Buck answered, nodding. He started to turn away, hesitated a second, and turned around. "I reckon you know Uncle Pollack is out-a jail?"

Dad didn't say anything, just nodded. He had gotten Pollock out of jail.

Buck nodded back and strode off down the driveway, moving like a soldier, his head up, his shoulders back. I've seen him walking all slumped down, shiftless looking, when he's around other white folks. Just like he always talks niggertalk to white people, excepting my family.

Before he got out of sight, I took off running behind him. "Hey, Buck, wait up," I yelled at him.

He waited in the shade of one of the magnolias until I caught up with him. "What you wanting, Sam?"

"I just wondered. What happens when somebody's in jail? Do you know? Do they beat him every day? I heard about what happened up in Jasper County. "

Buck nodded. He looked somber. "Yes. I heard no matter what you do, don't ever get in trouble up there. Leastways, our sheriff is better than that most of the time. Of course, your dad talked to him to be sure Pollock wouldn't have any more trouble. And to be sure they just turned him loose after a couple of nights in jail."

I heard voices, and Michelle and Molly came around the hedges at the end of the driveway. "Hey," I called.

"Hi," they both answered. Michelle, who was leading Lady, asked, "Do you have time to go riding?"

Michelle looks a lot like her mama, short and skinny and real pretty, but with black hair where her mama's hair is already gray all over. They have the same way of holding their heads to the side when they look at you or when they're laughing which seems like most of the time for Vicki. Michelle is more serious minded than her mama.

"Sure," I said. "I'll go catch Dolly."

Molly looked at Buck and then at me, and asked, "What's so important that y'all are standing out in this heat?"

"Jail," I said.

"Jail?" Michelle responded. "Howcome you're talking about jail?"

"Well, Pollock is out. I always wondered about jail, and what's it like."

"Did you ever go to jail in the Army?" Michelle asked Buck.

Buck's laughter, like a waterfall, tumbled all around us in the stillness; it was like running in the rain after a long dry spell—it took away all the gloom that had seemed to wrap around us.

"Nope, I never did. Actually, from working for the professor I knew how to do what I was told. And Miss Laura taught me what I needed to know to always be respectful. So even when the officers got ugly, I just kept silent and let them yell. They can't put you in jail if you just stand quiet.

"Of course, any colored who talks back to a white man is going to jail unless he gets lynched. Benny's the only one I ever heard of who didn't get lynched but never did stay quiet. And the white draft board never did catch him to put him in jail."

"Who's he?" Michelle asked.

"He was a colored man a little older'n me," Buck answered. "He was about the first nigra man in town to get drafted out-a here. When he reported to the draft board, they called him 'Boy.' He got mad— he'd heard them calling a white man just ahead of him 'Mister Adams.' He told them his name was 'Mister Tatum.' When they laughed at him, he just turned around and walked out."

"What'd they do then?" Michelle asked.

"They sent the sheriff out after him, but he was gone from home. He went by his house just long enough to throw some food into a croaker sack and leave out. The Klu Klux came after him that night for being so uppity. Burned a cross in front of his mama's house and tore up creation looking for him. Nobody's heard from him since. And three days later, the church where he went, over by where you go to school, got burned down. Every nigra in the county knew about it, knew the white men would never stop looking for Benny. So when they sent me a notice I was drafted, I went down. And I kept my mouth shut, except for saying 'Yassuh' and 'Nawsuh.' And I went on off to war."

"That's the place Flint is gonna pave over for his used cars," I said. "The big colored cemetery."

"That's so," Buck said. "Less your dad can get it stopped."

"Where's that?" Molly asked. "I haven't heard about it."

"Over where that church burned down, by the schools," Michelle said. "You know, over right across from Rufus Flint's car lot and Phil Snyder's Hotel. Mama and Danny are trying to help stop it from getting paved."

"Yeah," I said. "There's a lot of graves there. Cou'n Phil swears he owns the land and is selling it to Flint. Buck, you reckon any nigras will go there again to buy a car if he paves over the cemetery?"

"I wouldn't," Molly said. "You step on a grave, the dead person's gonna haunt your forever."

"I can't say about the coloreds, Sam. Most all the coloreds in town live in one of the houses that Mr. Rufus owns with Judge Phil. If they don't pay their rent on time, he takes them to court in Judge Phil's courtroom, and of course the judge makes them pay. Or he takes their furniture away and puts them out on the street. Might be they'll keep on going to his car lot even if it is on the cemetery."

"I heard Mama talking to Uncle Slim about Judge Snyder. He's supposed to've said those are not really graves, just places where dogs or Indians were buried."

Buck nodded. "Say the rest of it, Michelle. Dogs or Indians or niggers, and what's the difference? Every colored man in town has heard what Judge Snyder said. And we all know those are Flint's words too, but they still go to his grocery, just like I went to his car lot."

"You got folks buried there in town, Buck?"

"No, Sam, most of my folks are buried up on the cemetery where your granddaddy gave us the land, on this side of your grandma's place. None of my close family ever went to town to church, but some cousins did."

"Where do they go now?" Michelle asked.

"They've been using the colored school since the fire. They're trying to raise up enough money to build." He looked at me. "But Judge Snyder told them they can't build back where they were. He told them the church never owned itself, that it was just allowed to sit there on his granddaddy's land. So they don't have any land to build on, either."

"Why'd it burn down? There's a fire truck in town. Couldn't they put it out?"

I answered before Buck could. "Mama always said it was the Klu Klux who burned it, on account of the fella that sassed the draft board."

"That's right," Buck agreed. "The Draft Board was Roger Benson, Judge Snyder, Rufus Flint, and the mayor. I didn't expect to be called 'mister,' and I didn't say a word when they called me 'boy.' I've always wondered if one of them set that fire. Especially now that Judge Snyder is wanting to sell the land to Flint."

"I remember the fire," I said. "I watched it from the playground at school. Everybody stood around, but nobody did anything to put out the fire. Michelle, it happened before y'all moved here."

Michelle shook her head, and I knew she felt the same as I did about it. "What happened to Benny? Did he ever write to anybody?"

"Nobody knows. He could write a little, but his mama can't read, and if he's alive, he never wrote home that I heard tell of. I don't think the Klu Klux ever caught him, though. I think he's living somewhere, maybe Detroit. I sure didn't give them any sass when I got drafted cause I wanted to come home."

"Didcha go to church in the Army, Buck?" I asked.

"We went every week in training. They got regular preachers in the Army, and we marched off to church ever Sunday morning."

"Didcha like marching? I think it would be fun. Remember when the WAVES were in town? I used to watch them on the campus at college when I waited to ride home with Dad. And sometimes I'd get behind them and march with them. It sure was fun to keep in step and learn the 'hup' song they marched to."

"Marching's hard work," Buck said. "But all this talking is keeping you girls from riding. Y'all go along; I've got things to do."

"You wanta go with us?" I asked Molly.

She shook her head. "I was just out walking when Michelle came along. I'll be heading back to the house in a minute. Y'all go on."

So we did. Michelle stayed a long time and we rode way up the road to where the old ferry used to run across Big Hickory. She couldn't stay for supper, but she did go with me to bring in the milk cows before she went home.

When Dad came in tonight and said we've got some new shoats, Mama didn't want me go out to see them since it was getting dark and Pollock might be out there somewhere. I said he oughten to be mad at us, since Mama kept those Klu Klux from hanging him, but she wanted to be cautious. There hadn't been any word or sign of him since he got out of jail.

SAMANTHA

June 12, Wednesday

I went with Dad to slop the hogs this morning so I could see the new shoats.

We met Pollock astride a mule coming up the middle of the driveway. He pulled up on the rope reins as soon as he saw us.

Dad paused a fraction, walked on and said, "Morning, Pollock."

I stopped, too, my stomach getting all tight. I had to jam my hands in my jeans pockets to keep them from shaking. Time stopped and froze into my mind, so even tonight I can smell the stink of the slop digging into my nose, even though it was nothing but our table scraps plus a lot of corn meal that Dad put in for the pigs. I can feel the wind, just barely touching my face, carrying the smell of Pollock's fear, the smell of the mule, the smell of the fresh green manure the mule dumped on the driveway. I can still see the steam rising up from those manure balls, still see the horsefly sitting on the mule's face, just off from his left eye, where it was sucking blood; still see the worn overalls and the heavy shoes Pollock had on; still see the sweat glistening on his arms; still see where the hairs on his arms seemed to glitter with sweat; still see his eyes, looking down to the ground just in front of Dad.

When Dad just kept on walking down the driveway, I scuttled to catch up with him. But I knew from looking at Pollock that there'd not be much I could do if he got after Dad again. I wondered if he knew it was Dad who got him out of jail. He for sure knew Mama saved his life, and he wasn't mad then.

I tried to act like I wasn't scared. I didn't reach over to take ahold of Dad's hand like I would've when I was real little, but for a minute I really did want to. Dad stopped a few feet in front of Pollock and put down the buckets. I just stood there by him and waited. I tried not to bite my lip, and I shoved my hands deeper into my jeans pockets so Pollock couldn't see my hands shake. I hoped he couldn't smell my fear.

Pollock pulled off his hat and spoke up, looking down on the ground just in front of Dad and never looking up at him, even though

Dad and Mama always try to get folks they're talking to to look at them.

"Mista Professor, I'se sho glad to see you be doing okay. I wants to tell you how sorry I is fer whut I dun."

"I know you are, Pollock, and it's all right. You've paid enough for it. How's your back?"

"Hit dun't hurt too much no mo', suh. I thanks you fer sending in Dr. Morris to put the turpentine on hit."

"You want to come back to work for me?"

"You real sho you wants me outchere? I knows I dun did wrong, Suh. I sho dun did wrong. Ain't no white folks gonna want a nigger frum de jail to wuk fer em." He kept his eyes down.

"I'm sure, Pollock. You know I always need some help out here. You back up at Elvira's?"

From as far back as I can remember, Pollock has lived with his sister Elvira, who is Buck's mama.

"Yassuh. I means, yassuh, I knows you is always needing sum hep outchere. But Elvira, she dun put me on de road. I'se staying up to de wuk shed behind de Blanton place. Up de road on t'other side of St. John's Church. Dis here be Billy Blanton's mule what he let me use ta cum down here ta talks ta you." He patted the mule's neck like he'd missed being able to pat any mule for the days he was in jail.

"Well, I'll pick you up tomorrow about light. Can you bring along your dinner or should I have Miz Lawson fix you something?"

Pollock's black head was covered up with tight gray curls where they had cut his hair real short down at the jail, and he bobbed it up and down and flashed his teeth in a wide smile, like the whole world was a better and happier place for him than it was only a minute ago.

"Yessuh. I'se'll be ready by day, and I kin bring me a corn pone for dunner."

Watching him was like seeing somebody go from fear and being crushed down into a slump, to rising up, sitting tall, with pride and joy. He got up his courage and looked up at Dad for just a second, like he wasn't sure it was okay. He slapped his hat back on his head, kicked the mule in the sides while he turned it around, and set off back up the road to the shanty where he was living. I could see that shack in my mind, two rooms balanced on rocks at every corner; never-painted clapboards that look like part of the forest in winter when everything else was the same gray; windows that you couldn't see through in winter cause they had tarpaper tacked up over them, but in summer stood open and naked for whatever breeze wandered by and let in the flies, mosquitoes, and dirt daubers.

Dad let out a deep breath, like he'd been holding his too, the way I was. He picked up the buckets of slop and walked off to the pigpen.

"Dad, howcome you want Pollock to come back here to work? Aren't you scared he'll do something else? Besides, you're letting Buck go part time up the road to work."

Dad didn't say anything for a few steps before he answered. "Sam, a man like Buck has got to stretch himself and find something useful to do. He's got to stay busy to stay happy. He wants the extra work to be happy. Pollock needs work, any work, and nobody around here is going to give him a job. If he's got no money, he'll take to stealing corn and sweetfeed and making liquor and first thing you know, he'll be back in jail. But he'll behave himself now, and work harder than he ever has. Besides, I need him to keep up the fences." He laughed. "At least our neighbors will be happier if I can keep the bulls away from their cows."

I laughed with him. All our neighbors fuss when one of our canner-and-cutter bulls gets into the pasture with their pure whiteface or Jersey cows and give them some mixed-up calves.

When we reached the hog pen, I climbed up on the fence so I could see the new piglets. The sow got up when she saw Dad and left them squealing on their pile of hay while she came over to the trough to slobber up her meal. The babies kept wiggling their tiny pink bodies all around and over each other, oinking and trying to find their mama. Their pink skins were clean and pretty—and they were so little I wanted to pick one up, but I knew they'd be our breakfast by next fall so I didn't want to get to love them, just look at them ever once in a while.

When we told Mama about Pollock, she just shook her head, kind of smiling, saying better that Pollock work for us than that he go off mad.

June 17, Monday

At breakfast, Mama said she had to go to court for jury duty. She had been fussing with the Clerk of Court for two years because no women were on the jury list.

Now she had been called to serve in Rufus Flint's trial for killing a black woman two years ago.

She laughed and said, "I'm sure Danny will strike me."

"And he wishes he could leave you on. He was telling me the other day he can't stand Flint. He thinks Flint won't stop with this killing if he gets off," Dad said.

"He can't get off, can he?" I asked. "They gotta find him guilty."

But Dad said the same thing Buck did: White men won't convict a white man for killing a nigra.

Mama said it was the most important case ever here in Stanleyville, about as important as the trial of the century for the man who killed the Lindberg baby, cause this was the first time a white man was tried for killing a colored woman. Mama said whatever happened to Flint would mean the same would happen for another hundred years to any white man who killed a colored person.

I almost told Mama I wanted to go to the trial, but I knew if I did she'll tell me no. So I didn't say anything, just waited for her to leave for town. After she was gone, I got out my bike and headed for the courthouse, hoping I'd get there before the cloud off in the southwest caught up with me. I didn't dare go into the courtroom at first, but peeked through the window in the door. I saw Mama and a bunch of people go up into the jury box, but in a few minutes Mama was walking back down to the benches. She had her knitting with her and sat in the second row, where she started knitting.

Anybody watching would think she didn't know what was going on around her, but she doesn't have to watch her hands when she knits. Her fingers seem to know what to do without being told by her eyes. I didn't have to see her face to know she was focused on Danny.

It seemed like everybody was in that room. Even some farmers, who'd gotten their crops laid by, had come in although it wasn't a Saturday. Mostly, it was men; I saw a few women, but other than Vicki, I didn't know any of them.

When I eased the door open, I could feel the excitement, almost smell it in the courtroom, mixed in with perfumes, tobacco smoke, sweat, and fresh plowed dirt and manure on somebody's boot. Everybody was filling up the room with whispers, like an autumn morning when the wind first gets up and leaves brush against each other as they fall and settle down among others spread crackling over the ground.

I sat on the fourth row, across the aisle from Mama. If I got any closer, she might see me. I squeezed between a fat woman and a farmer in his overalls. He smelled like cows, old sweat, and plowed dirt.

The cloud I outran reached town and poured so hard the windows were closed. The courtroom became stuffy-hot. Didn't but one of the fans work. Everybody was waving one of those funeral parlor fans to try to keep cool.

Mr. Flint turned and looked at everybody in the room, like he was judging them, seeing who was there to be against him. He's got creepy eyes, a funny color of brown mixed up with green. They bulge out kinda like a bullfrog's would if it had been stomped on. His hair is too long for a man, but he's getting a little bald is why he lets it grow long—so he can comb it over his bald spot. But he looks shaggy. He's little, and even with his funny shoes that make him another two inches tall, he's not much taller than me and I'm only almost thirteen. He's little all over, real thin and gaunt like he just got up from inside his grave.

If I close my eyes a hundred years from now, I will still see everybody, see the room, smell the smells, and get a shiver from the look in Flint's eyes, like looking at a picture show running in my head.

It was kinda fun to see Judge Plummer in the black robe that everybody says he's naked under when it's brinjin hot in the summer, like today. He's a big man and leaned over to the side most of the time, his left elbow on the chair arm with his jaw resting on that hand. He held a pencil in the other hand so it looked like he was writing. I wondered if he was maybe just snoozing a little part of the time. He wears glasses that the light danced around on, so it was hard from where I was to tell if his eyes were closed.

For a criminal, Mr. Flint didn't look scared about what could happen to him. He just looked mad. I was close enough I could hear him fuss at Danny Murphy.

Collier Hancock, the solicitor general who made the case against Flint, is about the same age as J. D. and was in the war too, in the Marines with J. D. He looks like a soldier, with his back always straight and his hair in one of those crew cuts so you can almost see the skin on his head through his black hair. His black eyes can fix on you almost like a hawk's, but he can laugh too, like he thinks everything is funny, except a murder trial.

*   *   *

People told different stories about the same happenings. All the colored people told it the same about Rufus Flint and his hired man Sims, though. Even the little girl younger'n me, only nine years old, told it the same.

The nigras said Flint and Sims came out to their house with guns and threatened everybody, all over some money owed down at his grocery. Sims took some brass knuckles to the boy on the porch—the boy Billy wasn't but fourteen. His mama and two sisters ran inside. Flint followed them in and shot up the mother. She died. The two girls screamed and hollered and ran out the back door.

Billy said he couldn't do anything cause Sims had pulled a pistol on him.

The trial stopped for the judge to get something to eat, and I got out of the courthouse before Mama saw me. I don't know how much I missed cause after I went over to the drugstore for a grilled cheese and co-cola and snuck back inside the courtroom, Sims was up on the stand.

Sims swore he didn't have a gun, but everybody knows he totes a pistol all the time. I've seen him downtown with it showing on his hip. Flint said all he wanted was to get the money they owed him, and that they threatened him, said they were gonna get a gun and shoot him, so he had to protect himself.

Collier Hancock asked the sheriff if he had found a pistol in the house. He said no, and Collier asked him if he had looked for one. He said he had.

Danny told the jury they had to find Flint "not guilty," but Collier said that it was time to judge the facts, not color of the people, and that Flint ought to go to jail.

I about fell off the bench when the jury came back. Seemed like they had just gone out and walked right back in.

Guilty.

I didn't know what the difference was in "slaughter" and "murder," but they said "slaughter."

A loud whisper ran through the courtroom. Judge Plummer slammed his wooden hammer down once and it got quiet. He looked a bit addled and looked from Danny to Collier. He never looked at Flint and sentenced him to two years.

I couldn't believe it, just two years for killing somebody. He oughtta been hanged. If that woman had shot him, she'd already be on her way to the electric chair.

"Your honor, we will appeal," Danny said. "May the defendant remain out on bail pending the outcome of the appeal?"

"Of course," the judge said. He hammered once, stood up and left.

Flint turned to Danny. Even from the back of the room, I could see his eyes bulging out. His mouth was all twisted up and I would of sworn he was slobbering like a mad fox. He yelled, "You bastard! I'm not guilty! It's all your fault! Who'd you pay off on the jury so they'd find me guilty? You damn well better get me off on this appeal, you hear me?"

"Hold on there, Rufus. You know better than that. I'll do everything I can for you. But times are changing. You can't just shoot a nigra any more."

"You—you—." Rufus seemed too mad to be able to talk. His hands were tight fists, shaking up and down, like it was all he could do not to hit Danny.

Sims eased away and slipped out of the courtroom. Other people just stood around and watched. The sheriff had gone out behind Judge Plummer, so he wasn't there to hear any of it.

"I'll see you in hell before I go to jail," Flint snarled and stomped out, his little feet trying to make a loud noise.

Nobody moved. Even Mama was still in her seat.

As he stormed by me, the air chilled. I shivered.

June 18, Tuesday

Danny drove Vicki and Michelle out late this afternoon, and we all went to the side porch to fan and rock and hope for a little breeze.

"Laura, we came out to see Buck about his car. I want to handle the case. Get his money back from Flint," Vicki said.

"Can you do it, with Danny handling Flint's appeal?"

"Oh sure. Well, I probably shouldn't, since we're in the same office and all. We turned down Mattie yesterday afternoon."

"Mattie?"

"Yes. She asked Danny to file her divorce from Rufus."

"You aren't going to help her, Danny?" Mama asked.

"No," he said. "I suggested Vicki, but she said she wanted a man lawyer. I suggested J. D."

Vicki laughed. She throws laughter into the air like the wind dances the leaves, so it floats all around you and makes you feel good inside, like looking at the yellow leaves of the hickory tree against the blue autumn sky almost makes you cry they are so pretty. I like to hear her laugh; Michelle's laughter is just like hers, only more full of mischief than just plain joy of being alive.

Vicki doesn't act old, but she must be, cause her hair's turning gray. She runs her fingers through it all the time, like that's all it takes to brush it. Michelle does the same thing, like she's copying her mama. I wish I could wear mine short, like Vicki's, but Dad doesn't want me to cut it so I have to wear it in two long pigtails.

"She did tell us to keep it quiet, though. She wants to get Rufus moved out of her house the same day the papers are filed. She's a little scared of him," Danny said.

"I don't blame her," I said. "He looks scary to me."

They all turned to look at me for a minute, and Vicki suddenly laughed. "Me too," she said.

When they came out to pick up Katie last night, Sis and J. D. hadn't said a word about helping Miss Mattie get the divorce. I asked, "Is Miss Mattie still working at Flint's grocery store?"

"Yes," Vicki said. "She's not going to change anything until the papers are ready. She said he could be real mean."

"The house is hers. She inherited it. I don't think he'll manage to get it from her," Mama said.

"I've never seen hate like Flint's," Vicki said. "He seems to dislike everybody, but he really hates the nigras."

"You didn't see any racial hatred in South Carolina when you were growing up?" Mama asked.

Vicki shook her head. "No. I suppose it was there, but I didn't see it. Oh, they have the separate waiting rooms in the bus station, separate water fountains and all that. But my town is small, and all the nigras and white folks get along."

"Stanleyville's small," I said. "We don't even have a thousand people here."

She smiled at me, tossing her head and laughing a little. "We didn't have two hundred people in my town," she said. "And in California, nobody cares what you do, so nobody there hates people just to hate."

Vicki married a soldier and they lived in California for awhile; Michelle was born there, and still talks funny. One of her friends in California was Danny's daughter, and after Vicki's husband got killed in the war, she suggested Vicki move to Stanleyville and work with her father. Vicki said once that she didn't have any reason to go back to her home town and couldn't stand staying in California where all she thought about was her dead husband.

When they got to talking about the dances being planned for sesquicentennial celebrations, Michelle and I left for the pasture. Our plantation house is gonna be open for people to see during the town birthday party this August. During The War Between The States, Sherman's army stayed at our house one night before they reached the capitol and ran the State government out of Milledgeville, a little bit south of here. Some other houses in Stanleyville will be open for the party, too. But I know I'm gonna have to do a lot for the birthday party, like clean up in the house and yard, and wear special clothes to serve cookies and such. But I will get to ride Dolly in the parade.

We let my puppy out of the smokehouse to go with us, and like always, he sniffed Michelle, putting his nose right up to her front and then headed toward Buck's. We followed and found Buck cleaning fish for his supper.

"I see you let the dog out. Taking him with you to bring in the cows?"

"Yeah. You need to hang around the house. Vicki and Danny are up with Mama and they need to talk to you about the car."

"I'll be here. You oughtn't take that puppy with you for the cows. He'll chase them all over. Wait till he's older."

"You reckon?"

Buck nodded. "It'd be best, Sam. You need to train him some first."

So I took my red-bone hound puppy back to the smokehouse and we went to drive in the cows. Buck had raked hay today, so the air smelled like drying hay, and the wind picked up a little of the dust and swirled it around with tiny hay pieces. I wanted to lie out on the windrows just to feel the softness, but I knew better, cause air had to flow through to dry off the dew in the morning for Pollock and Buck to load it and take it to the barn. Buck never cut the back meadow but left it for the milk cows and the horses we keep in that pasture.

We found the cows at the back creek, laid out in the shade and chewing their cuds. The horses were there too, Dolly standing in the edge of the water hole, up to her knees in the mud, switching horseflies off her side, but they just landed on her ears and sucked out her blood there. Although she's with foal, I can still ride her. I sure hope it's born in time for me to ride in the parade with Michelle and all the other people from school.

We drove the cows into their stalls and fed them. The calves, like always, bellowed their dismay at being left outside.

When we got back to the house, everybody was inside, sitting under the fan Dad had gotten put in overhead last summer. Since Mama keeps the heavy drapes pulled during the day, the house stays a lot cooler than the outside, especially with that fan moving the air around.

"Has it cooled off any?" Mama asked.

"It's still brinjin hot," I said.

Vicki looked at me and said, "I've heard you use that a dozen times, but I never asked. What in the world does 'brinjin hot' mean?"

Danny laughed. "I always wondered where that word came from."

"I really don't know," Mama said. "I've heard it all my life."

Dad said, "It took me years to know what it means—hot enough to burn water and to singe off your eyebrows."

Vicki shook her head while her laughter tinkled its way across the room.

June 19, Wednesday

It cooled off late today so I rode my bike up to see if Molly would ride along with me on hers.

The house is about as dilapidated as any I've ever seen, with the boards hanging down and a piece of cardboard over one of the windows. The tin roof shows big rust spots, and it probably leaks. The inside has to be worse, cause Dad said the boys were so lazy they sometimes used the inside paneling for firewood. I think the only time they feed their two bantam hens is when they steal some of our feed.

Richard perched in a cane-bottom chair, tilted back on two legs. A cigarette dangled from his mouth so he had to squint his eyes to keep the smoke out.

"Molly here?" I asked.

Richard pulled his cigarette from his lips, used his little finger to flick off the ashes right onto the porch floor, put the smoke back in his lips, and talked around it.

"She dun gone off on that cycle. Dunno where at."

I figured she was off with Buck, but couldn't let on. She used to ride the bicycle with me all the time, sometimes with me riding Dolly, and sometimes me riding my bike. We'd go all the way up to the crossroads, sometimes both walking back. It's pure lonesome with Molly not spending time with me any more, especially in summer when I don't see Michelle every day.

I rode on by myself, passed the cabin where Ellie Mae and Amos live, but didn't see them out in their cotton patch. I passed Bessie's, but of course she was in town working at Vicki's. They'd gotten rid of the trash from that burned up cross, but I could still smell what was left of it in the back yard where they'd dumped it.

Buck's mama Elvira wasn't home either. She worked for Mama when she lived down in the slave house where Bessie stayed. Buck was born down there on a day when his daddy had gone down to the river to catch some catfish and saw a big deer, with antlers all over his head, and he called his new baby after that buck.

I didn't want to go any farther by myself. The crossroads was just ahead, where the left-hand road goes up to the Benson Place and straight ahead is the Snyder Place where Cou'n Phil lives with his wife and daughter.

Their places join up on a high hill where the Klu Klux burned a cross last summer. Mama and I were on the way back from getting some corn ground at the mill when it happened. If I went any farther up the road, I'd still smell the kerosene and burning rags and hear the Klu Klux men yelling up on that hill all the way from last summer. My mind locked onto that evening, onto that sunset with gray smoke curling upward, catching the breeze and drifting toward us like the shadow of some monster let loose on the summer twilight.

When I asked Mama what it was all about, she told me it was about hating people, that some men seem to live on hate instead of loving people. She told me some white men think they are following the wishes of Jesus when they burn a cross and beat or kill a nigra and don't stop to think that the people they hate in God's name are kin to them if they believe in the Bible.

She said we may not like some of our kin—we don't like Cou'n Phil cause of his politics and cause he's mean to his wife, and most of all cause he's in the Klu Klux—but we don't go around trying to do him harm. And nobody oughtta be trying to do harm to the nigras, she said.

The memories followed as I turned toward home. Smoke weaved

its way into my nose; the same crickets complained it was too dry; the same whippoorwill sounded desperate that it was alone and night was coming; the same hound still insisted it had treed a possum.

Men's maniacal laughter and shouts echoed from last summer.

The only good thing I can remember about that evening are the goldenrod and the orange butterfly bushes blooming alongside the road where we stopped that day, and I can still see the flowers moving in the wind that carried the smoke and the voices to us. I can see the lespedeza in the hay field swaying like the ocean waves in the breeze.

June 20, Thursday

It happened after dark today. I heard the crash in my room even over the sounds of the conjure woman's drums and the rattling of the train. Mama has always laughed about the train, how there would come a time that one of the railroad people would ask us if we didn't hear the train whistle, and we would have to ask them, "Yes, but what was that awful noise we heard first?"

I ran downstairs and out the kitchen door, to find Mama and Dad already at the truck. I piled into the back, and as we drove by Buck's cottage, Dad said, "The front door's wide open, so he heard it too."

We found him at the train tracks with a lantern. The caboose lights showed for a few seconds and disappeared around the bend toward town.

"I know somebody got hit, but I can't see anything it's so dark. I grabbed the lantern, but I don't have the first match," Buck said.

Dad pulled a box of kitchen matches out of the tool bucket in back of the truck and handed it to Buck, who struck one on the seat of his overalls to light the lantern. All four of us started down the railroad toward town. The lantern light reflected off something red and Dad said, "Taillights."

What was left of a pickup lay scrambled in the ditch, its wheels up in the air. "That's Everett's truck," Buck said.

"They must have been drunk," Mama said and grabbed me by the shoulder. "We'll stay here, Sam. Let them see to the Everetts."

"But, Mama—"

"You mind your mother," Dad said as he and Buck walked on. Even though they talked low, I could hear what they said. "Looks like they ran into the train instead of the train hitting them," Dad said.

"Two men inside," Buck said.

They were quiet for a minute or two while they pulled at the doors, but they were jammed shut. Buck reached inside the window and shook his head.

"I can't feel any pulse on either one, sir. The inside of the truck sure does smell like shine. Like they busted up a bottle when they crashed."

Dad called back to us. "Laura, y'all walk on up to tell Maude. It's her husband and Molly's dad. They're both dead."

We found Maude and Molly in the yard. "Maude. Molly. I sure am sorry. I guess you heard the crash, same as we did. Maude, it's your husband. And your daddy, Molly. Looks as if they didn't stop for the train. I'm so sorry. They're both dead."

Molly didn't look too unhappy about her daddy, seeing as he had beat up on her so much she'd had to move down here with Maude a long time ago. Maude didn't seem bothered too much either, except she said, "I ain't got no money to bury him plain, much less fancy."

"Molly, do you want me to go tell your mother?" Mama asked.

Molly nodded. "Please, Miz Laura. I don't reckon my ma's got any money for a funeral either. Were they drunk?"

Mama nodded. "I think so."

"They was," Maude said, her gray head nodding. "You reckon they'll let us bury them up at Trinity? Ain't no place else I know to put 'em. I gotta get a blanket—" She turned to Molly. "What you figure your ma's gonna wanta do?"

Molly shook her head. "Mean as he was to her, she probably won't much care."

Maude nodded. "Miz Laura, reckon you can git them brung up here to the house? I could get Richard to see to 'em, but he ain't likely to git home afore the next train runs. I don't want they should get hit again."

"We'll see that they are brought up here," Mama said. "Anything else I can do for you, Maude?"

"Maybe see somebody at the Trinity Baptist for me."

"I'll see about it first thing tomorrow. If you need me, now, Maude, you send Molly down to the house."

Maude nodded, and we started back home. Hadn't either one of them shed a tear for the men.

SAMANTHA

June 21, Friday

Buck spent all day making coffins for the two men. Buck told Maude and Molly's mama it wasn't right to bury anybody in just a sheet. He went down to the barn where old Preacher's house burned, pulled off some side boards and brought them up to Maude's. He got the sawhorses, he cut the boards to length, and he figured out how to put them together by using a one-by-one strip in the corners.

He spent almost all day working on the coffins.

At least Richard helped, but he sure got bossy with Buck, treating him like a nigger instead of a friend who was trying to help them. He'll never change, just always be white trash.

Richard never said thank you or any kind word to Buck.

Molly and I watched them most of the day, and we kept the well bucket full. Of course, though, Buck had to use a Mason jar that I brought up for him to drink from. Richard used the dipper. Every once in a while, Buck poured a jarful of water over his head, letting it run down his face and his back to cool him off, same as he does when we haul hay.

When the coffins were finished and Buck and Richard had put the men in them, Buck took our hay truck down to pick up Molly's mama. He and Richard loaded up the coffins in the back of the truck to go to the graveyard.

I wanted to go, but Molly told me no, that just the family would be there. The three women got in front with Buck, but I noticed it was Molly sitting next to him. Richard and the others rode in the truck bed with the coffins. I don't know if they had a preacher or not. Mama told me preachers charge to bury people.

Molly's mama is gonna move down with Maude. The only men left in their families are Richard and his younger brother Tommy, who's only fourteen. Molly's mama didn't want to stay a mile down the road without a man in the house to cut the firewood and plow the garden. I reckon she'll bring down their mule too.

June 22, Saturday

When Michelle and I got back from Aunt Tessie's this afternoon, a bunch of wagons full of colored folks filled up the driveway as they left. Danny's Cadillac sat in the shade of an elm. Leaving the horses ground-hitched, we went inside.

Vicki and Danny stood in the dining room, under the fan, talking with Mama and Dad. With the drapes closed to keep out the heat, no air was getting in and the room smelled like sweat. Somebody had tracked manure across the rug

"You girls look mighty hot," Vicki said.

"It's brinjin hot, and getting hotter," I answered as I wiped sweat from my face onto my shirtsleeve. Dolly's white, salty sweat had soaked all the way through my jeans and stuck them to my legs. I reached down and pulled them loose.

Vicki's laughter rang through the house, but her face turned serious again. "Well, girls, we've gotten ourselves into another battle. I knew it was going to happen, sooner or later."

"I've been expecting a group of them since Jackson came by to ask for help," Mama said.

Before anyone else could say anything, I asked, "Were they here about that cemetery? Y'all gonna be able to stop the car lot?"

"We're sure going to try," Danny said.

"It won't be easy since most of the graves are marked only with a rock, if that. They're mostly slaves. Hadn't been but a few new graves in twenty years or so. And of course none since the fire," Mama said.

"That's the problem," Danny said. "I've talked to Snyder and to Flint. They both insist there're only four graves up there. The city council voted to let Phil move those four. He didn't mention the rest of the graves. All we can do now is get a restraining order when they start up the bulldozer."

"Danny, you know Mayor Deason was there when the church burned. Remember? He was one of the firemen who just stood and watched the fire. He's just doing whatever Phil and Flint want," Mama said.

"Phil always gets whatever he wants," Vicki said.

"Yes," Danny said. "And he passes judgment on his own tenants when they're late with the rent, which is inexcusable. But he's got friends on city council, and he gets by with most anything. With half the town scared of Flint, they're not likely to go against him, either."

For a moment, nobody said anything; then Danny said, "I just wish I wasn't Flint's attorney. I don't like him, and I know he doesn't like me. In fact, he scares me sometimes."

"But he's not MY client," Vicki said. "So anything we can do to stop him will just be in my name."

I had to ask. "If he puts a car lot over the nigra cemetery, why'd any of the nigras ever buy from him?"

"Good question," Vicki said.

Danny had an answer. "Nobody else will sell to the nigras on time."

"Cou'n Phil may say there're not but four graves up there," I said, "but I've been in that cemetery, and there're graves going all over the place. You know, those sunk down places like down the hill in the slave graveyard."

"There're only four cement slabs in there. That's how he's getting by with saying there're only four graves," Vicki said.

"That's just like Phil," Dad said. "Danny, can't you just go on and get an injunction now to stop work there?"

"Not until they start with the bulldozer," he answered. "But I'll have it ready to hand Judge Plummer the minute they start work."

He turned to me. "J. D. tells me you and Michelle plan to ride in the parade on Sesquicentennial Day."

"I can't wait. I just hope Dolly doesn't have her foal before then. It's due in August, we think."

Michelle grinned. "If she does, I get to carry the flag."

"But I'm going to carry the Confederate flag," I said. "Buck's already fixed Mama's English saddle with a little box on the stirrup for me to put the flagpole into so it'll be easy for me to hold it up."

"Well," Mama said, "let's have some pie."

"It'll ruin Michelle's supper," Vicki said.

Mama just laughed. "It won't matter once, to eat dessert first."

So we ate pie and ice cream before they all left.

June 23, Sunday

Vicki drove Michelle out before daylight to go fishing with us. It wasn't long before Molly and Buck got to the house too, but just a few minutes apart. I wonder if they'd planned it that way, so nobody would know they had walked together from Buck's after Molly got there.

Mama fixed us all a fried egg and sausage sandwich out of her biscuits. She cooked extra sausages and biscuits for us to take with us, just in case we didn't catch anything to eat. Then we were off to Possum Creek for the day. Everybody toted a load—we took Mason jars to get water from the spring that fed the creek just a little ways from the pool we'd fish; we had poles, a pail of worms Buck made come out of the ground last night by hammering in a stob and rubbing the ax handle over the end of it; our food for later; and the rifle in case we ran up on a mad raccoon or fox.

Buck led the way and Molly walked behind him on the path. But when we got down to the wagon road, she moved up next to him. She reached over to touch him, but suddenly she looked over her shoulder at us and jerked her hand away.

Fear flooded her eyes, and she dropped a couple of steps behind Buck. I wanted to tell her it was okay, but I was afraid of Michelle knowing.

But Michelle said, "It's okay, Molly, if you and Buck like each other special. It's okay if you want to hold his hand. We don't care, do we, Sam? Besides, I think you two look real pretty together."

We stopped, me as surprised as Molly and Buck. I didn't know what to say, and for a long minute all of us just stood there, looking at each other. Like Michelle said, Molly was pretty, her hair colored the gold wheat turns to in summer up at the Simpson's dairy, and today it was tumbling in curls all down the back of her neck and almost falling into her eyes. Her face was a little pink from the sun, making the freckles stand out over her nose. But it was her eyes that were so pretty; until the darkness of fear clouded them, they had sparkled brighter than the sunlight off the summer leaves. Even so, you didn't even notice where her front tooth is broken off, from where her papa hit her that last time. She wore a cotton dress made out of some of our feed sacks that were all kinds of bright colored flowers, like the sacks Mama makes my school dresses from.

Buck stood tall and was thin like a real cowboy, his back naked except for the bands of the overalls crossing over his middle, his arms hanging like logs from his wide shoulders. He's got the prettiest skin of anybody I know—it glistens like Dad's purebred stallion's hide when the sun hits him and is the color of my four-poster bed that Mama said is mahogany.

But her words struck fear in us, a fear so strong I smelled theirs just as I felt my own rising up from my stomach into my throat and tasting foul. I stared at Michelle.

"Nobody can tell you two you can't like each other," she said.

Molly reached out and touched Buck's hand, but he backed up a step, and his smile was only an attempt, barely touching his lips, while his eyes stayed dark and almost cold.

"The Klu Klux can, Miss Michelle. They'll lynch a colored man for not getting off the sidewalk for a white person or for just looking at a white lady. Hadn't you been here long enough to know that?"

"Yeah, I reckon," Michelle said as her face reddened.

"Around here, most white men may put nirgras ahead of white trash, but not ahead of dogs or cows," I said.

She nodded. "I've been here more'n two years and I'm still trying to get used to all the differences between here and California. Out there, the coloreds are just other people, but here, it's like something's about to happen all the time. Bessie, the nigra working for Mama, acts scared all the time. She looks at me like I'm going to do something to her and she wants to be sure to please me so I won't."

"She's got a right to be scared," Buck said. "The Klu Klux lynched her oldest boy. She'll always be scared they'll come after another of her boys."

"Mama never said a word to me. And Bessie sure hasn't." She turned to me, "And you didn't either."

"I just never thought you didn't know," was all I could say. "I figured Vicki would've told you."

"You never get used to it," Buck said, "no matter how many crosses they burn or how many people they whip. The fear sits inside you all the time, same as in the war. You have to hold it inside and learn to live with it."

"Unless you're white and grown up," I said, looking at Michelle. "Then maybe you can do something about it. Mama and Dad want to make it better, and they don't want me to know what's going on. They think I'm still too young. But I sure do know that lots of white people still think the colored people don't count for anything. That's why we got to be sure nobody, and I mean NOBODY, not even our folks, ever hear about Buck and Molly."

I turned to Buck. "I don't care if y'all like each other. Y'all and Michelle here are the best friends I got. I for sure don't have any call to tell anybody, especially old Flint or anybody else in the Klu Klux."

"Flint sure is creepy." Michelle shivered in spite of the heat.

"He's evil," Buck said.

"But you bought your car from him. A no-good car," I said.

"Yes. And I'm going to sue him about it, too. Miss Michelle, your mama's helping me, your mama and her boss Lawyer Murphy."

"Yeah, I heard her talking to Uncle Slim, something about making Flint take a car back. I sure hope she can do it."

"Me, too," Buck said.

"Why didn't you go to the Chevrolet place?" Michelle asked.

"I did, but they wouldn't sell on time. We've got to get a move on if we're gonna catch any fish this morning. It's getting late. Come on, Molly."

Buck reached over for her hand and she moved closer to him, walking right up against him into the woods. The lanes in the wagon road were so narrow they had to walk real close together or one of them would have been in the middle, in the high weeds.

We had just come out of the woods into a small meadow when Buck stopped, pointed overhead, and whispered, "Look."

We stopped, silent, and watched. The birds, shadows against the sky, their necks curved to pull their heads back against their slim bodies and their wings stretched, glided, silent as the dawn. Not a sound, not a wing beat, just the flight of eight herons flowing like a stream in the sky, coming out of the sunrise, directly toward us, moving overhead and toward the west.

We didn't move except to watch the birds until they disappeared over the hill.

At the creek, we scattered around the big hole with our cane poles and waited for the fish to get hungry. Each of the four corks sat big side up, barely moving with the current because the washed-out hole was so big.

The morning was lazy. My mind wandered all around, and I listened to the crows go over, the song birds welcome the morning.

Michelle squealed when her cork went under. She jerked her pole so hard she threw the line and her fish right over her head into a bush. She had a bream about the size of my hand.

Then Molly caught a bream, and as the morning passed, we caught enough for lunch. Buck was the only one to land a catfish.

While Buck gutted the fish, I built up a small fire, feeding it until it got real hot, We let it burn while we packed the fish in red mud from the creek bank. Buck said you don't take off the head or the scales when you cook fish this way. As soon as the fire began to die down, Buck raked some of the coals back, laid the fish on those still in the middle, and covered them with the rest of the coals.

"Now, we wait," he said, lying back, his face in shadows, his hands folded under his neck.

We stretched out, watched the clouds and waited.

Molly said, "The conjure woman sure was drumming loud last night. You hear her, Sam?"

"Seems she's pounding all the time, nowadays," I answered.

"You're always talking about her," Michelle said. "If I didn't know better, I'd say you made her up, except I've heard that drumming when I spent the night with you. Buck, who is she? Do you know?"

"No, Miss Michelle, I don't know her real name. Everybody probably knows her. I've heard my mama talk like she knows her, but the one time I asked, she told me to 'hesh up.' So I haven't asked again."

"All I know is her drum," I said.

Her drumming has been the rhythm of my nights for as far back as I can remember.

"I'm a little bit afraid of her," Molly said.

"Does the conjure woman just hex colored people, Buck?" Michelle asked. "Should I be scared of her?"

"I never heard of her putting a spell on white people, but I reckon she could," he said. "Especially if they believe in her."

"But you don't really believe all that stuff about the conjure woman, do you?" Michelle asked.

"Oh, yes, I do. I've seen what she can do to folks. Most of us coloreds believe."

"That drumming scares me. I don't want to meet up with her, especially at night, even if she's not supposed to put a hex on me," Michelle said.

Sometimes I say I'm not scared, when I really am. And sometimes it's almost fun to be a little scared. But I don't want to meet up with the conjure woman, and I said so.

Buck laughed again, saying, "Come on, Sam. You know she won't hex you."

"I dunno. I always try to believe she won't put a hex on white people, but I know she could if she was a mind to."

He shook his head, smiled and said the fish ought to be ready.

We feasted.

We had started home when Michelle asked, "Buck, when are you and Molly gonna get married?"

"I don't reckon we will," he answered.

"Why not? Don't y'all love each other and want to? If you get married, the Klu Klux can't bother you, can it?"

"That's not it, Miss Michelle. I love Molly with all of my heart, and I always will. But Georgia has a law that says I can't marry her. So it's not just the Klu Klux."

"That doesn't make any sense to me," Michelle continued.

"A lot of the laws don't make any sense, Miss Michelle. Partly cause some people are scared that us coloreds are going to better ourselves. They think we'll take their jobs and their homes. They were scared of the same thing when The War ended back in 1865. But colored folks in the South haven't gotten any white folk's work yet. But the white folks sure don't want a darky grandbaby. So they made a law says I can't marry Molly."

"I don't think California's got a law like that. Buck, you real sure about it?"

"I'm sure. I knew some colored soldiers from the North, colored soldiers who married up with white ladies when they were in Europe. But they can't live down here in the South. I'd have to move up North if I wanted to marry Molly, and we haven't talked about leaving home."

Molly spoke up. "I'd be scared to go up north, Buck, not knowing anybody. My kin'd hunt us down and kill us if we left, I reckon. I'd rather stay here. We can see each other most all the time without anybody ever finding out."

"You could go to California," Michelle said. "Nobody there would bother you. And I don't see what anybody can do if you stay here and keep on seeing each other."

Buck stopped and said, "Miss Michelle, you've been here long enough to know this town. They'd not just put me in jail, they'd hang me in the middle of the night."

"They'd have to go to jail," she said.

"Maybe in California, but not here," I said. "White men who kill nigras around here don't ever have anything happen to them."

"But Rufus Flint is going to jail for shooting that nigra woman."

"Maybe. Maybe not. If he does, it's not but two years. But you wait. He'll win that appeal and won't anything happen to him. He may be the first white man around here tried for shooting a nigra, but by the time it's all over, he'll walk free. It'll be like up at the dairy, where Buck works. It didn't matter that the Simpson boy beat Mick up bad the day before, smashing him up real bad. When he shot the Simpson boy, Mick ran cause he knew he was dead. He was dead even before they found him and killed him."

"All it takes is for a nigra man to not get off the road when a white lady drives by," Buck said. "I've seen some boys here beat half to death for that. And us coloreds learned before we were five that we don't look a white person in the face. We have to look at the ground."

Michelle wants us to be like the California she remembers. So do I. "But you look at me when we're talking," she argued with Buck.

Buck took on the look of a beaten down field hand, shamed, slumped, like he expected any minute to take a beating, his eyes cut to the ground in front of Michelle. "Yassum, Miss Michelle, I sho' nuff do. And seeing as how I'se a nigger, iffen you was to tell yo' Unk Mr. Slim, I dun already be in de jail or wuss. And I sho' nuff better talk like a nigger, too, Missy."

"Oh, Buck, don't talk that way!" I said. "You're our friend, and we don't give a damn that you're not white!"

Buck suddenly whooped with laughter. "Sam, should your mama hear you talk like that, I would be in bad trouble for leading you down the wrong paths."

"Well, it's true, Buck. I can't remember not knowing you. Mama always seemed to treat you just as good as she does me."

Buck said, "Why don't you two run along on ahead, and Molly and I will be along soon. Y'all go on along to the house."

"You gonna kiss her, Buck?"

Molly got real red, and Buck acted kind of funny, for a minute looking like a colored boy instead of the army man he is. He said, strong like, "You know better'n to ask such, Miss Sam."

I felt myself blushing, like I would if Mama fussed at me in front of a lot of people. I did know better. "Now you two go along," Buck said, smiling. "I'll see you later."

I looked at Michelle and she looked at me. We backed up, turned together, and trotted off. After a few steps, she yelled, "Beat you to the house," and took off at a hard run.

June 24, Monday

While riding Dolly up the road toward Elvira's, I met up with Mr. Benson in his big white Buick, and I couldn't believe that Ellie Mae sat in the front seat. Nobody was in the back. I couldn't figure why Benson would put a nigra up front with himself instead of in the back. I'd never seen either Ellie Mae or Amos in his car, although they work for him sometimes.

I turned around just before I reached Elvira's, and when I was about half-way back home, I met Mr. Benson on his way back from town.

He stopped, leaned out the window, and said, "You're a long way from home by yourself, Sam. Nothing wrong, is there?"

I figured he might think something else had happened down to the house. "Oh, no. I was just out for a ride." He kinda smiled but didn't answer, so I asked, "Where's Ellie Mae? Didn't I see her in your car?"

"She's over in the asylum," he said, "with Amos."

"Really?" I said. "Howcome I hadn't heard Amos was there?"

"I just took them both in. He was laid out in the back seat. He thought he was dying, so I took him to see Dr. Atkinson. Nothing wrong with him, so I drove them both over to the asylum. He saw the conjure woman and then had a spell. She put a hex on him from what Ellie Mae said. You know how it is with some of the niggers. They're just plain crazy. Those two are so scared of the conjure woman I can't get a lick of work out of them. They really believe she put a spell on them, and there's nothing I can do about it. How does your daddy handle getting work out of them?"

"Oh, they think he can out-conjure the conjure woman."

"Well, they're just plain crazy," Mr. Benson said, shifted gears, and drove off in a storm of dust.

Dolly snorted it out of her nose, and I pulled my shirt up over my face to keep from breathing it in.

Back home, I told Buck what Mr. Benson had done, and I asked him, "Did they really come from Africa?"

"From Africa? Why in the world would you think they came from Africa?"

"Well, they always told me they came from across the waters. So I just thought they came from Africa, you know, across the ocean. But I don't think they're old enough to have been slaves?"

Buck laughed, touching my shoulder for a second. "No, Sam. They came from across the Oconee River. They grew up with my daddy, and I can remember when they weren't crazy. They were fun, always laughing. Until the Klu Klux got after them. First time, they burned a cross in front of their little old house. I don't know what all they did to 'em about a week later. Broke down the door, tied Amos to a tree and whupped him bad. I heard he almost bled to death, but I wasn't more'n ten when it happened, so the grownups never told me much. Just to be careful of white men."

"You think that's what made them crazy?"

"I'm pretty sure. They left here for a long time. Didn't come back till they heard your daddy undid a spell the conjure woman put on Old Man Nappy. All they wanted to do was live on your dad's place. But they never seemed as happy as I remember them being."

"Well, they've been working up the way for Benson."

"Huh. I didn't know that. He may be the one's got them too scared to work. We need to tell your dad. Maybe he can do something for them."

"How'd Mr. Benson get them put in the asylum?" I asked.

Buck started to explain that all Benson had to do was go see the county ordinary at the courthouse, and then I remembered. I was in there one day when a nigra woman came in to say that her husband was beating up on her when he got drunk. The little old lady ordinary said she'd have him put out in the asylum. I asked Buck if that was all it took, just asking down to the courthouse? He said yes.

"Let's go tell Mama and Dad. They've still got a cotton crop, and maybe Dad can get them out and back home. They're not gonna hurt anybody. They just need to stay away from Mr. Benson's place."

"Maybe they need some cash money. Maybe your dad can give them some work regular."

"I'll ask him," I said and turned toward the house.

It didn't take Dad long to get them out of the asylum and back into their own home. All he had to do was remind Amos that he could out-hex the conjure woman, and they were ready to go home. He also had to agree with the asylum people that he would watch out for them and be sure they didn't get into any trouble if he could stop it. Like Dad said at supper, they may be simple and uneducated, but they are decent and hardworking people.

June 25, Tuesday

After Michelle and I went to the picture show today, we headed to the Magnolia Dairy for ice cream. A soldier staggered out of the poolroom and almost bumped into us. We stopped, and he turned the other way and leaned on the wall for a few seconds, like he had trouble standing up. I didn't know him, but I sure knew the smell coming off him, the same smell that always stinks up the street outside the poolroom and that hovers around the pulpwood cutters on Mondays after they've spent their pay on moonshine over the weekend. His uniform still was almost neat, the creases down the front of his pants still looked sharp, but his shirt had dark spots where he'd spilled something. The tag from a tobacco bag hung out of his shirt pocket, and he had stuffed his cap into his back pocket.

The cripple man, who sits on his rolling board with a cup out for everybody to drop a dime in, used his hands to push himself away from the wall as if to give the drunk room, but the soldier stumbled over the man and knocked him off the rolling board. The soldier fell, too, and crawled back to the wall, which he used to haul himself up against.

Michelle and I ran over to stop the man's board from rolling off down the street, and when we turned around, Buck appeared from somewhere. The man doesn't have any legs—he gave them for our country in the war, and now he has to beg to get some money so he can eat.

He thanked us for getting his board and told Buck he was okay and could get himself settled without help. He just lifted himself up on his padded-over hands and swung right back onto his board. I wished I hadn't spent most of my 30 cents in the picture show—I'd paid 14 cents to get in and a nickel on my Ben's Bar, so all I had left to give him was 11 cents. That meant I couldn't go get the ice cream, but he seemed like he was glad to get that, and Michelle still had 14 cents that she gave him. Buck reached in his overall pocket and gave the man a dollar, and the white man looked at him kinda funny.

"You been in the Army, Boy?" he asked Buck.

"Yes, sir. I heard you were at the Bulge," Buck said.

"Yep, that's where I lost the legs. You get hurt?"

"A little. It wasn't nuthin, not like yours, suh."

"Much obliged for the help, young ladies," he nodded to us. "You too, Boy," he said to Buck.

I looked over to where the drunk soldier was holding onto the wall of the stores as he worked his way along to the corner, and we left, heading to the horses. Buck walked with us, only he stayed a step or two behind us all the way to the courthouse, where we had left the horses tied under an oak tree. While we untied the horses, I asked, "Buck, howcome you're in town today?"

"Your daddy sent me to the hardware store for some plowlines and trace chains," he said. "You girls going on home?"

"Well," Michelle answered, "we were going to the Magnolia Dairy when everything got messed up. Now I reckon we're going home."

Buck nodded, reminded us to be careful, and he strode off toward the hardware store.

June 26, Wednesday

Michelle rode Lady out to the house this morning to spend the day, and while we were talking about where to ride together, Dad came in and said we were missing some cows from the tin shed pasture. He wanted us to go looking for them, and if the fence is down, go across to find them. He didn't want Buck or Pollock over on the land that backs up to us to the west. It belongs to Cou'n Phil's kin on the other side of his family, and since their big house burned down last year, the family moved up north to Washington the Capitol and got Cou'n Phil to take care of the land.

We found where the cows got out. They just walked down the creek that goes under the fence. It wasn't just down—it was pulled back, like somebody had cut it and had taken a wire-stretcher or a clawhammer to pull it away from the creek crossing. Even our horses could go through. We had to get off to lead the horses, though, cause Dolly was set and determined to go across the creek, not down it. Just across the fence, we found where the cows climbed up the creek bank to a new path, with fresh cow tracks and cow piles on it.

CATTLE TRUCK DRIVER

Bobby John backed the truck up to the loading chute and stepped out into the stench of cow manure and the bellow of angry cattle. He scrambled onto the bed of the truck and untied the sides laid out on the flatbed.

In fifteen minutes, he had the side boards in place. All that would be left to attach was the tail gate when he drove the cattle into the truck.

He threw the pitchfork to the ground, scrambled over the wall separating the cab from the cattle, and slid down onto the hood. At the tailgate, he saw the rope he'd been told would raise the entrance to the loading chute and pulled it. He tied it off on the broken end of a board. An old broken board, he noticed. Not like so many of the fresh rough-cut two-bys used to tidy up the chute and wall of the barn.

A yearling bull poked his head out the opening, snuffling. But did not clamber up the chute.

Bobby John went around the old barn. It had been some ten years since he last took a load of cattle from here. Back right after Old Man Synder died and young Phillip sold off his pa's cattle. These, he knew, didn't belong to the Judge—they had strayed and Judge Snyder was going to make the professor pay for having a bad fence.

If the fence really was broken. Way the professor kept things, I just betcha Judge Phil got somebody to cut the fence and drive these cows up here. This trap and chute are too new. He thinks since he made judge he can do whatever he pleases. I don't know why Judge Plummer didn't lock young Phillip up when he came at him with a pistol that time. Or how anybody could have voted for him after that.

He pulled the door open, slipped in and re-latched the door. The cattle moved away. Light filtered between the boards and flooded through openings in the tin roof.

"Yii-yii," he shouted and flung one hand toward them. They backed away. An old cow bellowed and headed for the opening of the chute. Two yearlings charged away from the others, circled him, and headed for the closed trap door. The rest followed the cow, and she had no choice but to move up and into the truck as the others pushed her.

Bobby John followed up, dodging the piles of steaming manure one had dropped. The cattle bunched up near the cab, and he closed them off with his half-way gate.

Back down the chute, he had no trouble pushing the half-grown calves into the truck. They were already bellowing for their mothers. He closed the truck's tailgate. With it tied off with the last of his ropes, he headed for the cab.

As he pulled out, he glanced in the review mirror and saw two riders cantering up the hill toward the barn. He gunned the truck and raised a cloud of dust.

If they see me, I'll go to jail. I gotta get rid of these quick as I can.

Since he hauled cattle for everybody in the county except the professor, he didn't expect any problems while on the way to town. He parked in the alley behind Flint's Grocery and went into the store through the back door.

Flint rose from behind the cash register, waved him back, and came to meet him. He took Bobby John by the arm and led him back into the butcher shop.

"You got me some beeves?"

"Two, out on the truck. Judge Phil said you wanted anywhere up to four. You sure these are his cows?"

Flint glared at him. "Don't be stupid. Course they are. Two's fine. Wait in the cab. I'll have my men get 'em out."

He did as ordered and waited. Flint wasn't a man to anger.

Two hefty black men came out with ropes and wrestled the beeves until they had them both haltered. Each calf weighted close to 300 pounds, but the men simply lifted them off the truck.

Bobby John didn't wait to watch the butchering. He headed to Macon and the auction barns.

He'd see the professor when he got back. Rustling wasn't for him, not even for the Judge.

SAMANTHA

We followed the new path—it went west alongside the creek a little ways and then turned north, up the hill to where the old house burned. The path had been used a lot, and as we got close to the top of the hill Michelle suddenly pulled Lady up and said, "Sam, I think I hear a truck or something."

I pulled up Dolly and listened too, and sure enough I could hear something driving away from us. Kicking Dolly in the ribs, I grabbed her mane as she jumped into a gallop, and up the hill we went, right to the scorched chimneys and the old barn. A truck was driving away, a big truck like Dad's that we use to haul hay to the barn in summer and to haul cows to market in the fall. We couldn't see what was in the truck for the dust rising up, but I heard a cow bellow; the truck was around a bend in the driveway, leaving nothing but a cloud of red dust floating in the air around the old barn and along the drive, and seeping into our noses.

"You reckon that's your dad's cows in that truck?" Michelle asked.

"I don't know. Probably so. But how'd somebody catch them and get them loaded? Unless—Come on. Let's look at that barn."

We didn't know we might oughtta have been scared. But I had my knives so if we had gotten caught and tied up, I could have cut us free; Dolly would never go home without me, and Lady would always come back if Michelle whistled. When we got up to the almost tumbled-down barn, we saw where it had been fixed up; the holes in the sides had boards nailed over them. When we got around to the other end where the door was, we decided we better not go inside; the door had some sort of wheel on it, with a big rope, and there was a feed trough inside. The smell of cow and dust was strong and fresh. Manure still steamed. We figured it was rigged up to close down on the cows when they went in, and somebody had even built up a loading chute better than the one at our barn.

"Whose place is this?" Michelle asked me.

"It's Cou'n Phil's. Well, not really his, but he takes care of it for somebody. I bet Richard Everett trapped our cows for him. Let's go tell Dad."

It didn't take any more than turning the horses' heads toward home and they wanted to run, but we made them go kinda slow. Even with the path to follow it had a lot of low limbs, and we didn't want to get our heads thrashed. I could've gotten bumped right off Dolly's hind end like I was last year by a limb, if I couldn't duck fast enough.

When we told Mama about finding the trap and seeing the truck going off, she got really upset. Since Mama really owns everything, including the land and the livestock, she had to go to Macon. By the time we got the horses turned out to the pasture and fed, Dad was home. He had just dropped Buck off at the cottage, so on the way, we stopped to pick him up.

He jumped into the back of the truck with me and Michelle, and while we were on the way to Macon, the wind and dust blew us so much we didn't even try to talk.

"We're here," Dad said as he got out. We were over the tail of the truck onto the ground by the time Mama got out. "Ya'll wait here until I find out where the cows are," Dad continued. "Buck, you come with me."

They hadn't gone twenty steps when a white man in a suit came from somewhere and stopped them.

"Hold up there, Mister," he said. "You can't take that nigger in here."

Dad spoke so quiet I couldn't hear him, but I knew he'd get Buck in to help him find our cows. Sure enough, in less than a minute, the man raised up his hands, palms toward Dad, backed up about three steps, turned, and walked away.

We waited.

The air smelled like our barn when Dad finished milking. Dust sat on everything and hung heavy in the air. Bulls bellowed, calling to the cows in heat, on and on, deep bellows that stretched out like the shadows in the early morning. Somewhere in all of the noise I could hear some calves, away from their mamas for the first time, crying out, lonesome. Like I get sometimes, like a part of me is gone away and I feel kinda empty, even when the house is full of people.

Dad came back from the jungle of cow pens to say he'd found some of the cows, to come see. Sure enough, in a pen together were four of the cows I helped feed all last winter—the black cow with the back half of her almost white; the brindle cow with a broken off horn; a spotted bull that was two years old; and the red Hereford-colored cow with a tiny white-looking patch on her left shoulder, where she'd gotten her hide torn on a nail at the tin shed and we'd had to doctor her for screwworms last summer. But the two calves born late last fall that'd been running with the two cows weren't there.

"Who brought them in?" I asked Dad.

When Dad said they were in Cou'n Phil's name, Mama said, "Can't we load them up and just take them on back home?"

Dad shook his head. "No, I've already asked at the office, but we'll get the court to stop this sale." He was already walking away and said, "I'll have to get Vicki over here with the papers as soon as she can drive over. The sale's not until Friday morning. I got the trucker's name too, so we can find out where he took the yearlings. We need Slim's help too. Come on. Let's go."

We went straight back to town, to Danny Murphy's office. Vicki looked up at the crowd when we all walked in, and bounced up to greet us with a laugh and a toss of her head.

"Well, welcome to my office," she said. "And to what do I owe this delight? You all here about Buck's car?"

"Not this time. And I'm afraid it's not a delight," Dad said. "We've just come from Macon. Phil Snyder has taken some of our cattle to the market. Can you get an injunction to stop the sale? And find Slim? I want to get those cattle home today if we can. Buck here knows them from feeding them all winter, too."

Her eyebrows rose and her eyes widened. "You mean our very own Judge Phil Snyder is turning to cattle rustling?"

Mama said yes, and cousin or not she would do what it took to get her cows back.

"I'm afraid they won't accept Buck's word," Vicki said.

"I know the cattle too," Mama said. "I had to drive Buck to feed up everywhere last winter when Dad had pneumonia. Sam knows them too."

"Okay. Let's draw up the papers. We'll stop Friday's auction. But I'll have to file the papers in Macon to claim the cattle."

As they went to work, Michelle and I got tired of listening, and we slipped out the door, drifted down the hall, and glanced into offices. We stopped in where Sis works with her husband; the office door always stays open, so his name is against the wall and you can't read the big black letters: "Law Office of Jefferson Davis Stanley."

At the front desk, Sis stopped her work long enough to ask us what we were doing.

"Dad's getting Michelle's mama to stop Cou'n Phil from selling our cows he took over to Macon today."

She just shook her head and said, "I can't believe he's that stupid. He's in this morning. I heard him earlier out in the hall. He must've had somebody else do his dirty work. Probably the Everett boys."

Michelle and I went back out in the hall. The door across from J. D.'s was closed, like it always is. Michelle asked me if I knew what was behind it, and I had to say I didn't. Somebody said one time it led to another set of stairs, but I've never seen anybody use it.

We walked down to Cou'n Phil's office, where the front room was empty. Just beyond his door, between it and the steps, is a great big hose, almost cream colored, for the firemen to use if the place ever gets on fire, and we stood by it and listened. We could hear two men talking in the inside office, but I couldn't make out the words, so I said to Michelle, "Let's go in."

When we slipped inside to hear better, I recognized the other voice as Larry's and wondered when he got in from Savannah. He hadn't been out to see Dad. But his voice sounded tense, loud, and rough. Not at all like Larry.

"Phil, what's the matter with you? I waited up for you last night until after midnight. Where were you?"

"Larry, I just don't know what to do. Somebody's watching me. I keep seeing a car parked near the house, and it follows me sometimes when I'm coming to town. It's not the same car every day. Do you think Martha may be onto us?"

"Oh, come on, Phil. You know better. Where'd she get the money to hire somebody to spy on you? I know SHE's not the problem. So what is?"

Phil went on, like he didn't hear Larry's words. "Larry, Larry, the good Lord knows I'd rather be with you than with her. But I'm scared. You know this town. You know how it'd be if anybody finds out about us. I'd be good as dead. You know it. You know how careful YOU have to be. They'll accept anything but this—and I think Martha would, too. But somebody's watching me."

"Come on, Phil. Who'd be watching you?"

But Phil didn't seem to hear anything Larry said. "I can't afford a divorce. I can't afford exposure. I'd be off the bench, out of politics in this rinky-dink town. We just can't see each other for awhile."

"If she's the only problem, it's not a problem. But if it'll make you feel better I'll meet you in Macon or in Eatonton. Anywhere."

"No, I can't. Somebody's following me."

"That's crazy. Nobody's following you."

"I know it sounds crazy. I'm probably just too nervous. But I've had a car behind me when I go home late, and I see it turn around in my driveway. And sometimes it's waiting for me when I leave in the mornings. It's a different vehicle every time. Sometimes a truck, but mostly sedans. I'm afraid she'll find out about us. If she ever does, well, I'll lose Sunny, and I couldn't stand losing my little girl. It's going to have to end for us, at least for awhile."

"Quit acting like an old man, Phil," Larry said, and laughed. "Or maybe I should say quit acting like an old woman. Who'd Martha get to follow you? She's got nothing on you, except that you spend some time with me and we have dinner together a lot when I'm in town. That's nothing. I'm here a lot, to sell antiques to you, Lawson and a few others in town. Nobody thinks anything about seeing us together at the restaurant. And that's the only place they ever see us together."

"You don't understand, Larry. Nobody has to prove anything, just suspect. And start talking, start the rumor. Somebody's after me, somebody suspects something. I don't know. Maybe somebody's seen us out at the old cabin. I don't know. But no matter what, I'm not going to loose Sunny. I'd kill Martha before I'd loose Sunny."

For a second, it was quiet inside, and all I could think of was the time Sunny got on the bus crying, and told me her daddy had beat up her mama that morning.

"Look. I've got someone coming in a minute. You go. I'll see you tomorrow at the hotel for supper. We'll talk then. Go, go. I can't talk about this now. Not here. Not now. I don't want any trouble, Larry. This is the wrong place for this conversation. Now go. You shouldn't have come here to start with."

"Okay, I'll go. But I'll see you tomorrow, and I expect you to be there at six sharp. We'll talk about this. It's certainly not going to end like this, not after—what is it now, fourteen years? Since I was sixteen. So yeah, fourteen years. You be there at six, you hear?" There was something in Larry's voice that I'd never heard before, a hardness, like a threat of something bad that lay in wait for tomorrow evening.

A chair scrubbed across the floor; Michelle and I glanced at each other and tiptoed back into the hall. We barely got out of the door when Larry came up behind us. I turned, made like I just saw him, and said,

"Well, hi, Larry. When did you get to town? Do you have some things for Dad? He's up here with Vicki right now. Maybe you can bring them out to the house?"

"Hello, Sam. Hello, Michelle. Yes, I've got a few things in the car he might like. You think I might come out this afternoon?" He didn't sound at all mad, like he was with Phil. His voice was as soft as ever, but his eyes looked different, like they couldn't smile, like they were holding back something that bothered him real bad. They had sunk into his face, almost surrounded by black, like he hadn't slept much. I was sure glad he didn't know we had been listening.

"I think maybe after dark would be best." I didn't want to tell him Dad was going to be in Macon to get our cows back that Cou'n Phil rustled.

Larry grinned but it didn't seem real. His eyes didn't smile. I like him even if he is a little bit sissy for a man and different from most grown-ups. For one thing, his voice doesn't sound like he thinks we're still children. Most grownups talk to me with the same tone of voice they use talking to children and to the coloreds, and treat both me and Michelle like we're just kids and don't count at all. But one of the things I like so much about Larry is he treats me special, like I'm a grownup just like him.

"Well, I'll see you tonight, Sam."

"If you get out early enough I'll let you ride Dolly if you want to."

"Not this trip up, I think. It'll be dark when I get out, but maybe another time, when I can catch up with you earlier in the day. Tell you what, I'll bring up my jodhpurs next time for sure. But tonight it'll have to be a business visit with your dad. Okay?"

After Larry disappeared down the stairs, Michelle asked, "Do you think Martha is really going to leave him?"

"I don't know. But I'd leave anybody that was beating up on me."

"Me too. I don't think he'd really kill her, though, do you? He had to be just talking."

We had started back toward Vicki's office when footsteps sounded on the stairs, and we looked back. Rufus Flint went straight to Cou'n Phil's office, and the light from the door faded out as he closed it.

"I wonder what they're up to," I said.

Michelle said, "They're probably trying to figure out how to steal more money from the nigras."

"Maybe," I said. "And maybe they're trying to figure out how to bulldoze that colored cemetery."

"Yeah. But Mama and Danny will stop them, you'll see."

"What're you girls doing out here in the hall?" Mama asked as they came out of Vicki's office.

"Nothing. We saw Larry Huntington. He said he'll be out to see Dad tonight with some new things. After dark, so Dad won't have to quit early."

"Well, we'll have supper early and save him some dessert. You girls want to go back to Macon with us? Your dad and I are going with Vicki to take the injunction as soon as Judge Plummer signs it."

"You want to go, Michelle, or had you rather go fishing?" I asked her.

"Oh, I'd love to go fishing," she said. "But we might miss something if we don't go back to Macon." She was grinning all over. "Besides, I don't think Roy Rogers would go fishing when there's a bunch of rustlers to catch."

Vicki laughed. "I'll come out to the plantation house as soon as I get the papers signed. I'll pick you up. It'll be easier if we all go together."

When she got to our house, Vicki told us she had tried to reach Slim, but couldn't, and had finally left him a written note at the house, with the name of the truck driver. This time, Buck stayed home to do the chores.

In Macon at the barns again, Michelle and I wandered around, looked at everything, and breathed in all the cow smells, while Mama, Dad and Vicki went to the office. Mama told us to stay close, so we climbed up onto the top rail of the wide board fence where we could watch Vicki's car across the lot while we talked about the cows in front of us.

We didn't have long to wait, and were soon on our way back home. I wanted Vicki to leave Michelle with me to go fishing, but she said she might not be able to come back for her before dark. I decided to go by myself, and hadn't gotten any more than half-way to Buck's back porch when Slim drove up. I forgot fishing and ran through the hot stillness to reach the house by the time Mama let him in the kitchen door.

Slim is just like his name, tall and lanky, but his hair is still coal black and not getting gray like Vicki's. His deep-set gray eyes always seem to smile. He keeps his pistol on his left hip since he's left-handed, but he doesn't all the time pull it up the way most of the deputies do, as if they want everybody to see how heavy it is. "I found the truck driver, Laura," he said, spinning his hat with his left hand inside it.

Dad strode into the kitchen from down the back hallway at the same time. "What'd he allow?" Mama asked.

"He said he knew those were your cattle, but he didn't dare not haul them since Judge Snyder told him to. And he said he dropped two yearlings off at Flint's Grocery, at the back door down the alley. Two colored men came out, but he didn't see Flint at all."

Dad's face got redder as he said, "Let's go." He didn't bother to go back down the hall for his hat, just headed out the door with his head bare, which I've never seen him do before.

"I wanta go," I said, hurrying to keep stride with Slim.

He grinned down at me from under his hat as he pulled it on and snugged it over his right eye, his crowsfeet crinkling all up. "You got no call to be going," he said.

"You may as well take her with you," Mama said from the porch steps. "She'd be there on that bike by the time you drove in."

His laugh was a lot like Vicki's. "Okay. But you'll have to stay in the car when we get to the grocery. Right, Professor?"

Dad nodded, but I could tell he was more worried about the cows than about my going with them.

Slim had left his car in the sun, and it was so hot inside I could barely sit still, the heat scorching me through my jeans. I cranked the partly open window all the way down in hopes of getting enough air to cool down, but sweat ran down my face long before Slim got up enough speed to get the wind blowing inside the car.

I stuck my face, eyes closed, just outside the window to catch whatever wind I could so I didn't hear Slim and Dad talking. But I wanted to get cooled down.

Slim took the alley to the back of Flint's Grocery. I've never been down the alley before. It was lined up with barrels to dump trash into, and flies swarmed all over the barrels, those black flies that lay maggot eggs on everything. Stench rose up so thick I had to pull my face inside the car by the time Slim stopped.

"You stay here," Dad growled at me.

I knew he was mad at Cou'n Phil and Flint rather than at me, but I knew to stay inside the car. Where it sat, though, I could hear everything. And smell everything. I didn't dare close up the window to keep out the smell or I'd have baked just as quick as those apples I forgot to take out of the car one day last summer and they lay up there on the shelf under the back window and baked until they were done. If it was almost a hundred out at the house, it must have been a hundred-ten in that alley, and more inside the car, even if the sun wasn't directly on me.

Slim opened the screen door and started in, Dad behind him. They both backed up as Flint came outside.

"What the hell you doing here? You want something, you go to the front door, like everybody else."

"Where're those two yearlings got delivered here a while ago?" Slim asked.

"I don't know what you're talking about," Flint answered.

Dad stepped up. "You know—"

Slim's hand came out in front of Dad and halted his steps and his voice. "Let me handle this, Professor. If your yearlings're here, I'll find them."

"Don't you dare call me a rustler. I don't steal. Just because you can't keep your cows in the pasture, don't you think you can come in here like this."

"Let me talk to your butcher," Slim said.

"You got no call to be talking to my help."

"Rufus, let me talk to your butcher. Now."

I couldn't see Slim's face, but I could hear what he must have looked like, his voice getting hard and demanding. He moved his left hand toward his holster and hooked his thumb into his pocket, maybe to scare Flint, maybe just to rest it.

Flint yelled, "Hey, Nick, get out here."

Wiping a butcher knife on his already bloody apron, a black man, stooped with his years, moved outside and moved up beside Flint.

"These men say we've got the professor's yearlings. You seen any yearlings out here?"

The man looked at Slim, at the gun on his hip, then at Dad, and turned to Flint. "Nawsuh, I ain't seen no yearlings outchere." He clenched his hands together as if afraid the knife would jump away from him.

"Get back to work," his boss told him. The old man slid inside the screen and eased it to behind himself.

"Satisfied? Now y'all get on away from here." Flint turned and went inside, and I could hear him hook the latch as he closed the screen. He probably would have slammed the wooden door if it weren't so hot.

I got out of the car and without a word I went over to the barrel beside the screen, where the worst of the flies were, and pushed against the top, but I couldn't make it move. Slim shoved it off. I had to back away from the stench and the cloud of flies that rose as we interrupted their meal. It was full of cow guts.

"He'll have the hides salted down inside somewhere," Slim said as he turned and slammed his fist against the screen. "Open up, Rufus," he called.

"You got a warrant, I'll open up."

This time, he slammed the wooden door.

Dad shook his head. "Let it go, Slim. By the time we find Judge Plummer and get a warrant, he'll have the hides gone. At least we've stopped the sale in Macon and we'll get those cattle back."

The stench and the swirling flies seemed to fill up the car even when Slim got it up to forty-five on the way home and the wind tried to blow the smell and the sounds out the windows.

LAURA AND THE PROFESSOR

Laura was cutting up the frying-size chicken when Molly came into the kitchen from the sewing room to show off the dress she had finished making. It spoke of spring with its yellows and blues.

"It's beautiful, Molly."

A knock on the screen door pulled their attention from the dress.

"Come on in, Buck," Laura called.

Buck entered, his gaze going to Molly and a smile spreading over his face.

Laura looked at Molly and saw the reflection of Buck's delight.

Oh my.

"Do you have any chores for me, Miss Laura?"

"No, I'm just starting supper. Well, maybe see if you can find Sam and go with her for the cows."

"Sure will."

He looked again at Molly and Laura saw love pass between them.

Buck had not been gone a minute when Molly said she needed to be getting home and left.

Time to catch up with Buck before he and Sam go for the cows.

*   *   *

The professor walked into the kitchen, into the smells of frying chicken and baking biscuits.

"Smells like a good supper tonight," he said and set his briefcase on the floor.

Laura smiled, turned from the stove and the pot of butter beans to kiss him a welcome home.

"I'm worried about Buck and Molly," she said.

"What's going on?"

"I think they're having an affair. Or at least, in love with each other. It's the way they look when they're together. All smiles. They can't seem to quit grinning at each other. They act like they just want to dance all the time. I'm afraid for them. If anybody sees them together without Sam around, they could be in trouble."

"Buck knows better. He'd be risking Molly as well as himself."

"I know. And I'm sure he knows, too. But what can we do?"

The professor shook his head. "There's really not much we can do. They have to make their own choices. We can't say a word to them. But we can support them and protect them any way we can."

"Suppose..."

"What, Laura?"

"What if she gets pregnant? Those Everetts would kill him."

"If she gets pregnant, we'll take her in. And find some way to get them to a safe home. Danny's daughter lives in California. We could send them both there. At least they'd have support from her and not be alone. She'd find him work."

Laura smiled, hugged him, and turned to stir the pot of butter beans.

SAMANTHA

June 27, Thursday

I can't tell anybody what I did today. I had no business peeking in the hotel window, so if I tell, I'll get a whupping from here until next week.

I wouldn't have even been in town, except that I rode in with Mama for something to do because of the rain. We hadn't more than gotten to the Piggly Wiggly, though, than the rain slacked off. So while she did her errands, she said I could do what I pleased, just to meet her back at the grocery store when the train ran.

I walked over to the nigra cemetery that Flint is planning to pave over, and I got right in the middle of the sunk down places—they line up row after row, like we line up the cards when we play Fishing, going in all four directions at the same time, no matter where in the graveyard I stood. Last March, daffodils bloomed around some of them. Most have got rocks lined up around the sunk-down spot. I don't blame the nigras who've got folks buried here for coming to get Dad to keep Cou'n Phil and Rufus Flint from bulldozing up the graves. Dad's even told Mayor Deason that if they pave over those graves, it'll just show that Stanleyville is still living in slave days.

Between me and the street was what was left of that colored church—the rocks that held up the corners, and some of the bricks from the chimney that hadn't been taken off to make a fireplace for somebody else. I circled around it and, cause of the weeds and briars growing thick in the ashes, I had to be careful about where I put my bare feet. I followed the paths the nigras made when they pick blackberries or shortcut through. And I made sure not to step on any of the graves—I didn't want any of Buck's haints coming up after me cause I disrespected their graves.

At the edge of the cemetery, I looked across the street, where the Snyder Hotel sits on the corner of Main Street. The alley down the side of the hotel separates it from the small two-story building where Flint has his car-lot office on the ground floor. I don't know what's upstairs, but I think Sims lives up there.

Something moved in a hotel window that Michelle and I think

looks haunted, with a face looking out at us a lot of times, a face we can't make out. The light often turns the window into a mirror and lots of times the curtains are closed. Even when the wind gets up and blows them away from the window on warm days, I can't see who's inside; I see just a shadow moving around.

Black metal stairs in the alley rise up the side of the hotel, to a platform that wraps around to right under that haunted window. Michelle and I used to talk about sneaking up there, to peek in. So with nothing better to do this afternoon, I decided to climb up there, to see if anybody was inside.

Didn't anybody but Mr. Sims pay me any mind when I walked right on up to the street, like I belonged there and was just going on about my business. He leaned against the door jamb at Mr. Flint's car lot. He's too fat for his uniform; his belly hangs out over his belt, and his shirt was already sweaty-wet and turning dark under his arms. Even from the cemetery, I could see the big patch he had on his shoulder like the army patch on Buck's coat, but this one said, "Sims Security," with the words in a circle around a pair of crossed rifles. I've been close up to him once, and he smelled like what Mama would have called "rank as a sweaty horse" from his sweat, from tobacco, and from that stale kind of smell the hired men have on Monday mornings.

I didn't dare go across to the hotel with him watching, so I leaned up against a tree and waited.

He took off his hat, nodded, wiped his forehead with his handkerchief, stuck his cigar back in his mouth, hitched up his britches with both wrists, pulled his pistol up higher, turned, and walked back in his office. He sure does take short steps, I reckon cause his tummy is about as big as a watermelon and gets heavy to tote around. He walks like a woman going to have a baby, like he's got to get his legs out in front of his belly to keep it from pulling him down frontwards.

With him inside, I just hoped he wasn't still watching, and I walked across the street and on down the alleyway where the coloreds leave their mules when they come to town on Saturday to bring the moonshine to sell to the Snyder Hotel. I had to step around some lumpy piles of mule manure so old they had turned white from the heat. Even the rain hadn't softened them.

When I got to the steps, I looked around again, but I couldn't see Mr. Sims, or anybody else. I didn't figure anybody else would be in the graveyard with it wet as it was. The only other thing I could see from down that side alley was a little bit of street that nobody used except the coloreds, or somebody from the asylum getting off the train that ran right down the main street of town. But the train didn't run until four o'clock so I knew I could get up there with nobody seeing me. I walked up to the bottom of the ladder and scooted right on up it.

I tucked my shirt tail into my shorts to be sure it didn't get snagged on anything. Mama's always saying we don't have the money to buy any new clothes. Plus, Mama hates to sew. And besides, we'd never match the feed sacks today with the ones that Mama made this shirt out of. My bare feet wouldn't make any noise, but I sneaked up anyway.

The wind hadn't gotten up, like it usually does after the rain, but a lot of steam rose up from the street. My shirt was real bright, and if anybody looked up that high, even with the clouds and mist, they'd sure see me. Anybody in the room wouldn't know I was there unless he stuck his head out.

I got up to the little platform, way up almost to the top of the building—it must have been five stories high up there—where I could hear sounds coming through the haunted window. I squatted down, sat on my heels and leaned tight against the brick wall so I would be able to sneak my head close to the window and peek in from the side without being seen.

The air steamed. Mist lifted all the way up to the top of the building. With the wind not even a whisper, the mist just wavered around, like ghosts moving up from the graveyard. The fan inside turned real slow, making a soft whumping sound and moving the curtains out of the window just a little, so it seemed like the room itself was breathing and the curtains, like a shirt, lifted a little with every breath the room took. If anybody inside did look my way I'd be out of sight behind the edge of the curtains.

I was glad to see it was a real room and had real people in it, that it was not haunted. The "ghost-face" I'd seen behind the curtains musta been Larry, cause there he was. Maybe he always stays in this room when he comes in from Savannah.

I couldn't tell at first who the other man was, and even now I don't know what was the matter with Larry. He was lying on the bed on his back, without a shirt on, moaning something terrible. Even with the fan blowing, sweat shone on his face and chest, like on Buck and Pollock when we pitch hay in the barn in July. Larry looked like he didn't have on any britches either, and the man on the side of the bed toward the window was kneeling down over Larry, his head nodding up and down about something; Larry kept on groaning like he was hurting, and he reached his hand out to the other man, who held onto it. I figured the man musta been trying to calm him down cause Larry was sure shaking and groaning really bad.

When there was a kinda rattling noise at the door knob, Larry said, "Oh, my God, it's Phil!"

The other man jumped up, and Larry jerked the covers up over himself at the same time. As he jumped up, I saw the other man was Rufus Flint. He took three steps, turned, grabbed his hat off the dresser, and closed himself up in the closet before the hall door opened. As Cou'n Phil stepped into the room, Larry sat up in the bed.

Phil closed the door and stood there, his back to it, his hands behind him, looking at Larry for what seemed like a long time. Larry finally lay down on his back, pulled a pillow up under his head and folded his hands under his neck. I could of sworn I felt a cold wind coming out of the window. Cou'n Phil took off his hat and stood there, turning it around in his hands.

"You're a bit early. It's not even four."

"Like I said yesterday, I got a problem with Martha. She claims—"

"She claims? She claims?" Larry sat up again. "I don't give a damn about Martha's claims, Phil. I just don't. Why should I? You sure don't care about my claims to you." His voice rose. The words seemed to drip with anger, like I heard him in Cou'n Phil's office yesterday. "And I know the problem's not Martha, it's some cadet from the school, isn't it, Phil? Isn't it? Well, you just see about your little military schoolboy, and I'll tend to the other fish in the lake. And you can go to hell."

Philip stood against the door, his face beginning to look like it was sagging around the jaws, and his eyes were getting real shiny. Larry went on talking, holding fury back no better than a dam holding water in a lake when the rains are too much and water floods over the spillway. I just knew something was gonna happen, and it did.

Larry kept on talking, his voice rising. "I know it's not Martha. She's not a problem and never has been. You've always used her as your excuse when you wanted to play around, didn't you? She's too scared to start any trouble. It's somebody else, itn't it, Phil? Itn't it? After fourteen years you got yourself somebody else AGAIN. And— AGAIN—you thought I wouldn't figure it out. Just like I didn't figure it out last time. Didn't you?" He yelled.

He jumped up out of the bed. Cou'n Phil started across the room to meet him, looking like he was about to cry; his voice broke when he started to talk, "Oh, no, Larry, no. It's not that. I couldn't—"

But Larry strode across the room. He was naked but for his socks. His long thing was red and weird looking, all shriveled up and snuggled in a patch of jet-black hair that curled up as tight as the hair on Pollock's head. It looked like his insides were falling out.

The ghost inside wrapped the room with a nameless terror that sent chills all over me. Larry lunged, pushed past Phil, opened up a drawer in the chest, and turned back toward Phil with a pistol in his hand, a pistol like the one that my great-uncle brought home from the War to End All Wars before I was born. As Larry raised his pistol, his hands shook so much he had to use both to hold it even part way still.

"Who is he, Phil? Who's your new boy?" His voice faded almost to a whisper with the word "boy," and Larry looked toward the closet door for a fraction of time, almost slumping against the chest of drawers for a second. He lowered the pistol till it pointed at the floor. He looked back at Phil and almost shouted, "By God, it's Rufus, isn't it? You're messing around with Rufus too, you god dammed pervert! You're both damn perverts! I'll send you both to hell, damn you! Y'all're not gonna get by with screwing me like this. Neither one of you. I'll see you both dead!"

Phil's face went all over white, and he backed up until he hit up against the hall door. He tried to open it without turning around as Larry started to raise up the gun.

It all happened fast.

Phil tried to turn away, the closet door banged open, Flint slammed into Larry, Larry fired, Phil yelled, Larry and Rufus hit the floor, and I ran.

I ran down the steps without worrying about snagging my shirt or stumping my toes on the metal stairs. I took the steps two at a time, jumping from the last landing, over the last seven steps, falling on my hands, and skinning up my knees. I jumped up and kept on running, down the alley and across the street into the cemetery, where I ducked down into a low place behind a stump. I could look around the stump to the hotel door on one side, and by looking around the other side of the stump I could see Flint's car place behind the hotel.

Mr. Sims was back standing in the door, leaning on the jamb, with his cigar chomped down in his teeth. I wondered if he had seen me running, but I wanted to see what happened, even if it was almost time for the train to run and me to meet Mama. I couldn't wait but for a few minutes.

The police hadn't gotten there when I had to leave, but I did see Mr. Flint come out. He stopped just outside the door while he put his hat on, pulled it a little off to the left side, the way he always wore it, and walked across Main Street to his grocery store.

The train whistled just outside town, so I hurried through the cemetery and onto the sidewalk so nobody would know I'd been anywhere near the hotel.

I can't figure out what Larry meant by his claims to Phil cause Phil's got his wife Martha and his girl Sunny. Who else could claim him? Maybe Mr. Flint can, cause Phil mostly judges the colored folk who are behind on their rent for those shanties down in niggertown that he owns with Flint. So Cou'n Phil is judging to make the nigras pay him money they owe him, only he pretends it's just to make them pay money they owe Flint. So he really doesn't answer to anybody unless it's to Rufus Flint, who likely does have a claim cause they're partners.

I know he doesn't answer to Martha. He mostly just beats up on her, but if she really did divorce him, she might get all of his things— the farm, Sunny, maybe even some of those nigra houses, and all his money. I know Sunny would want to stay with her, from some of the things she's said on the school bus. Especially because she's scared her daddy will beat up on her the way he beats up on her mama.

I want to ask somebody about what was going on in the hotel room, but I don't dare. If Mama ever finds out I was looking in that window, doesn't matter that I'm too old for a whupping, I'd get one.

*   *   *

Vicki and Danny stopped by with Michelle this evening after taking Bessie home, and we all sat around in the dining room to talk. Dad was in the corner in his favorite chair, grading lab reports for his summer school students.

Vicki did most of the talking, telling Mama the injunction hadn't done any good, because somebody at the barns telephoned Phil at his office this afternoon and warned him. She ended up with, "So Phil just drove right over to Macon and sold them directly to a meat packer. The cows were hauled off from Macon, and probably already butchered, before Phil got shot this afternoon."

"Got shot? Who in the world shot him? How bad is it?"

"Not bad. Just his arm." Vicki glanced over at me and Michelle, and looked back to Mama, who seemed to catch some kind of signal from Vicki's screwed up face cause she frowned for a second.

Danny got Mama's mind back to the cattle by asking, "What do you want us to do about the cows? Just let it go, or do you want to have him arrested?"

"He may be my kin, but he stole my cows, and I want the money."

Vicki's saying, "You ought to have him arrested," just brought a long minute of silence.

"I can't do that, Vicki. He is my kin. It'd about kill him if we locked him up. I just want my money. Can't we just file a civil suit?"

"Sure." I thought she was gonna say more, but she didn't.

Danny started to say something and turned the noise from a word into a cough that he tried to hide behind his hand.

Mama looked at him funny, decided he was okay, and said, "I just wish there were some way we could get Flint. We know he got those calves."

They talked about some of the law stuff Vicki was going to do so Phil would give Mama her money, and I was getting bored with it all. I was just before suggesting to Michelle that we go play cards when suddenly Vicki said, "Why don't you girls go upstairs and play carroms?"

The way she said it, I decided I didn't want to leave. Vicki was going to tell Mama all about the shooting, I just knew, and I didn't want to miss anything. "It's hot up there," I said.

But Mama musta known Vicki and Danny didn't want me and Michelle around, and she said, "Y'all run along, now, Sam. Take up some cards if you don't want to play carroms."

"Aw, Mama."

"Sam, y'all run along now." When Dad spoke up, I knew I had to go.

I shrugged and went over to the chest where we keep the cards, pulled out a deck, and we started toward the front stairs. But I wasn't about to miss everything, so I laid a finger on my lips, and we tiptoed back to the dining room door, where we sat down with our backs to the wall and listened.

Mama was saying, "Danny, you hushed up real quick when I started to ask about Phil. What's going on?"

"Larry shot him, we think."

"Larry? Our Larry?" I could almost see Mama looking back and forth between them while she tried to figure it all out. "Why would Larry shoot Phil? It must have been an accident."

Danny said, "I don't think so. Phil is lucky that's it's just his arm that got messed up, when the bullet could've gone a few inches to the left and killed him."

Mama asked, "Danny, what's going on with Larry and Phil?"

He coughed, but didn't say anything. Finally, Vicki spoke up. "Laura, I think it's a three-way affair."

Again a long silence. Mama spoke first "You mean, Phil and Flint and Larry? They're all married, except Larry, and he's dated Sis. Well, I swan. I'd of never guessed, especially about Larry. Sis said he's always been a perfect gentleman. I just never thought of him like that."

"Rufus was in the hotel when it happened. I think he was in the room, too, and just slipped out, and now Phil is protecting Larry, saying it was an accident. And keeping Flint's name out of it all," Danny said.

"Slim went over with the sheriff, and told me a man who was in the room next door heard a lot of yelling and saw Rufus come out of the room," Vicki said.

Dad spoke up, "That would explain why Phil got some of our cattle for Rufus to butcher and sell."

"Right," Danny said. "If it was just Black Market, he could sell them anywhere, but Rufus is the only one in town who had beef all during the war."

"Our beef, I wager," Mama said. "You think it'll get all over town, about them?"

"I don't think so," Danny said. "It's just lawyer gossip right now, and I don't think the lawyers or Dr. Atkinson are likely to talk it up, even to their wives."

"Folks who think it's wrong are going to be afraid to say anything, afraid of Rufus hearing what they say. And those who don't care will never bother to say anything. They know it's not their business, no matter what the preacher has to say. And with Flint and Snyder both in the Klu Klux, nobody'll dare say a word. It's not like if they find out about Buck Steele and Molly Everett. If that gets whispered around, everybody'll listen," Vicki said.

How did they know about Buck and Molly? I know Michelle didn't tell her cause I trust her with my life and my horse too. How in the world did they find out? Mama always says she's got eyes in the back of her head, but she'd never tell anybody if she did see something. I know she'll never tell anybody else, and neither will Vicki or Danny cause they know what could happen if the Klu Klux finds out.

Vicki went on. "I've heard stories Phil and his wife Martha don't get on good, even if they come to church together every week."

"But I do wonder if Martha suspects or knows. If so, why would she stay with him, knowing he didn't love her?" Mama said.

"She's afraid. She's got no education, no way to make a living. All she's ever done is keep house and care for the child. She's trapped. As sure as if she were in prison for life. She's got nowhere to go, no way out, not unless she could get most of what he owns in a divorce. And I've been here long enough to know that Stanleyville is a man's town. It won't matter what her causes, she'd never win against Phil. She'd get nothing in a divorce. At church every week, she looks scared of doing or saying something wrong."

"But maybe this cow business will be worth it if we can use it to keep him from being re-elected for another term. We just have to hope someone will run against him," Mama said.

"I'll be sure the word gets around the courthouse about the cows, but you know we can't say a word about Phil liking boys."

I couldn't figure out what they were talking about. It didn't matter that Phil liked boys—all men wanted boys, not girls. Cou'n Phil woulda wanted a boy instead of just Sunny. But seems he's good to her, in a way. He takes her to buy her clothes, all the way over to Macon. But he won't let Martha go with them, and he even buys all the groceries. The only time Martha can go anywhere is on Sunday, when he takes her to church. To the big church in town so everybody can see them.

Martha can't get a divorce unless she can show he's running around on her—and he's not. All he does is visit with Larry over at the hotel.

Suddenly Vicki's voice came up louder and pitched higher with excitement. "I forgot to tell you, Laura! Slim's getting his own house next week. He's closing next Friday, and plans to move in right away."

Mama said, "Losing your chaperone?"

They all laughed. "You know Slim'll be back over a lot for supper."

"He might be a third party, what with Danny coming over all the time," Mama said.

They all got real quiet, and I nudged Michelle. "What's that about Danny?"

"I think he's courting Mama," she said. "He seems to be getting invited to supper a whole lot."

"Maybe Vicki is sweet on him," I said. "Reckon she'll marry him?"

"I dunno. I guess. If she wants to."

"You like him?"

"Yeah. He's mighty nice to me all the time. He doesn't care if I bust into the office or call Mama after school or anything."

I didn't get a chance to tell Michelle about what I saw today cause Vicki and Danny decided to go on home, and of course Michelle left too. So I'm still trying to figure out what's going on with Larry and Cou'n Phil, but I don't dare ask Mama. And I'm NOT going to ask Sis what it all means cause she'll just laugh at me. I do hope Cou'n Philip's not hurt bad and doesn't die cause I like Larry a lot and I don't want him to go to jail or to the electric chair.

July 1, 1946, Monday

When Dad asked Mama to go to the hardware store for some barbed wire this afternoon, I rode in with her for something to do, and when we saw a big truck pulling out from beside the hotel, Mama said for me to go see what was happening at the cemetery, that it might be the bulldozer was there.

It was. Cou'n Phil and Flint stood in some grass off to the side of where it had bit up the ground, so they wouldn't get their shoes messed up in the raw dirt. I eased over by the old oak snag that's still taller than my school building. It's got no leaves, is burned to jet black all around the bottom, and woodpeckers have made nesting holes all up and down it. I was close enough I could hear everything they said, and not once did either one of them even look my way. They just looked at each other while they talked.

Flint looked at Philip's arm, and reached out to barely touch his hand where it was stuck out of the sling. "How is that doing?"

Cou'n Phil raised up his elbow a little and looked like he was trying to wiggle his fingers, but they didn't wiggle much. "I don't think it'll ever be the same, Rufus. I can hardly move my fingers; they're bent up bad from where the bullet tore up the muscle in my arm."

What he said told me they hadn't been alone to talk since the shooting. "How in the world did you happen to be by that day?"

"You don't remember?" Rufus asked.

Cou'n Phil shook his head. "All I remember is that pistol pointing at me, Larry shooting, the noise, and me falling and cussing him."

"I was—in the hall and heard your voices. I knew from what I heard y'all were having a bad problem, so I slammed open the door. I think it surprised him so much it musta messed up his shot."

Phil musta believed him cause he said, "I'll be grateful to you for life, Rufus. Without your being there, I'd be dead now."

Flint touched him on the shoulder. "I'm glad, too, Phil. You've sure been easy on Larry from what I've seen in the paper, saying it was all an accident, inviting him to have an antique show in the hotel during the sesquicentennial weekend. Have you seen him lately?" I could see his eyes seeming to get smaller, but not from squinting at the sun cause it was cloudy. His hand moved down to Philip's bad hand and lightly touched his fingers.

"Not since I was in the hospital. I had to tell him to leave cause Martha got really upset with Larry's being there. She just can't understand friendship between men. She can't seem to realize it was really just an accident, you know?"

"Yeah, I know; Larry told —" Suddenly Rufus stopped talking, his eyes shifting off away from Phil's face.

"Whatda you mean? You mean you've seen Larry? Why? What'd you want to see him for?" Phil backed up a step, shifting his bad arm away from Rufus's touch.

"Well, I—I was just asking him when he's gonna come back to set up that antique showing. It was in the papers. I was just trying…"

I could feel the fury in Cou'n Phil's voice as it rose almost into a shrill shout. "It's you! I knew it! I knew Larry was seeing somebody else, so I took up with you. And all the time, it was you. You were laughing at us!" He paused for just a fraction, long enough for his mind to shift back to that day, and he seemed to remember. "And you weren't in the hall. That's not the door that opened. I was leaning against that door. You were in there with him and he was naked. Where were you? In the closet! You came at Larry out of the closet, not at me from the door. How could you?"

"Oh, shut up, Phil," Rufus snarled back at him. "You got no reason to bitch about me and Larry, considering what you were doing with me. So just you shut up unless you want me to walk away from you. Then where'd you be? You don't have the gumption to find yourself another man around here. And you're dead here anyhow. How could you be so stupid as to get caught selling the Lawson cows?"

Philip sagged like a half-full sack of sweetfeed when you try to stand it up on end. Leaning back on the oak, he covered his face and shook, like he might be crying. Rufus reached over to touch his shoulder, and when he did, Phil jerked away.

"No, don't do that here. Not now. I couldn't stand it now."

"Have it your way, Philly boy," Flint said. "You can go beat your own meat, or you can stay here and cry if you want to. But don't come crawling to me next week. I won't have time for you. And get that bulldozer going again. Get this land cleared up this afternoon, before Lawson gets on us again. You signed that contract, and by God you're gonna keep to it."

He poked Phil in the chest, took a cigar out of his jacket pocket, bit off the end and spat it on the ground at Phil's feet, struck a match on the behind of his pants leg, and puffed on the cigar until the little bit of breeze pushed the cloud of smoke toward me. The smoke got into my nose even with my being farther away than across the living room. I had to cover up my mouth and nose to keep from coughing. He shook out the match, tossed it my direction, and walked off right through the fresh dirt, getting the red goo all over his fancy shoes. He crossed the street to his car lot, went inside, and didn't bother to close the door. He stood inside, looking out, watching to see what Phil was doing.

Phil stood there for a time, took out his handkerchief and wiped his eyes and face. His hand shook. Staying on the brush to keep out of the mud, he eased back to the street and crossed over to the hotel. He didn't look toward Flint but walked with his head down. In a couple of minutes, a man came out of the hotel, got on the bulldozer, and went back to pushing up the graves.

I didn't waste time trying to figure out why in the world Phil would want to beat meat, cause I know he doesn't cook. I don't know why else would you beat on meat except to make it tender to cook it. I hurried back to the hardware store, where Mama was getting impatient, but when I told her about the bulldozer already there, we went over to Vicki's office.

"The bulldozer's pushing up the cemetery," I said as we walked in.

"I know," Vicki said. "Danny's over at the courthouse with the restraining order right now."

"You expect trouble?" Mama asked.

Frown lines crept onto Vicki's face. She hadn't smiled when we came in.

"I don't know. Danny and I talked with Rufus a couple of days ago. Of course, he was a mite angry."

It was like he'd heard his name. The door banged open and slammed against the copy machine, and Rufus barged in, his eyes bulging more than ever, his hair almost standing up where he'd raked his fingers through it.

Mama pushed me off to the side, getting between me and Flint. I could feel her trembling a little and knew she was scared. I wasn't scared, but just plain disgusted.

"Where's Murphy?" he demanded.

"Over at Judge Plummer's," Vicki responded. "Seeing to that restraining order."

"I'll kill that son of a bitch," Rufus promised. "He's supposed to be my lawyer. How dare he think he can stop me. I'll pave over his grave if he keeps on getting in my way. You tell him." He jabbed a finger toward Vicki, turned, and stomped out of the office.

Vicki let out a long breath.

"How did he know so fast?" I asked.

"I imagine Judge Plummer had his clerk call over to the car lot," Vicki answered. "At least he knows, and he hasn't really done anything."

"You think he will?" Mama asked.

Vicki shook her head, and before she could answer, Danny walked in, so Vicki told him about Rufus's visit. Danny simply walked over to his desk, pulled out a revolver, broke it, checked that it was loaded, and put it back in the top drawer.

"You gonna take it with you?" I wanted to know.

Danny smiled. "I don't think so. I want to be prepared. Just in case. But I don't think Rufus will really do anything. I think he's just mad because he lost this round of the argument. He doesn't like to lose."

Mama needed to get the fence wire back to Dad, so we had to leave.

Of course, when we got home, Dad wanted me to help Pollock fix the fence. All I had to do was hold the wire stretcher while Pollock drove the staples, or help him unroll wire by holding onto one end of an old broomstick. If you try to unroll wire any way but on an old broomstick the barbs will tear up your hands. I had to fetch the tools and staples for him, and it woulda been fun to use the hammer, but Pollock told me I wasn't strong enough to drive a staple into Osage orange trees, and if I would just hold the stretcher after he pulled the wire tight I would be a big help.

"Pollock, you oughtta put down that rifle if you're gonna get any fencing done."

He shook his head at me. "Missy Sam, I ain't goan habe nary haint gitting atter me."

"What good's that rifle again a haint?"

"Hit mighten be nairy good again a haint, Missy, but hit shore do make me feel better iffen I gots hit wid me."

"Well, you lean it over there, like you would if Dad was here."

"You ain't got nuthin to run off no haints, Miz Sam."

"I got as much magic as my Dad, Pollock."

"You is?" His eyes widened and his thick eyebrows rose, almost in fright.

"Yep," I told him. "Want to see me drive a nail with my eyes closed?"

I knew he didn't want to. Every since Dad had driven a nail with his eyes closed, with Amos and Ellie Mae watching, all the nigras thought he could out-hex the conjure woman. I felt it was okay to say I could, even if I couldn't, if it'd get him to lay down that rifle and get to work.

Pollock shook his head, "No'm," and propped the rifle against a tree until we finished the fence. He didn't even move it until we'd worked down a dozen panels instead of moving it every time we repaired a panel.

I asked Pollock what does he know about the conjure woman, and he said, "Miz Sam, you ain't got no call to eben be ackskin about her." He shivered.

Tonight, when I came up here to write, I went out on the upstairs porch to listen to the conjure woman pound her drum, a slow steady beat that every once in a while changed. It felt far away, like the wind when it's half asleep in the night. I've never seen her and I don't know what she looks like, if she is old or young, or if she came from across the waters with Ellie Mae and Amos, but for all of my life she has lived somewhere near our land. I don't know exactly where, but I don't want to cross over our fence line and run up on her.

Sis says that she just has one arm, that she holds one of her drum sticks in the toes of one of her feet. But I don't think so, cause she pounds that drum too good to just have one arm. Sis says she doesn't have a real drum, that she uses one of those fifty-five-gallon metal drums like the one Dad uses to keep chicken feed in down at the hen house. I don't know where Dad got our drum, but when I beat on it with a stick it sounds just like hers.

I shivered at the chills running down my backbone; I felt she was right there, watching me, seeing I was scared of her. I went back inside, still shivering in the heat.

July 2, Tuesday

Roger Benson has got bulldozers turning our wagon road into a highway and taking people's land. They're at the other end of our road right now, and Mother and I went up there with Vicki and Michelle this morning.

Dust rose faster and thicker than a winter rain could ever lay it down. As hot as it was, we needed to close up the car windows to keep from getting all choked up on the dust.

Vicki pulled in at a nigra's home, stopped, and got out. "I want to see if Roger's gotten a deed from any of the nigras."

I opened the door to get out too, but Mama said, "You girls wait here." She got out with Vicki.

Michelle and I rolled the windows down to listen, but the bulldozer noise was too loud even with the wind blowing the noise and dust the other way. They stood on the porch for a couple of minutes, talking to the nigra woman, and the woman called to her husband who was in the back yard sharpening up an ax on his grinding wheel. He came over, talked a few minutes, and Mama and Vicki came back to the car.

"What'd they say?" I asked.

Vicki backed out of the driveway as she said, "Roger hasn't bothered to even ask any of the colored people about widening the road onto their land. He's just bulldozing everything, like he thinks they don't count for anything."

Mama said, "Well, I'll be glad to see the road paved, but I'm not just going to have him run all over me. Vicki, I need you to tell Benson to stay off my place until we get everything settled. They'll have to keep the fences up all the time, and I don't want the road shortcutting through us."

I hope they don't want to put it through Wordsworth's Acre, where we've planted a million daffodils just in my lifetime. They spread all the way across the yard and down the hill to the pond, making the whole hillside yellow when they bloom. Dad said we'll put daffodils on the other side of the lake next year, so we can see them "beside the lake, beneath the trees."

Surely Benson wouldn't do that. Since J. D.'s in charge of the parade for the sesquicentennial birthday party for Stanleyville, he said all the people coming to town are going to come out here not just to see the house, but also to see the boxwoods and the slave houses and the other buildings that were here when Sherman came by. The Committee people are already selling tickets to the house tours. Mama will get some of the money to help pay for the cookies and punch cause we'll have a tea party for everybody that afternoon.

"We'll have to shoe the horses when they pave out here. I can't let Dolly run on pavement."

"You can get our blacksmith," Michelle said.

"I know, but Buck knows how to shoe horses. He'd do Dolly for me."

"Have you got a fireplace and anvil and all that?" she wanted to know.

"Yeah, we've got a little blacksmith shop down behind the cottage, the other side of the chicken house. Buck fixes all the old plows for Dad. He learned how before his Daddy died. Mama said that's one reason he's so strong. You know, from swinging that heavy hammer when he's working on something."

At the house, Mama and Vicki sat in the living room under the fan, and Michelle and I walked toward the kitchen. We hadn't gone ten steps when Vicki said Rufus Flint is trying to sell his grocery store.

I moved back toward the door, my finger against my lips as I signaled Michelle to come with me. If we went in the room with them, they'd be careful about what they said, so we sat down by the door to listen.

"Danny told him he'll have to go to prison for killing that woman two years ago if his appeal gets turned down. And also told him it probably will be turned down, since there aren't really any grounds.

Flint got mad as a setting hen. He told Danny, with me sitting right there, 'You think I'm going to jail, you better think again. You'll be dead before I see the inside of a jail. So you better get to work on that appeal, you hear?' And he slammed out of the office. I told Danny I'm a mite afraid of him." Vicki paused just long enough to catch her breath and continued.

"I wonder what in the world Flint's gonna do with all of his bottles of pee in his refrigerator in the grocery store?"

"What? You mean he keeps urine in his refrigerator? Why?" Mama asked.

"He thinks somebody's trying to poison him. He's trying to get somebody to test it for him. You know, to look for arsenic. I heard he even took some bottles over to Macon, to the health department. They laughed him out of the office."

"Do you think he's crazy, Vicki?"

"Oh, he's got to be. He ought to be locked up in the asylum, but it'll take somebody in his family to get him in there. Mattie's too scared to do any thing. And so is his sister."

"He's got a cousin in town, too, but she won't even admit to being his kin," Mama said.

Vicki changed the subject suddenly. "Laura, I really like Danny a lot, but there's a big age difference. Do you think ten years is too much?"

Michelle's eyes got big. She smiled and whispered, "I thought so."

I tried to squeeze my nose to hold back a sneeze, but it blew out anyway.

"Of course not," Mama said. "Sounds like the girls are back."

We walked back into the room so they wouldn't think we'd been listening. A few minutes later, Vicki said they had to leave.

Michelle laughed. "Mama's got to cook dinner for Danny."

Laughing, Vicki tousled her hair.

After they left, I went out to the smokehouse to get my puppy. Mama hadn't wanted me to get a dog, but I talked her into it when I told her I would pick out a boy dog so we wouldn't have a lot of puppies.

Buck says the puppy has the blood to be a good possum dog. He's a good kind of hound, a redbone, so I've been calling him Red.

I reckon Buck was right for me not to take Red when I go for the cows. He chases everything, even the chickens if I don't watch him close. He's the best dog ever. He goes with me everywhere though, and loves to follow when I go riding and always comes when I call him, even if he is chasing something. He's gonna make a great possum hound with Buck's help, and maybe Molly and Michelle can go hunting with us this fall.

July 4, Thursday

It's July Fourth! Today we can pull a watermelon out of the patch. Mama says they're no good until today. But before breakfast, Sis and J. D. drove up to tell us that Roger Benson's son Little Rog was killed in a car wreck last night. A nigra so drunk he didn't know he was on the wrong side of the road slammed Rog's car into an oak tree. Rog died before anybody got to the car.

The nigra's only hurt came from hitting his head on the steering wheel, and he bled all over his car from the cut. But the policeman took him on to the jail, not to the hospital. The nigra had a lot of moonshine in his car—three Mason jars full, and one open that spilled all over him and the car.

Rog mighta been drunk too, cause they found a half-empty Mason jar of homemade likker in his car, with the top off. But if he was drunk it hadn't helped him stay alive the way I've heard tell it would. Slim called J. D. cause he knew we'd want to know about it, even if Roger and Dad had bad feelings between them.

Ole Roger sure has set a store by that boy. Rog is not just his only son, but his only child. I hope he doesn't turn all his caring for that boy to hate for the nigras.

I wonder if the nigra was drinking likker from Mr. Benson's still at his candy factory. Everybody says he made his Ben's Bars for the Army during the war, so he could get all the sugar he wanted and used most of it to make likker. Vicki said that Benson sells it at his B&B Drug Store and that Phil sells it at the Snyder Hotel dining room in water glasses. Slim wants to bust his still, but wants to catch Mr. Benson there when he does.

As much as Dad hasn't liked Mr. Benson, I know he and Mama voted for him cause he's better to the nigras than the man who ran against him last election. But everybody liked Little Rog cause he was always nice to people, even to the nigras, and was always laughing. He's older'n me, but he rode the school bus with me for a long time. I can remember him making everybody on the bus laugh when he hooted like the train whistle to scare the bus driver. And one time he turned loose some of those bumblebees that don't sting you—the ones with the yellow noses that are always making holes in the beams at the barn— and he nearly got put off the bus. Sis dated him one time, right when he was finished high school, and she told me he'd wanted her to have a drink out of the Mason jar with him but she wouldn't. She'd made him give her the car keys that night, and she'd driven herself back out to our house in his car and left him sitting in our yard, and had told him she'd never go out with him again. Mama didn't know about that, and I'm not about to tell her.

Mama and Dad had to go pay their respects to the Bensons at their house and take some food today. I was glad I didn't have to go and could stay home. I didn't want to have to put on a school dress to go calling.

Since Buck went off up toward Athens to visit with his friend George from when he was in boot school during the war, and Molly went to town with her Aunt Maude, I didn't have anybody to go fishing with, so I just stayed under the fan today and tried to stay cool.

It was so hot tonight I've had to sprinkle my sheets with water just to try to get cool enough to go to sleep. I keep my windows open all the time now, and draw the drapes every morning. But on nights like tonight, when the wind's asleep, the sounds of the conjure woman's drum seem to beat with my heart so I can't sleep.

July 6, Saturday

Mama didn't make me go to Little Rog's funeral but she and Dad went. So did Vicki, Danny and Slim. Mama hadn't been home but long enough to get out of her good dress when Vicki stopped by the house from taking Bessie home, and she and Mama got to talking about how bad Big Roger looked, like he was about to die.

He's always been kinda like Roosevelt, smiling and chomping on his cigar and slapping everybody on the back, but Mama said there didn't seem to be anything good left inside him now that his boy was dead.

Just a couple of days before Rog got killed, I saw him laughing in town, in front of Flint's furniture store, when I went to the picture show. His voice rolled down the street, like thunder; only his voice never did grumble; it sounded like he was always having fun—until he choked himself on his cigar and started to cough.

I hope he doesn't get to hating all the nigras the way Cou'n Phil does. Mama says if he turns all his passion for life into hate, he won't leave any nigra alone that crosses his path.

Buck and I finally got to go to the field and get some watermelons. Buck thumped a bunch to decide which four were best. We had one for my family, one for him, one for Vicki, and one for Molly's family. As soon as Buck put ours on the back porch table, he was off to Molly's. Mama cut ours, and I sat on the back steps to eat, so I could spit the seeds out for the chickens.

July 7, Sunday

When Dad came downstairs today, the first thing I noticed was he hadn't shaved. He said he was gonna grow himself some Burnside sideburns. Mama laughed and said he looked like he might be trying to be the "strawberry roan," which got me to singing the song while I set the table.

Dad laughed, saying he had a head start on the "Brothers of the Brush," who are gonna collect money from any man who comes to town without whiskers during the week of the big birthday party next month. All week long, they're going to have a jail cell right in front of the courthouse so everybody can see who hasn't grown some whiskers. The men who get locked up have to pay real money to get out. I don't know if they'll arrest any nigras, though.

On Saturday there's a big parade, and I get to dress up like a Confederate soldier, ride Dolly, and carry the Confederate flag. Michelle says she oughtta be the one carrying the flag since she'll be on Lady, who's got the fanciest walk of any horse in town.

But having a brother-in-law in charge of it all, I get to carry the flag.

SAMANTHA

July 8, Monday

As soon as Michelle got here on Lady, we cantered up to see what's going on with the new road. Red ran in circles around us, his short legs blurring with his speed and excitement. Then he was off to see what he could sniff out of the bushes.

The nigras used to make up a separate group on the chain gang, but today both groups were there. One of the guards was napping, and one was playing cards by himself. The crooks had a set of dice and were rolling for kitchen matches. Nobody was working.

I threw my right leg over Dolly's shoulder and sat sideways. Michelle did the same, and we just sat and watched the crap game. The guards glanced over at us a couple of times, but mostly nobody paid us any mind. Those dice didn't care if a colored or white man threw them—they lost matches for the white crooks just as much as for the colored crooks.

We were fixing to go—I was tired of watching the chain gang do nothing and listening to the guard snore in the shade—when a car rattled the planks of the bridges over Big Hickory and Little Hickory creeks up at the other side of the old train station. A cloud of dust rolled toward us, and a big old white Buick came ripping up the road. As soon as the car stopped Roger Benson got out in the cloud of dust that settled all over his suit. He didn't bother to even brush it off.

I hadn't seen Roger since before Little Rog got killed, and he sure did look poor, like he'd not had enough to eat, or like something was eating away at him from the inside, so his whole body shrank. His face was as pale as his hair, that's gotten pure white, but his heavy black eyebrows stood up like bushes over his glasses. His eyes have sunk in so much all I could see of them was his mad. He hadn't bothered to get his hair cut in a long time, so his army-style hair cut has grown upward like his eyebrows and stands up all over the top of his head. He's bald in the front, his hair peaking down in the middle and up on the sides, like Melanie's in *Gone With The Wind.*

His face didn't used to be lined except when he was frowning, but now two lines have run down between his eyes like train tracks. Others have crossed his forehead and slid down his face, where he's gotten skinny and his face is falling in. His cheeks have sunk in so much he looks like he's taken out false teeth. He's turned old, and angry. He's probably mad at everything around him he can't keep a hold over.

Benson flapped his arms like a mad setting hen's wings when he stomped over to the sleeping guard and kicked him in the side.

"You're not getting paid to sleep, you damn bastard. Get up from there!"

The guard scrambled to his feet, and the dice disappeared as the prisoners all stood up, shuffled around, and moved toward the equipment. The guard with the cards scooped them up and into his pocket with one easy motion, like he'd hidden them lots of times before.

"You goddamned niggers. Get to work or I'll haul every one of you over to Jasper and see you dead in the river! Move it, you bastards!"

"What's he gonna haul them to Jasper for?" Michelle whispered.

"He means he'll haul them up to the river, shoot 'em, and dump 'em in the river, like that man did up in Jasper County."

"Didn't he get caught?"

"Not for a long time. Since the river took the dead people on off downstream, when anybody ever found one of them, nobody knew who they were. Figured they were maybe just some nigra that fell in the river fishing. It wasn't until somebody told what was going on that the man got caught."

"He go to jail?"

"Yeah. Funny thing, though. A nigra who worked for him, who wasn't a crook, helped the sheriff send him off to jail. But they made him a "trustee" right away, so he wasn't treated like the rest of the crooks. They let him help chase prisoners who escaped. And one day, he was out helping chase two nigras who knew him. They stole a truck from somewhere, but the dogs were right behind them. Anyhow, when they saw him, they pointed that truck right to him and ran over him."

"Served him right. I hope they killed him."

"They did."

We sat in the heat a minute or two longer just to see what might happen. The wind still slept. It was still as death and brinjin hot. I stuck to my jeans where they touched Dolly's side, and Dolly's neck turned dark up under the reins. The only shade up the road where they're working is from that one Chinaberry tree they hadn't pushed off yet, where the guards and all the crooks had been sitting around.

Benson flapped his arms toward the bulldozers and yelled, "You bastards get this machinery moving!" He kicked his foot toward the bulldozer and screamed, "Get moving, get moving!" A prisoner climbed on one of the machines and cranked it; it coughed and sputtered and spewed out black smoke. He turned toward the creek and our land. Not once did he look toward Roger, just toward where he was guiding the machine.

I knew it wasn't gonna take that bulldozer long to knock down our fence, but at least they had a pile of posts and barbed wire to put it back up.

Michelle said, "Let's go. Benson's making me edgy."

I was getting on edge too, the way Benson was acting so crazy. Besides, I was getting tired of watching and was ready for a co-cola. When Dolly tried to grab the bit in her teeth, I kept her to a trot. Michelle just kept right up there with us. Lady seemed to shrink down in the rear end and to try to throw her front feet right off her legs as she settled into a fast running walk. I couldn't let Dolly really run; she was too heavy with her foal.

It sure was a good day to be out riding, but when the pavement's finished I can't ride up and down the road as much.

July 9, Tuesday morning

Boy, did we have a time of it last night, what with the cows out and the trucks running again. Buck heard the cows in his yard in the middle of the night, and he yelled at me from just below my window, "Cow's out." I piled out of bed, got into my jeans, and ran to help him get the cows put up before they stomped down or ate the boxwoods planted by the slaves when the house was built back in 1800.

I wasn't about to wake Dad since he teaches at eight o'clock. But I didn't think to get a flashlight, and I stomped on an Osage orange thorn. It hurt terribly, but I still had to keep on after the cows, so I ran on my toes on that foot until we got them back into the pasture. We didn't have to even open the gate; the chain gang had left about six panels of fence laid out on the ground, and the cows just ran back in the pasture over the barbed wire.

When Buck saw me limping he said he ought to send me home, but it was going to be too much for him to fix the fence by himself. I said, "If you'll get the tools, I can at least stand here and keep the cows inside."

The conjure woman's pounding echoed in the stillness and sent shivers up and down my back. The night wind barely moved, but it brought the smell of fresh manure from the pasture. The stars seemed to crackle they were so close. The moon drifted in and out from behind the few clouds as if it, not the clouds, moved. A calf bawled for its mama, and somewhere a hound barked as something came into his yard.

I heard a truck before Buck got back, and its lights flashed up the hill from the train tracks. I ducked down behind a privet hedge, but kept my head where I could see. Somebody in the back end of the pickup, with a cigarette glowing, held what looked like a rifle. I hoped it wasn't the Klu Klux out looking for somebody.

Buck came back after the truck was out of sight.

"You know that truck?" I asked.

"No, Sam, I don't. It doesn't belong out thisaway. And no stranger's got business out here this time of night. Looked like the man in back's got a rifle."

"You reckon they're looking for somebody? You heard anything about trouble?"

He said no, and we went to work on the fence. He brought a crow bar, a hammer, some staples, and a piece of barbed wire to piece out the strands if we couldn't pull them tight enough. It took us almost an hour, working in the moonlight, and twice we heard cars going by up at the fork at Molly's.

A truck rattled across the train tracks. We hid.

The truck eased up the hill and rolled by us real slow. Somebody around here was in bad trouble.

When we got back to the house, Buck pulled out the thorn. It's as big as a nail, and about two inches long. It hurt a lot when Buck got that thorn out, and I had to struggle to keep from crying cause I sure didn't want him to see me cry and think I'm a sissy. He heated up some water and I found the carbolic acid to soak my foot in. He went back to his cottage, and I soaked my foot until the water got cold.

Instead of going to bed, I stood at my bedroom window a few minutes. I don't know what we'd of done without Buck. Pollock is too scared of haints to put down his gun, especially on a night like this one, with the moon turning the night blue and the light wind making the shadows move and sway just like a haint walking.

I went to sleep feeling my heart beating with the drum as the sound flowed into my room and seemed to wrap me with its rhythm.

By morning, my foot was sore as everything, and Mama looked it over real good to be sure it didn't have any red streaks going from it. All I have is a big red circle, but even so she made me sit in the kitchen and soak it for another two hours before she'd let me take my foot out of the foot tub. The water had gotten cold anyhow.

Buck had to do all my chores this morning.

*   *   *

Vicki drove out to tell us about two nigra boys breaking out of jail and killing somebody. If the truckers had seen us last night, they mighta shot us.

I can't ride by myself now, or even bring in the cows alone, until those two colored boys are caught.

"If they'll shoot a man for no reason, you won't be safe," Mama said.

They shot a man and stole his truck, but they could've just taken the truck cause the key was in it. They've probably gone to Atlanta. They're still free. So I'll be stuck inside till they're caught.

Vicki and Mama decided Michelle can't ride Lady out, and I can't even ride Dolly or my bike. I can't go anywhere at all outside unless it's with Buck. I told Mama I ought to be okay if I just took the rifle, but she said no.

So Buck went with me to get in the cows this afternoon, and before we got them to the barn, it'd started raining.

"I don't expect anybody's out here looking for those boys. At least not the way they were after Mick. They'll be looking up toward Macon or Atlanta," Buck said.

"If it rains much, they won't be getting down the road anyhow," I said. "The road's already mucky."

Where the chain gang bulldozed the road, the inches of dust had turned to mud. When Mr. Hightower, our neighbor up the road, drove by us, he left deep ruts, so anybody on the road is gonna get stuck tonight. I don't think even our truck can get through it.

July 12, Friday

No word on the killers. If they're still around here, they've probably drowned after two days of rain. The road is a muddy mess, and every car digs deeper ruts in what was dust just a couple of days ago.

Driving the cows to the barn this afternoon, Buck and I packed so much mud on our feet we had to wipe it off on the side of a tree before bothering to rinse the rest of it off in the driveway mud puddles.

The radio news tonight said it was the most rain in ages, almost six inches already. Even Camper's Creek is running all over town, and the river's flooded too.

When Mama went to the kitchen to cook supper she hollered and I ran in. Muddy water ran out of the faucet. We never had mud in our spring water before. I went for Buck and we got a hoe and shovel and slipped and slid down the hill to the spring. Muddy water rushed like a river through the woods to the spring, so fast and heavy that we couldn't begin to turn it back. Only place it could go was to the spring—everywhere else was uphill. We headed upstream through the downpour, and Buck laughed at me when I held the shovel over my head like an umbrella.

The chain gang had dammed up the ditch that usually carried water from the rain to a drain that missed the spring. But now it was washing a new gulley to our drinking water.

Buck shook his head. "I'm no engineer, but I know enough not to do something like that. I reckon the deputies running the chain gang aren't any smarter than the prisoners."

"They'll have to fix it with the bulldozer, won't they, Buck?" I asked. "Looks like a lot of dirt making that dam."

Buck nodded. "Yep. Let's go tell your mama. With all this rain the chain gang won't be back until Monday."

We told Mama what we found. She bit her lips to hold back her words. I know she was about to cuss, but wouldn't in front of me. She picked up an empty Mason jar, filled it with muddy water and capped it. Then sent me to turn the water off under the house.

She doesn't want somebody to forget we can't run any water and open a faucet, letting the red mud into the pipes. It's probably already into the hot water tank.

I walked back into the kitchen as Buck read aloud: "Could you make your prescriptions or candy with this water? My family can't drink our faucet water because your road workers dammed up the ditch and forced water into our spring. Get the road crew out here right now so my family will have water."

He glanced up at Mama and continued. "Yes, I can read your writing." He grinned. "I noticed you didn't ask if he could make his likker with it."

We all laughed.

"Don't you think I should take it to him now?"

She shook her head. "No, wait until morning. It'll be dark soon."

"If I wait until morning, he may be gone off. His road isn't a mess like ours."

"Take one of the horses."

"I can cut across country and be there quicker than if I take time to catch Daisy."

"Okay," Mama agreed. "Let's put the note in a Mason jar so it'll stay dry." She reached up to the shelf where she kept her empty canning jars and took down one with a lid.

"Can I go too?"

"No, Sam, you may not go." She put the note into the jar, closed the lid, and handed it to Buck.

Buck laughed. "You stay here, Sam, and get out of your wet clothes. I'll be back soon."

"You got on wet clothes," I said.

"Yes, but I'll stop at my house and put on a dry shirt and get my slicker."

"You be careful. The creeks'll be rising. And night's coming."

"I should be back before it's plum slap dark."

He stepped out onto the porch and headed for his cottage.

I put buckets under the eaves to catch roof water, and while I was out, just got naked and took an outdoor shower.

BUCK

In dry clothes and his slicker pulled on, Buck stepped onto the porch of his cottage. The wind lifted the tail of his rain gear. *I'm gonna get wet. Good thing we got the note in that jar.*

He stepped into the yard, into the growing mud, and instead of attempting to walk the mud hole that was the road he kept to the yard until he reached the pasture gate, opened it, and followed the fence until he reached the other side of the pasture, at the railroad. He found the place where the top wire was broken, snugged the slicker up to his chest with one hand, and with the other pushed down on the top unbroken wire. He stepped over without tearing his slicker, and slogged through the runoff in the railroad ditch.

The route down the tracks might be longer, but he would not be in the muck of the road. He set off as if on a command hike in basic training. In about three miles the track crossed the road going up to Benson's.

Twilight deepened and darkness fell before he reached the crossing. He turned left. At least this road was hard-packed, even if a little slippery in the tire tracks. To avoid slipping, he stayed in the middle of the road and walked on the hump of small gravel thrown up by tires and sprigged with weeds and grass.

Another mile to Benson's house. Light from a front window guided him up the driveway, but he slogged around to the back door. He might be there for Miss Laura, but he knew better than to knock on the front door. Mrs. Benson opened the kitchen door and released the sizzle and smell of steak frying. His mouth watered.

"Why, hello, Buck. What are you doing out in this storm?"

"I brought a message from Miss Laura for Mr. Roger." He pulled the jar from his overall pocket, removed the note, and handed it to her. And realized he'd forgotten to talk nigger talk to a white lady.

"He's taking a nap," she said as she unfolded it. She read the note, looked up at Buck, and said, "Oh, my! Well. He's got to get this fixed right way. Oh, poor Laura! No water. That's awful. I'll wake him."

She hurried from the kitchen. Moments later she returned. "He'll be here in just a minute. He's writing a note for the sheriff. He wants you to take it to town."

"Yessum."

"Tonight," she said.

He nodded. "Yessum."

"It's dark. You'll need a lantern. Do you have one?

"No, M'am."

"One's on the porch."

"No, M'am. Ise'll be fine."

"Well, I—"

Roger walked in with Laura's note and a new one. "Take these to the sheriff . He'll tend to this. I can't drive those roads in this weather. You got one of the professor's horses?" He held out the two notes.

"Nawsuh. I be walking." He took the notes and placed them into the Mason jar and it into his pocket.

"Get going, boy."

"Oh, Roger, he needs a lantern. It's going to be dark before he can get home."

"A lantern won't help him in the rain. The glass'll blow. Get going, boy. "

Roger stomped from the kitchen.

"M'am, your steak—"

Mrs. Benson grabbed a towel, jerked the pan off the stove and set it on a metal-topped table. Smoke rose from the steaks. She flipped them over to reveal scorched meat.

"I reckon we'll eat well-done tonight. You best go along, Buck. And get the lantern off the porch out there. There's a box of kitchen matches on the shelf. If Roger doesn't like your taking it, he can be mad at me."

"Yessum. Thank you, M'am."

He lit the lantern while on the porch, stepped back into the rain and headed toward the railroad. Shortest way to town and the only way to avoid the two red hills that turned to slick in a light rain. The road would be more slippery than a moonshiner brewing for the sheriff's brother.

He whispered a thanks to Mrs. Benson for the lantern. It shone golden-orange on the water in the roadbed, and when he reached the tracks it glowed along the rails. As he slowed his stride to fit the uneven spaces between crossties, the walk stretched out in time.

The rain slacked off to a drizzle a half-hour later. In another half-hour, he reached the jail. He pulled the screen open, pushed the wooden door into the office, and stepped inside. Water dripped from the slicker, his brogans and his hands. He set the lantern on the floor.

"Whatcha need, nigger? You step outside and quit dripping on this here floor."

" I got a letter from Mr. Roger Benson fer the sheriff."

"Well, why didn'tcha say so? Give it here."

"Mr. Roger told me to give it direct to the sheriff."

"Well, if you're gonna be that-away about it, you jest head back outside. He's over to Flint's grocery."

"Thank you, suh," Buck replied. He picked up the lantern, turned, and stepped back into the mist.

Wondering with every step why the sheriff would be at Flint's this late, he strode the three blocks to Flint's Grocery. Lights from inside flooded the sidewalk in front of the store. The overhead awning blocked most of the mist, but wind drifted some against the door. He touched the knob to see if it were locked and discovered it wasn't. He set the lantern down next to the wall, pushed the door open and stepped inside.

Flint sat behind the counter at the cash register. The sheriff leaned against the counter but stood erect when he turned and saw Buck. He held a tall glass filled with clear liquid, and a matching glass sat on the counter. Buck knew neither contained water. Must be some moonshine from a still the sheriff had busted.

He spotted the .38 caliber revolver lying on the counter to Flint's right.

"What you doing here, boy? You got the money you owe me?" Flint almost barked. His eyes, protruding anyway, looked to Buck as if they would pop out.

"Nawsuh. I got a letter fer the sheriff from Mr. Roger."

"Gimme here," the sheriff said and held out his hand.

Buck fished out the Mason jar, removed the two notes, and handed them to the sheriff. He waited in the silence.

"You tell Miz. Laura I'll have the men out first thing in the morning. Soon's the rain let's up enough we can get there. You remember that, boy, or I need to write it out for you?"

Buck nodded. "I can remember, suh."

He turned toward the door.

Flint snapped. "You wait, nigger."

Buck did not turn around. He stopped, his hand on the door knob, and waited.

"You got my money?"

"Nawsuh."

"Boy, you signed a paper. You getting me mad now. I may just have to take care of you if you don't pay like you ought to. You hear me, boy?"

"Yessuh. I hear you, suh. But Miss Vicki, she said she gonna take ker of hit, suh."

"She can't take care of anything. She's just a dumb bitch. You get my money in here or else."

The hammer clicked on the pistol. Buck knew it was pointed at his back. Flint had killed over money owed him before—a lot less money.

Am I next? Can I get out of here before he shoots? He can't shoot me in the back. Not with the sheriff there. Or will he? He's just trying to scare me.

"Yessuh. I'se'll shore nuff tell Miss Vicki, suh." He jerked the door open, stepped through, slammed it closed, and stepped over the lantern beside it, away from the front window.

Flint's laughter floated through the door.

"I'm gonna kill me that nigger."

"Well, don't do it in front of anybody. I got enough problems with you and your man Sims already," the sheriff replied.

Buck shivered and headed home as the rain intensified again.

SAMANTHA

A long time after dark came I figured Buck oughtta be back, but he hadn't returned when it got to be my bedtime. I worried. Had he run up on somebody who thought he was one of the killers? Who'd be out on a night like this?

Just as I crawled into bed, I heard his knocking on the back door. I jumped up and ran downstairs to the kitchen.

"Mr. Benson sent me to town to take his note and yours to the sheriff," Buck said as I got there.

Another ten miles, and after dark in that rain. No wonder he took so long.

"Buck, what's wrong? What happened?" Mama asked.

Buck wasn't looking at her but off to the side, his eyes shifting around as if he were looking for something or somebody who might be in the shadows down the back hallway.

He shook his head, and when Mama repeated her question he finally met her eyes.

"I ran up on Mr. Flint and he got on me about paying for the car."

"Vicki told you to hold up on that since she's filed that suit," Mama said.

Buck nodded. "I best be going and getting into something dry."

"Try not to worry, Buck. Vicki and Danny'll take care of everything."

He nodded, turned, and walked out into the night. But even after he left, I could smell his fear, a rank odor like a rattlesnake and a sweaty horse all mixed up together.

"I don't want anything to happen to Buck," I said.

Mama nodded. "Me neither. Go on to bed, Sam."

I did, but I couldn't get Buck out of my mind. When I closed my eyes, I could see his, glancing off into the darkness looking for Flint to jump out of the shadows at him.

July 13, Saturday

The rain finally stopped during the night, but Mama said it won't be two days before the dust is back, what with the wind blowing so. As soon as I got my chores done, I sat out on the front porch, reading, and waiting for the chain gang to get here to fix the road.

When I heard a car making so much noise it sounded like it was stuck down toward the train tracks, I walked along the fence line to stay out of the mud and went to see who it was. Benson was stuck, his very own white Buick convertible covered all over in red mud splatters, sitting smack between the bad ruts, doing nothing but spinning mud all over everywhere and digging itself in even deeper.

He still hadn't gotten his hair cut and it was sticking out from under his hat, which he didn't even bother to take off while he talked to me. His voice was almost shrill now, almost like an old woman, mad, screaming fury.

When he yelled and waved at me to come over, I moved a little closer, but I wasn't about to go into all the slop to get next to his car.

"Go get that nigger of yours to come push me out!"

"He's not my nigra, Mr. Benson. He's his own man. He's not here, anyhow," I told him. "It's Saturday, and he's off today. I reckon he's gone on to town."

"Goddamn niggers. Always gone off when you need 'em. Well, go get your horse to pull me out."

"She's about to drop her baby and she's never been harnessed up before. Maybe somebody'll be along in a few minutes."

Sure enough, here came the chain gang truck, with a bulldozer, three prisoners, and a deputy. The prisoners got behind Benson's car and pushed while he gave it the gas. He yelled back at the men, "Rock it, you fools!" So they pushed and let off, pushed and let off, and suddenly the car slid off to one side, seemed like it caught and moved a little, and kinda jumped out-a the ruts. The three nigras were covered with mud splatters, on their jail overalls, their faces and hands. Their brogans were just big wads of mud, with muddy water running inside them cause the slop came over their tops. Benson yelled back at them to leave the prison truck and walk on up the road, and get that damn ditch fixed.

I told Benson they'll have to push him out again if they don't bulldoze out the mudhole he was just stuck in. He glowered at me like he was mad, but when I glared back, my hands on my hips, he nodded.

I watched them fix the runoff down by the spring so the water went down the ditch like it always had, instead of into our spring. They went back to where Benson got stuck and pushed mud around some, but I bet it won't hold cause all they did was push mud into the ruts, so it'll just stay soft. Anything can still get stuck in it. When I told Benson he oughtta make a trench for the water to run off the road, he said he knew what he was doing, that I was acting like an uppity nigger and to mind my own stupid business.

July 14, Sunday

Mama was right. The dust is rising, and the wind brings it right back into the house faster than Mama can keep it wiped off the furniture. We can't hang clothes out to dry when Lillie Mae washes Katie's diapers or anything else either, cause the red dust lands on them so fast it turns right to mud on the wet clothes. So we can't catch up on the washing, but at least the spring has cleared up. Mama's running water through the pipes today to get out all of the grit, but still won't let us drink any that hadn't been boiled.

All anybody is talking about now is the birthday party they call the sesquicentennial, for the 150th year of Stanleyville. It's gonna be on the 10th of August—that's the closest Saturday to the date old Willie Stanley carved on a tree down near where the courthouse is. The tree fell down about fifty years ago, but somebody wrote down what was carved on it: "W. S. here aug 12 1796."

Everybody born in Stanleyville knows that W. S. stands for Willie Stanley, the first person to build a cabin here. It rotted down years ago, long before the tree he built it under had died. He's J.D.'s great-great-something granddaddy.

After the parade, when a lot of people come out to the house, Buck has to wear a fancy suit and tell everybody about the two slave houses and help people up the steps so they can see inside. He's got to tell them the pile of dirt—three feet high—under the houses is what's left of the topsoil that was here when Willie Stanley first came. It shows how much the plow has caused to wash down the river.

Molly, Michelle and I all have stuff to do. So do Elvira and Lillie Mae. The nigras'll be in the old kitchen, with its five-foot-wide fireplace, telling how people used to cook, and they'll have to wear long cotton dresses and head rags. Course, they wear headrags all the time anyhow, but they don't wear long dresses nowadays.

I reckon J. D. being in charge of all of the celebration is why we have to have the big tea and show off the plantation. Mama said she knows what people pay for their tickets won't be enough to cover her costs of all the sandwiches, cookies and hired help.

For the parade, Vicki is making Michelle a Confederate uniform out of real Confederate gray and is going to put gold braid on it. Mama's making me one out of butternut so I can be a real soldier, not just a dress-up soldier. She teases Michelle about being a dress-up soldier, but Michelle says that means she's the boss soldier and since officers don't get to carry flags, only enlisted people do, she's gonna outrank me.

July 15, Monday

Mama went off this morning, and just as I started reading Zane Grey's book *Spirit of the Border* about Lewis Wetzel, somebody knocked on the back door.

When I answered the knock, I found a ragged, dirty man on the porch. He looked like something the cat dragged in after it was through with him, not at all like the tinkers I'm used to seeing wandering around looking to sharpen scissors or put dams in frying pans and pots. This man needed a shave, a bath, and some clean clothes. I could smell him through the screen. He musta slept in his clothes a week. He had a big knife stuck on his belt. When I looked down, I saw one of his toes stuck out of the end of his shoe.

But it was his eyes that gave me the willies; they weren't still, they shifted from side to side and he seemed to be trying to look behind me, all the time looking everywhere but at me. The look in his eyes brought to mind the mad fox that chased me up the tree. I felt a coldness trickle down my back, and my stomach got a hard knot on the inside that seemed to rise up and burn the inside of my throat so I could hardly talk.

"Whatcha want?" My words were as croaky as a frog's.

"Is your pa home?" he asked.

I don't know what made me lie about it, but I said, "Yes, he's in the dining room off the kitchen here. Can I call him for you?"

He looked right at me, and I could see an emptiness in his eyes, like he wasn't there behind them. He reached out for the screen door, and I suddenly realized it wasn't hooked. I reached for the hook, but he already had the door coming open. I started to back up, suddenly knowing he had figured I was lying. I felt a trembling start in my hands and my mouth filled up cause I couldn't swallow.

"Miss Sam!"

"Buck!" I managed to whisper back.

The man turned around, put his hand on the handle of his knife, and looked at Buck.

For a long minute they looked at each other like that. Buck's hands tightened; his shoulder muscles moved in the sun, swelling up and rippling down his arms; his eyes got smaller. I could see Buck was readying himself for a fight, but he never took his eyes off the white man's face. Nigras for sure don't glare and look at a white man the way Buck did.

"Whatcha doing here, nigger?" he demanded, kinda pulling himself up a little. He was shorter than Buck and nowhere near as strong looking. He might've run off from the asylum and been out in the woods for a week or he might've gotten aloose from a jail somewhere.

"Mista, you best be getting on down the road," Buck said real soft.

"You trying to tell me what to do, nigger?" he shouted at Buck.

"No sir, not trying. I'm telling you. Get on down the road. These folks here don't want you around. You best not stop for at least three miles cause I'll be watching you every step till you're long gone. You could walk north up the rails about a half-hour and hop the freight when it stops up to the station."

Buck's words were soft spoken but his voice had a chill to it I've never heard before. I've never heard a nigra talk back to a white man, but I've never had a white man scare me out of my mind before either, and Buck could see I was plum scared, what with my hands shaking and my voice stuck somewhere inside and not coming out right.

With a quick look back at me, the man said, "I ain't needin' nuthin'," and walked down the steps to the yard.

Buck stepped off to the side, to stay more than an arm's reach from the man. As he went around the porch, Buck drifted into the yard behind him.

I just shrank down onto the floor and shook until I could get rid of some of the fear that still ran cold all over me. Finally I got to my feet, hooked the screen, and ran through the house to the front door, closing it and throwing the thumb lock on it. I'd never locked up the house before in my life, but I've never been scared out of my wits either.

I went upstairs to the front porch to look out down the driveway.

The man was headed off in the direction of the train tracks, and I could see Buck moving through the trees, staying behind the man and off to the side.

Mama came home to find the house all locked up, and when I told her why, she hugged me and said she was sure glad Buck was close by or the man might have robbed me or killed me or, like Dad said at supper tonight, "something worse." I don't know what could be worse.

So now I'll keep the screen hooked and won't open it even to feed a hobo. Mama's never been scared of the depression hobos, but fed them if they stopped by and let them chop wood or do some little chore to pay for their keep. They were always polite.

Buck got home when I was leaving to bring in the cows, and he called me. "Hold on there, Sam. I'll go with you."

"Did you follow him all the way up to the station?"

"Yes. I waited until he hopped a boxcar. He won't be back."

"Suppose he comes back when you're gone off?"

He smiled. "I don't think so. Let's get the cows in."

*   *   *

After supper, Vicki and Danny stopped by with Michelle after taking Bessie home. All they could talk about was the sesquicentennial party and the tea out at our house.

All the nigras who have ever lived on the plantation house grounds or who have worked for Mama and Dad in my lifetime will be out here helping.

The party is a really big thing for us, with all those people coming out. Of course, if Sis had married Larry, we probably wouldn't be doing anything for the party. Sis would be living in Savannah now instead of in town.

J. D. came by his name honest, I reckon, seeing as how his daddy is Robert Lee and his older brother is Bedford Forrest. They all call each other by their initials. J. D. got out of the Marines when the war was over, but B. F. didn't. When he was here for the wedding he said he'll stay in the Marines for all of his life cause he loves the Marines next to his wife. He's not going to be here for the party, and neither is J. D.'s daddy.

Maybe the party will help make times get better, and maybe Molly and Buck can get married one day.

July 16, Tuesday

At breakfast, Dad said it was okay if I wanted to get Buck to go fishing, since we won't be working hay for a few days. As soon as I thought Buck would be back from the dairy, I went down to his cottage to see if he would go. We went to the barn, where we turned over some boards and just grabbed earthworms before they could crawl back underground.

On the way down to Possum Creek, Buck asked, "Have you heard about Amos and Ellie Mae?"

"Heard what? Last I heard, Dad got them out of the asylum after Benson put them away."

"Well, Benson put them back in a couple of days ago. Seems he went to get them to come work for him, and he found Amos in bed saying he was gonna die. So he dragged them back to the asylum, but Amos died that night, and Ellie Mae the next morning."

"Howcome we hadn't heard?"

"Billy Blanton's nephew, who works at the asylum as a brick layer, told Billy, who told Pollock, who told me when he got to the house this morning. He said he'd tell your folks."

"Who's gonna bury him? What'll happen to Ellie Mae? You think Dad will tend to them?"

"Oh, no, he won't have to. The asylum has its own cemetery. Well, it's not like a real cemetery, like the one where my folks are buried or where yours are, down by churches. It's a big field, and every time somebody gets buried there, they put up a stick with a number on it. If you go to the office at the asylum, you can get that number for your kin and find the grave. They don't put names on any of the graves. They bury everybody there—the nigras and the white folks."

"Reckon the conjure woman's hex really is what killed them?"

Buck kinda smiled, shaking his head. "I don't know. You know how they were, maybe not quite right in the head. If they got in mind that they were gonna die, then likely the idea was enough to kill them. They thought your dad could undo her hexes, but if she did come back by, she could have scared them to death."

I asked if he'd ever been over to where she lives, and he laughed, shaking his head no. "And I don't reckon I want to, either."

"Buck, I thought you didn't believe in hexes and haints."

"Sam, believing's a sometime thing, like I've told you before. I believe in her enough I figure it's best just to leave her be."

We fished until we had a good string, and headed home. I asked him howcome with all he can do to make a living did he come back to Stanleyville, where the only kind of work he can get is farm work. He laughed and said it was because the whole time he was gone all he could think about was Molly and wanting to come back here to see her. He never thought she'd care for him; he just wanted to be around her some and watch out for her.

He asked, "Sam, you'll go off to college one day, and you'll either come back here or stay away, take a job somewhere else. What do you think you'll do?"

"Oh, I know I'll come home. I don't want to live anywhere else."

"Yeah," Buck said. "And you'd be coming home to your folks and the land. I came home to Molly."

Then I understood. Even with all the bad things that can happen to colored people here in Georgia, it's still home if you love somebody.

Buck offered to clean my fish for me, but I told him no, just to clean them for himself. Maybe he could fry them up to share with Molly. He seemed to like that idea.

*   *   *

After everybody else had gone to bed, I went out my window onto the roof. I don't go out there much and nobody else ever goes. I sat for a long time, hugging my knees, leaning back on the wall of the upstairs, looking at the stars, watching them disappear in the west where the clouds were coming in like a dark blanket the night sky was pulling up over itself to sleep under. I watched the lightning flash against the tree line of the horizon, and I felt that maybe the souls of the two dead nigras were out there in the storm, way off, trying to sort themselves out and find peace. The night was hot and still. The storm way off flashed lightning, but was too far away for me to hear the thunder rumble or feel the wind.

All I heard was the drum, kinda soft tonight, like a whisper talking to the darkness. It stirred at my sadness cause I won't see Ellie Mae and Amos again. They won't be here to help pick up a sick horse or to watch Dad undo one of the conjure woman's spells.

I can't let myself ever forget them. They won't really be dead unless nobody remembers.

July 18, Thursday

Pat, the only other girl who will ride in the birthday parade, came out with Michelle. I didn't even know Pat got a saddle for Misty on her birthday back in June. But all she could talk about was the Klu Klux, that she called "The Klan." She didn't even want to talk horses or the parade—just about The Klan. They're gonna burn a cross on her daddy's hill, the highest one in the county, right after dark tonight.

"They told Daddy a nigra man is walking around with a white girl. The Klan is gonna be sure all the nigra men know they better watch out," she said.

The bottom went out of my stomach. "Did they say who it is?" I managed to ask. All I could think about was Buck and Molly. If they know, what'll the Klu Klux do to her? I know they'll kill Buck. They think there's nothing worse than a nigra man looking at a white girl unless it's a white girl looking at a nigra. They might do her the same way they do Buck.

"They didn't tell Daddy," Pat answered. "I don't know if they even know or if it's just a rumor."

I knew I had to warn them both, and for the first time I can remember, I just wanted my friends to leave, to go back to town so I could see Molly.

A cross burning up on that hill can be seen everywhere. Not a tree anywhere is tall enough to cover it up. I knew I could see it from my bedroom window.

When Michelle and Pat finally left, I turned Dolly aloose and walked up to talk to Molly, but I met her down at the train tracks, on her way to Buck's. The sunlight turned Molly's hair almost gold, and her eyes flashed with excitement—I knew it was cause she was going to see Buck.

"Molly, I heard something today. You know Pat, lives over on that high hill?" Molly nodded. "Well, the Klu Klux is burning a cross there tonight. Pat told me they've heard about a nigra walking with a white girl, and they're after the nigra."

She looked kinda funny, her eyes going wide for a second, but she shook her head and said, "It can't be Buck, Sam. It just can't be." But her eyes had narrowed with her fear, and her hands seemed to find each other, holding on as if to keep courage tight in them.

"You better stay home and as far away from Buck as you can," I said. "Promise you won't go near him? Please promise, Molly."

"But why, Sam? Why'd they be after Buck? Nobody knows about us but you and Michelle."

"Well, I dunno about that, Molly. Michelle and I haven't said a word to anybody, but other folks know. Mama and Dad know. And Vicki knows. And I've seen Mr. Hightower look at y'all when he's up and down the road. Y'all been out around anybody else?"

We were walking up the hill and were almost in front of Buck's cottage when Buck walked out of the driveway to my house, saw us, and came over. I told him what I'd heard.

"We've been down to the cafe on McIntyre Street, but nobody's there but us coloreds. It can't be me they're after. Don't you fret so much, Sam. I'll be fine." He looked away a minute, then down, then at Molly, and finally at me. "You walk Molly back to her house. And quit your fretting, Sam. Nobody knows anything cause we've been careful that there's nothing for anybody to know."

Molly and I didn't talk all the way up to her house. I wanted to talk to her, to warn her better, but I didn't know what to say. I could feel my insides starting to fret from my being scared for them both.

Not long after dark, the flames of the burning cross bounced off the clouds and lit up the whole sky like the Devil had come up out of hell to burn the world.

I thought back to the day last year when I saw the Klu Klux whip a white man for stepping out on his wife. They whipped him until he bled down his back, and left a burning cross in his yard, maybe for the wind to push the flames into his house and burn it down. They'd do worse to Buck.

When I saw the fire, I called Mama and she came upstairs to my room to look. I told her it was the Klu Klux, cause of a nigra liking a white girl, and Mama put her arm around me, hugged me and told me not to worry, cause the Klu Klux didn't know who it was.

"How can you know that?"

"If they knew it was our Buck, that cross would be burning down at the cottage, not way off like that."

"Mama, I'm scared of what they'll do if they find out it's Buck."

I held onto my stomach with both arms hugging myself. All I could see was Buck dead, like one of the cows the train runs over, all cut up and bleeding like the cows, laid out dead on the ground. I shivered.

The drum started. The beat was different, slow and low, then louder and faster, and then dropping back again, like anger building, dying, and then erupting all over again.

"Mama, it's the conjure woman again. She's changed her drum."

"Maybe she's going to hex the Klu Klux, Sam. It'd serve them right if she did."

"She can't hex a white man, can she?"

Mama shook her head. "Sam, if she can't do anything else, she can scare them. I know she sees the fire from her cabin."

"Who is she, Mama? Have you ever seen her?"

Mama smiled a little, still hugging onto me. "All l know is she's been here since I can remember. My mother used to talk about a nigra named Agnes whose mama was a young slave direct from Africa. Her daddy had been a witch doctor, and she was supposed to know how to cast spells. So that slave passed her knowledge on to her daughter. But no, I don't know who she really is. The nigras trust us, but they've never told me who she is."

"Do you think she can protect Buck?"

"Sam, I just don't know. Buck's got to be careful, or nobody can help him. Sweetheart, why don't you sleep in Sis's room tonight? You won't see the fire from there, and you'll be closer to our room."

I got my pillow and went to Sis's room, and in a few minutes, I heard Dad going down the stairs. I was quick to go find out why, and Mama must have heard me cause she met me at their bedroom door.

"Your dad's gone down to talk to Buck," she said. "We don't want him out on the road alone, going up to the dairy. He's to take the truck tomorrow."

I went on back to bed, but every time the wind blew one of the crepe myrtle limbs against the side of the house, I sat up in bed, scared.

July 19, Friday

"You get Buck to take you and Molly fishing as soon as he's back from the dairy," Mama said at breakfast. "I don't want him around the house until things quiet down."

"You worried too, Mama?"

She smiled. "Just being a bit cautious." She took a deep breath. "Yes, I am a mite scared. I worried over Buck all night."

When I heard our truck rattle into the yard, as Buck came back from Simpson's, I trotted outside.

"You sure are up and about early," he said.

"Yeah," I said. "Mama wants us to go fishing! Can you stand it? Dad even said no work this morning, just tend to me and Molly at the creek."

"He still worried over me, Sam?"

"Yeah, I reckon a little. We don't know if it's you they burned the cross about. I think they don't know who they burned it for. They just want to make a fuss. But Mama said for us to be safe. If you'll get the poles, I'll run up for Molly and see you up to the house. You had breakfast?"

"Not yet, I was just fixing to go fry me up some eggs. Y'all eaten yet?"

I nodded. "Yeah, but Mama said come on in. She's making biscuits and frying up some sausage so we can take a lunch with us if we don't catch enough fish. I'm going to go get Molly."

Molly was in the yard drawing water at the well when I got there and told her to come with us. She looked back at the house. "Maude's figuring on going to town and me staying here to mind Tommy."

"Tell her Mama wants you down to the house. That's true, it won't be lying. She said to come up and get you."

It didn't take Molly but a minute to get that bucket of water into the house and be ready to go.

"You see the cross burning over to Pat's last night?" I asked her.

Molly nodded. "Yeah, I did. It was up high enough to light up everything, bouncing off the clouds like that."

"Mama said if we spend the day fishing, won't anybody know where Buck is and he oughten to go to town tomorrow. But he's not worried about anything."

"He wouldn't worry. He tries to be a little cautious sometimes, but he's not the kind to worry over the Klu Klux less'n he thinks they'll be after his mama."

"They got no call to be after Elvira," I said. "Not less Flint gets after her about something."

"I don't know, Sam. She's bought a table from him on time."

We were walking pretty fast and were getting up to Buck's yard. Molly went on. "I don't think Buck knows it's bought on time, so don't tell him. Okay?"

I nodded. Molly looked worried. All I could think of was Flint killing that nigra woman two years ago for owing him money.

Buck came around the house with the poles as we walked into the yard. "I got new string on the poles," he said. "Y'all ready?"

"Yeah," I said. "And I'm ready for those biscuits."

In a few minutes, we were in the dining room scarfing down biscuits, Georgia cane syrup, and some of the sausages we stuffed last winter, when it was so pig-killing cold your hands would almost freeze.

I bet not another white family would let a nigra come in the house and eat breakfast with them, but Mama had Buck come eat a big breakfast cause she said it's gonna be a long day. Molly and I had already eaten, but we didn't care, we ate biscuits and Georgia cane syrup too.

Mama told us to take the leftover biscuits and sausage with us, to stay away all day, and cook our fish or eat sausage and biscuit, but not to come home until real late. She gave us some Mason jars to take by the spring for water on the way.

Then we were off to the barn for our worms. I got to tote the rifle.

Early as we were, the wind was already stirring the water and the sunlight was dancing on the edges of every ripple, making the surface almost white. Buck said to go around to the east side so the glare wouldn't be in our eyes.

It didn't seem like anything could be going on bad around us it was such a pretty morning and the air smelled like the boggy edges of the pool. None of the smoke hung in the air from last night's cross burning, and the leaves seemed to turn the air almost green under the trees. It was so peaceful there that when a red-bellied water snake slithered into the water, I jumped at the splash.

July 20, Saturday, just before supper

In spite of Mama telling him to stay home and out of sight, Buck said he was gonna go to town to see the new movie *Song of the South*.

"Don't tell your mama," he cautioned. "She'll just worry over nothing."

Michelle, Molly, and I planned to go upstairs to the nigra section to sit with Buck, and knew we had to be careful not to be seen by the boy who takes up the tickets. They were a little scared we'd get caught, but I told them nobody would do anything even if they did see us. I didn't tell Mama about our plans.

Like most Saturdays, everybody was in town.

I'd never seen J. D. in jeans before, but he was on the square, already building the jail cell. Some boys from the Stanleyville Military School and a couple of the other lawyers were helping him. Danny was swinging a hammer. They all had whiskers. Even Buck is letting his mustache grow, he said just to be sure he doesn't get locked up, but I don't think they'll lock up any of the nigras.

Some wagons sat in the shade of the oaks, where the colored women sit around the wagons and talk about their kinfolks and babies, and the children chase each other around their mamas. The older boys go down to the café on McIntyre Street, and the men mostly go to the nigra poolroom next door. By dark, some of them will be in fights and have to drive all the way up to get Uncle Morris to stitch up the cuts.

Today one of the babies cried and cried, until it got to screaming really loud, so I went over to see why. Its mama kept sticking her tit in its mouth, but it kept pulling away; and when its mama felt inside its diaper, it wasn't messed up or wet or anything, so I could see she got plum worried, like she figured the baby was sick and she didn't know what to do. She wasn't more'n about fifteen, and she just sat there, her head all hidden in her head rag and her tit stuck out in front like it was supposed to be showing out to everybody in town, like a soldier standing at attention.

I hadn't even seen Elvira until she got up and started over there. When I heard her laugh I knew it was Elvira, cause there's nobody who can laugh like that except Jethro. They both always chuckle at everything that happens, and their bellies seem to shake the laughter right up from deep inside.

"Tain't nuttin' wrong wid dat baby, honey. He jest gots a bug in his air. Lookit how he grab fer his air." He was clawing at his ear and I hadn't noticed until Elvira talked about it. "Now jest you squirt some ob dat milk in his air and float out dat-air bug, and he's'll hesh up his crying."

As soon as the mama squirted some milk into the ear, up floated a drowned mosquito, and the baby hushed up.

On my way to the B & B Drugstore, I saw Benson go into Flint's store on the corner, and right behind him went Cou'n Phil. As I walked by, I saw them going way back in the store, to where Flint has his office.

They're up to no good was all I could think about as I went on toward the B & B to get my sandwich before I hunted up Molly and Michelle. Molly was down there somewhere on McIntyre Street with Buck, and I just hoped didn't anybody see her.

The second B in the drug store name was supposed to be for Little Rog, but now that he's dead, Benson's got nobody but some far-off cousin that might want to take over the drug store. After he got to be the county commissioner, Benson didn't go to the store much, and now after Rog got killed, he doesn't go there at all.

There's really not anywhere else in town for me to get a sandwich. It costs too much at the dining room in the Snyder Hotel, and I don't dare even think about going to the nigra cafe on McIntyre Street, or the white poolroom.

When I passed him in front of the poolroom, the legless man smiled at me and said, "Howdy, Miss."

I took out my money and said, "I'm sorry I can't give you more'n a quarter."

He smiled. "You keep your quarter, Miss. It's Saturday, and you need to be having a good time, not giving me your spending money." He rattled his cup to show me he had some money in it.

"You sure?"

He nodded. "You run along. I remember how much you helped me, you and your little friend, the day that drunk soldier ran over me. Have yourself a good time today. You going to the movie?"

I nodded, said goodbye, and went on.

The B & B has a regular eating place, where you can sit on a spinning stool and turn around while you eat, and you can get a co-cola there too. There's a big sign in the window that says, "Have a little, have a lot, have it cold or have it hot." One of the girls at school is always laughing about the sign, saying it doesn't have anything to do with eating, that it's about the women upstairs. She says you can buy women up there, but people can't be bought any more. It doesn't make any sense to me.

Mama had given me a dollar for dinner, and I had some of my own money for the picture show. I decided to have a grilled-cheese sandwich, a co-cola, and a piece of chocolate pie. I still had plenty of extra money to spend at the picture show if I could figure a way to buy the popcorn and slip upstairs.

As I came out of the B & B, I ran up on Pat and June, who were on their way to the Magnolia Dairy, and Pat said, "They're gonna burn another cross."

"Up on your hill?"

"Not this time. I don't know where. Daddy told them he was scared the hay fields might catch fire."

"You mean, your daddy told them 'no'?"

Pat nodded, and showed her pride in her father with her tone. "Yep, he sure did. You wanta go with us to the Magnolia Dairy? We're meeting Selma, Hardie, Dale, and some of the other girls. We're going to eat banana splits. Coressa's gonna make them."

I wanted to go with them cause I sure do like the banana splits down at the Magnolia, but I said, "No, I'm meeting Michelle to go to the picture show." I hoped they weren't going to be looking for me there, seeing as we'd be upstairs.

"We're going tonight," Pat said, and with a goodbye wave, headed off down Main Street.

I decided to give the legless man at least a quarter. When he objected again, I told him I had enough left over for the picture show. He thanked me a lot, saying that not many girls ever stopped by to be friendly with him. Mostly, he said, the girls seem to be scared of him, since he's different. I didn't tell him I had been scared of him too until the day he got knocked off his rolling board.

When I got to the picture show, they were both waiting out front. Molly said Buck was already inside and would save us a place. I knew the woman who sells tickets probably heard her, but she didn't know who Buck is, so it was okay.

We almost got found out when we tried to go upstairs. The boy who takes up tickets wanted to talk. He didn't have anything much to say except he was sure gonna like the picture, but he kept on talking to us while we were wanting to get away and slip up the stairs with nobody seeing us. I don't know him, except that Buck told me once he's a little touched. His eyes kept moving every which way, looking all around like he was watching for somebody, and he kept on pushing his hair out of his eyes. But finally he had to take up some tickets from three boys, and when he turned around to take their tickets, we scooted up the steps behind his back.

We had slipped halfway up the steps when Little Jethro said, "Miz Sam, whutchu doin' up heah with us niggers? Ain't you goan git in trubble?"

I told him no, not unless he went home and told his Grandma

Elvira we were up here with his Uncle Buck. He allowed he'd not tell on us cause Buck'd whup him if Big Jethro didn't, and we all laughed as we went on up the steps to join Buck.

When the picture ended, everybody was singing "zippy-de-do-dah" right along with Uncle Remus. We had to wait until most everybody was out before we tried to leave. Buck went first, and we girls snuck out so nobody'd know we were with him. We went on around the corner, down toward McIntyre Street, where we caught up with Buck and stood while we talked about the picture.

Buck thought it a lot of fun, but he didn't think everything had been all that nice and fun way back when his grandpappy was a slave. I said it isn't that much fun to be a nigra now is it, and he said no, it isn't. I told them I remember Mama talking about Sherman, a slave's son, who worked on her daddy's plantation; he told her and her sisters stories about Brer Rabbit and Brer Fox every night, when they'd finished supper. He'd bring the stovewood into the kitchen, and all the girls would sit on the floor around him while he smoked his pipe and told them the stories. Mama said the stories we call Uncle Remus today had come from Africa with slaves a long time ago. The African people had changed their own stories to fit the animals here, so their children could understand their meaning.

A white man from Eatonton had heard the stories, so he wrote them all down cause he liked them so much and thought the nigra stories ought to be kept cause they teach you so much.

Buck said that Sherman, who had been his granddaddy, had told him the stories too when he was little, right on up until Sherman died. He told Buck to learn a trade, anything other than cutting firewood and toting water. I didn't mention that one of Sherman's jobs was to tote out the slop jars every morning.

All of Buck's uncles but Pollock have gone off to Detroit to get work besides farming. His mama Elvira got married when she was real young, and she had to go to work when Buck's daddy got killed. I didn't know until today that the Klu Klux killed him.

When Mama was little life wasn't much different than in slave days, except they had to pay the nigras for working. But it couldn't of been much money, cause even now you don't have to pay anybody even a dollar a day to be in the kitchen cooking or in the fields working. Pitching hay isn't fun when its brinjin hot. It's hard, sweaty work, even if you do like to hear people tell stories when you stop work to walk down to the spring for a drink of water.

I said it musta been hard to chop cotton or pick it, or to cut firewood all day and not get anything for it but some food and clothes, with never any time off, and never any chance to learn to read.

He said, "Learning to read is the most important thing for anybody to do. Until all the nigras take up reading and schooling they'll be nothing but field hands like Jethro."

He said Jethro couldn't ever be anything but a field hand or a moonshiner until he at least learned how to read and figure some. He said that way back, when nigras were slaves, they were held back by not being allowed to learn to read. He said again how he was lucky to've been able to study on Mama's porch when he was growing up. He learned more there than he learned in school. I said that's cause he never had books in school like the ones Mama was always getting for her porch classes. She'd even check some out of the bookmobile for him every week when he was growing up. But Buck said it was hard to have some learning and not be able to use it in his work, and all the work he can get is farm work since everybody thinks all a nigra can do is things with his hands. Buck's smart. Why, he could do better than old Benson at being the county commissioner cause he's not just smart, he's honest and fair.

We stood at the corner of McIntyre Street, still talking about the picture, when the voices and laughter that fill Saturdays faded into silence. A mockingbird called, and across the street in the courthouse yard, a squirrel barked at one of the children, flicked his tail, and bounced around on a small limb, thrashing the leaves.

I heard a soft shuffling sound moving towards us.

We all saw them at the same time. The Klu Klux in their white sheets and pillowcases turned onto McIntyre Street up at the next corner. They weren't chanting or anything, and they didn't carry a big cross; they just walked real quiet, like they had their minds on something, but each one kinda dragged his feet, keeping in step, to make the shuffling noise that seeped through my skin like water through a roof, drop by drop, until the sound of the drops hitting into a tin pot is enough to make you want to scream.

Everybody down on McIntyre Street slipped into doorways, and everywhere up and down the street doors closed and shades came down. The mockingbird quit his singing, and the squirrel went still. Nothing moved except the silent ghosts gliding up the hill.

We backed up against the side of the bus station and watched. Not one of us said a word. I got in front of Buck, trying to back him up around the corner of the bus station, but he's so much taller and wider than me I knew I couldn't hide him.

When they got up to our corner, they turned in front of us, going directly along the side of the courthouse, and finally Buck backed up down the alleyway between the Piggly Wiggly and the bus station, with the three of us backing up with him.

Brenda, Cou'n Phil's sister, came out of the Piggly Wiggly with Carolyn, who's still real little, and Carolyn said, "Look Mama, there goes Uncle Phil under that sheet."

Her mama said, "Hush, Carolyn!" I knew she wasn't supposed to know who was under the sheets.

Carolyn said, "But Mama, it's Uncle Phil right yonder. And there's Mr. Flint, right by Uncle Phil."

Brenda put down her sack of food and jerked Carolyn back against the front of the Piggly Wiggly, saying, "How can you know who they are? You don't. You can't tell who anybody is under those sheets."

Carolyn said, "But Mama, nobody else in town's got shoes like Uncle Phil and Mr. Flint. See?"

She pointed, I looked, and she was right. There's not another man in town would even think of wearing those slide-on shoes with that little floppy thing on the top like Cou'n Phil wears, or those lace-up black shoes that Flint wears, that have the thick soles and almost high heels, like the WAVES used to wear to march in.

Nobody else said a word, and if any of the Klu Klux heard Carolyn, they didn't let on. They kept on shuffling down pass the courthouse and turned left at the corner.

They'd gone out of sight before the shuffling sounds faded. Buck said, "Last time they got out like that they all went over onto Washington Street and burned a cross in front of the Gaylord's house."

"They burned one in front of the Walker's too. And whupped him for beating up on Roger Benson's sister. That's the only time I've ever heard of them doing something to white men," Molly said.

"I heard Gaylord was beating up on his wife. She's cousin to Rufus Flint. The Gaylord's maid is daughter to one of Ma's friends, and she said Mr. Gaylord hadn't taken a hand to his wife since. That's all the good I ever heard of about the Klu Klux. Mostly they just kill us colored men."

"Danny told us they take a food basket to the Widow Simms every Thanksgiving and Christmas," Michelle said.

"I heard that, too," Molly said.

"But I don't think that food makes up for beating on people," Buck said. "I reckon they're marching today to remind everybody us coloreds are supposed to be like Uncle Remus and not better ourselves. I hope that's all."

"Well, they're not after you, Buck," I kinda laughed, but not real much. "If they had-a been, they'd grabbed you right here off the street corner."

"You're right, Sam, but I do fret a mite sometimes." He turned to Molly and smiled, his eyebrows pulled together. "Molly, you want to go on home, what with them out?"

Molly shook her head, "No, Buck, let's go on over to Buddy's like we planned."

"Got yourself a laughing place down there?" I asked, smiling at them.

Molly answered, her eyes on Buck, "I got me a laughing place anywhere I go with Buck."

He sure did look happy as the two of them went on down McIntyre Street toward Buddy's juke joint.

All the way over to Michelle's house, we sang "zippy-de-do-dah." I've never liked a song so much, but I know I'll never have a bluebird on my shoulder—the real bluebirds are too scared to sit on somebody's shoulder. The closest I've ever come to one is to those that nest in the fence post up the road by Molly's house, but every time I look into the hole in the post to see the nest, the birds fly off and yell at me.

BUCK AND MOLLY

Molly walked ahead of Buck down McIntyre Street to Buddy's Place and strolled in as self-assured as if she were entering the Rose's Dime Store over on Main Street instead of the Negro cafe. The room went silent.

She stood to the side of the door to wait for Buck.

Smoke from the barbecue pit, cigars and handrolled cigarettes floated in the air like mist rising with the sun over a meadow in autumn. Smells so like home greeted her—hot cornbread, frying chicken and hot lard, steaming turnip greens, and baking biscuits.

A dozen tables, their pine tops glistening from lard that had soaked in the wood and been wiped to a polish, stood scattered round the room. On the left two tables had been pushed against the wall.

Buck entered, waved at Buddy, took Molly by the hand, and led her through the crowd to the only empty table, by the wall. He pulled it away from the wall, and they sat beside each other, their backs to the wall.

Buddy came to the table. "Whatcha wanting, Buck? Miss Molly?"

Sweat had put a shine on his medium-dark skin. He wiped at it with a red handkerchief he pulled from a back pocket.

"Miss Molly'll have a barbecue and a co-cola. I'll take a barbecue too and a beer." He reached into his pocket for money and laid down a half-dollar.

Buddy nodded and walked away.

Conversation started up again.

Buck heard the whispers and smiled at Molly. "They're talking about us."

She smiled back and placed her hand over his on the table top.

A large white-haired man in overalls at a nearby table shook his head. He removed the cigar from his mouth, pointed it toward them, and said, "Buck, you be axing fer truble."

All other conversation stopped. The man's voice filled the room and seemed to echo from the ceiling.

"Them white men don't ker you work fer the professor. They gonna kill you, boy."

"They don't know."

"You crazy, boy. They know. They knowed afore you come in here with her the first time. Ain't nobody in town what don't know."

"You scared?" Buck whispered to Molly.

"Not so long as I'm with you. How can anybody know? We've been careful."

The old man said, "You don't know about kerful. And you better be scairt and lay low."

Buddy returned with their drinks, set them on the table, and left without a word, but with his mind in a frenzy. Was he gonna be in trouble for serving them? Did Buck always sit with his back to the wall in case some of the Klu Klux came in? If they did get Buck in here, were they gonna burn down his place? Maybe he better go see the collection man and get some insurance on his place. He couldn't rebuild if he got burned out. He'd just need insurance for awhile. Till they killed Buck. If they didn't burn him out before then.

"Yes, sir, Mr. Perkins. We'll be more careful."

Buddy arrived with their sandwiches and they set about eating. The silence faded as conversation started up throughout the room.

Finished eating, Buck said, "You think you better go on out ahead of me and see if you can catch up with Sam?"

"I'm not scairt," she said.

He nodded. "Okay. But let's be a little careful. You go ahead, go up to the courthouse corner, and I'll come along in about five minutes. Just in case. If Sam's left, we'll head home. I'll just lag behind a few steps, make it look like I'm just going the same way."

Unable to find Sam, they walked toward home. They had gone only two miles along, with Buck ten paces behind her, when a car pulled up beside Molly. All windows were open to keep it almost cool in the afternoon heat.

"Give you a lift, Molly?" Mr. Hightower asked.

She looked back at Buck. Fear gripped her. Buck nodded slightly.

"It's okay, Molly. He can't bother you. Get in."

If he thinks I'm scared of Buck he can't know anything. She reached for the door handle and as she opened the door, something white caught her attention in the back seat. She cut her eyes to Mr. Hightower, but he was looking down the road.

He's got Klu Klux sheets back there.

She swallowed fear, and got into the car. Even with the windows open she smelled whiskey.

Hightower pushed the gear shift into first, jerked the car forward, and went into third gear. He left a cloud of dust over Buck and the road.

She was grateful that he did not speak until they reached Maude's house. All he said there was, "You're home. Safe from that nigger."

She got out and trotted to the porch through the dust cloud.

SAMANTHA

July 21, Sunday

I didn't have much of anything special to do this afternoon, so I settled down in a rocker by the window and started reading *The Last Trail*, about Lewis Wetzel and Jonathan Zane. I hadn't any more gotten started good when I heard voices.

President Grimes from the college brought some of his friends out, who won't be in town for the town's birthday party. They wanted to see the house and the boxwoods and the slave houses.

Since Buck is going to be the tour guide for the slave houses, Dad asked me to find Buck, so he could guide the visitors, for practice. But I reminded him Buck had gone to visit with his friend George and wouldn't be back until the last train ran tonight.

So I was stuck and had to give them the tour. I really don't know as much as Buck does, but they gave me a quarter. When I told Buck tonight, that I had earned enough money to go to the picture show and get a bag of popcorn, he just laughed and said he was too old to get in for fourteen cents. The quarter would take him to the picture show but leave him with only a penny.

I asked him about his friend George up in Walton County, and he said George's brother-in-law is in trouble for taking a knife to a white man. He's in jail, and may never get out alive. I kept asking questions, but he just shook his head and said, "I don't know, Sam. He's being held for murder. If that white man dies, they'll drag him out of the jail and lynch him. I just can't think about it, much less talk about it. Things are worse up there right now than it was here when Mick got in trouble." Worry lined his face.

July 23, Tuesday

We've started cleaning everything, getting ready for the big party, even though it's not until the 10th of August. Seems all I did today was my regular chores and polish silver until my hands got black.

Molly and I have to help clean up the house, but Buck gets to do all the fun stuff, like cut the grass with the swing blade. It'll take him and Pollock all of the two weeks to get the yard ready.

Mama wants everything perfect in the house as well as in the yard and all the outbuildings when everybody who comes to town for the parade and the pageant comes out. Even the governor will be here. Mama said we'll have to work steady to get everything finished by time of the sesquicentennial whoop-de-do.

Today Molly waxed the ballroom floor with paste wax and old towels, rubbing and rubbing until the floors shined. I'll have to do a floor every day, too, as soon as I finish all the silver.

Elvira and Lillie Mae took down the drapes and the sheer curtains today from all the upstairs windows, as well as the skirts from the four-poster beds. They'll get everything washed and ironed and back up in about three days.

Lillie Mae and Elvira's biggest job will be the day before the parade, when they bake cookies. Every time we have a party, Lillie Mae bakes cookies, throwing flour all over the kitchen and herself, so I always tell her she's just trying to turn herself white or why else would she cover herself all up in flour. She just giggles and shakes her head at me.

It was late afternoon before Mama finally said we'd done enough for one day and let us go outside. I rushed to the kitchen for a co-cola, and Molly came along slower. We found Buck in the kitchen, where he'd come inside to get water for all the men. When Molly walked in, I could see both their eyes light up. Lillie Mae poked Buck in the ribs with an elbow and said, "You chulren quit making eyes at each other."

We all laughed, got a co-cola apiece, and went outside. Buck took the water on out to the other men and came around to join us in front, where we were sitting on the porch steps trying to catch a little breeze and weren't even talking until a snake came out of the boxwoods, lifted its head to look around before it slithered across the yard. Molly froze, watching it. But I stood up, taking a couple of steps toward it. Making loops in the air it ran off so fast, the snake slithered under some more tree-boxwood.

Buck laughed, "It's a coachwhip, Sam. Don't you know you'll get yourself in trouble chasing that one?"

"Why?" Molly asked. "She hadn't gotten in trouble with all the rest of those she chases."

"Well, if you run after it, it's like any snake. It'll run away from you. But if you ever run away from a coachwhip snake, it'll turn and come after you. And since it can crawl faster than you can run, it'll catch you. And when it catches up with you, it'll jump on you, wrap around you, squeeze up on you, and whup up on you at the same time, until it whups you to death. You can't just make like you're dead, cause when you fall down and get still, it'll run its tail in your nose to tickle you to see if you're dead. If you sneeze it knows you're not dead, and it'll whup you some more."

Molly laughed. "Yeah. I believe that one. It's as crazy as the one Sam tells at school, about taking eggs out of a chicken snake, putting them back under my hen, and the eggs hatching out."

We all laughed. It was mighty good to just sit around awhile with my two best friends.

When I started out for the milk cows, I asked Mama if I could tote Dad's pistol today instead of the rifle. I could put the pistol on my hip like Roy Rogers, but she said no, the rifle was safer for me to tote.

July 24, Wednesday

Men shouted. Light danced against my widow. I yelled and ran down the stairs, afraid we had a forest fire, but Mama and Dad beat me to the front door.

A cross blazed at the end of the driveway, right where it goes across Buck's yard. Black kerosene smoke rolled up, and what wind there was seemed to push the stink right toward me.

Barefooted, like always when he's in the house, Dad ran to get on his shoes. I snatched up the rifle from the back hall and headed for the door. Mama grabbed the back of my shirt, pulled me back and yanked the rifle out of my hands.

"No, Sam! I couldn't stand it if you got hurt. They're mean as snakes, they don't care—No, Dad, don't you go down there!"

But Dad had already run by her, the shotgun in his hands, and he vanished into the shadows. In seconds I pulled away from Mama and ran behind Dad.

Fire rose as high as the roof of the cottage, danced into the oak overhead, threw shadows and light into the yard, and turned the world orange.

Before I got anywhere near the end of the driveway, Dad shot off one barrel of the shotgun.

White-sheeted men rushed across Buck's yard toward the trucks.

One came out of Buck's front door, yelling, and as Dad fired the second barrel, the men tumbled into the trucks and raised dust as they tore off toward town.

Running toward Dad, I screamed, "Did you hit one? Did you hit one?"

Dad shook with anger and, unaware that I was there, shouted, "You god-damned bastards! Don't you ever come here again or I'll kill you, you sons of bitches."

As he started toward the cottage, I followed, looking for Buck. Dad called a couple of times as he went in, but there wasn't any answer.

Buck was dead. I knew it. The horror of it all rushed up inside me, and I slid down the wall by the front door, my face in my hands. I shook with crying.

I couldn't go into the house, couldn't bear to see him dead.

Dad didn't let me sit long. "Buck's not here," he yelled. "Sam, go get the hose from up at the house. We'll get this fire out and then find Buck."

I ran back to the house, still crying, and ran into Mama. "Buck's not there," I told her. I couldn't stop crying, but I stammered out that I was to take the hose down there to try to put out the fire, and she helped me get it.

When I got back, Buck was standing there, talking to Dad.

I threw myself against him, still crying, "Oh, Buck, you're okay. Thank God you're okay."

"Hush, now, Sam. I heard 'em coming and got out the back window and off in the woods. You hush now. It's okay. They won't be back. I'm fine. Let's get that fire out."

Mama came out of nowhere. She grabbed my arm and pulled me toward the big house. "Come on, Sam. Let them handle this."

"Mama, they'll come back. They'll kill Buck."

"No, Sam. You go on back to the house with your mama. They won't be back," Buck said.

Dad was pulling the hose toward the faucet by the back door, so Buck ran off to help, and Mama said just what Buck did. "No, Sam. They won't kill him. They'll try to scare him to death. But they're people we know. I just can't believe they'd kill Buck, no matter how much they hate the nigra. Buck's not hurting them. This isn't Jasper County."

"But, Mama—" I wanted to remind her it wasn't but a few minutes since she thought they'd kill me and Dad.

She didn't let me finish. "Sam, I know why they came out here. So does your Dad. He'll be talking to Buck about it. And I'll talk to Molly."

I went on to the house with Mama, and in a few minutes, Dad came back. Buck walked in with him.

"I'm not letting Buck stay in the cottage for a couple of nights. He'll sleep in our guest room."

"Sir, it's too much trouble for Miz Laura. I can stay down at the barn the rest of the night."

But even Mama insisted that he couldn't sleep in the barn with the rattlesnakes and wasps. So he's staying in the guest room.

I peeked in a few minutes ago, after everybody was gone to bed, and the two yard lights invaded the shadows just enough that I could see Buck sleeping on the floor, flat on his back, using his hands for a pillow.

The sound of the conjure woman's drum, like the smell from the watered down burning cross, seeped into my insides. I just lay in bed, smelling the stench, while my heart caught up the beat of the drum.

July 25, Thursday

The smell from the burned-up cross stayed in my room all night and was all up inside my head when I woke up. The wind might blow it out of the house by this afternoon, but it'll never get out of my head. It's jammed in there as strong as the Vicks Salve that Mama puts on me when I have a cold.

I wanted Buck to stay in the house, hidden, but he wouldn't. Soon as he'd eaten, he was down to the cottage to clean up the mess. He wouldn't listen to Dad about staying out of sight.

"I can be scared, or I can keep on living. And I aim to keep on living."

I tried to argue with him too, all the way down the driveway when he headed to the cottage, but all he'd say to me was, "Sam, don't you go fretting about me. I'm like Miz Laura. I don't think they'll do any more than burn crosses and parade around and make a fuss. Besides, they're all people I know."

"Mick knew them all, too," I argued.

He nodded. "Yes, but he killed Junior. I hadn't killed anybody."

I wanted to say what he was doing with Molly they'd think was worse than killing a man, but I didn't.

We were still arguing while he raked up the stuff when Mr. and Mrs. Hightower drove by, stopped, and backed up to look at all the burned up stuff still on the ground. When I got his extra yard broom and helped, the Hightowers drove on.

I wondered if he was one of the men who burned the cross.

July 26, Friday

After breakfast, I started out on my bike to see Aunt Tessie, who always gives me a co-cola, and the next thing I knew, I almost ran over Buck and Molly when I topped a hill. Buck pushed Molly's bicycle, and they didn't even look at anything but each other until I yelled, "Whoa!" braked to a stop, and raised dust with my heel sliding on the road.

Without thinking, I said, "What're y'all doing way up here?" How could they even think of being out like this, together, where anybody driving by would see them?

Molly got red and looked around a little then said, "I was just out on the bicycle and met up with Buck."

"I was heading back home from the dairy," Buck said, looking at his feet for a second, not at me.

I wanted to say he was mighty late leaving the dairy and why was he walking when he was supposed to take the truck, but I didn't. I forgot about Aunt Tessie and the co-cola and I fell in beside them.

We moved over to the side of the road when we heard a car behind us, and Mr. Hightower drove by on his way to open up his shop. He slowed down and looked hard at us, then went on. What scared me was the way he looked at Buck, walking beside us instead of two steps behind white folks. It gave me a bad feeling.

I was scared he might be one of the Klu Klux. But I didn't dare say anything to Buck and Molly about it. They've just got to be more careful. Why can't they just visit in his cottage, not off somewhere? Are they scared maybe Mama or Dad would walk in on them? But Mama and Dad know.

When I got to the house, Mama sent me down to get Buck. If he hadn't gotten back from the dairy, "wait for him on the porch." I knew something was bad wrong from the look on her face, but when I started to ask her something, she shushed me and said, "Just go find Buck."

Buck was home. I figured Molly had gone on to her house. When I told him Mama needed to see him, he looked down at his brogans and shook his head. "Can't go in the house with these on," he said.

We walked up to the house and he kicked off his shoes before we went into the kitchen. She waved us both to chairs.

Buck asked, "What's the matter, Miz Laura?"

"Oh, Buck, I'm so sorry. Danny just left. He got a phone call from a lawyer friend in Athens and came out to tell us. It's your friend George Dorsey." She got up, wandered over to the sink, and looked out the window, away from Buck as if she couldn't stand to see his face.

"Yessum?" he tried to coax her to go on. His face was all screwed up in a worry frown. I figured the man had died that George's brother-in-law had stabbed. But I was wrong.

Mama said, "It's bad. Real bad. George is dead."

I put my hand on his shoulder. Buck leaned forward. His shoulder tightened under my palm.

"Dead? How? How can he be dead? I was up to see him last Sunday. He was fine, except for worried sick about his sister's husband in jail for cutting a white man. What happened? Did that man die?"

Mama turned around from the sink and sat down herself. I decided I ought to sit down and not just stand there with my hand on Buck's shoulder. But Mama couldn't sit still and she got back up, poured herself and Buck a cup of coffee. She set the sugar bowl on the kitchen table and got them both a spoon. He likes two spoons of sugar in his coffee.

She looked at me, opened the Frigidaire, and handed me a co-cola. She's never let me have a co-cola this early in the day before.

He sat stirring that cup of coffee for a long time, just stirring it until the silver spoon took up the extra heat from the cup and it was cool enough for him to sip without burning his tongue. After he set the cup back down, he looked Mama straight in the eye and asked her, "Miz Laura, did Mista Danny know what happened?"

Mama nodded. "Yesterday, a white man—I can't remember his first name. Somebody Harrison bailed Roger out of jail. Dorothy was there and so were George and his wife. This Harrison said he wanted Roger to go to work for him, and he'd drive all four of them home. He drove them over the River Bridge at Moore's Ford. The bridge was blocked by a mob.

"Buck, all four of them are dead. I'm so sorry. So sorry."

The room got real quiet. I could hear the faucet dripping where Mama hadn't turned it off tight. Outside, a hen clucked to her biddies and they cheeped back to her. A crow flew by, and way off a hawk screamed. From across the road, one of the bulls bellowed. Not a breath of wind stirred.

The kitchen smelled like Buck's sweat and Mama's coffee.

Buck lowered his head and hid his face in both hands for what seemed like a long time. Then he sat up, gulped down the last of his coffee, rose, and said, "I ought to go up there, Miz Laura. I know I can't help George, but at least I can go see him buried. He was my friend."

"Take all the time you need, Buck. But you be mighty careful. Those men don't care who they kill. And I don't want anything to happen to you." Mama tried to smile, touched Buck on the shoulder. "We need you, Buck. We depend on you. Just come back safe."

"I will, Miss Laura."

"Do you need any money? Train fare?"

Buck shook his head. "I ought to be okay, M'am. If it's okay with you, I'll head on out on the 10:00 o'clock train to Eatonton now. I got time to pack and get to the crossing to flag it down. Did Mr. Danny know anything about the funeral?"

Mama shook her head. "I asked, but he said no. Do you know anyone else up there?"

"A couple of George's friends. I'll find them."

Mama nodded, and Buck turned and walked out.

I sat there, looking at Mama for a long time, and suddenly I remembered, jumped up, and said, "We'll have to send Pollock up to the dairy. I'll tell Buck."

I took off running toward his house, and got there just as he did.

"Buck," I called, and he stopped, turned toward me.

"What is it, Sam?" His voice almost cracked with his sadness.

"The milking. We'll send Pollock up to the Simpson's."

He frowned, closed his eyes, shook his head, and said, "No, Sam. If you would, just tell the Simpsons I had to go off. They've had time—I can't let Pollock go up there. They'll goad him into something. Would you see about getting them word I'm gone?"

"Don't fret, Buck. We'll tend to it for you."

He nodded, turned, and went inside.

Mama and I drove up to the Simpson's. We didn't tell him that Buck was going up to Walton County to his friend's funeral, just that he wasn't going to be able to help with the milking any more. Old Man Simpson seemed a little put out, but Mama said we needed Buck all the time now, and hadn't Mr. Simpson had most of the summer to get himself some more help? He walked off in a huff, but we didn't care.

BUCK

July 26, Friday

From the train station in Athens, Buck walked to the bus station and caught the next bus heading to Atlanta. He got off at Aycock's Store, where he had met George on his earlier trips. He was unsure about which way to go from there, but knew the best source of information would be either the local black undertaker or the cafe down in the black section of town where he and George had enjoyed barbecue and beer. He went to the cafe, pushed the screen door open, and stepped inside, his duffle bag in his left hand.

Silence greeted him. More than thirty men stood inside; smoke had fogged the room. Sun outlined him at the door and revealed their harsh faces to him. The scent of fear-sweat overpowered the smoke.

He set his bag on the nearest table and said, "I've come up from Stanleyville for George's funeral."

One of the men said, "You Buck Steele?"

"That I am."

The man came out of the crowd, his hand extended. "I'm Bill Kindle. We met last year when ya were up here. You was in the army with him."

Buck took his hand. "We were in training together, but he went to the Pacific and I got sent to Europe."

The men crowded around him, pumping his hand, patting him on the back, their voices running together as they welcomed him.

Bill asked "You got a place to stay? The funeral's tomorrow."

"No, I don't. I just packed up my duffle and flagged down the train."

"Well, you gonna stay with me tonight. And I'll get ya to the train Sunday after the funeral."

"I'm sure obliged," Buck said.

A man thrust a glass of iced tea toward Buck. "Here ya go. It'll cool ya down."

"Thanks," Buck said and took a swallow of the cold sweetness. The familiar sweat on the glass comforted him

"Can you tell me just what happened? I was up here right after

Roger got locked up. Next thing I hear is that George and Roger and both their wives got killed."

"We think it was all started when Roger got the idea Dorothy was having an affair with Barney Hester," Bill said.

Another man continued. "Yeah. It was just about two weeks ago, Roger went out to Hester's place, got in a fight over Dorothy and stabbed Hester. Can't no nigger get by with that. He got put in jail. And Mr. Hester had to go to the hospital. Everybody thought he was gonna die. He been real sick."

"How did this Harrison get involved?" Buck asked. "Why'd he get Roger out of jail?"

"You visited with George, you know where he lived at. It's Mr. Harrison's place. He and Roger sharecropped the place. Dorothy asked Mr. Harrison to get Roger out of jail. He didn't at first. Wouldn't anybody bail him out. Not even our undertaker."

Someone said, "He be the richest nigger in town, and he wouldn't help none."

Another voice added, "Seems like old man Harrison wouldn't help till atter it look like young Mr. Hester ain't gonna die. Ten days he wouldn't help, but he did all-a sudden. Put up his farm, somebody said. And took Dorothy and George and their mama Moena and George's wife to bail out Roger."

"That doesn't make sense at all. Why?"

"We think he got told to. By the Ku Klux. Or Mr. Bob. Barney Hester's daddy. Don't nobody know, and iffen dey do, they ain't saying. Mr. Harrison told at the jail he was taking them home, so they could get back on the fields in the morning. Only reason Moena weren't in the car, there wasn't room. Mr. Loy Harrison didn't head home. He drove around and about. And stopped in the middle of Moore's Ford Bridge acrost the Apalachee river. They was men all in the bushes at both ends."

Bill's brother picked up the story.

"They was a bunch of men. They dragged all four of 'em out-a the car and tied 'em up to trees down at the river and shot 'em. They even cut out Dorothy's baby and smashed it all up."

Bile rose in Buck's throat and he reached for his now-empty tea glass. Only a few lukewarm drops left, but the flavor of the tea remained and helped wash out the bile taste.

Bill suddenly stood and paced the room, his fists shaking up and down. "I just want to kill old Harrison and all of them."

"Anybody talking? Know who any of them are, other than Harrison taking them out there to the ambush?"

"Nobody's saying a word. The white folks are scairt if we know, we'll kill 'em. And if any of us coloreds know, they ain't talking neither. They're scairt of getting shot up. You know how it is. The law run everybody off the streets, scairt we'd mob up against 'em"

"Yeah, I know how it is," Buck said, his mind back with Mickey. "I got a friend, a lawyer, down in Stanleyville. She's a white lady and helps out us colored all the time. Reckon she could help here?"

"Good God man, no. They'd kill her quick as they kill us," Bill said.

"Amens" rose from across the room.

* * *

Jenny Mae, Bill's wife, placed supper on the table—a platter of pork chops, a tureen of turnip greens, and plates of cornbread and sliced tomatoes. Darkness fell and then erupted with light that danced outside. The three diners ran to the door. The sky swirled with light.

"God shore must be mad," Jenny Mae said.

"Never heard of it coming this far south," Buck said.

"What is it?" Bill asked.

"They're called northern lights. Miss Laura showed me pictures of 'em in a book when I was growing up. There's something in the air at the north pole that causes them. But not down here."

They watched while supper cooled. Buck wondered if Molly were watching them too. Surely she wasn't afraid and wouldn't think it was cause God was mad. She had seen the pictures in the book too.

Maybe, though, the mob would be scared. Maybe those white men didn't know about the northern lights and might think God was after them.

July 27, Saturday

Buck and Bill arrived at Young's Funeral Home the next morning in Monroe, to find a line that stretched more than two city blocks. They joined it, and saw the line grow even longer behind them. After the sunlight, the inside of the parlor seemed dark, but after a few minutes Buck realized that heavy curtains accentuated the dimness, and only a few light bulbs burned.

He had expected the caskets to be closed, but the bodies lay on stretchers, not in caskets. Their heads were uncovered.

He grimaced at the damage to the Roger's face, and shuddered. Could he bear to walk by George's stretcher, see his friend dead by the hands of the Klu Klux when he had fought and survived the Japs? No, he decided, and looked at the floor until he had passed all the bodies.

Outside, the sun glared. People went about their business as if no one lay dead just inside. People went in and out of the cafe, the beauty parlor and the barber shop.

Life goes on. The world doesn't stop for anyone.

July 28, Sunday

Bill drove Jenny Mae and Buck to the Mount Perry Baptist Church in time for the funeral scheduled for 2:00 p.m. Some of the morning worshipers stood outside with the arriving mourners. George and his sister Dorothy were to be buried together at Mount Perry's cemetery; their mother, Moena, belonged to the church. People stood in groups scattered around in the churchyard.

Conversations centered around the lights in Friday night's sky and curiosity about where was Moena Williams and her husband Jim.

Buck was surprised to see white reporters and cameramen trying to talk to the other mourners.

Many men wore full suits in spite of the heat, and a few were in shirts and ties. The ladies wore summer frocks and mourning clothing, all with white gloves and hats. Children had on their Sunday-go-to-meeting outfits with white shoes and also carried gloves.

"Howcome all these white people are here with cameras?" Buck asked. "You reckon the news has spread out of town?"

"Don't talk to them white folks," Bill cautioned. "Ya don't know what they might say you said. Them folks is trouble for us."

They walked through the crowd, Bill nodding to acquaintances, and entered the church. As many mourners had entered as stood outside. "I'm surprised this many folks came, what with everybody scairt," Bill said.

"I reckon they know fear can be as bad as death," Buck said.

They hung their hats beside others and settled into a pew.

"Howcome Dorothy is being buried here and not with Roger?" Buck whispered.

"Roger never did get a divorce from his wife. I don't even know if they planned to get one. She's been gone a long time, and Dorothy jest called herself Mrs. Malcom. Moena said her daughter had to be buried with her family. Moena goes to church here."

Time passed. Nothing happened. The front pew, reserved for Moena Williams, remained empty.

Undertaker Dan Young left to find her, and the service was delayed.

The air felt thick, hot and heavy with sadness. Even the children, too young to comprehend death, carried fear in their eyes. They had been born into their family's fears—fears that forever had hovered in their imagination. They constantly turned one way and another as if in search of an unknown danger.

Whispers spread through the church, then increased in volume as people stood and walked up the aisle to the front door.

People stirred, but no one left. Rumors spread through the crowd. Some shook their heads and said, "No" to the rumors. Others seemed to become gripped by fear. Buck and Bill rose and moved among the crowd to listen. Someone said, "I hear the Atlanta radio and papers done told about the lynchings."

"That's howcome the reporters are here," Bill said. "The white folks can't get enough reading about us getting killed."

Dan Young returned, without Moena.

At 4 o'clock, the preacher stood to began the services.

Behind him, Buck heard the loud whisper.

"A damn shame. Everybody knows who dun it, but ain't nobody going to do any talking. Ain't no white man ever gonna pay."

* * *

Buck and Bill followed the other mourners to the cemetery, where the graves lay open beside a massive pile of fresh dirt. Buck stood silent with the crowd around the double graves and when the final words had been spoken, he was one who seized an end of the rope and helped lower his friend into the grave.

He removed his coat and tie and lifted a shovel to help cover the graves. Sweat soaked through his shirt. Tears mingled with the sweat that ran down his face. He felt shamed over crying and hoped no one noticed. The dirt clunked onto the coffins, and each sound seemed to slam into his chest.

When the graves were covered, two vases of flowers appeared and were placed over the mounds of dirt

It was too late to catch the bus back to Athens and the evening train. The Kindle's invited Buck to stay another night.

Next day, on the train back to Stanleyville, Buck found a seat in the Negro car. As he dozed to the sound of the clacking wheels, he thought about George and Roger. Both should have known better than to accept the offer of a ride. He wondered if the same fate lay in store for him and Molly if the KKK in Stanleyville really did know. He just couldn't let anything happen to Molly.

SAMANTHA

July 30, Tuesday

Buck got home last night, after what seemed like a powerful long time. We started another cutting of hay while he was gone, and if it wasn't for Jethro's coming down to help Pollock, we couldn't of started at all. While Buck's been gone up to George's funeral, the Macon paper has had a lot of stories about what happened. Buck said it was more horrible than the paper said.

I think the killing was planned right along, and that's why the man bailed Roger out-a jail.

We hadn't had time to talk at all, with the hay needing to be raked and thrown into shocks until we can haul it By the end of the day, we're all so tired we just go home. I wanted to drive the truck, but Dad said I'm not old enough yet. I had to jump on the hay when the men pitched it on the truck, to pack it down so more could be piled on.

We beat the rain with our last load today.

August 3, Saturday night after midnight

Mama and Dad drove her car over to Aunt Tessie's right after supper, and I was in the house by myself. They dropped Lillie Mae off to her house when they left, long after Sis had picked up her baby Katie. Remembering that crazy hobo, I hooked the latch on the kitchen screen door before I went upstairs to read.

It had gotten dark when I heard knocking from the back porch, heard the kitchen door being jerked, and Molly's voice rose up like she was scared, frantic. As I ran downstairs, I could make out her words.

"Dr. Lawson! Sam! Anybody! Help!"

She was sobbing when I got to the door, and kept pulling on it so hard I had a time getting the hook aloose.

"What's the matter?"

"Quick, Sam, get your gun. They're killing Buck. Hurry."

I ran to the back hall where the rifle and the shotgun always lean up in the corner and pistol stays on the shelf. I'm not supposed to ever touch the pistol because it shoots more than one time, but I grabbed it and ran toward the cottage with Molly right behind me. At the end of the driveway, I stopped so quick Molly nearly knocked me down, but I told her to stay back. I snuck up closer to where I could see the men, three of them, in white sheets by the oak tree in front of the cottage.

I could hear their voices, one of them saying, "He'll never stick it in a white girl again."

They all laughed.

I couldn't shoot at them without hitting Buck, so I shot toward the truck parked at the edge of the road.

One of the men hollered, "Let's git out-a here!" I shot again.

Even with them running away, I shot again toward the truck, but I was so mad I knew I couldn't come near to hitting anybody. At least I could shoot enough times to run them off, even if the truck was really too far away for the pistol to do any good.

Moonlight shone on a blue pickup, kinda rusty on the left back fender.

They whooped like they were at the Stanley Military School football game. One of them yelled, "It's just that little gal Sam." It sure sounded like Cou'n Phil's voice to me. They hollered again. One rolled over the tailgate into the back end and the other two jumped into the front seat.

Tires spun and squealed on the new pavement, leaving lines of rubber. Laughter floated back.

We ran to Buck. He was tied to the oak, his back against the trunk, kinda leaning forward.

He looked at the pistol. "They're gone, Sam. Unload that thing. Molly, they dropped the knife. Cut the rope."

His voice quivered and his breath came out between clenched teeth. He kept leaning forward and rocking back, his eyes closed. He was hurting.

She reached for the big pocket knife at Buck's feet and started sawing at the plowline while I broke open the pistol and took out the one bullet that I hadn't shot. Buck was moaning a little, deep down, and as the ropes came apart, he slumped over, reaching his hands down between his legs.

Then I saw the blood. And that he didn't have on any pants. I wanted to look, but I made myself turn away.

"Molly, I'm cut bad. I need a bandage."

She pulled up her skirt tail and ripped off a piece while Buck said, "Sam, go get your daddy's truck. You'll have to drive me up to your

Uncle Morris." He took the cloth from Molly and held it against himself between his legs.

"Go on, Sam. Hurry," he said, and to Molly, "Sweet, get me my coveralls."

I ran through the darkness, tore into the kitchen, dropped the pistol on the table, grabbed Dad's keys where he hangs them just inside the door, snatched up the flashlight and ran out to the truck. I'd never driven before and I wasn't sure what to do.

I put the key in the switch, turned it, pushed the starter, and the truck jerked forward. The gears. I had to fix the gears, and when I pulled on the stick, it ground like the meat grinder on a bone. I thought of the clutch, stomped on both foot pedals, and pushed the starter.

The truck cranked, and with both feet still on the pedals, I moved the gear but wasn't sure exactly which way to move it, and when I took my feet off those pedals, the truck jumped forward. I finally jerked my way down to Buck's yard.

Together Molly and I got him in the truck. Molly had folded up one of Buck's sheets for him to sit on so he wouldn't bleed on the truck. She closed the door, came around and crawled over the gearshift to sit next to him. With one hand he held the flashlight, and with the other he held himself, down between his legs where Mama says nice people don't touch themselves except to clean off.

Between breaths he told me how to drive and change the gears. I had to sit way up on the seat to see over the steering wheel. By the time we got to Aunt Tessie's, Buck had his head forward, leaning on his arm on the dashboard. Molly's arm was around his shoulder.

I turned into their yard, honking, and drove across the grass before I got the truck stopped.

When Uncle Morris opened the front door, I was already out of the truck. "Quick," I yelled. "The Klu Klux cut up on Buck. He's bleeding to death."

Uncle Morris ran into the yard, and Dad came flying out right behind him.

Buck struggled out of the truck, leaned up against the fender, held onto himself and kind of rocked. He tried to stand up but bent over with his pain. Blood was all over his overalls, a dark stain sharp against the bleached-out cloth.

Dad and Uncle Morris took ahold of Buck, one on each side of him, and started toward the house, all of them talking, and Dad asked

Buck, "Think it was the same as from the other night?"

"It was the same men, sir."

They went down the hall to the kitchen, where Aunt Tessie already was getting Uncle Morris's stuff ready. He uses their metal-topped kitchen table to sew up the razor cuts and to take care of the sick people. When Molly and I tried to follow them in there, Mama said, "No, Sam, they'll take care of Buck. You and Molly stay out here."

Molly stood with her hands twisting all over each other. She didn't even bother to try to wipe off the tears rolling down her face. Blood all over her hands had dried up and was flaky looking.

When Mama saw that one whole side of her skirt tail was torn off, she asked, "Molly, what'd you do to your skirt?"

She looked down at it and started to just shake all over with sobbing. Mama put an arm around her, talking to her the way she always used to talk to me when I would start to cry over getting hurt when I was real little. Finally Molly just cried herself out on Mama's shoulder and told about what had happened. She couldn't seem to think straight about it all.

"We didn't think they'd come back, and we were down to the cottage when they came up on us not long after dark. Buck said they were in a 1940 blue Ford truck. They busted into the front door. Buck told me to run out the back and keep quiet. He made a lot of noise. Musta wanted them after him and not me.

"They knew he was with a white girl cause of what they said to 'im."

She stopped a minute like she wanted to catch her breath. "Do you want to go on, Molly? Maybe talking about it will help," Mama told her.

"It was three of them. One of 'em has got a bad arm, so I know he was Judge Snyder. We think the others were Commissioner Benson and Rufus Flint, but I can't swear. They had pillowcases over their heads. We didn't hear the truck, didn't hear them till they smashed the door. They caught Buck and dragged him out the front door, and when I saw they were gonna tie him up to the tree, I ran up to the big house to get some help. I didn't know you were gone off. When Sam and I got back, she ran them off shooting the pistol. They'd-a killed him, Miz Lawson, if hit warn't for Sam.

"They yelled he'd never stick it to a white girl again, and even when they drove off, they were laughing. Sam shot at them, and they just laughed. They left him to bleed to death. I had to tear off my skirt and make a bandage for him to hold on himself till we could get over here. Sam drove.

"He's hurting something awful," Molly went on. "He told me he kain't never have babies now," she went on. "I did so want his baby, Miz Lawson. Is he gonna be all right?"

"They'll take care of him, Molly. Try not to worry. I know he'll be fine. After all, you stopped the bleeding, and he was able to walk into the house. We'll drive him to town if Dr. Morris thinks he needs to go to the Clinic. But let's just wait to see what Dr. Morris does and what he has to say."

I wondered if my Aunt Tessie had put turpentine on Buck the way she usually does on every raw place. It hurts something awful when you first put it on a cut place or a skinned knee, but it does kill the pain, cause you don't get sore there later.

If they'd put turpentine on Buck in there in the kitchen, he couldn't have helped screaming from the pain of it. But we hadn't heard a sound.

I could smell funny medicine smells when Aunt Tessie opened the kitchen door to come tell us that Buck was going to be okay. We would be able to take him to his mama's for her to look after; he shouldn't stay by himself, she said, but he wasn't going to need to go to the hospital for blood, thanks to Molly getting that bandage on him.

Mama said, "I'm taking him to our house."

"He said you'd want to, but he insists he wants to go to his mother's," Aunt Tessie said.

Mama shook her head. She wanted to take Buck home with us to protect him. There wouldn't be anything she could do at Elvira's.

"I'm going with him," Molly said.

"Molly, we'll all go. You can go inside with him if it's okay with Elvira. But we really must take you on to your Aunt Maude's. You can't stay at Elvira's. Suppose they come back looking for Buck and find you there? It just won't be safe for you. Or for him or his family."

Molly looked from my mama to my aunt and nodded. "Can I see him?"

"Sure," Aunt Tessie said.

As they started back toward the other room, Mama called to Molly, "See if you can talk him into going to our house."

Molly glanced over her shoulder before the door closed. "I'll try."

"Mama, what did she mean about he can't have babies?" I asked. "Does it mean the men—?"

"Sam, a lady doesn't ask such."

"But Mama—"

"Samantha!"

"Yessum." I sighed and walked off to the window, looking out into the dark yard. The moon had gotten up enough to turn all the yard into a kinda yellow except the shadows were a deep black, and the little wind seemed to make things move under the trees. I felt myself shudder, thinking about the men almost in our own yard, doing all that to Buck. I was thankful he was alive. While I watched, one of Tessie's cats, the calico, trotted by in the moonlight with something in her mouth, going toward the barn, and I wondered if she was taking a mouse to her kittens out there.

I sure hoped Molly would get Buck to agree to go with us to the big house. Wouldn't any of those men ever think of coming into our house to bother him. But it seemed forever before Molly and Aunt Tessie came out of the kitchen.

Aunt Tessie went up to Mama and said, "He insists on going to his mother's."

Mama nodded. "Okay. We'll do what he wants. But I don't like it."

Right behind them Dad and Uncle Morris came with Buck between them. Buck was walking like that drunk soldier, but at the same time like he had a board shoved down his backbone and legs. I knew he was still hurting a lot. But he looked at me, tried to smile, and whispered, "Sam, thank you."

I nodded back, tried to smile at him, and hurried outside ahead of everybody so I could get the car door open. They helped Buck into the back seat, and Molly ran around to get in the other side, sliding over to let him rest against her. I eased the door to on Buck's side. Buck didn't even so much as say "ouch," when I know it had to hurt him to move around so much.

Mama told me to get in the truck with Dad, she'd drive the car, and Dr. Morris would ride with her. We all went right on over to Elvira's.

When I opened the door for him to get out, I heard Molly ask Buck if he was hurting bad. He told her no, that Doctor had given him some strong medicine; he was so sleepy he was having trouble sitting up.

Dad told them to stay in the car while he and Uncle Morris went to the door and called out to Elvira. I went up on the front porch too, and when Elvira came to the door, Dad said, "Elvira, it's Buck. He's gonna be all right, but we've got him in the car. He's hurt. Bad. Somebody cut him, like a stud horse."

"Oh, Gawd, no!" Elvira wailed like somebody lost in a cemetery, calling on God to help her find her way out of a darkness filled with nothing but sadness and ghosts. I hurt inside even more for her than I had for Buck and Molly.

Buck never did cry out with all his hurting, but his mama tore up the night with her shrieking, like she was in a worse sorta pain than he'd been in from getting cut. Her hands covered her mouth for a few seconds, like they were trying to hold her scream inside, and she clutched her stomach like the pain there was too big for her belly to hold it without her hands helping.

Uncle Morris told her to calm down, that Buck was all stitched up and was asleep; she needed to fix him a bed where the other boys wouldn't have to sleep with him. Elvira said Jethro lived next door now, so it was just her and her girl at home.

"First thing tomorrow, I'se goan see de conjure woman. She'll hex de men whut dun did dis to my boy."

Mama came up on the porch. "It was the Klu Klux from what Buck said. I don't think the conjure woman can help you, Elvira. We just have to take care of Buck."

All the coloreds listen to Mama. She grew up with a lot of them and she talks with them the way they talk cause her folks had a lot of colored people to help out with the firewood and the cleaning and the planting, and Mama had to talk to all of them when she was little, like I have to.

Mama said, "If you've got a bed we can put Buck in, the men will bring him in now and you take care of him. Don't leave here to go calling on the conjure woman. Just stay here and take care of Buck. He needs you tonight and for the next few days."

"He got a bed in de back room," Elvira said, as Dad and Uncle Morris walked back to the car to get Buck. She went inside, and when I heard her pushing a table to the side, I hurried inside to help her. But she was already through the kitchen and into another room with two double beds in it. She lit the kerosene lamp and pulled the covers back on one of the beds. I was too late to be any good to her, and I had to get out of the way for them to bring Buck through, held up between Dad and Uncle Morris. Buck was still half asleep. Molly came in with them and stayed even when Dad and Uncle Morris left and made me go with them.

Mama called Elvira out of Buck's room and told her about how to give Buck the medicine Uncle Morris had for him. She explained how to tell time by looking at the little hand on the alarm clock she had brought over from Tessie's so Elvira wouldn't give him the medicine too many times. Mama told her she HAD to use the clock, not to use sun time cause it wasn't close enough. Mama told her the medicine and the clock went together, and if Buck was asleep when it was time for the medicine, to wake him up. Course, Mama knew they didn't have a clock—I don't know any nigra with a clock. They don't need one. They can tell by looking at the sun what they're supposed to be doing, when it's time to milk, or feed the chickens, or come back in from the fields for supper, or even to go down to the house to work for Mama and Dad. Even when it's raining or it's winter, they still know what time it is. I wish I could tell time by the sun, but I can't. Mama wanted to be sure that Elvira gave Buck the medicine right, and she even showed Elvira how to wind up the clock.

"Elvira, I want him to get up tomorrow afternoon and walk around the house some. Tell him it'll hurt, but he'll have to get up. I'll be out before supper tomorrow to see him" Uncle Morris said.

"I'se'll git mysef over to de conjure woman in de mawning," Elvira stated, nodding her head. "She'll gibe dem men dair comeuppance."

Mama's voice got firm. She said, "Elvira, you best stay and tend to Buck."

But Elvira wasn't paying Mama much mind. She cut her eyes around like she wanted to find some words waiting out there for her to say, but instead looked down at her feet, muttered, "Yessum," and went back to Buck's room. I knew she was gonna go off first thing tomorrow.

As we started outside to wait, I said, "Mama, she'll be going to get the conjure woman to cast her spell."

"I hope not," Mama said, shaking her head. "We got trouble enough without tending to voodoo spells."

"Can she hex white men if they don't know they're hexed?" I asked.

But Mama shook her head. "Don't fret so about it, Sam. Put your mind to something else and quit worrying."

Uncle Morris leaned on the fender of the truck on one side, with Dad on the other, while Mama stood by the door of the car and I sat on the car's hood and wished the night were cool enough to sit inside with all the windows rolled up so I wouldn't have to smell where Elvira had been burning her trash. That smell always bothers me, getting inside my nose and staying for what seems like forever. It's a lot worse to me than any pipe smoke, kinda like some food and rags burning. I don't know why they'd throw away food, unless they leave some in their tin cans and it's burning. With the war over we don't have to save the tin cans any more, and I reckon all the nigras burn theirs with all their other trash. It's a different smell from the trash piles the po' whites burn, but theirs smell pretty bad too. Mama makes me take the trash down to a big gulley way down behind the house, where it can all rot away.

I looked over to Jethro's house, off to the side of Elvira's, but it was dark, and I figured they'd already gone to bed. He gets up way before day to cut pulpwood.

"That boy is lucky to even be alive. If Molly hadn't been there to stop the bleeding, he'd have been as dead as a horse if Mule Wilson cut him," Uncle Morris said.

Then I knew what they did to Buck.

I felt something swell up inside me as my hands began to shake and tears started down my face. My belly tightened up. I wondered if my mad at Cou'n Phil was turning into hate. Mama says it's wrong to hate, that hate will eat up your insides. I felt like my insides were getting eaten up, so I knew I hated Cou'n Phil and Flint and Benson. Wouldn't anybody else in town do such a thing to anybody, not even to a nigra.

"Did Buck tell you anything about who it was?" Mama asked Uncle Morris.

"I don't think he wants to say. I know it's hard to recognize a voice if it's muffled behind a sheet, but I think he knows. At least, however, we know it wasn't Molly's family. All Buck would say is they sounded educated."

"Molly thinks it was Cou'n Phil, Roger Benson, and Mr. Flint. And don't forget the blue Ford truck," I said. "I bet if we looked on Flint's used car place we'd find one there. It has a brown rusted-up fender."

"It has to be Klu Klux. Nobody'd dare dress up like them. And unfortunately we know both Judge Snyder and Roger Benson are in the Klan," Uncle Morris said.

"Flint for sure is Klu Klux too," I said.

Mama asked, "Who told you that?"

So I told her about seeing them marching in town and what Carolyn, Phil's niece, said about their shoes, like nobody else in town wore.

"The three men in town who absolutely hate the coloreds. Benson cause of his son; Phil and Flint cause of the colored cemetery. And this is something they'd do. It's worse than killing. It's an attack on all nigras, not just Buck. They want Buck to be an example: Stay in your place. Keep your hands off white women," Dad said.

Dad left with Uncle Morris, but I wanted to ride home with Mama and Molly. We waited in the yard, not saying much, each of us just thinking. Jethro's old redbone hound wandered over from his house next door and sniffed up my front before he let me pet him. He smelled like he'd been down in the creek, but wasn't wet all over. I scratched him behind the ears, right where a dog always wants to be scratched. When my fingers ran up on a fat tick, I pulled it off and used my pocket knife to kill it. I hate ticks.

In a few minutes Molly came out. When she got in the back seat, I got in by her so we could talk on the way home. I told her I thought Buck was a mighty brave man, to be hurt that bad and still be able to tell me how to drive and all. She told me it seems like everybody forgets Buck fought in the war and got to be a hero. He was all cut up from a bayonet, but he still carried his officer on his shoulder like a sack of sweetfeed, picking him up from a ditch were he was shot almost to death, and carrying him back to what Molly said was the "line," where he could get to a doctor. Buck got a decoration for that, but Molly said he'd never shown it to her cause Elvira keeps it tucked away in a box in her bedroom. She doesn't put it out cause the sunlight might fade the colors.

She'd told Elvira about how Buck hadn't hollered or screamed when they cut him, and that's when Elvira showed her the medal. It was some sort of congress medal showing special honor that Elvira told her it was the best of all medals given to any soldier.

Before we took Molly home, we went to the plantation house, where Mama had Molly wash up to get off all Buck's blood, and put on one of Sis's dresses to go home. That way, her Aunt Maude wouldn't know what had happened unless Molly wanted to tell her tomorrow. Mama went with Molly to the door, to tell Aunt Maude that Molly had stopped by the house and had been helping her this evening, so everything would be okay for Molly at home. I never heard Mama tell a lie before.

August 4, Sunday Night

I went to church today with Mama. She said to pray for Buck and to pray to find inside ourselves forgiveness for the men who hurt Buck. I don't want to forgive them; I'm like Elvira, I just want them to get their comeuppance. Get it real bad.

We got to church early and stood under one of the oaks to wait for Vicki. Like every Sunday, all of the town people Mama knows came over and talked about Sis and J.D. and the pageant next week. Some of the husbands said the "jail" was gonna open on the courthouse on Monday, with the SMS cadets making the arrests for the "Brothers of the Brush." Every one of those old ladies in the U.D.C. and the D.A.R. who go to the Methodist Church tried to pat me on the head, like they think I'm a puppy. When I ducked away from one of them, Mama told me to mind my manners.

Vicki, Danny and Michelle finally came in sight down the sidewalk, and I went over to meet them. As we walked together to Mama, I told them about last night.

"I got a letter yesterday that Flint's appeal has been turned down, so he'll go to the state prison for killing that nigra woman. For a couple of years at least," Danny said.

"When?" I asked.

"Just as soon as the marshal can get here from Atlanta," Vicki said. "I thought sure he would've been here yesterday, right along with that letter."

"I haven't told Rufus yet," Danny said. "I don't want to stir up his mad until I have to. I may just call him to come to the office when the marshal gets here. I don't think he'll run off, but I'd rather not give him any warning."

"Howcome laws are so much harder on a nigra?" I asked.

"That's because white men made the laws. When women get to write the laws, we'll make life a lot more fair," Vicki said.

Danny looked at her, shaking his head, but Mama laughed and

said, "Better watch out, Danny. I think she likes to make the rules."

We hadn't any more gotten inside and sat down than Flint slithered up the aisle and sat on the front pew. Benson and his wife followed Flint, walked in front of him, and sat beside him. Preacher Randall had gotten up and raised his hand like he was about to pray when Cou'n Phil did what he does every Sunday—he strutted in like the peacock that lives on a neighbor's farm, and he pulled Martha along on his arm. He grinned just a little, to show he knew everybody was there just to see him. He sat on the front row next to Flint, as usual.

I struggled to stay awake till the preaching was over, as I have to do every Sunday.

Vicki and Danny stopped by the house after dinner, on their way to see Buck about his case against Flint. It goes to court the Monday after the parade. Mama let me go with them so I could visit with Buck too.

When we got there, only Buck and his sister Willie Jo were home. Elvira was gone off to they didn't know where, so we sat around in Buck's bedroom a few minutes to visit. While Vicki and Danny talked about the court case, Willie Jo and I went out onto the front porch where we sat in the rockers and fanned.

"Buck never did get that car running again, did he?" I asked, pointing down to the Chevy sitting by the mimosa tree.

She shook her head. "No'm. Hit weren't no account when he got hit. He ain't been paying Mr. Rufus nuthin since Miz Vicki said she'd settle it up fer him."

"Hey, there comes your mama," I said.

Elvira strode up the road like she was going somewhere in a hurry. Big as she is, with those long legs, she can out walk anybody else I know. Little puffs of dust rose around her bare feet and settled onto her lower legs and ankles, so they looked reddish compared with her brown skin. With the sun bright behind her, I could see she didn't have on a petticoat, and her legs showed up real clear through her feedsack dress.

"Ma, where you been?" Willie Jo asked as Elvira started up the porch steps.

"I dun been to see the conjure woman," she said, her lips turned down for emphasis. She nodded her head twice.

"Mama!" Willie Jo got up from her rocker and backed toward the door. "You ain't dun dat, is you?"

"I did. Dem Klu Klux whut cut my Buck, dey goan pay fer hit. She dun promise me, dey goan git dair comeuppance."

"But, Mama. Her spells scare me. And dey ain't no good against de white man. Whut spell she put on de white man is for shore goan come right back here on us."

"You hesh yo' mouf, Willie Jo. Hit's whut I wants. I wants dem Klu Kluxers dun fer. And she dun said she can do fer 'em."

Vicki came out onto the porch as Elvira said her last words, and she asked us, "Who's doing what to the Klu Klux?"

"Elvira's been to the conjure woman to get her to hex the men who hurt Buck."

"You think she can do that, Elvira?" Vicki asked. She knew about the spell on Amos.

"I knows so," Elvira answered. She nodded her head twice, firmly sure. "She dun tell me hit goan cost me a heap, but I tells her I dun't keer whut hit costs. Jest to put de hex on dem."

"Who is she?" I asked. "What does she look like? Where does she live?"

"You got no call ta be ackskin, Miz Sam. You ain't wanting her to put no spell on you fer ackskin."

I rolled my eyes around like I didn't believe her, and I shouldn't have. Elvira saw me, and she said, "You quit dat, Miz Sam. Somethin' bad goan happen, you keep on lak dat."

Elvira nodded, her lips in a tight line, as if to tell us to go off and tend to our business, not hers.

SAMANTHA

August 5, Monday

The world turned around the wrong way today, even if it did start out with almost the coolness of September slipping in to promise better times when I got up this morning. The promise was gone forever before the day ended.

Molly came by early to tell me she was going up to see Buck, and Mama told her to wait until she fried up some chicken for him. So we caught two of my fryers, that are almost big enough to sell, and while Molly held them with their necks on the chopping block, I swung the hatchet and chopped their heads off. By the time we had them cleaned, Mama had the bacon grease hot, and it wasn't long before we were ready to go to Buck's.

We wrapped the chicken up real good in a clean cloth and put it in a clean chicken-feed sack to tie closed real good so no dust could get to it. Molly wanted it in her bicycle basket, so I let her take it. Red had been watching all the goings-on and decided he'd trot along with us. He was in and out of the bushes along the road, and he had to run hard a few times to keep up with us.

Molly was real quiet while we pedaled up the road, not wanting to talk. I knew she was worried about Buck. In the quiet, with the only sounds a few birds and a far-off hound, I could hear the conjure woman's drum. Molly looked up that way a couple of times, shook her head and stayed silent.

We rode to the sounds of the bicycle chains and the soft whirr of the wheels intermingled with the rustle of leaves from limbs that hang over the road. A few Queen Anne's lace blossomed along the ditches, and we passed one bright orange clump of butterfly bush. Red yelped once and darted off when he spooked up a rabbit, but we went on, figuring he'd catch up with us.

When we got to Elvira's, Willie Jo came to the door at Molly's knock, and we all went down the hall to the back bedroom where Buck sat, propped up against a pile of pillows. His face softened when he saw Molly, his lips curling easily into a smile.

Elvira sat in a rocker by the bed, and when she saw us, she got up to offer me her chair, but I shook my head at her and leaned against the inside of the door jamb, my hands behind me for my bottom to rest against instead of the wood. Molly went straight over to Buck, knelt by the bed and whispered, loud enough for us all to hear.

"Are you all right?"

Smiling wider, he reached his hand out to touch the side of her face, and she leaned into his palm.

"I'm fair to middling, Molly." He looked up at me. "What you doing here, Sam? Don't you know you can get in trouble, coming here?"

"I came to see you."

A truck rattled into the yard, and I leaned around the door but couldn't see anybody.

"Want me to see who that is?" I asked.

"Dat jest be Jethro, gitting a ride to next door," Elvira said. "He wuking funny times, cutting pulp wood."

I know about the hours they cut pulpwood. On Mondays, almost nobody works cause they've got too much moonshine in them left over from Friday and Saturday, when they use up all their pay to get likker. Even if Jethro doesn't drink up his money, he can't work if the rest of the cutters lay out. He likely walked to work and thumbed a ride home when nobody else showed up.

We talked about different stuff for a few minutes. Pointing to the sack Molly had put on the floor, I asked her, "You gonna give Elvira that chicken?"

She laughed and handed the sack over, and Elvira looked inside. Saying, "Much obliged," she rocked herself forward, out of the chair, and headed for the icebox. I stepped inside the room to let her get by me.

"Oh, God," Elvira yelled. "You kain't take muh table off, Mr. Flint. I goan pay ya fer hit."

"You ain't paid a penny for a month. I'm taking the table and I'm taking that car your no account boy ain't paid for."

"You ain't taking dat table, I tells you."

Willie Jo took off for the front of the house. Molly jumped up from the bed, from beside Buck, but he grabbed her arm. "No, Molly. I'll go."

I looked around the door. Elvira swatted on Flint with the flat of her hand as he held onto her new table and tried to get it out the door.

Sims had backed halfway through the front door as he tried to get the table turned sideways so it would pass through the opening. Flint dropped his end of the table as Willie Jo got to the front room.

Just when the table thunked onto the floor, the bedsprings squeaked and groaned as Buck struggled up, but Molly tried to push him back down. "No, Buck. You stay in bed. I'll see what's the matter."

Flint pulled out his pistol and shot, not once, but three times, and I heard something fall. Willie Jo screamed, turning back toward the bedroom, and Flint shot again as she ran toward us. He looked up, saw me, raised up the pistol and I jumped back into the room. I heard him laugh.

Willie Jo got to the bedroom door and fell, her head inside but her feet still in the other room. Buck tried to get by Molly, but she grabbed him. I did too. We pulled him back. From the floor, Willie Jo grabbed at his foot and held on while begging him not to go through the bedroom door.

A truck door slammed, and we turned Buck aloose.

I left Molly kneeling beside Willie Jo and followed Buck to the front room, where Elvira lay, blood running onto the floor under her.

Buck stumbled to the front door, turned back to the fireplace and took his daddy's rifle down from over the mantelpiece. Running toward the door, he cranked the lever on the 30-30. As he raised up the rifle, I could see the truck, from under his arms, as it started off, towing Buck's car. He tucked the rifle tight to his shoulder and shot through the back window of the truck, busting the glass into a million cracks so we couldn't see inside it any more.

The truck, and Buck's no-account car, were gone.

Buck propped the rifle against the door jamb and turned toward his mama. Molly and Willie Jo were already by Elvira, but Buck's mama was dead right there by the table. I could tell she was dead because she had that same funny non-seeing look to her eyes that a cow has when you kill it to butcher.

Even with one arm dangling, Willie Jo pressed a piece of cloth to her mama's chest where the blood was seeping out. She paid no heed to the blood coming out of her own arm. Buck knelt down to his sister, took the rag from her, and quickly tied it over her arm.

"Sam," he said without turning back to me, "go get your mama. I can't stay here. They'll be back after me as soon as Flint gets to town.

Molly, I need you to stay here to look after Willie Jo. I gotta get out-a here or I'm dead."

"You can't go anywhere, Buck," I said. "You're not able."

He looked at me. "Sam, go get Jethro if he's home. Then go get your mother, you hear me?"

I nodded and tore for the door. I almost fell as my foot hit the empty shell from where Buck had cranked his rifle for a second shot. But I caught my balance, got around the table, across the porch, jumped to the ground without using the four steps, and ran across the yard toward Jethro's house. Elvira had raked the yard just today, had raked her careful patterns in the dust, the patterns broken up by tracks of those pointy toed shoes Flint always wears as well as the boots Sims always has on.

Jethro stood just inside his door, peeking around the jamb to look into the yard. "Whatcha doing here, Miz Sam?" he asked. "What's all dat shooting?"

"It's your mama," I said. "Flint's gone and shot her dead. Buck shot back and he's gotta run. He needs you to come hep 'im."

Jethro's never run so fast. He might be fat, but he juked across that yard like a scared chicken snake, and I was hard put to keep up with him. I followed him into the house, where Buck was in the kitchen putting stuff into a croaker sack. I could tell he already had some cans in it, and in the minutes I was in the kitchen, I saw him stuff in some cornbread and the chicken we brought.

He told Jethro, "Get my nasty overalls out-a the bucket on the back porch. We'll use them to fool the dogs. If nobody's dead, I can come back in a couple of days. Sam, you get on after your mama now."

"Where you gonna hide, Buck? They find you, they'll kill you."

"You go on along, now, Sam. Best if you don't know anything. Then you don't hafta lie."

"But Buck—" I started.

"Don't you fret, Sam. Just go."

"I'm going, Buck," I said. In the front room I stopped by Molly where she was just now getting Willie Jo onto her feet. "You need me?" I asked.

"No, you go get your mama afore Flint gets the sheriff here," she said. "I'll tend to things here."

"I'm going," I said, and ran back outside to where the bicycles were still leaning on the side of the house. I pushed off and started pedaling as hard as I could.

My mind kept seeing Elvira on the floor, blood everywhere, Flint pointing that pistol, fire and noise erupting from the gun. I started to shake all over, remembering him pointing it at me, and I nearly fell off the bicycle. I had to stop for a minute, just stand there in the road and try to stop shaking. I tried to erase the pictures from inside my head, tried to think about Buck. Where could he hide? Would he tell Molly so she could get him food and stuff he might need? And tell him when it was safe to come home.

Had he killed Flint? Or maybe Sims? If Buck hit one of them, not even killing him, then he was in really bad trouble. But I'd never tell where he's hiding, even if I did know. If either Flint or Sims is dead he needs to be, after what they did to Buck Saturday and to Elvira and Willie Jo today. Probably wouldn't either of them have to go to jail for shooting Elvira dead or for cutting Buck or hurting Willie Jo, but Buck would go to jail and be electrocuted for just shooting at a white man, whether the shot hit or not.

BUCK

Buck and Jethro headed north, away from town, and kept to a path cut deep by generations of cattle and mules since the land had been settled shortly after the Revolution and war veterans received hundreds of acres of wilderness for their service.

Neither spoke. Buck set a faster pace than Jethro was used to when he followed the hounds after coons and possums.

The wind slept. The sun bore down with the same fierceness they had known in the hay fields as they crossed the cotton patch behind Jethro's home.

The shadows of the hardwoods along Muddy Creek broke the heat. They followed the creek downstream to its merger with the infamous Murder Creek, once called Simmons Creek. But after Simmons, in a rage, chased his wife carrying her unborn baby into the stream where she drowned, it became known as Simmons' Murder Creek and later simply as Murder Creek.

No one fished here after the drowning. To the locals, it was haunted by the ghost of the unborn child who moaned when the night winds blew. The wind rose. Jethro stopped.

"We ain't gonna cross Murda Creek is we?"

"Don't fret, Jethro. I'm going into the edge. You're going home."

"I ain't gonna go with you?"

"No."

He put his load onto the ground and spread the slicker. He put his bag of food on it and tied it into a watertight bundle with the rope. His extra cartridges and pocket knife went into the top pocket of his overalls. He would carry the rifle at the ready.

"Them dogs're gonna smell you iffen you keep to the edge."

"No. I got it planned." He hoisted his bundle over one shoulder and gripped the rifle in his other hand. "You follow along on the bank a ways, dragging my overalls. The dogs'll follow that scent. Go up about as far as you'd shoot a possum and then turn off and head back home. Take the east path. The dogs'll follow that scent. It's stronger than mine in the creek."

"Where you going?"

"I can't say. If you don't know, they can't make you tell 'em."

Jethro nodded. He reached his arms out to his brother and hugged him. Buck set the rifle down and hugged him back.

"You be kerful, ya hear?"

"I will. Don'tcha worry over me. I got plans in mind. Now you get along on home."

Buck stepped into the water's edge. It rose over his brogans. He nudged the bottom, found the gravel to be smooth but not slick, and angled into deeper water, until it reached his knees.

Jethro followed along on the bank and dragged the overalls. When it snagged on briars, he stomped the stickers to the ground and pulled the clothing on. When Buck raised his hand holding the rifle and waved him away, Jethro headed up the path to his right and toward home. He looked back only once, to see his brother disappear around the bend and the thick underbrush.

Buck splashed his way down Murder Creek for two miles, until it reached Hickory Creek.

Darkness was closing down. Hickory Creek had seen high waters that cut under the banks and left no shallows for easy walking. Buck had to leave the water.

His feet sloshed in his brogans when he climbed ashore.

Maybe that water'll help hide my scent if they get around here. Huh. I know better.

The almost grown-over path through the brush alongside the creek hindered his speed. One limb after another barred him and he had to push them away. Blackberry branches snagged his overalls. He moved his pack to his front and hugged it against his belly to prevent snags in the slicker.

The sun dropped below the trees but flamed the scattered clouds on the horizon.

At last. There's the mill pond. Big Nate wouldn't be at the mill this late. I can get around it to the dam.

He stood a full minute at the road side to listen for any sounds—somebody walking, a distant car coming, even the sound of a hound that would betray him.

No human sounds. Only the barred owl up the hill, the crickets calling to the night, a bullfrog asking others to join in.

He hurried across the road, passed the mill and across the mill yard to the runoff from the paddle wheel that ran the grindstones.

Again he stopped to listen, but heard only night sounds, whispers from water in the spillway and the soft roar of the flow over the dam.

The wooden dam angled outward and upward for fifteen feet as it rose from its bottom. The overflow provided a white, moving curtain for the fifteen-foot hidey-hole.

With the sun down and only reflected light, he searched the spillway for the rocks he knew were there. He had come here as a child to fish the mill pond and to splash in the overflow. And had discovered the misty tent the dam created. Crossing the spillway then, in full light and with short legs, had been a fun challenge. His feet seemed to remember the rocks as he stepped across.

No way to avoid getting wet as he ducked under the end of the dam and into the cavern beneath. At least he was safe, had food, a weapon and cover.

Molly would bring him food in another couple of days.

In two or three days, Flint's posse should give up and figure he'd gotten out of the county. Or Vicki would get Prosecutor Hancock to put the shooting on Flint.

Dream on. And pray God they don't hurt Jethro and they don't think Molly knows where I am.

He curled up with the slicker over him and an arm curved under his neck for a pillow. No worse than a battlefield bed. He'd stretch the food for at least a couple of days.

When darkness fell, he slept.

SAMANTHA

When I got to the house and told Mama about the shooting, she didn't want me to go back with her at first, but I told her I had to, that I couldn't stand staying at the house by myself and worrying myself sick over Buck and Molly. She finally said I could go, and I was in the car faster than she was.

Mama tore up the road, speeding like I've never known her to, and in a few minutes we were back at Elvira's. Molly came to the door when she heard the car drive up, and Mama gasped, "Oh my God," from seeing the blood all over her front.

Inside, Mama took one look at Elvira, told Molly to find a sheet, and they laid it over her, but blood soaked right up into it from the floor. Then we went to the bedroom where Willie Jo was laid out on the bed with her arm all bound up.

"Can you walk?" Mama asked Willie Jo.

"Yes'm," she answered as she eased herself up. Her face had gone pale as she started to sit up, and Mama and Molly both reached down to help her stand. Mama was real careful about touching the shot-up arm and not mindful of getting herself bloody as she helped Willie Jo.

"Let's get you in the car and up to Dr. Morris," she said.

Molly crawled across the back seat to help Willie Jo sit still and not sway around when the car moved, and I sat by Mama.

She asked, "Where's Buck gone, Molly? Do you know?"

"He and Jethro took off," she said.

"To where? If he's hiding out, he'll need food."

"I know. But he took a good amount. He'll be okay for a couple-a days."

"Not if the sheriff gets the dogs after him. You know how good those bloodhounds are at tracking."

"Yessum, I know. But I think Buck can get away from them, with Jethro's help. They took Buck's bloody overalls. Jethro's gonna drag them when Buck gets into a creek. The dogs'll go after those overalls, not after Buck."

We didn't say anything else until we got to Aunt Tessie's, where Mama drove right up to the back door. Aunt Tessie and Uncle Morris were out in their garden plowing, with Tessie hauling the plow behind her and Uncle Morris making it stay in a neat row like they've done for the past two years, since their last mule died.

When Mama honked, they looked up and saw us getting Willie Jo out of the car, and they almost ran to the house. We got Willie Jo into the kitchen, and onto the table where Dr. Morris had tended to Buck. Tessie told me and Molly to wait in the living room.

I tried to find a way to calm Molly down and spotted Aunt Tessie's special viewer that make's everything look real—you look through two eye pieces at two pictures of the same thing. Its like magic. Molly had never seen one. So I got out the pictures of nigras in the cotton fields, of the Grand Canyon, and of Niagara Falls, that showed how long the rows of cotton are, how deep the canyon is, and how wide the falls are.

Before we had looked at any more pictures, Mama came in to say Willie Jo was doing okay. Uncle Morris had gotten her arm sewed up, and none of her bones were broken. He'd said she could go on home, but he and Aunt Tessie are going to keep her with them until everything was taken care of back at her house.

We started to take Molly home, but before we got to Maude's place, Mama said, "Molly, I can't let you get out looking like that." Blood was dried all down her front, smeared over her hands and arms. "And I can't take you to town with us. The sheriff is going to try to find Buck, and I just know he is going to be looking for you."

She drove on down to our house, right up to the back door, and said, "You girls stay here at the house."

Molly got out, but I didn't move. "Sam," Mama said. "You stay here with Molly."

"She'll be all right, Mama," I said. "You might need me for something. I'm going with you."

"No, Sam. Molly'll need you more."

"I'm all right, Miss Laura."

For a minute I thought Mama was gonna insist I get out of the car, but instead she turned toward Molly, who was leaning against the car's front door to look in and talk to Mama. "Okay. Molly, get cleaned up real good. Take a bath. Find something of Sis's that'll fit you good, and take those clothes down to the trash gully. Wrap them in some newspaper and take the trash out of the barrel in the yard to dump over them. I don't want anybody finding out you were up there and trying to get you to say where Buck is. Okay?"

"Yessum, I'll do that, Miss Laura. Thank you." Molly started for the door.

Mama yelled behind her, "And don't answer the door for anybody, you hear?"

"Yessum." She waved from the open screen door as Mama turned the car around, digging out two ruts in the yard as she sped up.

At the sheriff's office, we found out Flint had already been there and told them that Buck had shot Sims in the back of the head when he was leaving there today—killed him for no reason, Flint said. The sheriff had already gone out to look for Buck.

Mama really gave that deputy sheriff something of her mind, and we drove around the block to park in front of Vicki's office building. We found her working on some of the papers to use in court next Monday, and I blurted out, "Vicki, you gotta help Buck. They're saying he killed Sims, but Sims and Mr. Flint killed his mama and shot his sister and stole his car out of his yard. You gotta help him."

"Whoa, just a minute, Sam," Vicki said. "Slow down and tell me what's happened." She looked up at Mama. "Laura?"

Mama told her. She said we've got to call the undertakers to go out to pick up Elvira.

"No, no. We've got to make Collier Hancock go out there so he can make a case against Flint. Then Buck'll be safe." She picked up the phone and called the solicitor general.

"Flint's killed another woman, Collier. I'm putting Laura on to tell you how to get out there. You come right on out, you hear?" She nodded at what he said, and handed Mama the phone.

Vicki followed us to our house to leave Mama's car, where Mama ran inside for a minute to check on Molly.

Vicki drove us to Elvira's and parked in the shade of the big mimosa tree in Jethro's yard. The sheriff's car was parked right out in the middle of the yard, in the brinjin hot sun, along with a truck that had a dog cage open in the bed, so we knew that they had dogs out looking for Buck. When we got out of the car, we leaned against the car hood to listen, but we didn't hear the dogs barking. In fact, even Jethro's dogs didn't bark, so I figured he had them penned up in the back yard, pretty far from the house. There didn't seem to be anybody else around, so we sat down again inside the car and left the doors open to catch some air while we waited for Collier Hancock.

I kept looking over toward Jethro's house, and thought one time I saw his face in a window, for just a second. I almost said something, but decided not to. If Jethro had gotten back, he didn't need anybody going over to see him. I hoped if it were him at the window he would slip out his back door and get himself off into the woods aways.

It wasn't long before Collier Hancock drove up, and behind him came a hearse and some colored undertakers.

"Where's the sheriff?" Hancock asked.

"Off chasing an innocent man," Vicki said. "Come on in, Collier." She walked toward the door, and I started to go in, too, but Mama reached out, grabbed my arm, and said, "No, you don't. This is as close as you go this time."

They hadn't been in there very long when the sheriff and two deputies came into the yard with a dog that looked like it was part coon dog and part blood hound and wasn't big enough to fill up its own skin. Its hide wrinkled up and its ears fell over its eyes. It drooled slobber all over in front of where it was going, and its head seemed to hang down. It was too tired to pull the man on the other end of the rope. The men's uniforms were torn up from briars—probably not only blackberry bushes but also those sawbriars that can cut up on you bad if they grab you, cause you can't break them they're so tough—they've got thorns as big as Osage orange thorns. Bad as they are, Buck said you can eat the leaves.

It looked like the dog had pulled the deputies right into the vines. Blood spotted their shirts and pants where the thorns had not only torn their clothes but had also dug into their skin.

The one holding the dog's rope was soppy wet, like he'd fallen in the creek. I didn't know him, but the other one's Deputy Warren. His son is in my class at school is how I know his name.

Hearing their voices, Mama came out, and the sheriff asked her, "Mrs. Lawson, what're you doing here?"

"I understand you're looking for Buck. You ought to be locking up Flint for killing Buck's mama and shooting his sister," Mama said back.

Vicki appeared on the porch, with Collier right behind her, and she said, "Sheriff, what are you doing out there with that dog?"

"We're looking for Buck Steele for killing Sims. Shot him in the back of the head."

"Have you been inside here and seen what Sims and Flint did?"

"Come in, Sheriff. And leave the dog outside," Collier called over Vicki's shoulder.

The sheriff hitched up his britches, like his pistol was too heavy, as he walked toward the house, and said over his shoulder, "You boys stay out here, you hear?"

"Yes, sir," they both said. They went over to the well and pulled up a bucket of water. The one I don't know said, "Wrench out that dipper real good. I ain't wanting to be drinking behind a nigger."

After they drank they plopped down under the oak tree by the house. Sweat darkened their shirts and rolled down their faces. One of them wiped his face on his sleeve. I walked over, sat down by the dog, leaned against the tree, and pulled up a piece of sour grass to chew on while I waited. I petted the dog, even with it smelling bad from being so hot. It slobbered all over me and tried to lick my face.

My mind ran over the idea that Red was supposed to be there with me, but I couldn't hold onto the thought long because I wanted to find out about Buck. "Did you find anybody out there?"

The deputy I didn't know shook his head, "No. We just got dragged as fast as we could run down to Murder Creek. When Frisky there jumped in the creek, he pulled me right in with him and then he just stopped. Like he couldn't decide which way to go. I've never seen him like that. He came back out of the creek, sniffed around, went back to the creek, came back out, and started to circle back this way, still tracking with his nose down. It just don't make any sense. That nigger wouldn't of come back here, but old Frisky here thinks he did. If I didn't know better, I swear that nigger took to the treetops. But we looked there too and didn't see him."

"What'd you do if somebody killed your mama?"

"I'd kill the ess oh bee," he said.

"What's an ess oh bee?"

His face got red, like he was suddenly sunburned, and I really wondered what he was talking about that I wasn't supposed to know. When he didn't answer, I asked him again. "What's an ess oh bee?"

He coughed, looked down the road at nothing, back at me, and didn't say anything. Deputy Warren said, "It's a really bad person, and don't you go calling anybody that, or your mother'll skin that boy alive." He jerked his thumb at the other deputy. "And she might get ahold of me, too. You hear?"

I laughed at him, "You mean, it's something bad, like cussing?"

Deputy Warren poked at the other deputy's side. "Answer her, Bud."

"Yeah," he said. "Real bad. And you never heard me say it, okay?"

"Okay, I won't call anybody that. But if you would kill somebody for killing your mama, why can't Buck?"

"Cause he's a nigger," the deputy said, like he was telling me Buck was a grasshopper or a rattlesnake, something that didn't matter at all.

"He's my friend," I said. "He fought in the war."

"I fought, too, but the niggers mostly sat around at night and scairt themselves with their ghost stories. Half of them ran off in the night. Couldn't any of them be officers cause they're all cowards in the dark. I got no use for niggers, them running off when I was getting shot at. Buck is just a nigger, and don't you go trying to make him out better'n he is, you hear, Sam?"

"Yeah? Well, there was one man Buck met, a nigra that got to be a big officer. Name of Robinson. He went to a big California white college, too. Don't go saying a nigra can't be an officer. They even made Buck an officer for awhile."

"Sam, you hesh that kinda talk," Deputy Warren said. "Buck's in enough trouble. You keep on, you'll just make matters worse. You ain't forgot Moore's Ford, is you?"

"Who can? But white men better start remembering what happened up at Simpson's dairy. I heard it was Junior who started it, beating and kicking Mick. And it's all over town the nigras are saying it'll teach white men not to beat up on nigras.

"White folks can shoot the nigras and it's not murder. White folks can steal from nigras, and it's not stealing. Flint is stealing from every nigra in town that has ever bought anything from him. This makes four women he's shot up. He sells those no-account cars and then takes them back to sell again when he still hasn't fixed them. He killed Buck's mama cause she owed him less than ten dollars for a table. Flint's just a crook."

"Don't be saying that about a white man, Sam," the deputy said. "I don't wanna hear it. Fact is, I don't wanna hear any of your nigger-loving talk."

Mama and Vicki came out, and Vicki said, "Collier's going to charge Flint with murder."

If that prison marshal had been here Saturday, like he shoulda been, none of this would've happened.

When we got back to the plantation house, Vicki came in to talk with Molly, and told her she and Danny would be Buck's lawyers if he ever had to go to trial, but she didn't ask Molly where he was or even if she knew where he was.

After she left, Mama and Molly went to the kitchen to see about some supper, and I went to feed my puppy. I called Red, but he didn't come. I remembered he'd gone off chasing a rabbit before we got up to Elvira's, and if he'd gotten up to her house, he'd have barked when Flint and Sims drove up. And he'd have gone over to Jethro's dog pen and barked at those dogs. He never got up to Jethro's. He must be lost somewhere out there, but I hoped he'd find his way home for his supper.

He didn't.

Upstairs in my room, my mind was on Buck, out there somewhere by himself, hunted, alone in the dark, listening for the conjure woman's drums. She might have put a hex on Flint, but it sure didn't take. Her spell just turned inside out and not only killed Elvira but also put Buck out of the house and into the darkness.

I hadn't been able to go to sleep for listening to the sounds of the trucks, ripping up the road, the white men yelling, their voices like a coon hunter's as he whoops on his dogs. I knew if the trucks stopped, if the yelling stopped, they had found Buck.

Not even the moon gave light tonight. The wind was still as a graveyard when the haints are too scared to come out. The drum was silent. Nothing but darkness.

August 6, Tuesday

"We can't do a thing for Buck right now, so let's get our work done and you both can come to town with me. I have to go to Piggly Wiggly, and you can check out the jail, see who hasn't grown whiskers. Okay?" Mama tried to cheer me up at breakfast.

All I did last night was fret and worry over Buck and wear a hole in the mattress from turning over a million times.

Molly came downstairs before seven o'clock, while breakfast was cooking. After we ate, we went to work on getting everything ready for the celebration. At least the work kept our minds off Buck. Except when we worked in the same room, and we'd both bust out crying.

It was late when we went to town. Molly wanted to stay at the house. "I just don't feel like going in, Miz Laura."

Mama didn't have to get a whole lot of groceries, but she wanted to be ahead on her shopping before everything in town got all jammed up with the festivities. After Friday, cars won't be let on the streets except the ones to be in the parade. J. D. said he'll make the "Brothers of the Brush" let the nigras park their wagons at the courthouse, like they always do, even if the jail cell is right there. Dad won't go to town for anything but to teach his summer school classes—it's just too much going on.

Right across the street from the courthouse, the Piggly Wiggly people are keeping open until eight o'clock all week cause of the jail cell being so close. I reckon the store figures they'll get some extra business when the "crooks" get freed. They'll be open Saturday, but only until time for the parade to start. All the stores are gonna close as soon as the parade starts.

The whisker growing is silly, just like the long dresses the women are supposed to wear, but I wanted to see who they've got locked up. Most everybody has grown some kind of whiskers. The prisoner has to stay in jail until somebody pays $5.00 for him to get out, and he's not supposed to use his own money. Some of them do, though. Cadets from the Stanleyville Military School serve as the jailers cause the head of the school got put on the birthday party committee, and he can make the cadets do anything he wants them to.

I went over to the jail. The duty cadet leaned up against an oak tree and talked to a girl, not paying any mind to the jail or to the one prisoner, a man who once ran against Mr. Benson for county commission. I asked him howcome he didn't grow himself a set of whiskers, and he said he tried to come to the courthouse every day to see if somebody would bail him out of the fake jail.

Mr. Benson walked up and had to holler at the cadet, really scaring him. But he wasn't at attention like he was supposed to be. Benson paid the money to get the man out, and then glared at me, but I didn't let him scare me. He asked, "They catch that nigger of yours yet?"

"He's not my nigra or anybody else's. He's his own person. And I hope they never catch him after what you men did to him!" I squinted my eyes real hard at him to let him know how mad I am, and I blurted out, "Little Rog would be so ashamed of you."

Benson's face paled around his whiskers. His sunk-in eyes got even smaller, his thick brows ran closer together, and his hands trembled. He didn't say anything, but he cut his eyes away, turned, and walked off around the courthouse. I'd never seen him all slumped over like that.

When Mama came out of the store I went to help her load up the groceries. I got in the back seat and made like Mama was my driver. I said, "Home, please, James," and Mama and I got to laughing a little. But when we came around the bend just south of where Maude lives, we almost ran into three cars parked all whichaway across the road.

"Get down, Sam!"

I didn't. I stuck my head out of the window to see what was going on.

Slim stepped from behind one of the cars, walked over to us, bent down, and said "Sorry, Miz Lawson, but we have to check every car to be sure Buck's not running out of the county. I hate it being like this."

Two other lawmen rose up from behind the other cars, Deputy Warren and the officer who went in the creek with the dog when he was chasing after Buck. Slim looked in the back at me and asked, "You okay?"

I nodded. "I'm fine, Slim. Especially since I told off old Roger Benson."

"That so?" Slim asked.

"What?" Mama asked and turned around and looked at me. "What did you do?"

"I told him he was terrible for what he did to Buck. And he didn't say anything. Just walked off."

"Why're y'all out this way? Don't you reckon Buck's long gone by now?" Mama asked.

"Well, there're deputies and GBI on all the roads, and I got pulled in to help. No matter how we feel, we have to look for Buck. I think he's gone, like you said. We've searched all the colored houses, and didn't find the first sign that he was staying around here. But you might need to go on along, Miz Laura. Is the professor out anywhere that we should watch for the truck?"

"No. We left him grading papers, so he's home."

He dropped his voice to a soft whisper. "Is Molly still at your house? How is she?"

"She's holding on. I'm keeping her with us for awhile. At least till all this blows over."

"Good. I'm glad," Slim said. "She's a fine girl."

"Howcome Flint isn't in jail? He killed Elvira and he's free. Buck just defended his family and he's had to run to stay alive," I said,

"Phil Snyder went to Judge Plummer and posted his land as bond. Flint didn't even spend a night in jail. I agree it isn't fair, Sam. But that's the way it is."

"When I grow up, I'm gonna change it," I said.

"Sam, Vicki is working for the same thing. By the way, did your dog ever show back up?"

"No, and I can't figure what coulda happened."

Deputy Warren stepped up to the car.

"Sam, I've heard about your dog, heard it's a fine redbone. I'll lay odds somebody just picked him up. How'd he go missing?"

"He went off after a rabbit when I was on my bike, and he never came home."

"Well, I'm sorry, girl, but somebody probably picked him up. If he gits away from them, he'll likely come on back. If he don't, just try to know he's likely got a good home. Most hunting folks set a store by their dogs."

Mama decided it was time to go and said, "Goodnight, Slim. Goodnight, Deputy."

Slim said "Goodnight. Sam, you behave."

I can't believe somebody would steal my puppy, but Buck said from the start he's gonna be a really good possum dog. They've gotten where they cost money now, cause you can't get 'em free off farmers any more. The only free dogs nowadays are the ones the town people bring out and throw away.

Tonight when I heard the conjure woman's drum, I crawled out of the bedroom window to sit on the roof to listen. She pounded louder, faster. Fury seemed to rage into the night from the distant drum; it galloped loudly into the darkness, seemed to change direction, and paused as if to look around, to see where to go, to gather up more anger before it started up again to release fury into another direction.

All I could think of was she hadn't yet given the white men their comeuppance and already it had cost Buck and his family more'n they oughtta have to pay.

I crawled inside and pulled that window down. I didn't care how hot it was, I just didn't want to hear that drum any more.

August 7, Wednesday

I was so tired last night that when I put down the window, even the heat didn't keep me awake. Once, a bad dream about Buck getting caught and hanged out in the woods woke me up, and I shivered in the heat.

How I miss Buck. I wish he could be here so he could go to his mama's funeral with me tomorrow. I don't know what to do, cause I've never been to a funeral before, but I do remember when a great-uncle died and was laid out in the parlor when I was real little. When the Cape Jasmine bloom in the front yard, their smell reminds me of that funeral and makes me think of dead people.

Mama's not going. She's gonna stay home with Little Katie so Lillie Mae can go. I know as old as she is, Lillie Mae's gone to funerals before and she'll help me not do anything wrong.

Molly and I rode up to the mill real early this morning, to get ahead of anybody bringing their corn out to get it ground. Only person we saw was Big Nate, who runs the mill for the Simpsons. Standing at the door and looking out at the morning, he greeted us with a smile when we got there. Big Nate is the tallest man I've ever seen, taller and wider and stronger than Pollock. His short hair twists into gray curls, but his face doesn't seem old enough for him to be going gray.

He dropped down from the mill platform, where the wagons back up, to meet us, and as soon as he saw the croaker sack in Molly's basket, he knew why we were there.

"That's for Buck," he said, nodding toward the bike.

I didn't answer, but Molly didn't hesitate. "Yes. I reckon you know where he is?"

"Miz Molly, I ain't about to go looking, and I ain't about to stay round and watch. Thataway, I can be truthful iffen I gits acksed." Placing both his hands onto the platform almost as high as his shoulders, he hefted himself back inside and vanished into the shadows.

The top of the dam slants away from the pond, making a kind of roof that throws the water away. The bank going down toward the dam isn't real steep, and it's easy to get under there just by walking down the slope and stepping over the sluice where the wheel pours water when it's turning. I've been under that waterfall a couple of times, when I came up to the pond to go swimming. The dam is like a lean-to in the woods in the rain. You get some mist from the water falling, but you don't get really wet, just damp. But I knew if I had to stay there a long time, I'd likely be wet and cold.

We parked the bikes over against an elm tree and I waited with them while Molly took the food to Buck. She stepped down the bank at the end of the waterfall and disappeared under the gleaming mists. Seemed to me she was gone an awful long time.

On the way home, we went by Elvira's house to see about Willie Jo. Jethro had let one of his hounds out into the yard, and it barked a greeting as we pedaled up. The noise brought Willie Jo out of Jethro's house.

"You doing better?" I asked her.

"Yessum, Miz Sam." She nodded. "Miz Molly."

We just stood there a minute, looking at each other, none of us knowing what to say. Willie Jo said, "Miz Molly, Ma set a store on de letters Buck send from de army. I can't read dem, and Jethro can't neither. Does you wants em?"

She did not expect to see Buck again.

"Oh, Willie Jo, yes. Oh, yes, I do. I do."

She led us across Jethro's yard to Elvira's home. Inside, she went to the bedroom where Buck had been recovering when everything went bad, and opened a drawer to a scarred old chest. Lifting out a box, she turned and handed it to Molly. "Dat-air's everything frum his army times."

Tears rolled down Molly's face and she didn't try to hide them. She wrapped one arm around the box and the other around Willie Jo, and they just broke down and sobbed on each other's shoulders until I was crying too. It was like we were all saying goodbye to Buck.

When we finally quit bawling, Molly wiped her face on her sleeves, same as me.

"I take him something every day," Molly told Willie Jo. "If he can hold out a few more days, I think he can slip off down the river."

"Me and Jethro shore do 'preciate all you is doing fer Buck," she said. "You be mighty kerful, you hear?"

Molly nodded and turned toward the front door. We all walked out, and it seemed there wasn't anything else left to say. Molly and I got on the bikes and pedaled home.

I wondered if the letters Buck wrote me were in the box. I used go over to Elvira's to read her every letter that I got, and she wanted to keep them, to save for Buck when he got home from the war. Early on, he wrote about George, but George is dead. I wonder about the other friend of his, the nigra Lieutenant Robinson who'd been born in Georgia but moved to California. I hope the Klu Klux doesn't get after him too. Buck says he's a fine man and had to put up with a lot of sass from white men, but he knew how to pay them no mind.

*   *   *

Vicki, Danny, and Michelle came out to the plantation house for supper with us tonight. We had pork chops, butter beans and sweet taters, and of course Mama's biscuits. Vicki said it was the best meal she had eaten in she didn't know when, and Mama told her that food always tastes better if somebody else cooks it. Danny didn't say quite the same thing; he patted his belly and said the fixings sure were good. He didn't dare say it was the best he'd had, cause he's always eating at Vicki's. She almost led him into a trap.

Flint came by their office this morning about his appeal, and when he learned it was turned down, he went on a tirade, yelling at Danny it was all his fault, that any half-wit lawyer would have gotten him off in the first place, and anybody else could of done the appeal and kept him out of jail. He slammed the door open so wide it crashed into the copy machine and then stomped out of the office. Storming up and down the hall, he cussed everybody, including J. D. and Sis, and even Cou'n Phil. He raged down the stairs and across to the courthouse, where he went up and down the halls and yelled into every office, "You'll all be dead for this!"

Danny said, "Rufus got it in his head I bribed the jury to find him guilty. He's gotten crazier since he shot Elvira and I wouldn't help him get bonded out."

Vicki told us to be extra careful. "I worry about what Flint might do. He's mad at everybody now, including you, Professor."

She didn't smile at all when we were talking about Flint; her eyes shrunk up some, and I could see she was worried from the way the lines in her face seemed to go real deep with her frowns. Danny said he takes his pistol with him now when he leaves the office. Until today, I didn't think Vicki or Danny was scared of anybody.

August 8, Thursday

The rain was just enough to make me squint my eyes, and I had to scrunch down under an old rubber raincoat on the wagon seat between Molly and Lillie Mae on the way to the church where my Grandpa gave the nigras some land to build it on. Every nigra I know goes up there to church.

Lillie Mae drove the wagon, keeping ole Daisy moving right along. Molly and I each held onto a vase of flowers that Mama drove all the way over to Macon for early this morning. She said she thought Molly and I should both carry some up to the church for the funeral. If it were springtime, we'd have plenty of flowers in the yard—daffodils or dogwoods or Chinaberry blossoms or fruit tree blossoms. Something blooms from late winter all the way into summer around here. But not many things bloom in August.

In the wagon bed, Pollock held onto a churn full of crepe myrtle blossoms that he and Lillie Mae had cut. He didn't have anything to keep the rain off except an old Army coat that Dad gave him. It had to be hot, but it did keep the rain off.

The rain broke for maybe five minutes, but got to be a real hard shower as we reached the church. Pollock tied Daisy off to the side, along with the other wagons, and we hurried onto the porch with the crowd. Since the porch wasn't very big, most people were already inside. I was the only white person there except for Molly. All the nigras nodded to me, respectfully, but some of them went over to Molly, whispered to her, and touched her arm. I couldn't hear what they said cause they kinda moved her off toward the door, away from me and Lillie Mae. One of the men took her flowers inside.

Lillie Mae and I stood out on the porch a few minutes, her talking to some of the women, and me just standing there with her, holding my flowers. Pollock went inside with the big churn.

Some of these people here I've known a long time cause they've worked for Dad off and on. They looked real different all slicked up in shiny clothes—I'm used to seeing them in overalls in the summer, working on fences, pitching hay, or cutting wood, with no shirt on. And likely no underdrawers either, and their arms hanging bare, like coils of rope bulging to escape from their black skins. I can see their skins, like black satin, shining in the sun with their sweat.

Lillie Mae told me to take my flowers inside, and as I went in, I was hit by the sickly-sweet flower smell that choked the air. The windows were closed to keep the rain from blowing in, and with just the open door to let any air stir, the room was stifling. People had brought in all sorts of blooming things—a jug of cattails, some orange butterfly plants, lots and lots of churns full of crepe myrtle, and a couple of jars of Queen Anne's lace.

I didn't know what to do with mine, so when I saw Molly I went over to her. She took my jar, walked it over to the corner and put it on the table by hers.

I didn't want to stay inside cause I could see Elvira, laid out in a big box, wearing a pink dress, with lace all around her face, and a flower in her hand. I'd never seen anybody dead before, and every time I looked toward the coffin, all I could think of was seeing her sprawled out on the floor with blood everywhere. I thought I might be supposed to go up to the coffin and kiss her goodbye, or do something like that. But I couldn't. Not even for Buck. I hoped he'd forgive me.

I just wanted to go back outside. My insides knotted all up. I wanted to cry.

The Elvira up there was not the Elvira I knew. She was pasty and cold, deader than she looked when she got shot. I had to struggle to keep from crying. I got shivery-cold all over, and hurried out to the porch. I looked down, hoping nobody inside saw me crying. I specially didn't want Molly to see me cry cause it might make her cry.

Out on the porch, even though I know I'm too old to want to hold onto somebody's hand, I reached over and took Lillie Mae's. Kinda like Pollock takes his rifle even when he knows it won't kill the haints, but it makes him feel better to have it close by, I knew holding Lillie Mae's hand wasn't gonna keep me from being sad. But I felt better just touching the hand that had been so good to me all my life. It was a comfort.

I barely recognized Big Nate cause he'd shaved off the stubble of whiskers he always has during the week, like it was Sunday instead of a Thursday. Lillie Mae told me that Big Nate grew up on Grandma's place at the same time Elvira did. "Dey was chulren together." I could see he was hurting inside. His eyes were sorta extra bright, like from tears he was holding back, and his voice sounded like he had something stuck in his throat that wouldn't let his words come out right.

The men mostly talked to the men and the women mostly to the women. But they all talked about what a good woman we were celebrating today. The women talked about how good Elvira had been to them, how she had sewn clothes for those who couldn't sew; how she had kept a baby for a man whose wife died giving birth just about the time Elvira's new baby died, so Elvira had milk. She had nursed and cared for the baby for two years and sent it home to his papa. She never got anything for all that, not even for the food and clothes, except a lot of love from the boy. They talked on, about things I never knew about Elvira.

She was such a good woman she never thought of herself, but just of her friends and her children. She hadn't had a chance to learn books and wanted better than the cotton fields for her children, and they talked about how Jethro always played hooky even after she got him sent off to school, so he never got any learning. He couldn't do much now except cut pulpwood, run his hounds and fish. But she'd pushed Buck and he was a fine man.

I'll forever see some of the nigra ladies who were there, forever remember the sadness on their faces, the pain in their voices, how they looked down, shaking their heads, sorta mumbling "uh-uh-uh" to show their sadness, to show it was beyond their thinking, what had happened to Elvira and Buck.

I saw something move over by the dug-out grave, and at first I thought it was a grave digger. But whoever it was didn't have a shovel. All I could make out was a long black coat and big black hat. I moved over to the front of the porch to see better, and watched whoever it was just slip closer to the church and stand by an old oak tree, just stand there in the rain.

I pointed and asked Lillie Mae, "Who's that, over in the cemetery? Just on this side of the grave, by that big oak?"

Lillie Mae stepped up to the edge of the porch, looked out, grabbed me by the arm, jerked me toward the church door. "Don't you fret yo-sef none, Miz Sam. She ain't got no truck wid you."

"But who is she?" I persisted.

Somebody behind me whispered, "Lawd, Lawd, look-a dere who dun come to de cemetery."

Everybody backed up toward the door, and whoever it was seemed to disappear behind the tree. I kept looking, starting to wonder if she was the conjure woman herself, and if today was the cost of her giving the Klu Klux their comeuppance. But hadn't anything bad happened to any of the white men, while Elvira was dead and Buck had gone off hiding to keep from being lynched.

Maybe she was here because her hex had gone all wrong.

The undertaker's black Buick came up the driveway, passing the grave. Big enough to hold ten people, it drove on past all the wagons, mules, the two Chevrolet pickup trucks, and the few other small Buicks that the nigras own, and parked right at the door.

Jethro, his wife and children, and Willie Jo got out of the car and hurried onto the porch. Like the rest of us when we came in, they stepped in the puddles of water, some running over the tops of their black shoes that had been polished to be like mirrors. They were all dressed up fancy, more'n I'd ever seen.

Today is the first time I've seen Jethro not smiling.

As soon as the family members all got out of the car and started up the stairs, nobody on the porch talked at all. The undertaker man passed out white gloves to some of the men, telling them to go inside. One of the young men had been trying to fix his tie, but couldn't, and another man had to fix it for him—I knew it was cause the coloreds don't have a tie on much, so he'd never had a chance to learn. I'd tried not to stare at them and instead looked down at my shoes, seeing they were as wet as everybody else's, shiny with rain like theirs were shiny with grease and polish. I thought of how Pollock always uses grease off of the wagon wheel to work over his plowing shoes to keep the water out.

When everybody started inside, I tried to kinda hold back, to see if I could spot the conjure woman again, but Lillie Mae hauled me in behind the men, pushed me into a pew, and told me I had to sit still and be quiet. So I sat, looked, listened, and didn't say a word. Molly was up front, next to Jethro.

A man got up to the altar and said to bow our heads, and I did, but tried to peek. As soon as my head tilted up, Lillie Mae poked at me, and I ducked my head real quick. I might be in a colored church, but she was gonna make sure I didn't do anything to make myself go to a white man's hell, but stay obedient to her God, and therefore to mine. So I kept my head down and tried real hard to hear what he prayed. It wasn't that I couldn't hear him, cause he spoke his prayer loud enough I could of heard him if I'd been outside in the rain, even with the thunder starting to roll. But I just couldn't understand much of what he said cause of the chant he put in his voice, making the words roll together and come apart at the wrong places. His voice rose and fell, like a woman calling out at something she can't see in the dark but knows is there. His words were so different from regular talking that I had to really think and listen close to understand. I missed a lot.

When he started to pray the Lord's Prayer he was still talking so fast, I could hardly understand him, but I almost started to pray with him out loud the way we do at my church. I'm glad I waited for somebody else to pray with him, but nobody did, so I kept quiet. After every few words, someone said "Amen," and I could hear Pollock's voice and Big Nate's among all the others. And I could hear the crying in Big Nate's voice. He musta loved Miss Elvira like she'd been his wife, and not just a woman who lived down the road from him. I knew from what Mama told me that these men were the amen corner.

I've tried to write down what I remember, but I know I can't remember all of it real good. I can't begin to put down how it made me feel; it was mournful and joyful both, their voices saying how deep they felt. I knew they loved Elvira cause so many of them had to choke back tears. It's the most special praying I've ever heard prayed. This preacher didn't just speak out a prayer he'd memorized, or read one he'd written down, and he didn't try to make his voice sound special. He just spoke out a prayer from inside himself, from inside his love. All the "amens" told me everybody else loved Elvira too. Never once did an "amen" get said when a "yeah Lawd" was being said. I was glad I didn't have to say it with them, cause I sure couldn't of got it right.

Our father who art in heaven (yeah, Lawd) whose very name is blessed (amen) your good kingdom come and everything you wish for oh Father (yeah Lawd) be it done here on this poor earth (amen) like You have it oh Blessed Father (yeah, Lawd) done in Your good kingdom in the Holy Heaven (yeah Lawd) and Oh Lawd (yeah Lawd) give us today your holy bread of life (amen) and forgive us, oh Lawd, forgive us (yeah Lawd, yeah Lawd) for our sins our terrible sins (amen) like we would like to forgive them that does us harm and oh Lawd (yeah Lawd, yeah Lawd) keep us from the temptations (amen) Oh Lawd (yeah Lawd, yeah Lawd) keep us away from the temptations of sin (amen) and of evil (amen) for yours is the kingdom forever (amen) and the power forever (amen) and the great glory forever (amen) and bless those sick at home who couldn't be here today (yeah, Lawd) and bless those in the hospitals who lie dying (yeah Lawd) and bless those of us who are here today to pray for our dear departed Elvira (yeah Lawd) as she goes on her way to her home with you Oh Lawd (amen) and blessed be your Name oh Lawd, and bless the family of our dear departed Sister (amen) who are here to say good-bye to their mother and their sister and their auntie (amen), so they can know relief from their sorrow and understand that she only sleeps. Oh Lawd (yeah Lawd) blessed be your name. (amen)

Somebody got up and said we were to sing hymn number 488, but there was no book to read from anywhere. I looked at Lillie Mae, and when I reached over and took her sleeve she looked sharp at me and "shushed" me, so I didn't say anything, just stood up with everybody else.

Pollock sat down in the front, off to the left of where the preacher was standing; he shared a bench with some other men—they were the amen corner people, almost hidden by the big churns of crepe myrtle, the limbs standing up almost over their heads when they were sitting down.

The nigras were singing, but I couldn't tell what they were singing, their voices rose and fell, like a chant the Indians might have had for a death chant. The people warmed up the church with all their feelings, and I felt what they felt, a rhythm that made me want to sway with them, to chant with them, to cry and mourn with them. At the same time their song made me want to rejoice, to praise God, and to feel His glory and His greatness. I never felt that humble and at the same time that magnificent in a white folks' church. I could almost feel Buck and Elvira's faith around me, like a cloak warming me up on a cold night, or the sunrise coming up in all kinds of peach colors on a spring morning.

I felt Lillie Mae moving with the sound. Every time her shoulder would sway toward me I would sway a little away from her, and then the lady on the other side of me would sway against me, and I would lean over toward Lillie Mae. I told myself it was so I wouldn't get smuched up between them, but it was really cause I felt the death they felt, the pain they felt, the movement in the chant, the angels dancing a soft gentle dance with their music that raised up my spirits—and must have been right then lifting Elvira's spirit. But at the same time the rhythm was kind of like the conjure woman's drumbeat—it wrapped around me and took over all of me, my thinking, my breathing, everything. It made even my heart beat with its rhythm.

Some of the people cried. Ladies had their nice handkerchiefs out, and one man blew his nose real hard on a red colored handkerchief. But the swaying and rhythm and sound seemed to release their sadness, and when the song ended, the tears seemed to end and the nose blowing stopped. Everyone sat still and silent as the preacher stepped up.

Tall and skinny, with gray hair making a circle around his shining black skull, he wore white robes that reached to the floor, and each side of the front had a big cross, just like the cross on a shield for a knight in a picture in my Ivanhoe book.

He read from the Bible, about a time for everything, about faith and about hope. I thought of how much Buck lived on faith, on hope that life would be better for him and for all the nigras. But the preacher said there isn't enough of the greatest of all things, love.

He talked fast, like my Aunt Kittie, who moved up north, talks every time she comes home. Nobody can understand her for a long time, at least until she has been here for more than a week and gotten her talking slowed down to Georgia speed again. Only his talking was so fast he ran his words together and almost sang his sentences. He talked like he had a lot of learning.

I can't remember whatall he said. Mostly, he talked about hope, love, and sharing love with your family. And a lot of the things everybody talked about on the porch, about how much Elvira did for people. He never talked about hell or about evil in people, like the white preachers always do. He didn't ever say "do what I say, or else," like the white preachers do. He only talked about love and joy, and going home to Jesus.

He ended his preaching the way our preacher does, saying "May the Good Lawd cast his blessing onto you. And may the good Lawd keep you safe, and make His smile fall on you for now and forever. And may the good Lawd put a special blessing on the families of Miss Elvira and let them rejoice in her rising to the Lawd this day. Amen."

I squirmed a little, and Lillie Mae poked me in the ribs and said, "Shush. Don't you be disrespectful." I got still and didn't move anything but my eyes, watching.

Everybody stood up and started humming real soft. Six of the women from the front bench each picked up a flower and started up the aisle in a row. The men in the amen corner rose up together and started up the aisle too. Big Nate stood higher than anybody. At first, only Big Nate sang, but did he ever sing. I didn't have any idea he had such a beautiful voice, like one of those radio singers—deep, filled with love and power and sadness. His voice made me shiver with its depth, as if he were reaching out to God Himself with the plea and prayer in his music. "Swing lo, sweet cha-ri-ot, cummin fer to car-ri me home," he boomed, and everyone else picked up the words, softly at first, the volume rising until the small room swelled with his faith and the promise of God.

Elvira could not have asked for more love than she got today. I could feel their love, their faith, and I know, I just know it for a fact, that at that moment Elvira was standing right up there by God, and they were both watching us all in the little church, and smiling together cause of everybody's love for her.

The pallbearers got on each side of the coffin, picked it up and rested it on their shoulders. Big Nate stayed inside the door and kept on singing, and kept everyone else singing, until the coffin passed out of the wide open doors, into the rain.

It rained like God Himself would cry forever and we were going to have another flood; red mud ran like little creeks across the yard, and when the rest of us followed the coffin outside, the mud squished under our feet, and ran into our shoes. Mama was gonna be mad at me cause that was my only good pair of shoes, and I never was supposed to wear them out in the rain. But when I pulled my foot up like I might be going to pull off my shoe, Lillie Mae yanked at my hand, almost pulling me down, and told me to leave my shoes on for Miss Elvira.

Just as the pallbearers reached the side of the grave, the rain stopped like somebody cut off the faucet. The undertaker had put some logs across the top of the grave for the pallbearers to put the coffin on before it got buried, and by the time they had gotten it off their shoulders and onto the logs, the cloud moved away just long enough for sunlight to wash over us, and everybody looked up.

I looked all around to see if the conjure woman was still close by, and thought I caught a glimpse of something black behind the biggest oak tree on the place. But with all the tree trunks black from the rain, I wasn't sure.

Everybody stood around while the family got right up by the coffin and the preacher read something that I didn't know—I don't think it was from the Bible but from some sort of burying book. The undertaker took a flower from one of the ladies and handed it to Jethro, and he took another one and handed it to Willie Jo. He laid the other flowers on Elvira's coffin.

He told everybody to go home and to be careful, there was trouble going around.

Jethro was the first one of the family to move, and he turned, looking around until he saw me and came straight to me. His eyes glistened with tears he was trying to hold back, and when he got up to me, his voice shook as he said, "Miz Sam, I'se much obliged to yo pappy fer all he dun did fer Ma. You tells him fer me?"

"Sure, Jethro. Sure. But he hadn't done anything special."

"Yessum, he is. He dun paid Mista Marcus dere fer all dis here."

Dad had paid for it all. He wouldn't want it known that he had gone into his own pocket to pay for "all dis here." I said, "Jethro, Dad does what he thinks he oughtta. You know that. I'll tell him what you said. You just take care of Willie Jo, okay?"

He nodded and turned toward his wife and sister, his shoulders slumped into his grief and pain.

Everybody came over to Jethro and to Willie Jo to speak, to say how much they'd miss Elvira too. Lillie Mae and Pollock talked to them both, and then to everybody else before they were ready to go. Molly was standing over by Willie Jo for a long time, and all the colored people talked to her like she was part of Elvira's family. I'm so glad they don't blame her for what all has happened.

While they were talking I tried to kind of wash the mud off my shoes in the big puddles. Finally, Molly came over to Lillie Mae and said she reckoned we better go if we were going to be getting up the road.

When we got on the wagon, Lillie Mae let me take off my shoes, and while the wagon moved along with old Daisy heading down the driveway, Lillie Mae dried them on her petticoat and tucked them up under the wagon seat.

All the while, I looked to see if I could catch sight of the conjure woman, but if that's who it was I saw, she was gone off. I couldn't see any sign of her anywhere.

At the end of the driveway, Lillie Mae didn't turn the wagon toward the house even with Old Daisy trying to go home. We turned up the other way, toward the mill.

There wouldn't be anybody at the mill, with Big Nate at the funeral. The Simpsons don't ever go to the mill except to collect money. You never know when a farmer might drive up, but with the rain, nobody would be hauling a wagon load of corn today.

When we got there Molly just stepped down from the wagon, took the box out from under the wagon seat, went to the end of the dam, and walked into the mist.

She wasn't gone long this time, and Buck slipped out with her, waved to us, and vanished again under the waterfall. He had to be cold even if it is August, cause I was chilly from being wet and just sitting in the wagon with the wind waking up.

I just hope the conjure woman isn't gonna make Buck pay any more for giving those three white men their comeuppance.

August 9, Friday

Dolly had her foal today, just in time to keep me out of the parade. We found it when Michelle rode out on Lady, to ride back to town with me when I took Dolly in to her barn for the night, to be ready for the parade.

"What about tomorrow?" Michelle asked.

"Maybe I can ride Charger."

"You think they'll let you ride that stallion? He's half-wild."

"I'll have to ask Mama. I don't know." I couldn't ask until later this afternoon, though, since she and Dad were both gone to talk with Sis and J.D. about final plans for tomorrow.

We stayed out in the pasture a long time, just sitting up against one of the oak trees to watch the foal butt Dolly as he nursed and then run around her and kick up his hind legs. When I eased toward them, Dolly whinkered and stepped away, so we went home. I'd catch her after the parade and start taming the baby.

Michelle and I were back at the house, upstairs, reading and eating cookies we had sneaked from the boxes full for tomorrow's tea, when I thought I heard somebody yelling outside, toward the driveway. I stepped across the hall to Mama's room to look out on that side of the house, and I saw Rufus Flint walking back and forth in front of the house with a pistol in his hand, yelling for Dad to come on out.

I ducked back down below the window and almost crawled back to my room. Michelle looked up from her book.

"What's the matter with you? Is there somebody there?"

"Be quiet. It's Flint, and he's got a pistol. He's yelling for Dad. I reckon he doesn't know Dad's not here since the truck is sitting in the yard. I hope he doesn't try to come in. None of the doors are locked up."

"I thought you locked 'em now, after that man tried to get in and Buck had to run him off."

"Yeah, but that's if you're here by yourself."

Michelle pulled off her boots and tiptoed across the hall into Mama and Dad's room where she could look down. Flint stood by his car, parked near the cistern but with the engine running and fumes flowing up into the air, and stared at the house.

"I'll find you, you damnyankee bastard. You'll pay! You'll pay like the rest of them for what you did."

Michelle looked at me and frowned, forming the words, "The cemetery?"

All I could do was shrug and halfway nod, "I guess so. Or those two half-grown calves he butchered."

"Look, he's going off. Maybe he won't be back."

He got in the car and drove off. We leaned out the upstairs window until we saw it going down the hill toward the train tracks and heard it bounce over the rails. I hoped he was gone for good.

"C'mon, let's lock up the doors in case he comes back."

"Where're Lillie Mae and the baby?" Michelle asked me as we started down stairs.

I had plumb forgotten them, and we hurried to the dining room where we found Lillie Mae had gone to sleep rocking the baby, and Katie was asleep in her lap, just as quiet as could be. I sure was glad she wasn't squalling when Flint was here.

When Mama and Dad got home they found the house all locked up and the wooden doors closed, even with it so hot we were all sweaty cause the breeze couldn't go through the house. It was late enough we should have opened the windows to let the cooling evening breezes into the house. I thought Mama was gonna be mad at me, but when we told her Flint had been outside with a pistol, she and Dad looked at each other, and they hugged us both and said we'd done the right thing, and where was the baby. Mama went off to see about Lillie Mae and Katie, while Dad went to the back hall where he kept his shotgun and the .22 rifle. He brought both guns out, got some bullets, loaded up the .22, then loaded up the shotgun. He propped up the shotgun in the kitchen by the hall door. He stood the .22 by the door in the living room that goes to the front hall. He checked the load in the pistol and left it on the shelf, and told me not to touch them. They were just in case Flint came back and started something, the way he had when he killed Elvira.

We told Dad about Dolly's colt and the first thing he said was, "You'll get to watch the parade tomorrow. She can't go to town with a day-old baby, Sam."

"But Dad, can't I ride Daisy or Charger? He's pretty tame."

Mama walked in and said, "No, you aren't riding Charger. J. D. may ride him a lot, but he's still half-wild. And he's not gelded. He'll start a fight. And Daisy would go crazy with all of those drums and the marching bands. You know how she is. I'm sorry, Sam, I know how much you've looked forward to the parade. But you'll just have to watch."

For two years, I've waited to be in the parade and now, just my luck, the colt gets born at the wrong time.

Michelle tried to cheer me up, saying she'd be a good enough Confederate flag bearer for us both, and I felt like pouting, but I knew it was what a kid would do. A grownup would just take the disappointment, go watch the parade, and have fun seeing Michelle ride Lady and wear her Confederate uniform. I could let out a Rebel yell when she goes by. From in front of the picture show, I can see them come down the hill from the military school where it'll start and then turn at the corner by the courthouse.

Michelle and Lady had not been gone long when Vicki and Danny drove out. They'd met Michelle on her way home, and she told them about Dolly's foal and about Flint coming to our house. They came to tell us that Flint stomped his way all around Collier Hancock's yard late this afternoon, toting a pistol and yelling for Collier to come outside. Lucky for Collier, he had gone to Macon.

"We'll have to work tomorrow," Danny said. "I have to meet with Rufus about his appeal. I sure will be glad to see him hauled off to prison."

"Let's hope he doesn't run up with Mattie," Mama said. "Sis and J. D. meet with her tomorrow and hope to get finished by parade time. Their divorce goes to Judge Plummer on Monday."

"Rufus is staying in Mattie's house," Danny said. "I should've planned to go there so I could finish up and leave when I want to."

"I just wish somebody else would be willing to take him on," Vicki said. "He scares me now."

"I don't understand why Judge Plummer let him out on bond after he killed Elvira," Mama said.

"That was Phil's doing. He put up his whole farm, all two thousand acres, as bond. The charges are like before, manslaughter. So it's not as if he were accused of murder. But I won't take that case," Danny answered.

As they left, Vicki told me how sorry she was I wasn't going to get to ride Dolly in the parade, and for me to come to their office if I wanted to.

"Ya'll be careful around Flint," Danny said. "You never know with him what he might do."

When I came up to go to bed, I closed the windows, to try to close out the drum, but I couldn't leave them closed. It's too hot. I sprinkled the sheets.

The drum scared me, especially after she vanished like that up at the cemetery. She scared everybody at the church. If she had been trying to help Elvira, the hex sure did turn topsy-turvy.

August 10, Saturday

"Slim caught Roger at the still in the candy factory," Vicki called as she walked into the house without even knocking on the kitchen door.

I nearly dropped the dish I was drying. Slim's been after that likker still ever since Benson cussed him when Slim warned him to close down the one on his farm cause it was so close to his house it was practically in his back yard.

Roger told Slim it wasn't his still, but Slim argued with him.

Everybody in town knows about the still in the candy factory. Slim told me once he'd bust it when he could catch Roger inside. And last night, he did.

Three Federal agents helped him, and now Old Roger is sitting in jail in Macon, waiting for Cou'n Phil to get to his office this morning so he can call Phil to come bail him out.

"I bet he's having a real conniption fit," I said. "Did they bust up everything?"

Vicki just smiled all over herself.

"They sure did. And they poured everything out, so the candy factory's out of business. There won't be any more Ben's Bars. The whole factory's covered with fermenting mash. I can't wait to see Roger's face when he gets back."

"That'll be soon as Phil gets to town, I reckon," Mama said.

"I'm not about to make it any sooner. I'm not going to ride up the road to Phil's to tell him about Roger. Slim has worked too hard for me to be making it easy on him," Vicki said.

Mama smiled. "Me, neither." She turned to me, "And don't you go telling anybody, Little Miss."

"Don't worry, Mama. I don't like either one of them."

"If he had just listened to Slim, he wouldn't be in trouble," Vicki said. "But he wouldn't close down either of his stills, he's so greedy. Now he'll have to sit in the Macon jail. He'll probably miss the parade." Vicki looked like she was gonna dance across the room.

"I bet he won't be our commissioner much longer," I said. "Vicki, you oughtta run against him."

She shook her head, "No. But Danny might. He's said we need three commissioners, not just one. He's making noises about running."

They couldn't stay—Michelle has got to get ready for the parade. I didn't go back to town with them; I'll go in with Mama and Dad later. Molly and I will take some food up to Buck before we go to the parade.

*   *   *

When Molly got to the house, we loaded up biscuits, a fried chicken, sausages, and oranges that Mama bought last night.

The sun warmed on our backs as we pedaled steady along. We talked off and on, and I called at Molly to stop when I saw a snake crawling up a crosstie fence post. I could see it already had its head stuck in the hole where some bluebirds nested, so I went over and pulled the snake out. It had eaten one of the babies, so I took it off aways and turned it aloose. After all, I can't kill a king snake. It does too much good, eating up the rattlers and copperheads, even if it does eat some birds off and on.

We rode on up to the mill. It being Saturday, and the day of the big parade, it'd be closed and wouldn't anybody be around. We saw a lot of people walking towards town and met up with some wagons and a few cars. The white folks waved, yelled and laughed as they walked along. But the nigras got quiet when we pedaled close by and looked at the sack in Molly's bicycle basket, as if they knew where we were going.

When we met his car going toward town, I said, "That's Cou'n Phil."

"Yeah," she said. "I know. But he's got no call to think anything about you and me out on our bikes."

"I hope not," I said and glanced over my shoulder to see if he turned around. I thought he slowed up, but he went on over the hill in front of his dust cloud, and I tried to forget about him. We pedaled past Phil's house, and I looked back a few times, but didn't see any sign of a car. When we got to the top of the hill, almost to the forks where we turned to the mill, I looked back and saw a cloud of dust coming our way. I figured it wouldn't be Phil this far out, beyond his house.

The mill isn't far down the side road from the forks, and when we turned off into the mill driveway, I glanced behind us, and saw two cars go by on the main road. The front one was Phil's but the second one I didn't know, and with it moving in the dust of Phil's car, I couldn't see the driver.

"Molly," I whispered. "Phil just drove by behind us. He musta followed us all the way up here."

Molly stopped her bike, dragging one foot, and I did too.

"Think we better leave?" I asked.

"I dunno," she said. "Maybe we can go on to the mill and wait a few minutes to see what happens. We're okay if he doesn't come down there, and if he does, we can say we're having a picnic before we go to town for the parade."

I nodded, and we pedaled on. At the mill, we leaned our bikes up against one of the oak trees and just sat down on the ground to wait. It seemed like we waited forever, and nothing happened.

"I think we're alright," Molly said and rose. She took the croaker sack of food out of her bicycle basket and started toward the falls while I got to my feet, still a little hesitant about going to Buck just yet. She hadn't gone ten steps when two cars raced down the driveway toward her. I froze by the oak, but Molly was cut off from me by the cars and she ran toward the mill.

Cou'n Phil and Flint didn't bother with pillowcases over their heads. Flint jumped out of his car and grabbed ahold of Molly, and she screamed, "Run, Sam. Run! Get help!"

I tried to get my bicycle turned around, but Phil spotted me right off. I didn't think he could move so fast, but he was practically on top of me before I could straddle it. I pushed it at him and ran into the bushes. He stumbled around the bike to follow me, but Flint called him.

"C'mon back. I need help with this hellcat!"

When I heard him thrashing the bushes and going away from me, I sneaked partway back. Maybe I could do something to help Molly get away. Flint had her by one arm, and was trying to catch her other hand, but she was flailing at his face with it so fast he couldn't catch her. Phil came up behind her, real quiet, and grabbed that free hand, pulled it around and up behind her back so high she screamed and bent over. Flint cackled, turned her other arm aloose, and trotted back to his car.

While Flint was at the car, Phil managed to turn Molly around and grip her arms from the front. The arm he twisted backwards looked almost broken. Flint strolled over with a shotgun in one hand and a riding crop in the other, a smile plastered on his face as he cracked the riding crop with each step.

I looked around for a stick, a rock, anything I could find, and was trying to pull up a rock when Flint took the whip to her. I heaved the rock, but it didn't even come close, and Flint just laughed and stuck her again. Each time he swung the quirt forward or backward, he yelled at her.

"Nigger whore. Nigger whore! Nigger whore! Damn any white girl messing with a nigger. Oughtta kill you, nigger whore."

I scrambled around, still looking for a weapon—I couldn't even turn over the next rock I found. Finally, an oak limb. I ran as hard as I could toward them, holding the stick like a baseball bat. Phil saw me and hollered at Rufus.

"There comes that Lawson bitch. Get her!"

Flint turned toward me, and all I could see was the shotgun, the end of the barrel as big as a canon.

"Run, Sam!" Molly yelled.

I threw the stick at Flint and ran.

I zigzagged across the parking area and dropped down behind Phil's car just as the shotgun went off. Flint pumped another shell in as Phil shouted, "Yell, Molly. Yell so your black nigger lover'll come out here. Yell."

Molly didn't yell again. She cried, and from under the car, I could see blood soaking into the back of her dress. But she didn't yell. If she did, Buck'd hear her over the sound of the waterfall. She kept trying to get away, but Phil was stronger than he looked and he held her, not letting her move away from the quirt. With Flint behind her and Phil in front, she couldn't get away.

But she didn't have to yell to bring Buck out from under the falls. He heard Flint's shotgun, and before the quirt hit her again, Buck splashed out from under the lean-to of the wooden dam, his .22 in his hand.

"Fall down, Molly! Drop! Drop!"

He couldn't shoot with her in the way, and she tried to fall, but Phil jerked her around, his bad arm around her neck, and held her between himself and Buck. She couldn't move.

Flint got behind the two of them.

"Why don't you shoot, you nigger son of a bitch?" Phil laughed. "Scared you'll hit your whore?"

Buck stopped, brought up the rifle, and took aim. I thought he was going to shoot Molly, was willing to kill her to keep them from hurting her any more. She twisted against Phil and tried to pull his arm from against her neck, but he just pulled tighter and tighter until her face got real red, like she couldn't breathe. He hissed at Flint, "Kill the son of a bitch!"

Flint laid the shotgun on her shoulder and shot, the noise busting the morning, and then Flint slammed the shotgun into her head.

Buck fell, his arms out to the side, almost like he was flying backwards. Molly crumpled to the ground.

I screamed.

Flint yelled, "Find that damn Lawson girl and kill her!"

I ran off into the bushes.

A little ways into the woods, I could tell there wasn't but one person behind me, and I got real quiet, listening. At first, I didn't know which one was after me, but at least he finally stopped thrashing around. It was Phil—he called, "I can't find the bitch."

"Well, c'mon. I dragged the nigger into the creek so he'll float right down to the river and be gone for good. Let's just get out-a here."

As Phil blundered his way back to the mill, I followed, but way back behind him, so if he turned around he couldn't see me. I could smell him from where he'd been just in front of me, the smell of sweat and fear and hate and something I couldn't place, something I smelled only one time before, that afternoon I saw Rufus and Larry up there in the hotel room. It smelled a little like a rank boar hog.

Both cars were driving off by the time I got to the edge of the woods. Molly lay out in the parking lot, blood trickling down the side of her face.

I couldn't stop my crying as I ran over to her. I didn't know much about what to do. I knew Roy Rogers always wrapped a handkerchief around a gunshot, so I took off my neckerchief and rolled it with the sweaty side out, and found it would just reach around Molly's head. I had to pull her head up onto my lap to wrap the kerchief over the cut. I eased her head back down onto the ground, tore a piece of my shirt tail off, and ran over to get some water from the creek.

There was blood everywhere, drag marks in the dirt going right to the creek. I stepped off to the side of the drag mark and went to the water's edge, but there was no sign of Buck. Everything looked like Flint had really killed him and dragged him to the creek. I sat down hard and tried not to cry. Molly needed help.

I wet the rag, went back to Molly and let some of the water dribble over her face. She didn't wake up like the people do in the movies, so I wiped her face with the wet cloth and talked to her, all the while hoping she would wake up. They must have thought they had killed Molly. They knew they had killed Buck.

My hands trembled as I wiped Molly's face.

"Sam?" Molly whispered. She reached one hand out to my arm.

"Molly! Oh, thank goodness you're awake."

"Have they gone?"

"Yes." How could I tell her about Buck getting shot?

"Buck? They shot him, didn't they?"

"Yes. I heard Flint say he dragged him to the creek. I found where he—where— Molly, I think he's dead."

"He can't be, Sam. He can't be." She tried to sit up, holding onto my arm, but groaned, eased back down, put her good hand to her head, and closed her eyes. "Go get Jethro. We'll find Buck."

"It's Saturday, Molly. Remember the parade. Everybody's in town. Even Jethro was taking his children in to see the parade. There's nobody. Maybe I can find Mama and Dad. Maybe we can get Pollock to help us. He and Lillie Mae weren't going to town today."

"I'll start looking," she said. "You go on." But she couldn't sit up.

"You can't do any looking if you can't even stand up," I said. "And look at that arm Phil twisted up your back. It looks broken."

Molly tried to lift the arm and slowly it came up from the ground. But it musta hurt something fierce cause she groaned as she moved it. "I'll get up, Sam," she insisted. "Please, just get somebody else here to help me find Buck."

"I'll help you look," I said. "But you need a doctor, Molly."

She rolled over onto her good side and slowly pushed herself up until she was sitting, but real slumped over. "See? I can get up. Now go on."

"Okay, I'll go. But you need some looking after, Molly. I'll get you somebody as quick as I can. But I'll have to go all the way to the house at least. Maybe even to town."

I ran over to the bicycles and started off. At the edge of the parking area, I looked back, waved once at Molly who was still sitting where I'd left her, and I went on down the road as fast as I could pedal, hoping to get some help before I had to go all the way to the house. Mama might have already gone off to town for the parade and I didn't think I was gonna find anybody until I got all the way to town.

Nobody was anywhere. I stopped at every house on the way to yell, but no one answered. Everybody was already in town.

* * *

I didn't figure on stopping at Cou'n Phil's cause he'd probably be there, but just before I came up to his driveway I met up with the nigra boy who sweeps up at the B & B Drug Store. He waved me down, and I slid one foot off the bicycle pedal and dragged it in the dirt as I stopped.

"Miz Sam, whereabouts do de judge lib?"

"What you want him for, Jorja? Don't you know he's in the Klu Klux?"

His eyes widened, and he looked all around us, across the fields where the cattle seemed like there was nothing wrong in the world, the way they grabbed at the grass, their heads bobbing as if they were just nodding "yes" to the day.

"Well? Whatcha need him for? I got to be getting some help for up the road."

"Mr. Benson done called down to de drug sto'. He in jail over in Macon. Mr. Slim dun cotched him making likker and gots him in jail. He need Mista Judge to cum git him out-a jail."

I thought if Cou'n Phil were home and went to town with Jorja, maybe, just maybe, Martha might help me get to town. I know they have a truck as well as the car Phil drives around in. I could maybe take the truck myself.

"That's his house up the driveway you just went by, but he's mad at me. You go on, and I'll come along behind you to be sure everything's okay and you find him."

Jorja looked at me like he wasn't about to go up there alone, what with the judge being in the Klu Klux, and he shifted from one foot to the other a couple of times. "You go on," I said. "He's not gonna bother you. He ain't mad at you. It's me he dun't like." I wasn't about to go up that driveway where Phil might come after me with a shotgun.

"Iffen he be the Klu Klux, he might kill me. Lak dem men killed dem niggers up the road a little time back."

All I could think of was that no white man would ever pay for killing those four nigras up near Athens, so since Phil had already killed Buck, why wouldn't he kill Jorja? But I said, "He's got no call to be mad at you. I'll be right behind you." I pushed the bike off into the ditch and laid it down so if Phil were up there at the house he wouldn't see it when he came down the driveway. "C'mon. I'll go up there with you."

I shoulda been going on to town, but maybe, just maybe, I thought Phil might leave and Martha would summon up the nerve to drive me to town in the truck if Phil took their car.

The driveway curved just enough that I didn't see Flint's car until we were almost at the house. It was parked over by the cabin that Phil's and Mama's great-great-granddaddy built way back in the early 1800s. His daughter, Sunny, told me on the bus that he would go out there sometimes and sit by himself or with Flint or maybe Larry for a long time, just the two of them. Sunny told me nobody, but nobody, was to go out there when her daddy had company, unless he invited them. There's no water out there, and their gas generator doesn't have a line to the cabin, so at night all they have there is a kerosene lantern, like Aunt Tessie.

"You go on to the door," I told Jorja, and gave him a little shove in the back. As he walked toward the kitchen door, I eased backward into a hedge so I couldn't be seen if Phil came to his knock.

Martha answered, with Sunny looking over her shoulder. "Well?" she said.

"Miz Judge, I'se Jorja. I wuks fer Mista Benson at de B & B. He dun sent me from Macon——." He paused, as if he were trying to sort out what he was saying. His voice trembled he was so scared.

"You came here from Macon?" Martha asked.

"Noam. I dun come frum Stanleyville. Mr. Benson, he be in Macon. He in de jail over dere and asked me to cum git de Judge to go over to Macon to git him out-a de jail."

I think Martha smiled just a little. "You wait here, Jorja. I heard him come in a little while ago. I'll let him know. Maybe he'll drop you off at the Macon road on his way. Save you some walking."

"Dat be aright, M'am. I'se used to de walking." Jorja started to back up, too scared to get in the car with Phil.

Martha came down the steps, with Sunny right behind her, and they started toward the cabin. Jorja backed up some more, turned and began running down the driveway. He didn't even look my way as he darted past. I didn't blame him—all I wanted to do was run, too, but I knew Martha would get me some help just as soon as Phil left for Macon.

I could see the front door to the cabin, and watched Martha open it and step inside. She screamed, a belly-twisting howl like a woman being eaten alive by a painter.

The words came while the scream still rattled inside my head. "You bastard! You goddammed bastard! How could you! I'm leaving and I'm taking Sunny. You'll never see either of us again! You bastards. Both of you! You'll rot in hell."

She turned from the cabin, saw Sunny, and yelled at her. "Sunny, get in the house. Right now. Get some clothes together. We've leaving that bastard. Move!" Martha stalked her way toward the house.

Sunny's eyes widened with fear but she obeyed, ran for the house, and disappeared inside the kitchen door as Phil came charging out of the cabin to run after Martha, who had not looked back once and didn't see him coming.

I don't know how he ran, his pants half off, one hand trying to pull them up and the other hand holding an ax handle. Just before he reached Martha he yelled, "You're damned if you think you're taking Sunny!" He swung the ax handle.

Martha jumped as he yelled, and the handle missed her when it swished downward. Phil almost fell flat on his face as his weight behind the handle pulled him forward and sideways. He was running again before Martha could get away. When he grabbed her arm and jerked her backwards, his pants fell. He shoved her to the ground.

Blood showed rusty red on his white shirt; some was splattered over his whiskers. His hair flew all over his head like somebody had pushed it to make it stand up. Martha seemed to see the blood for the first time as she lay on the ground looking up, for one hand went to her mouth as if to hold in her screams while the other rose up toward Phil, palm up, to hold back the ax handle.

For a moment everything got real quiet as Phil fastened up his britches, but the darkness of the cabin belched out the bloody-white form of Flint, and when Martha saw him across the yard, she screamed again. Phil looked over his shoulder toward Flint, who yelled, "You better take care of your problems. I'm going to town."

Flint laughed.

I backed even deeper into the hedge, but couldn't take my eyes off what was going on in the yard. Martha was trying to crawl backwards away from Phil while he and Flint grinned funny at each other and talked a few words that I couldn't hear. Martha was trying to scramble up, but Flint pointed, "Your bitch is getting away."

When Phil turned toward Martha, Flint strolled, without any apparent concern, toward his car, pulled on his coat and buttoned it closed over his bloody shirt. He checked his tie, reached inside the front seat for his hat, which he put on carefully, tugging it just right over his left eye, and he got in and drove right by me without looking my direction.

Martha screamed, "No, Phil!" She rolled away as the ax handle came down, but it smashed into her arm.

Phil raised the handle again, but as it went over his head, Sunny yelled, "Daddy! No!" and ran toward him.

He spun in her direction, clutching the handle and pulling it even farther over his shoulder as she approached.

"Don't you dare tell me what to do!"

Sunny dodged away and tore off toward the house, and Phil took off after her, screaming, "Get back here! You're not going off, you hear me, young lady?"

As the back door slammed behind Sunny, Martha struggled to her feet. "Phil! Leave her alone."

Phil stalked toward her as Martha backed away, one arm dangling. She ran to the other side of the pyracantha bush, away from him. Twice as he tried to circle the bush, he slammed the handle into it. Suddenly he dashed toward her, the handle swinging in front of him. As scared as she was, Martha wasn't faster, and he managed to hit her in the side of the face when she looked over her shoulder as she headed for the kitchen door.

Martha fell, hitting her face on the steps, but managed to push herself up just a little.

Sunny stepped out, yelling, "No, Daddy!" She held a shotgun, pointed over her mama's head right at Phil.

Surprised, Phil stopped. But only for a second. "You little bitch, you don't know anything about guns. It's not even loaded." He raised the handle and stomped toward Martha again.

The shotgun blast caught him in the chest. He fell backwards. The ax handle clattered onto the bottom step.

Martha screamed.

I yelled.

The two mules brayed.

The cows jumped up and ran off.

I tore off through the brush and across the pasture to the road and my bicycle and headed for help.

I pedaled as fast as I could toward the house, but when I got there, wasn't anybody home except Lillie Mae, Katie, and Pollock. I asked him to go to the mill to see about Molly.

"Her arm's broke, and I think Buck's dead."

"Lawdy, lawdy," Lillie Mae muttered. "I best git some towels so's you kin fix up her broke arm." She scurried off.

"Take one of the horses," I said, but he shook his head.

"I kin git there a heap faster through the woods, Missy. I ain't wanting on de road what wid the Klu Klux out."

He took the towels—our best company towels—from Lillie Mae, got his rifle off the back porch, and was trotting off as I got on my bicycle.

I headed for Vicki's office since it was closer than my cousin's house where Mama and Dad might be.

FLINT

Flint giggled as he rolled down Phil's driveway. Time to take care of everybody else. All the men who tried to hide from him yesterday.

I have to get these nasty clothes off before I go to town.

Bitch Mattie thought she would get me out of the house. Hah! I scared her and all her clothes out. And now it's all mine. He headed home. The closer he got to town, the more people seemed to be headed the same way—walking, in wagons and in cars.

They're going to see the parade. I'll give them a parade to see. The good Judge Plummer can just lead it right down to hell.

He parked in his driveway and entered the two-story, nine-room house where he had lived for twenty years. Upstairs, in his bedroom, he glanced overhead, at the sheet of lead that lay over the four posters of his bed. Still there. He stepped to the left-hand corner of the room, picked up the 30-30 rifle and checked its load. He then checked the 12 gauge pump shotgun leaning beside the rifle. Both loaded.

He repeated the procedure in each corner. He knelt beside the four-poster, double bed and touched the edge of the sheet of lead that lined the floor beneath the bed. It matched the overhead sheet. Nobody could kill him with X-rays while he slept.

Good. Nobody's been here. I'm still safe. At least here.

So far, though, can't find anybody to check my urine to see if somebody's slipping me arsenic. Napoleon died from arsenic, a little at a time. Maybe tomorrow I can find out. Take some of it over to Macon to that new hospital. I'll get somebody there to check it. If I can find anybody who's honest.

He stripped off his dirty clothes and headed for the bathtub, determined to be as clean as always when he went out in public.

Moments later, smelling like soap, he looked over his best black suit for any smudges. *It better be ready since it just came in from the cleaners yesterday.* He began dressing. White boxers that had been ironed. A starched white shirt and black tie. The suit. He sat in a gold-upholstered Queen Anne's chair to put on his shoes; he looked them over for any specks of dirt. He could see himself in the shine on the toes. *Good enough.*

He took his briefcase from the closet and three pistols and two boxes of cartridges from his dresser. Perched on the Queen Anne's chair again, he loaded each pistol, clicked the safety on for each, and stowed them in the briefcase.

Time to go start my parade.

Flint headed for his grocery, where he parked his car and walked two spaces over to Miss Chapman's. She had left the key in the ignition, as usual, because her severe arthritis gave her so much trouble to insert it. Nobody would bother her car since she worked for him and everybody was scared he'd go after them, or have Sims take care of them.

He giggled. *Her car's so old nobody else would want it, even it is going to be in the parade.*

He drove toward the courthouse. Already some of the stupid volunteers were trying to block cars off the parade route. He didn't slow down—they would get out of his way or get run over. At the corner, he turned right. Plenty of parking space there. Not many people going in the Piggly-Wiggly. They didn't want to have to deal with groceries while the parade was going on.

He parked, shifted into neutral and reached for the switch.

No, I'll leave it running. I might want to get out of here in a hurry.

He stepped out and leaned into the back seat. He opened the briefcase, took out one pistol, stood, and turned to face the courthouse. The upstairs window, to Judge Plummer's office, was wide open and the fan moving.

Old bastard's there. He'll get his comeuppance now for thinking he can send me to jail. I'll check on Stewart. If he's available for the parade, I'll visit the judge, and come back to Stewart and then go tend to Murphy.

Wonder if the judge's got his clothes on. Be fun to let him head the parade buck nigger naked like he is under that robe.

He strode to the corner, crossed with the light, and as he approached the courthouse, one of the military school boys grabbed his arm.

"Sorry sir, but you have to go to the jail. You don't have any whiskers."

Flint jerked his arm free and shoved the boy's chest so hard the boy stumbled back and fell.

"Don't you touch me, you hear?" He pointed the pistol at the boy and said, "Bang, bang, you're dead, soljer boy."

The cadet shivered, his face paled. He did not move.

Two women in long dresses and bonnets tied under their chins watched from the sidewalk as Flint turned and stomped toward the back of the courthouse.

"I wonder what Mr. Flint's doing in the pageant tonight?" one asked.

"I do too. I didn't know he was supposed to be in the pageant. He sure did scare that cadet. Do you know the boy?"

"Yes. He's my cousin's son. I need to see if he's all right."

They approached the youth. "Jesse, you alright, son?"

"Aunt Emma. That's a real gun he's got. It's not a play one. I could see the bullets in it."

"Oh, Jesse, you're just imagining things. It can't be real or he'd never point it at anybody. Let's get you dusted off. You need to head up to school to get in the parade, don't you?"

Flint reached the back door and found it closed, but not locked. County offices had to be open on Saturday morning since they closed on Wednesday afternoons. He sashayed down the hallway, his shoes clipping on the tile floor. At the clerk's office, he pushed open the door and stopped on the threshold. Steve Stewart looked up from the back of the room, nodded, and went into his office. Two men Flint did not know went in behind Stewart and the door closed. Three women worked at desks between the counter and Stewart's office.

"Can I help you, Mr. Flint?" one of the women said; she stood and came toward the counter.

"I'll be back," His voice dripped with anger. He scowled, pointed the pistol at the ceiling and waved it.

The woman backed away, fear flooding her face.

He left. At the courthouse door, he pushed it wide and kicked the door stop—a triangle-shaped piece of wood—under it to jam it open.

He headed for Murphy.

SAMANTHA

I had gotten to the courthouse when I saw Miss Chapman's car. The motor was running, the front door was open, and exhaust made a fog over the car. I dragged my foot down and stopped.

Her car's one of those real old square-topped Chevrolets with four doors, big square windows, and real narrow tires like wagon wheels. It's the oldest car in town, and she never lets anyone else drive it. Not even her sister the school teacher cause she can't remember anything even if she is a teacher—she pushes her eyeglasses up over her forehead, and then can't find them, so she goes from classroom to classroom to ask if anyone has seen her eyeglasses. I reckon Miss Chapman figures her sister's just apt to forget what she's doing and has got no business driving a car.

All kinds of flags tied on the car flapped in the wind: a Confederate battle flag; a Spanish flag cause they think DeSoto might have gone down our river; a French flag for when Lafayette came through on his way to Milledgeville; the Georgia flag; a flag for when we were under the British; and the flag for the United States. I knew the car wasn't supposed to be over here by the grocery store—it should be in line for the parade—and Miss Chapman should be driving.

Howcome it was parked here? I bet Miss Chapman was having a hizzy fit over it being gone.

Unless it was Flint.

It was. He came from around the courthouse to the car, where he leaned in and pulled out a briefcase. It looked like Uncle Morris's doctor bag, with a wide bottom and narrow top and made out of black leather. I'd never seen it before.

He was all dressed up in clean clothes. He had his hat pulled down low, but he couldn't hide who he was. Seeing him scared me. I dropped my bike and hid by one of the oak trees in front of the courthouse.

Howcome Flint didn't turn it off? Or close the driver's door? When the wind dropped, that cloud of exhaust wrapped itself around the car like the blanket Lillie Mae used to wrap up Katie when it was cold last winter. As stinky as it had to be, Flint didn't once try to wave it away from his face. He didn't stand there even a minute, but set out like he knew where he was going.

He held the briefcase in his left hand and something else in his right hand that I couldn't see good.

FLINT

Flint scurried along the sidewalk, his shoes clicking and drawing attention.

"Hey, Mr. Flint," someone said. "who you gonna play in the pageant? You gonna shoot somebody?"

Flint suppressed a grin and waved the pistol into the air, muzzle up, as if in greeting. *They'll learn it's not just a play, it's for real. Real for Mr. Smart Murphy and the rest of them. I'll go to Murphy's office first. He and that bitch Vicki can lead my parade. It's farther down the hall. Then get Mr. Jefferson Davis, president of the Confederacy he thinks.*

SAMANTHA

Even though it's brinjin hot, Flint had on his coat and a black tie, like Dad always wears in his classroom, even when it's so hot he sweats right through his coat. I thought about the slaughter case, and wondered if he were meeting with Danny.

He'd shaved off his beard, and where it had been his face looked almost flour white. He had the neatness about him that he never shows except on Sunday at church.

When he went on down the street around the corner, I had to hurry up to be sure he was going into his furniture store. But as I got around the corner, he disappeared behind the picture show ticket booth, where the stairs go up to all the lawyers' offices.

I tip-toed behind him up the stairs. I didn't want him to hear me. But I needed to see Vicki, to get her to find Slim to help Molly.

The heat got worse as I went up, and so did the smell of sweat, dirty people, and tobacco smoke.

Sis and Vicki were gonna work all morning to get ready for Monday's court. They'd watch the parade from their offices. One of them could get help for Molly, or at least they'd know where I could find Dad.

At the top landing, I peeked around the corner, but I couldn't see much except darkness after coming in from the sun. The only light in the hall comes in through the windows on the back or from offices if the doors are open; but most doors were closed, so it was twilight dark. Finally I saw Flint near the little jut-off that went to the bathrooms just a little way down the hall, and about that time Vicki poked her head out of Phil's office and looked down the hall away from me.

"Larry, it's only Flint going down the hall," she said over her shoulder.

I started to move away from the shadows of the water hose, to go into the office, when I heard a hoarse whisper, "Hush! Don't let him hear you!"

The fear in the voice was enough to make me freeze against the wall. "What the hell's the matter with you, Larry?" Vicki asked. "You've got no reason to be scared of Flint, have you? I thought you were friends."

Larry musta come to watch the parade with Phil. He said, "We are,

Vicki. But he's been real strange the last couple of days. He's angry about having all those court hearings next week."

Again I took a step forward, but Flint was knocking at a door. I jumped back into the shadows. Nobody opened the door. He looked back my way, but I pushed myself into the shadows in the corner by Phil's door, where the big fire hose was wrapped up, hanging on the wall, so even my face had something to be a part of. He couldn't see me.

He slammed open the next one, blamming it against something, and Vicki said, "Somebody's gone in Danny's office and hit that copy machine. I've got to find a better place for it cause everybody hits it when they open the door."

FLINT

Flint didn't bother to nod or tip his hat at the lady in the ticket booth but headed up the stairs for Danny Murphy's office. The tapping of his shoe on the steps preceded him up the stairs and into the hall.

He didn't pause at Phil's office but continued down the hall.

Three steps beyond, he heard Vicki in Phil's office say, "Larry, it's only Flint going down the hall," and he smiled.

She won't be saying "only Flint" after today. I'll give Larry time to get out and I'll stop by and see her later. After I go see that s.o.b. Mr. Hot Shot Jefferson Davis Stanley. Thinks he owns the town cause of his great something granddaddy. I'll show him he can't cross me.

He swung his briefcase and skipped along the hallway, delighted as a child approaching a birthday cake.

I should have done this a long time ago. I know Danny bribed the jury to find me guilty. No white jury ever finds a white man guilty of shooting a nigger. He and Stanley. Oh, Danny boy, the pipes are going to call you."

He paused outside the prosecutor's office, but the door was closed. He tried the knob and realized the door was locked. He heard voices inside. He banged on the door. "Hey, it's Rufus. Open the door."

The voices hushed.

I'll tend to him later. He must have heard I was out to his house yesterday. Well, Danny boy's in his office. His woman's in the building so he's in.

He stopped a few feet before reaching Danny's office door. It was half-open and light drifted into the hallway. Flint set his briefcase on the floor, put his right hand, holding the weapon, behind his back, slammed the office door open and stepped inside.

The door hit the copy machine and the sound echoed down the hall.

The outer office was empty. Flint scooted to the door to Danny's private office.

Danny, sitting at his desk, jerked his head up and stared at Flint. "Did we have an appointment?"

"Yes indeed-ee, we do. I just didn't get it done when you sicced that jury on me. You bastard."

Flint pulled his hand from behind his back and leveled the pistol at Danny. Danny grabbed the handle to his right-hand desk drawer, but before he could pull it open, Flint fired. And fired again and again.

"Son of a bitch."

Flint turned, stepped out the door, picked up his briefcase and hurried back down the hall with the pistol still in his hand.

SAMANTHA

I heard another, much louder "blam." Another "blam," and then another. Somebody was shooting.

But Vicki said, "Sounds like Collier's playing with that Revolutionary war musket again." Even I knew what she was talking about—it was the one he'd inherited from his grandpa, that he'd put some gunpowder in like he is supposed to do in the pageant and pretend to shoot somebody, and when the gunpowder goes off it sounds like a real gun even if it's not loaded. But after the third "blam" I knew there were too many, too close together, for Collier to be shooting off a muzzle-loading musket.

Too scared to move, I stayed shrunk back into the nook in the hall.

Flint ran out of Danny's office and scooted down the hall, straight toward me. He pushed against two more doors—and then reached J. D.'s office, where light flooded the hall from the open door. Flint stopped, shoved something into the briefcase, and pulled out something else.

A pistol.

FLINT

Flint stopped, replaced the .38 in his briefcase and pulled out a .45 semiautomatic.

That'll take care of the soljer boy better'n the .38.

He left the briefcase outside J. D.'s office and entered with the pistol behind his back.

"Good morning, Mr. Flint. What can I do for you?" Stanley's wife greeted him from her desk. J. D. stood beside her, reading something on her desk.

Now I can kill two with one stop. This is bettern'n getting the professor. Get her instead.

Flint pulled his hand around and began shooting—first at her, twice.

J.D. tried to pull her to the floor but too late. Flint hit him in the shoulder, but J. D. dropped to the floor and fumbled with one of the desk drawers.

Flint came around the desk as J. D. rose with a pistol. Flint shot twice.

J. D. fell. Flint scooted for the door.

J. D. pulled himself up by using the desk chair for a handhold and staggered to the office door. Flint was bent over his briefcase. J. D. leaned against the door jamb.

"Flint!" J. D. shouted.

Flint turned.

J. D. raised his pistol with both hands and shot once.

As he slid down the wall dying, J. D. thought Flint's finally dead.

SAMANTHA

Flint shot.

"No!" I screamed.

He shot more times than I could count and ran back in the hall. He looked up my way—he musta heard me yell. I was out from behind the hose and had started to go down the hall when Flint pointed the pistol toward me. I heard it click. He threw it away, reached into his big satchel, and pulled out another pistol.

J.D. stumbled out of his door, leaned his back on the wall, and slid down till he sat on the floor.

I backed all the way into the corner again. Flint raised the pistol toward me.

J. D. lifted his arms up, both hands gripping his pistol. He shouted "Flint!" And shot.

Flint's head blew up to the ceiling like the blood from that cow the train hit when they cut her throat and blood pumped everywhere.

I heaved up breakfast.

Everything went quiet, and in the quiet the smoke from the shooting drifted down the hall. Vicki ran out of Phil's office, but Larry grabbed at her, trying to stop her, and she was trying to just get down to her own office.

"Let me go, Larry, let me go!"

"No, Vicki, no. He'll shoot you too."

Then they saw me, and Vicki pushed Larry toward me. "See about Sam," and she tore off down the hall.

Larry grabbed my arm. "Get out, Sam. Get out of here while you can. Rufus must have gone crazy. He'll be here next." He hadn't seen Rufus fall with his head blown off.

I shook so hard I couldn't even think of trying to get aloose.

Danny come out of the door to his office, held onto the doorframe, swayed. He dropped to the floor just as Vicki reached him. She knelt down, and blood showered her as it erupted from Danny's mouth.

Collier Hancock slammed out of his office with a man right behind him. Collier reached Danny at the same time Vicki did, and Collier stopped, pointed back to his office, yelled, "Call the police."

The man ran back into the office as Collier bent down over Danny for a second. He shook his head and ran down the hall toward J.D.

I heard the man on the phone yelling about everybody got shot.

"Danny! Danny! Speak to me!" Vicki shook with sobs.

The man came out of Collier's office and said the police were coming with doctors. He bent down to Vicki. "I told them to find Slim."

He tried to help her up, but she said, "He's dead. He's dead, and he won't turn me aloose."

Collier ran over and knelt down by her; I could see his shoulders moving as he pried her hand out of Danny's.

When she stood up, even though I was down the hall, I could see she had blood all over her front. She was crying, her face buried in her hands, her whole body shaking. Collier ran back toward J. D.'s office and went inside.

I tried to go to Sis, but Larry kept on pulling me back, pulling me toward the stairs, trying to force me down the stairs.

"No. Sis's down there too. I gotta go."

But he held on to me real tight. "I know, Sam. They'll look after her. You stay with me."

He dragged me down the stairs, to the outside, and across the street to the corner. He pushed his handkerchief into my hand and said, "Here, wipe your face."

Cars from the sheriff and the police came from every which way, with their red lights flashing and their sirens so loud they hurt my ears; they parked all over the street, and one even ran halfway up on the sidewalk before it stopped.

The officers didn't even bother to close car doors—they jumped out and ran up the steps, their guns in their hands.

More sirens split the air as cars careened around the corner. Highway patrol officers, here for the parade, jumped out and ran up the steps. One policeman, pistol in hand, stood by Miss Chapman's car— the driver's door was still open, the motor was still running. Smoke from the tail pipe still smelled up the whole street.

Store owners and clerks followed customers onto the street, stopped, stared, asked questions that no one seemed to be able to answer.

I couldn't speak. I clutched Larry's hand. Worry chewed at my stomach. I shook so much inside I couldn't tell if it was my hand or Larry's shaking the most.

I'd never get back upstairs, even if I could get away from Larry—a deputy and a policeman stood at the steps behind the ticket booth, and I'd never get by the officers cause they both know me, as well as Sis and Mama and Dad. One of them is the one who said "ess-oh-bee" is something bad and not to ever say it.

Nobody paid me and Larry any mind as long as we stood against the corner across the street. I was trying hard not to cry and to see what was happening, just wanting to see Sis come walking out of there. We could see both ways down the street and see who came out of the building.

Slim's car screamed up, stopped, and Slim jumped out, looking pale, like he'd been throwing up and was sweating from being cold with a fever. He left his car in the middle of the street, the door open, but it kept moving like it was still in gear. I told Larry I had to stop the car, but he wouldn't turn me aloose even when we ran over, until I jumped in and turned the key off. The car sputtered, coughed and stopped, and I found the hand brake and pulled it like I'd seen Dad do.

Larry and I stood there by Slim's car in the middle of the street and waited while the noise from upstairs fell to silence. A sound like a swarm of bees swelled up as all the people stirred, whispered and moved.

I turned to Larry. "Flint and Cou'n Phil killed Buck this morning, Larry. We got to get somebody besides Pollock out to the mill to help Molly. They beat up on her, too."

I leaned into his chest. "I'm so scared for Sis." A sob erupted from me, and Larry's arms folded behind me as he pulled me close. I stammered out, "Phil's dead, too."

Larry stiffened against me for a second and I felt him shudder. A sob tried to erupt from him, but he managed to hold it down. He leaned his head forward to rest on my shoulder. We clutched each other, and suddenly the quiet blared with drums, trumpets and bugles.

The parade started.

I leaned away from Larry to look toward the military school, and here came the cadet band, the drums blamming, the girls from our high school throwing up batons and stepping high in their white boots and their short skirts, with the sun glistening all over the spangles on the uniforms, with flags flying. Right behind the girls, and leading the band, the drill team made a lot of noise, throwing their rifles from shoulder to shoulder, thunking their guns onto the pavement and back onto their shoulders.

Cars honked and people yelled as the parade approached.

In spite of the noise coming toward us, I heard more loud voices from the open windows overhead, but couldn't understand anything that was being said.

People kept coming out of stores to see the parade and to find out what had happened. They milled over the sidewalks and into middle of the street. Children ran here and yonder, mostly up toward the parade so they could march with the band.

The ambulance that is really the hearse from the funeral home came up, and a policeman pointed it away. Policemen brought somebody down on a stretcher all covered with a sheet, as a pickup pulled up. They put the stretcher in the truck while the hearse backed up, turned around, and went down the side street.

When the band got up to cars blocking most of the street, the cadet officer made the band shrink up and move over to the side of the street to get by. Right behind them came the Confederate soldiers with Michelle in the lead carrying the flag.

"Let go!" I told Larry, and when he saw it was Michelle, he turned my hand aloose, and I ran out into the street, yelling to her to stop.

She pulled Lady up, but Lady was still trying to high-step, prancing right there while Michelle tried to handle all four reins with just one hand. I grabbed Lady's bridle and pulled her to a stop.

"Danny's been shot. Vicki's okay, but Danny's hurt bad. Flint shot Sis too. And I think J.D.'s dead."

She turned, handed the flag to our friend Pat who was beside her, and reined Lady out of the parade. Nobody else stopped. The parade kept on down Hall Street and turned onto Main.

Policemen brought two more stretchers down with bloody sheets over them, and loaded them up into another pickup, and slammed the tailgate. A policeman stepped over the tailgate, leaned both hands on the cab roof, and the truck pulled off. The hearse had long gone.

Slim and Vicki appeared from behind the ticket booth. Michelle dropped Lady's reins, and we ran to Vicki. She took one look at Michelle and me, then busted out crying, that deep shaking crying that comes out from way down inside, and turned her face into Slim's shoulder.

Michelle and I stood there, not knowing what to do. But after what seemed forever, Vicki managed to swallow down some of her crying and turned to Michelle and me, pulled us up against her and squeezed me so hard she almost made me hurt. "Oh, baby, what'll we do? What'll we do?"

"What—is Sis?" I managed to say into her bosom.

Vicki couldn't answer, but Slim did. "Sis's hurt. Bad, I'm afraid, and J. D.'s dead. Danny's dead. Where're Professor and Laura?"

"I don't know. I was hoping you'd know. I don't know. Where's Sis? Is she still upstairs?"

"They took her down the other stairs, the private ones, that go into the alley behind the Piggly Wiggly," he said.

"Will she be okay?"

"We don't know," Slim said. "She ought to be at the Clinic by now. We've got to find your mama."

Vicki pulled herself back from her crying and looked up at Slim, "I can't go home until we find Laura."

The parade kept coming, the sidewalks stirred with more and more people—people watching the parade, people dressed in their farm clothes, women in long skirts like back in the 1700's, bearded men I'd never seen before, everybody trying to see the parade and what was going on in front of the picture show. I wondered where Mama would be in the crowd.

Slim told Vicki, "You need to be with Laura as much as she needs you. But you have to go home and get cleaned up. You don't want Laura to see you like this. She'll be more upset." He turned, "Hey, Johnny," he called to Deputy Warren. "I'm taking Vicki to the house to get changed and bring her over to the Clinic. Will you be okay, Sam? Michelle, stay with her. Johnny, help them find Professor Lawson."

Vicki reached over to Michelle, and said, "Sweetheart, stay with Sam. Help her. I'll be okay."

Slim led her to his car and in seconds, he had the red light turning, and the deputy stopped the parade long enough for Slim to get his car off the sidewalk and onto the street.

Michelle and I didn't wait for Deputy Warren, but got on Lady and managed to get through the people, onto the edge of the street, where we went against the parade. The deputy crossed the street between two floats and pushed his way through the people on the other sidewalk.

People, noise, and running children filled the streets and sidewalks. We checked both sides of Hall Street, almost all the way up to the school, and finally I saw my Dad's red head. Michelle kicked Lady, and somehow the mare found her way through the crowd to Mama and Dad.

They took one look at the blood on our fronts from hugging Vicki, and Mama got real pale. I was saying, "I'm okay, Mama, but Sis's hurt," when Deputy Warren ran up to us.

He took Mama's hand and said, "We hope she'll be okay. She's already at the Clinic by now. Slim's taken Vicki home, but she's okay. Come on, I'll get you to the Clinic."

They hurried down the side street beyond the crowd, and once they were away from the parade, the deputy found a car with keys in it. He just took it. He drove Mama and Dad to the Clinic while Michelle and I trotted along behind on Lady.

Mama was at the front desk when I got inside, and the girl there was saying, "The doctor's with her right now. Please, M'am. Sit down. Please. He can't help her if you go back there. He'll be out to see you as soon as he can."

Mama pushed through the door into the hall behind the desk, but the girl ran after her, saying, "Miz Lawson, please. You can't help her if you don't let Dr. Atkinson tend to her. Please!"

Dad followed.

Michelle and I just stood there in the waiting room. The hospital smells that floated out of the hall when the door closed behind Mama and Dad almost suffocated me. I could smell blood and medicines and even the same ether smell like the stuff Dad put on my fever blister to make it go away. He always told me not to breathe while he held that cold, burning piece of cotton to the blisters. I haven't had one in a long time now. But the smells bothered me, made my stomach burn and twist, made me think Sis was dying back there somewhere.

We were still standing in the middle of the room when Mama and Dad both came back and brought even more of the smells with them. Mama came over to me and hugged me real tight and asked Michelle to sit down with me.

We waited.

Mama couldn't sit still. She walked around the room, moved chairs one way and back another. Dad got up and took her hand and got her to sit some. She talked about Katie, out at our house with nobody there but Lillie Mae. We had to get somebody to go out to be there this afternoon when people started coming out for the tea. Mama said she wasn't leaving Sis for any tea, not even for the governor.

We hadn't seen the doctor when Vicki and Slim hurried into the Clinic waiting room. They both had on clean clothes, but the glitter and laughter were gone from Vicki's eyes. They looked empty except for a dark sadness. She went to Mama, sat down by her and took the hand Dad wasn't holding.

They each asked, "What can I do?" Each just shook her head, and suddenly they were sobbing on each other's shoulder.

Mama finally stopped crying enough to ask her if she knew anybody who could go see to little Katie and find Tessie or somebody to stay at the house to turn people away who came for the tea.

Vicki said, "Don't you worry about anything, Laura. I'll see to things for you."

"You need to take Michelle with you," Mama said.

"No, let her stay here. She can help Sam."

Vicki left. Slim stayed.

Mama told him she'd never seen anyone as strong as Vicki, to have so much loss herself and still be worried about others.

Vicki wouldn't be able to not cry, though. When she walked out, the tears were sitting at the edge of her eyes, waiting till she was by herself to come spilling out.

Mama said tending the baby would help Vicki hold up with her pain and would be the best thing anybody could do right now. But the tears came back on Mama, and as she started crying, she buried her face in her hands. Dad put his arm around her and pulled her into his chest.

Somehow Aunt Tessie and Uncle Morris heard what happened and came over to the hospital not long after we got here. Mama asked them to stay at the house to turn away people coming out for the tea. They both went in to see Dr. Atkinson before they left. I guess somebody'll have to give all those people their money back. Tessie said they'd come back up here before dark.

The nurse finally let Mama and Dad go in to see Sis, but Dad came out in a few minutes and said, "She's sleeping, Sam. We'll just wait."

We sat for awhile. Dad looked up at Michelle and asked, "Where is your horse?"

"Outside. I tied her to a tree. She'll be okay."

"We may be here a long time. Why don't you ride her home, give her a good feed and a rubdown. You can check up on your mom too."

Michelle nodded, stood up, and turned to me. "You be okay if I take Lady? I'll be back soon as I can."

"Yeah, go on. I'm okay."

She left. I felt such an empty space on the inside, I wanted to cry too.

The nurse came out to me and asked if I wanted to wash up. I was so glad to have a chance to wash off the vomit that dried on my shirt. I still smelled myself, and still tasted it, even after scooping water into my mouth with my hands and rinsing.

I asked the nurse for some paper and a pencil, and when she looked at me funny, I told her that when I get sad I try to write stuff down to keep from crying. It's the only way I know to keep from just sobbing myself to death. She nodded like she knew.

* * *

While Michelle was gone, Larry came into the hospital with Martha Snyder and Sunny. Martha's face was all swole up, one of her eyes closed, the side of her face black. Dried blood covered the front of her dress, where it had run from the cut on the side of her head, and even her hair was all bloody. She carried her arm wrapped up in a bunch of newspapers tied up with a piece of plowline, like it was broken.

None of them said a word to me or Dad or Slim. They just walked through the sitting room and on out into the hall, where we could hear their voices when they were talking to the nurse. In a few minutes, Larry and Sunny came back out.

Sunny stood in the door a minute and looked around. Larry pointed to me and gave Sunny a little push my way, saying, "Sit with Sam." She came over and sat next to me. Larry didn't. He looked at Slim, nodded toward the door, and the two of them walked outside. Dad didn't go with them; he kinda watched me and Sunny from across the room. Mama was in back with Sis.

Knowing what had happened, I didn't know what to say, but she looked at me, tears rolling down her face. "Daddy's dead," she blubbered. I put my arm around her shoulder, and she shook with her crying. I just let her talk, let her tell me what I already knew.

I took her hand, squeezed it, and tried to help her. I knew kinda what she was feeling, cause I was hurting on the inside, with J.D. dead and Sis back there somewhere, getting tended to. "Your mama's gonna be okay," I whispered to her. "She walked in here, so she can't be hurt too bad."

"There was so much blood everywhere," Sunny said, looking down at the blood dried all over her skirt. A fancy store-bought dress she'd put on this morning just to come to town for the parade. "I didn't know there was so much blood. I'll never get it off." She was rubbing her hands together like she was trying to dry them off, and some dried blood flaked off onto her lap.

After a little while, she started talking again about what happened, only this time it was what happened before I got there. "I heard Daddy's car when he came home, but he didn't stop at the house. He went on out to Grandpa's cabin. You know, that old log cabin just off the edge of the yard. Mr. Flint was right behind him. They were really loud. I've never heard Daddy like that before, not even when he'd go out to the cabin and get drunk with Mr. Flint. They were yelling and laughing and even cussing about 'nigger whores.'

"I couldn't see them real good, but they both looked dirty. I've never seen Mr. Flint when he was so rumpled-up looking. Mr. Flint shook his fist, holding this riding crop, saying something like, 'That'll teach the whore.' And he popped it like Lash La Rue, making it sound like a pistol.

"Daddy said something kinda like all the excitement had gotten him horny. I don't know what he meant, but Mr. Flint said he'd be glad to take care of that, but he had a list of things to do in town, so let's not be too pokey about it. They both almost fell over laughing, both of them leaning on each other, and then they went into the cabin."

The nurse came out with a box of those paper handkerchiefs for Sunny, and asked if she wanted some water or wanted to wash up her face. Sunny nodded and went off with the nurse.

Slim and Larry came back in. Larry sat down by Dad and Slim sat on his heels while they talked so soft I had to move closer to hear them real clear.

Slim said, "Professor, Larry went out to see about Phil." He glanced at me. "Sam told him something was wrong out there, and Phil hadn't kept his appointment with Larry. He found Phil dead, Martha beat up pretty bad. I'll get the sheriff or a deputy and go out there."

"What happened?" Dad asked.

"We're not sure. All we know is he got violent with Martha and one of them shot him. We don't know which one. Martha says she did.

But Sunny told Larry she shot him. Maybe Martha's trying to protect Sunny. I don't know. But it doesn't matter anyhow. The shotgun looks like it's been shined up. There'll be no fingerprints on it."

I could see Larry's eyes, almost shiny with tears he was holding back. Slim went on, "And we know it wasn't Larry. He was with Sam this morning when I found her during the parade. I'll be back quick as I can."

Then he and Larry left together.

Sunny soon came back into the room to wait with us. She'd gotten most of the blood off of her hands and arms, but not all. She'd never get it out of that dress. I asked her, "Did you get to see your mama while you were back there?" But she shook her head no.

In a few minutes, she began again, mostly repeating herself. I didn't want to hear any more about what happened. I could still see it all, running over and over in my mind, all the shooting and killing and blood never stopping. I knew that for Sunny, this morning would never be out of her eyes, just like it would forever be inside mine.

She stopped talking and wiped at her tears, snuffling and shaking all over. I knew how hard it was for her to talk, but it was like my writing—I sometimes have to write about something to help get the hurt out, so her talking ought to help her get out some of her hurt. Her hurt had to be at least as bad as mine.

I tried to close off the sound of her voice, not wanting to see it all again. But I heard her words when she said, "Oh, Sam, I killed my daddy."

"But he was trying to kill your mama," I said. "You did the only thing there was to do."

Sunny didn't say anything. She just sat slumped over. Her hands twisted in her lap and turned and pulled at her handkerchief until it was shredded. She didn't even wipe the tears sliding down her face.

Dad had heard all of what she said, and he came over, pulled up another chair close to her, and wrapped his arms around her. "Sunny, you saved your mama. He might have killed her. You did what you had to do. It's all right. It's all right. You are a brave girl, a brave girl. You did right. What you had to do."

Sunny threw her arms around Dad's neck and began to cry and cry, her whole body shaking and her crying loud enough to be heard way back in the back where the nurse was. When she came hurrying out, Dad shook his head at her, and she backed away, through the door, and left it closed. Still Sunny cried.

Finally, she just leaned back with her eyes closed and clutched my dad's hand like she wouldn't ever turn it loose. I wondered where Brenda and Carolyn were cause she could go home with them since they're her closest kin. They shoulda been there.

Slim and the sheriff walked into the waiting room from the outside door and went right on through to where Dr. Atkinson was tending to Sis and Martha. They both came back out in almost no time.

Sunny looked up at the sheriff and started bawling. But he went to her and knelt down in front of her. "Sunny, Sunny, it's all right."

"I don't want to go to jail," she cried.

"Oh, no, Sunny, you won't go to jail," he said. "Your mama has admitted to shooting your daddy."

"But she didn't. He was trying to kill her and I shot him when he came at her with that ax handle."

"You, Sunny? But Martha says—"

Slim reached over and touched the sheriff's arm and shook his head. "No, Sheriff, let it go. Doesn't matter which one pulled the trigger. It was needed. Let it be."

The sheriff nodded, rose, and patted Sunny's shoulder softly. "I'll find your Aunt Brenda," he said, and left by the front door. Slim stayed with us awhile, talking to Dad.

Sunny whispered to me, "Do you think I won't have to go to jail, Sam?"

"No, Sunny. You don't have to worry about anything. You heard what Slim said to the sheriff. It doesn't matter if it was you or your mama, they're not gonna do anything to either one of you."

"Oh, it was me, not Mama. He'd broken her arm. I know it was broken, the way it was hanging down, like mine was that time I fell down the steps. Why'd she tell them she shot him?"

"She didn't want them after you. But you don't have to worry. You're not even thirteen so they can't do anything to you anyway. You're not old enough to know any better than to shoot somebody, especially if somebody is beating up on your mama. It's gonna be okay. Slim's gonna see it is. And Vicki—Mrs. Gordon—Slim's sister will too."

A few minutes later, Sunny looked up at me and asked, "What are you and your Daddy doing here?"

"It's Sis. Rufus Flint shot her this morning." And suddenly I felt tears come up in my eyes and slide down my face, and I couldn't talk good.

Slim left to go to J. D.'s house, to call J.D.'s father and brother. He said he'd be right back. He was back by the time we had all finished up a sandwich and some cookies,

He said J.D.'s mama and dad were driving in from their Marine Base over in South Carolina. They'll be here by midnight. His brother will get into the Atlanta airport sometime in the early morning, and one of the deputies will drive up to meet him.

Before I could stop crying, Michelle walked in with a big sack full of sandwiches and cookies that had been fixed for the tea. I wiped my face as I realized I was hungry, and was sure glad Vicki had gotten the food while she was out to the plantation. At least we could all have something to eat. Sunny hadn't eaten since early this morning, and we had plenty for her to have some sandwiches too.

Slim said he needed to leave, so Dad asked him to go out to the house, to tell Tessie to have Pollock feed the chickens and not to bring in the milk cows until we got home.

I suddenly remembered and said, "Pollock's not there. He's up at the mill, helping Molly."

"What're you talking about?" Slim asked.

"Molly. She's hurt. Oh, Dad, I was to get her some help. I sent Pollock up there. But she—Buck. They killed Buck. I—." I couldn't go on.

"What? Who killed Buck?" Dad asked.

"Cou'n Phil and Mr. Flint. I was there. With Molly. We'd gone up to see about Buck—"

"I'll go right up there," Slim said, and started out.

Dad called him back. "Slim, stop by and get Dr. Morris to go with you."

Like all of us, Slim was worn to a frazzle, so tired his eyes were sinking into black pockets when he left, after being up all night over in Macon locking up Benson and now all day with the shootings.

Dad looked worse. I've never seen him like this—sitting awhile, and staring at his hands, and walking around the room and stepping out onto the stoop before coming back inside to sit.

We've waited until afternoon. Mama came out once and told Dad all Sis does is sleep. She's not waked up even once.

A really hard part of the waiting came late today when some of the people who worked with J.D. on the pageant came by. They were all dressed up in their 1700 clothes, the two women in long dresses and bonnets, and the men in tight pants, long coats, and whiskers. They had gone out to the house for the tea, and Aunt Tessie sent them away. I think they were a little peeved about the tea cause Mr. Johnson, who used to be mayor, told Dad, "We think J. D. would want us to go on with the pageant."

Dad just looked at him. Mr. Johnson fidgeted a little and glanced over at the other man. The silence seemed to go on forever, with the only noise the whumping of the overhead fan. That fan wasn't going to make enough noise tonight to drown out the whooping and Rebel yells or the drums and the guns.

"Don't you think so, Professor? He put so much into it, I'm sure he wouldn't want us to just cancel it." Mr. Johnson turned his hat around and around in his hand.

"You go on with your pageant," Dad said. He didn't look at them, but got up and walked into the back of the clinic.

Before those four people got out of the waiting room, one of the GBI agents brought Brenda to see about Martha and Sunny. Dr. Atkinson made Martha stay in the Clinic for the night, and maybe longer, but Sunny went home with Brenda. She seemed to be feeling a lot better when she left.

When everybody was finally gone, I told Michelle what all had happened up at Phil's.

Larry came by to check on Sis a few minutes ago, so I asked him if he knew anything about the shotgun getting wiped down, and he just touched my shoulder and said, "It was dirty. I thought it oughtta be cleaned up some." He smiled a sad smile at me and walked over to talk to Dad.

August 10, Saturday, sometime near midnight

Darkness fell through the windows when Slim came in with Molly. Blood had run down from under the handkerchief I'd put around her head and had dried all over that side of her face, which was all swole up and turning black from where Flint had whomped her with that shotgun. Briar scratches all over her arms and legs still seeped blood, and her dress was torn from briars and snags. Dirt and dried mud stuck to her feet and legs, and bloodstains smeared her dress where she'd used her skirt to wipe off her face.

She busted out crying when she saw me, before she could say anything. The nurse heard her crying, that kind of deep crying that you can't stop, that shakes you all over, makes you curl up over yourself cause you hurt so much on the inside. One look at Molly, and the nurse took her to the back to see the doctor.

She took Molly off before we even got to say a word to each other.

After Molly came in, I couldn't stop thinking about Buck, about seeing him fall backwards. I shivered. Had Sis fallen like that? I didn't want to know.

The next time the nurse came in, I asked her about Molly, and she let me go see her. They had put her to bed. When I walked into the room, she busted out crying again, but she finally told me what happened after I left her.

Molly's eyes were empty except for pain and sadness. The emptiness was like the shadows on the lake, turning water to blackness, or like the night when the moon isn't out and clouds cover the stars. A part of her soul had left her.

She had looked all over for Buck, even knowing she'd likely never find him. She'd been down under the waterfall; when she tried to find some tracks, all she saw was that smear of dark brown, where it looked like blood had dried off, where Flint had dragged Buck.

She had seen Buck fall, but was knocked out when Flint dragged him into the water.

She followed the creek downstream, on and on through the bushes and briars and the soft wetness from where the creek sometimes made pools off in the brush. Along the banks where the moccasins lay curled in the sun.

She couldn't find any signs that he was alive, and when she had heard Pollock yelling, she had worked her way back to the mill and walked back to the house with him. Her bicycle had disappeared, maybe stolen, maybe taken by somebody who would bring it back to her. She and Pollock got off the road every time they heard a car coming, and it was getting close to dark when they reached our house and found Slim waiting for them.

"I'm scared to tell anybody else, Sam. The sheriff would lock me up for not telling where Buck was hiding."

From the doorway, Vicki said, "Nobody's going to say a word, Molly. Slim'll take care of everything that I can't do for you."

Dr. Atkinson stood just behind Vicki. "I need to talk to my patient," he said. "You folks want to go back to the waiting room?"

"Please let them stay," Molly said.

He nodded, frowned and said. "I hope it's good news for you, Molly. You're going to have a baby."

Molly said, "Oh, I've so wanted Buck's baby." She started crying all over again, but this time she was trying to smile too.

Dr. Atkinson told us to let her rest, so Vicki and I went back to the waiting room. Seems like we've been at the hospital forever. The noise of the birthday party flooded into the hospital about the time I got back to the waiting room. It would of helped to close the windows, but it was just too hot, and even the whumping of the overhead fans didn't help keep that noise down. There musta been five thousand people across the street yelling, and at least a hundred pistols getting shot off and I don't know how many other guns and cannon from the noise going on and on. Every time one went off, I jumped, seeing Flint's head blow up and seeing J. D. falling down, all over again and again.

Mama's in the room with Sis now and only comes out once in a while, when Dad goes in to sit with her. A nurse comes by every few minutes to see what we need, but we hadn't needed any food with all the tea party food here. Vicki even brought a big Thermos jug of coffee for Mama and Dad and some co-colas for me and Michelle. Vicki just sits with Dad when Mama's in back, and stays by Mama while Dad is gone.

*   *   *

As soon as J. D.'s mama and daddy got to town, Slim brought them over to the Clinic, and they stayed up here a long time, talking soft to Dad. They've got to see to the funeral for J. D. When they were fixing to leave, Mama told Vicki to stay home the rest of the night and get some rest. But Slim stayed behind, even when Dad encouraged him to leave.

The door hadn't closed good behind them when he pulled a piece of paper from his shirt pocket to show Dad. I went over to look too, and so did Michelle.

"We found it in his coat pocket," Slim said. "It's his plans for today. Thank God J. D. put a stop to him."

It was a list of names. They had been listed once, and then numbers written beside them. Flint had re-written the list all over, in numerical order.

1. Plummer
2. Stewart
3. Murphy & Gordon
4. J. D.
5. Prosecutor Hancock
6.. Sheriff
7. Slim
8. Lawson

The list included everybody who had crossed Flint, from his arrests to his trials. I shivered—Dad might be lying all shot up in the hospital with Sis. I busted out crying.

Michelle didn't leave with Slim but stayed on. She finally went to sleep curled up in a chair, but I couldn't sleep, so I got some more paper from the nurse so I could try to write out my pain. I have used my pocketknife to keep the pencil sharpened, but when she brought me the paper, she brought me another pencil. It helps me clear out my mind to put things down on paper, and I don't fret so much over Sis if I'm writing.

The noise outside is over. The pageant that J. D. and Sis worked so hard for is over, and even the sounds of cars have gone away. Only heat, silence, and darkness seep through the windows now.

We're too far away to hear the conjure woman's drum.

August 11, about Sunday

It was getting light Sunday when Dr. Atkinson and Dad both came out from Sis's room at the same time, and I knew what had happened. Dad's face looked sadder than I've seen anybody ever, except Mama when she saw him. He didn't say a word, just came over and put his arms around her, and she started crying. He was crying too.

Dr. Atkinson came over to me, put his arms around me, held me close, and said, "I'm so sorry, Sam. There just wasn't much we could do."

I couldn't stop from crying for the longest time, and I felt like I just wanted to bend over cause my insides seemed like they hurt too much. I wanted to scream bloody murder and to pull my arms over my belly and hold on real tight to try to squash away all the hurting.

I could feel Dr. Atkinson almost crying too. He's known all of us so long; he and Mama grew up together. He took out my tonsils, delivered us both, and even took care of Sis when she had her baby. He's like my Uncle Morris, just extra special.

It hurts me on the inside so much that Sis's never gonna be back here picking at me and telling me how to do things. I start crying every time I think about Sis.

Mama asked me if I wanted to go in and tell Sis goodbye, but I didn't want to go look at her. Looking just that little bit at Elvira, I knew what was in there wasn't Sis any more. Michelle reached over for me, and Mama hugged us both and we all cried some more.

Mama said we needed to see about Molly, and Michelle and I went with her to Molly's room. Mama just flat out told Molly she was going home with us and will live with us from now on. She'll have her baby, live with us, and Mama will see to it that nobody bothers her again.

Molly told Mama it's Buck's baby and it's gonna be a nigger, but Mama told her that was fine, that Buck was a good man and we'd make him proud of his baby.

When we got home from the hospital, Red ran off the back porch and jumped all over me, slobbering and begging for something to eat. He was real thin, like he hadn't eaten in awhile, and he had a piece of rope around his neck that he'd chewed in two. Just like Deputy Warren said, he'd been stolen, but he got away and came home. I wish it coulda been Sis coming home. I miss her more'n I ever thought I could, even with her living away from home the last three years. I start crying every time I see anything that makes me think about her.

I fed my dog, and Michelle helped me treat him for screwworms while Dad talked to Pollock and Jethro. They had been tending to the milk cows and chickens, even my fryers. Dad just told them to keep on doing what they saw needed doing. They allowed they could manage.

Vicki drove up with Katie and Slim. Dr. Atkinson had called her right after we left the hospital. Her eyes were real shiny, and when she spoke, her voice trembled. "I had to be with you," she said, hugging me. We both cried. She said she was here to help.

In a few minutes, Vicki had everybody—herself, Aunt Tessie, Mama, and Molly—in the kitchen, fixing something to eat, while Slim sat in the living room with Dad and Uncle Morris.

August 13, Tuesday

Danny's grown daughter came home from out west to settle his things, and Vicki has helped her some, but mostly Vicki's stayed out here with us. Vicki, Mama and Molly all cry a lot. Aunt Tessie and Mama's younger sister Aunt Sandi do, too. Uncle Morris keeps trying to get everybody to take some of his medicine, but Mama said she doesn't want to be sleepy all the time. One of them will start, and one of the others will try to help her stop and the next thing, they're all crying. Vicki told Mama it helped her to be out here with us, that she couldn't bear to watch Cindy packing up Danny's things. I think tending to Katie is keeping them all going.

I cry too if I stay around them, so Michelle and I sit outside a lot, just sit. Michelle will reach over and take my hand once in a while, just to let me know she's there.

Dad stayed inside to sit with everybody for awhile Sunday, but he hurt too much to sit, and soon left to go outside. He said he had to get the haying started, but it was to keep from crying.

All kinds of people have come out, but Mama couldn't talk to them for long without crying. Different ones of us would go to the door, sometimes Molly, sometimes one of my aunts and sometimes Vicki. The people always would come in the living room, sit a spell, talk to each other, tell Mama how sorry they are, and go on home. Everybody brought food, and there's nowhere else to put any food, so Mama has sent a lot of it home with Jethro and Pollock.

Last night Aunt Tessie finally got us to take the stuff Uncle Morris had to make us all sleep, so Mama finally slept for awhile.

This morning, before Sis's funeral, Colonel and Mrs. Stanley came out with J. D.'s brother Bedford Forest and his wife. They had found some papers signed by Sis and J.D. that gave Katie away to Bedford Forest. The papers said Mama and Dad didn't need the burden of a child at their age if Katie was an orphan. Mama just busted up crying all over again, losing Katie like that. I'm so glad Mama's got Molly cause she's needing another baby to look after.

Mama didn't want to bury Sis from the church like the funeral J.D.'s mama and papa had for him yesterday. She didn't want all the moaning and wailing that would go on if it was in a church, so we just had a funeral at the grave, with the preacher reading the 23rd Psalm and saying a prayer.

Everybody we know was standing out in the hot sun today, and as far as I could see across the cemetery there were people—from Sis's school, from my school, from the courthouse, from Dad's school, and town people who grew up with Mama. I even saw our neighbors, the dairy family who gets mad when our bulls get across the fence and breed their good cows.

All the colored folks from out on the farm who ever helped us or even took our sweetfeed for their likker stills were standing there, back of all the white people, with the men holding their hats in both hands and turning them around and around like they didn't know what to do with them. The women who had their babies with them wouldn't let them cry but hushed them up by sticking a tit in a mouth and letting the baby suck. All those colored folks made me think back to the love they showed when they buried Elvira, and I could feel their love by looking at them. Jethro was there, and I could see tears in his eyes.

When the funeral was over and we were all leaving, Big Nate started singing, his voice filling up the spring air, and the rest of the coloreds sang with him.

Right after dark, the drum started. Slow as an old horse plodding, slow enough that sadness would pass it in the night. Low enough to be a whisper to Elvira about the promise kept.

I shivered.

August 15, 1946

None of Flint's kin—not his sister nor his cousin and not even Miss Mattie—would see to burying him. Cause he'd been out of the ground so long and stunk up the funeral parlor, the sheriff had to spend the county's money to have him buried, over where they bury the crazy colored people who died in the asylum. They dug his grave fifteen feet deep and buried him face down, so he'd have a head start to hell.

EPILOGUE

November 8

Miss Samantha Lawson
Stanleyville, Georgia

Dear Miss Samantha,

My father was Buck Steele, Jr., the only son of my grandmother Molly Everett Steele. I'm writing to let you know that he died. I can barely remember the stories Grandma Molly used to tell me about your friendship, but I well remember how she laughed about the time she helped rescue you from a fox.

I knew her only as a wonderful grandmother when I was real little. Daddy always talked about how hard she worked so he could go to college and to medical school. But Daddy never knew his father, and I would like to know something about the first Buck Steele.

I hope you can help me. I remember that Grandma Molly was a white woman, but, since my parents and I are African-American, I have wondered a lot about my grandfather.

Did you know him well when you and Grandma were growing up together? What can you tell me about him? All I know is that he earned medals for bravery during World War II. I also have the letters he wrote Grandma during the war.

Would you please tell me what you know about him? If the child reflects the parent, Grandpa Buck must have been a really good man, because my father was a loving, kind man and a very successful physician. I miss him terribly.

I look forward to hearing from you.
Sincerely,
JoLynn Steele

*   *   *

Stanleyville, GA.
November 12

JoLynn Steele
San Francisco, CA

Dear JoLynn,

Your letter to my Aunt Sam came to me. She often talked of your grandmother and your grandfather. Please accept my sympathy on his death.

When Aunt Sam died last year, I found a diary she kept during 1946. It has a lot about your grandparents. It will explain why your grandmother Molly moved away and never returned to Stanleyville.

I hesitated at first about sending it to you because those were terrible times, but I feel you have a right to know what happened. Perhaps if we remember our yesterdays, we won't make them our tomorrows.

If you ever get east, please stop in for a visit. You have numerous kinfolks here, on both sides of your family. I'm going to share your address with them.

Please stay in touch.
Sincerely,
Katie Stanley

FACT AND GLOSSARY

FACT

George Dorsey, his wife Mae Murray Dorsey, his sister Dorothy Dorsey (Malcom) and Roger Malcom were victims of a lynch mob at Moore's Ford Bridge in Walton County, Georgia, on July 25, 1946. The massacre was probably the most brutal lynching in the 1900s. George Dorsey was a WW II veteran who had served five years, including in the Pacific war zone, and had been home less than six months. Roger had knifed a white man and was in jail when Harrison bailed him out and drove the family to the bridge. No one has ever been charged. President Truman sent FBI agents to investigate.

Although Dorothy was considered Roger's wife, they were not legally married because Roger had been married and not divorced. That relationship is probably why Dorothy was buried beside her brother George rather than with Roger.

Laura Wexler spent years investigating the events and has documented them in her book *Fire in a Canebrake.*

FACT

In 1953, during the sesquicentennial celebrations in Milledgeville, Georgia, a shop owner named Marion Stembridge killed two attorneys and then himself. One of the attorneys had been on his defense team when he was tried for murder and convicted of manslaughter in the death of a black girl while he attempted to collect money he claimed was owed him for a car. He was supposed to have kept one or two firearms in each corner of his bedroom and to have installed lead sheets above and below his bed as protection against X-rays. He also was supposed to have kept bottles of urine in a refrigerator in his grocery, stored until he could have it tested for poison. A friend has told me of seeing the bottles in the refrigerator in his grocery.

FACT

This book is fiction. The only real persons mentioned are Jackie Robinson and the four victims at Moore's Ford bridge and the undertaker who handled their funerals. All other characters are purely imaginary and do not represent real people, living or dead.

Although some actual events have been "picked up" for this story, but characters here do not portray any of the real persons involved in those events.

GLOSSARY

Brinjin hot: Local term for hot as blazes; first syllable rhymes with "singe"; second syllable rhymes with "gin" (as in cotton gin). Defined as hot enough to singe off the eyebrows and to burn water.

Canner-and-cutter: A mixed-breed, lower quality of cattle

Cape Jasmine: Gardenia

Carroms: A board game popular in the 1940s

Carrying rights: The maid/cook usually had the right to carry food home each day.

Chilren, chullun: Children

Ground Hitched: Trained, a horse will stand when the reins are dropped to the ground

Haint: Ghost

Klu Klux: Ku Klux

Lespedeza: A thick-stalked grass used for cattle feed and hay

One-by-one: A board one inch wide and one inch thick, of any length

Painter: Panther

Screw worms: A parasitic fly larva that eats flesh of live animals. Now extinct.

Shoats: Baby pigs

Shocking: Piling hay into "shocks" or sloped stacks so the rain will drain off.

Sticking plaster: Common name for adhesive tape

Strawberry roan: A color for a horse; a mix of red and white. A song from the 1940s about a bucking horse.

Stumped toe: Stubbed toe

Trace chains: Used to attach the mule/horse/oxen harness to the wagon.

Two-by-six: Board two inches by six inches.

Wetzel, Lewis: A frontiersman in the 1700's. One of his feats was to rescue Daniel Boone during an Indian attack and carry Boone to safety. See Zane Gray's books ***Betty Zane, Spirit of the Border*** and ***The Last Trail.***

Whinker: Whinny

Yard broom: a yard rake.

ABOUT THE AUTHOR

Growing up some six miles from town on a 2,500-acre ante-bellum "plantation," Susan once again writes from experience. Characters in this book come not just from imagination, but from memory — bootleggers, cattle rustlers and interracial courtships. Her debut novel, *The Bottom Rail*, was chosen as a finalist for the 2013 Georgia Author of the Year's best first novel. Before publication, it won awards in the Dahlonega Literary Festival as well as the Southeastern Writers Association Workshop. This is her second novel and ninth published book. Her non-fiction articles have been published in various local, state and national publications. Her rural life was influenced by scientists and writers such as her neighbor Flannery O'Connor and her aunt, Sue Myrick, who went on to become technical consultant for Southern authenticity for the making of the movie "Gone With The Wind."

Other Books by Susan Lindsley

The Bottom Rail, trade paperback, $14.95, ThomasMax Publishing. Susan Lindsley's debut novel, winner of the 2013 ThomasMax "You Are Published" award and honorable mention for Georgia Author of the Year in first novel category. Seeking a future, the Carter families move from their home in the mountains to middle Georgia. By 1946 they expand their bootlegging enterprises to include murder, cattle rustling, election fraud and interracial affairs. Kindle/Nook, $4.99.

Susan Myrick of **Gone With The Wind:** *An Autobiographical Biography*, hardcover with dust jacket, $29.95, ThomasMax Publishing. The story of Susan Lindsley's aunt, Susan Myrick, who served as technical consultant for Southern authenticity in the making of the movie "Gone With The Wind." Contains letters, including correspondence between Myrick and Margaret Mitchell, clashes with David O. Selznick, Myrick's diaries and dozens of photographs. Also available on Kindle for $9.99.

Margaret Mitchell: A Scarlett or a Melanie? Trade paperback, $14.95, ThomasMax Publishing. Susan Lindsley presents works by her aunt, Susan Myrick, in answering the title question and also explores other articles by Myrick, including three feature stories about survivors of the War Between the States. Also available for Kindle or Nook for $4.99.

Blue Jeans and Pantaloons in Yesterplace, Trade paperback, $16.00, ThomasMax Publishing. A slice of rural life in the "Old South," Yesterplace inhabitants included Flannery O'Connor, Susan Myrick, cattle rustlers, shady politicians, world-renown scientists, murderers and a conjure woman. With neither TV nor telephone, Susan and her sisters made up their games and songs, rode horses to the picture show, and played at Roy Rogers and Jesse James. Kindle/Nook, $5.99.

Christmas Gift, Trade paperback, $10.00, ThomasMax Publishing. Lindsley has created a classic collection of family-friendly Christmas poetry with illustrations, including "A Deer with Funny Feet" and twenty other poems. Kindle/Nook, $3.99.

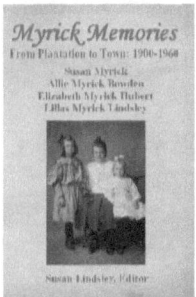

Myrick Memories, Trade Paperback, $10.00, ThomasMax Publishing. Learn about race relations, including interracial marriages, in the early 1900's. Explore courtrooms and visit an old-fashioned prom. Learn about housekeeping and child care in the late 1800's. Read Susan Myrick's only published short story. Kindle/Nook, $5.99

All books shown are currently in print and available virtually everywhere books are sold. If your favorite bookstore doesn't have a copy, ask them to order it for you. Also available through Amazon.com and other online book sellers, including Barnes & Noble, Books-a-Million, and many other websites. To purchase autographed copies and see or purchase other works by Susan Lindsley, contact the author through her website, yesterplace.com or via email at yesterplace@earthlink.net.

www.ingramcontent.com/pod-product-compliance
Lightning Source LLC
Chambersburg PA
CBHW020739250626
47155CB00003B/833